Also by David Nix

JAKE PAYNTER SERIES
Dead Man's Hand
Devil's Ride West
To the Gates of Hell

TO THE
GATES OF HELL

DAVID NIX

sourcebooks
casablanca

Published by Sourcebooks Casablanca, an imprint of Sourcebooks
P.O. Box 4410, Naperville, Illinois 60567-4410
(630) 961-3900
sourcebooks.com

Printed and bound in Canada.
MBP 10 9 8 7 6 5 4 3 2 1

I wish to dedicate this novel to my children, whose love of stories guarantee I always have an audience, and whose strengths mean I never lack for character inspiration.

CHAPTER ONE

March 1870, Wyoming Territory

REPRIEVE FROM DEATH NEVER ERASES GUILT, BUT IT sometimes illuminates a path toward redemption. Jake Paynter's path came with a badge and a steady supply of uninvited violence.

"What's eatin' ya, Paynter?"

Jake cut his eyes to Gus sitting at his right. The repetitive clack of the railcar chewing up track, coupled with the engine's persistent *chug-chug*, forced any conversation into a moderate shout. As Jake was not fond of shouted conversation, he and Gus had lapsed into silence for most of the two hours since the train had left Laramie. As a result, his friend's question dislodged Jake from a cavernous solitude.

"Nothin'," said Jake.

"Tell me another story so I might feel rightly entertained."

Jake looked away from Gus's growing grin to find the woman across the aisle peeking at him. The black of her dress and bonnet didn't hide the fact that she was young, pretty, and discreetly curious. When he dipped his chin at her, she turned her cheek as if finding the repetitive landscape rolling by her window abruptly fascinating. Jake responded by staring ahead in silence. After a few seconds, Gus nudged his shoulder.

"C'mon, now. You still riled about the ticket master in Laramie?"

"Maybe."

"Thought so. I've forgotten it. You should too."

Jake stabbed Gus with a mild glare. "He said 'your kind' weren't allowed on this train. I took offense. More offense than you took, I might add."

Gus chuckled. "Sure. But you didn't hafta break his nose over it."

"He sold you a ticket, didn't he?"

"He did. But if you'd given me thirty seconds, I'd a worked a ticket from him without resorting to haymakers."

Jake lifted one side of his lip. "Maybe. But the man needed his nose broke."

"Won't argue that. Stacy woulda done the same if she'd been there. She'll be sorry she missed it."

Jake kept his eyes pinned forward. From his position on the back bench of the coach car, he could lay eyes on the eleven rows in front of him—including the thirty or so passengers occupying them. Another minute elapsed before the expected second volley came from Gus.

"It's those men on the front row. Am I right?"

Unlike Gus's opening question, this statement failed to surprise Jake. Over the course of their eight-year association, Gus had proven every bit as suspicious and pragmatic as Jake. Of course, he would've been eyeing the same men for the past two hours.

"You are." Jake tipped his head sideways toward Gus. "I've a bad feeling about 'em."

His friend fell silent for a moment. "A bad feelin'? Like the one you had at Poison Springs in '64?"

Oppressive memory invaded Jake's study of the men, folding in layer upon layer as the events of that dark day paraded through his mind in a death march of snares and cannon fire. He'd spoken to Gus of his unease that April morning before the battle. By nightfall, both of them lay shot in a ditch, listening impotently to the ongoing slaughter of their wounded comrades. He swiped a hand downward from forehead to chin in dismissal of the apocalyptic vision.

"Yah. Something like that."

Without a word, Gus retrieved his Colt .44 from its holster and laid the weapon across his lap. Jake exhaled and followed Gus's lead, laying his British-made Kerr across his thigh. The startled intake of breath from the woman across the narrow aisle drew his attention. She twisted away while fixing wide eyes on the pair of revolvers. Jake pried open his coat to flash the star pinned to his shirt as he leaned nearer the woman.

"We're marshals, ma'am." He held his voice low while keeping the men at the front in his sight line. "Out of South Pass City, but headed back there now."

Relief swept her features as a gloved hand found the middle of her chest. "My apologies, then. I thought you men of business, given your suits."

Jake's lips quirked as he thought of their getups. He'd never worn a suit so fine in his life and likely wouldn't have until his burial if not for Judge Kingman's insistence.

"I can see your point, ma'am. This is not our customary attire. But when an associate justice of the territory makes a point about what to wear in court, it ain't exactly a suggestion."

She blinked twice before her eyebrows shot up. "Judge Kingman?"

"The same."

"Then you were in Laramie for the seating of the juries?"

Jake cocked his head before eyeing Gus. His former company mate smirked. "Seems like everybody knows about that."

The woman leaned toward them with renewed interest, nearly invading Jake's armrest. "And why not know of it? Justice Howe and Judge Kingman seated the first women jurors in the world. I heard that even the prince of Denmark sent his congratulations. Were you present for the proceedings?"

"We were," said Gus as he leaned across Jake's lap. "Some folks didn't think much of havin' women on juries. The judge asked us in to help keep the peace until they were done."

"And did you meet with any trouble?"

"Not much, but we thumped the skulls of a few knuckleheads to help 'em see reason."

Jake pried Gus off his lap and placed him firmly back in his seat. He clutched his revolver tighter and tossed the woman an apologetic glance. She eyed the piece, her jaw working back and forth.

"Are you expecting trouble from those…knuckleheads?"

Jake frowned and shook his head. "No. Not them."

Jake leaned forward as the men at the front grew restless.

He caressed the hammer of his Kerr like a patient lover. Without diverting his attention, he motioned with his left hand toward the woman.

"Are you in mourning?"

She smoothed her black skirt as her gaze found her lap. "Not really. My husband was a drunk. And when he drank, he liked to throw fists at whoever fell into his path." She touched a cheekbone absently, perhaps remembering. "Anyway, he was killed in a bar brawl in Baltimore. So I sold everything we owned and headed west to start again. Oregon perhaps. Or maybe even California."

Jake nodded approvingly. "That's a brave undertaking, Missus…"

"Everly."

"Mrs. Everly. It takes courage to leave behind everything and everyone you know to blaze a new trail. Musta been a hard decision." He knew just how hard, having done the same more than once.

She lifted her chin. "It was."

In the lull of conversation that followed, the world shifted on its axis. The train began to slow as it entered a long curve in the line near Hanna Basin. Within seconds, the four men at the front rose from their benches and made prolonged eye contact with one another. One laid a hand against his holster, a sure tell of its imminent removal. Jake pulled back the hammer of the Kerr, ready. One of the men opened the door at the far end of the coach and proceeded through with his associates in his wake, parading toward the baggage car. Beyond that was the express car housing a Wells Fargo agent transporting something of importance. Jake and Gus stood from the bench as one and slipped into the aisle. Jake paused to face the woman.

"Raise your right hand, ma'am."

She blinked twice before lifting the hand. "Like this?"

"Yep. I hereby deputize you. When Marshal Rivers and I go through that door, bar it shut and don't let anybody through but us. And if you hear shootin', tell everyone to find the floor. Think you can do that?"

Though clearly alarmed, she stretched her spine. "Yes, sir. I can."

"Thought so."

He swept down the aisle between upturned, anxious faces and burst through the door onto the gangway between the coach and baggage car. On the far side of the door, the churn of the steam engine pervaded his senses, rattling his eardrums and filling his nostrils with the acrid odor of billowing smoke. Despite the bright midday sun, the chill of late winter air moving at twenty-five miles per hour assaulted his nose and cheeks. He crossed the gangway to squint through the glass of the baggage-car door just as the last of the four men slipped beyond the far exit toward the express car.

"They're robbin' it, ain't they?" shouted Gus.

"Pretty sure of it. You ready?"

"Always."

Jake slipped through the baggage car door with the Kerr raised, lamenting not bringing his Henry rifle from the coach. What the weapon lacked in mobility, it made up for with its sixteen-shot carrier. Gus nudged up behind him as they surveyed the baggage car. Nothing but stacks of canvas bags, boxes, and trunks roped to either side of the car.

"Forward, then," he said.

He and Gus moved in unison toward the far door, crouching as they went. They had covered half the distance when the door window shattered. Jake careened into the baggage before the first shot rang out. Several slugs dug tunnels in the floor between he and Gus, and two more found the trunk behind which he crouched. He exhaled a pent breath and put a lead ball through the car to the right of the door. A string of blue curses erupted from the shooter, audible over the din, as the man fell back across the gangway. Seconds later, a string of alternating fire burned through the baggage car as a second shooter joined the first. Jake and Gus returned mostly blind shots over their baggage shields for half a minute before Gus snared Jake's attention.

"Cover me! I'll go for the door."

Before Jake could stop him, Gus bounded over a wooden box toward the door. He took two steps before a loud report rocked the train. Gus wobbled and went prone. His surprised eyes cut back at Jake.

"What the hell was that?"

A second eruption shook the baggage car. Jake's frown grew deep. "They blew a hole in the express car."

"Why?"

"To throw out the safe, I reckon. Let's take a gander."

Jake retreated to the rear door and onto the gangway between the baggage car and coach. As he leaned over to peer along the side of the baggage car, a shot whistled into the wood above his head. He dropped to a crouch as the train flashed past a knot of men and horses crowded against the tracks—no doubt the source of the shot. Three seconds later, the train passed a bouncing safe, followed by four men rolling out into the snow-covered sage in various states of disarray. More shots pinged the car above Jake's head. He looked back over his shoulder at Gus, shouting above the staccato sneeze of the engine as it began accelerating out of the curve.

"Go scout the express car! I'll meet you here in thirty seconds!"

He bounded across the gangway and thumped the door three times. "Mrs. Everly! It's the marshal. Open up."

The widow unbarred the door and he was through it, sprinting for his berth. Frightened faces peeked up from the floor where Mrs. Everly had apparently sent them. He snagged the Henry and Gus's Spencer carbine, threw a saddlebag stuffed with cartridges over a shoulder, and raced again for the door before stopping beside the woman with urgent instructions.

"You did good, Mrs. Everly. Have the conductor put out our baggage at Fort Steele, and let them know we'll be along shortly to claim it. Our horses are already there where we stabled them."

She nodded, eyes wide. "Yes, sir."

He touched the brim of his hat and stepped through the door. Gus emerged from the baggage car carrying a canteen he had liberated from the baggage.

"Well?" said Jake.

"Wells Fargo man is beat up pretty good, but he'll live. That safe we saw rolling through the snow holds forty thousand dollars in railroad and army payroll." Gus peered back along the track toward the thieves, now lost to sight. "So how do we do this?"

Jake shrugged the saddlebag off his shoulder. "Hell, I don't know. You ever heard of anyone jumpin' off a movin' train?"

"Nope. But I reckon there oughta be a first for everything. We should throw the weapons out first. Getting shot by our own guns don't seem like a fittin' end after all we been through."

"Good thinking." Jake holstered his Kerr, stripped the belt, and began hurling weapons and the saddlebag from the train, aiming for drifts of snow and hoping for the best. His hands empty, Jake hesitated as his eyes scanned the ground sliding by at an increasing pace. Gus crowded up behind him.

"No sense waitin'. It'll only get worse."

Jake inhaled and jumped. The ground flew up to meet him and yanked his feet violently sideways. He slammed to the earth, went airborne briefly, and found the ground again as grasping sage tried desperately to arrest his runaway momentum. The world spun—earth, snow, sage, sky, repeat—until he came to blessed rest. He stared at the wash of blue sky overhead bereft of clouds. He sucked in a pained breath and exhaled slowly.

"That was a terrible idea."

With deliberate movements, Jake struggled to his feet. His left ankle howled in pain but seemed to function. A jagged hole in the right elbow of his suit made him glad for the jacket. Only then did he remember the proper overcoat stowed in his baggage now headed toward Fort Steele some twenty-five miles distant. With a curse at his lack of foresight, Jake looked down the track to find Gus emerging from the brush, walking gingerly.

"Anything busted?" he shouted.

"Just my pride. And we plumb forgot our overcoats in our baggage."

"I know."

"That was addlebrained."

"It was."

Hobbled as they were, Jake and Gus trotted down the tracks to retrieve hats, canteen, saddlebag, and weapons one by one. Everything seemed to have survived the fall, although the Henry bore a new scar stretching along the stock. Nearly a mile distant, the robbers were loading the safe onto a wagon. Eight men, all mounted, and the wagon with two riders. Jake began to run toward them as the wagon rocked into motion but realized after three hundred yards he'd never get within rifle range on foot. They were widening the gap at a pace he couldn't overcome. He coasted to a halt, breathing hard with hands on knees, and watched in frustration as the bandits beat a path directly away from the tracks, headed due north.

"Dammit all."

Gus huffed up behind him and grabbed Jake's collar to bring him upright. "I been yellin' at you for the last minute. Didn't you hear me hollerin'?"

"Don't suppose I did. Why were you hollerin'?"

Gus pointed into the distance north and west. "Whadda you make of that?"

Jake squinted against the glare of snow across a treeless stretch of ground to find a slash of red running along the hip of a barren hill perhaps a mile away. Everything else within eyesight was a blanket of white and brown. He eyed Gus speculatively. "The trail they made comin' in?"

"That's the way I see it. They're circling around a rock outcrop and doubling back westward. Maybe we can get to that trail before they do and waylay the sons a' guns. Two against ten, kind a' like usual."

Jake hitched his rifle over a shoulder and launched into motion toward the trail. "Right. Looks like it's just us, then."

Gus belted out a laugh as he fell in behind Jake. "Been that way for a long time, Paynter."

CHAPTER TWO

EVEN AS THE BANDITS DISAPPEARED FROM VIEW, JAKE loped toward the red gash on the hillside with Gus at his elbow, sending forth columns of frosted air with each breath like a miniature steam engine. Within a couple of hundred strides, he and Gus began laboring from the distance, fresh injuries, and the uneven blanket of late winter snow. Mostly, their feet sank mere inches into the white stuff as they dodged sagebrush and rocks. However, the seemingly flat ground concealed rolls in the terrain that had filled to the hip with windblown snow. After ten minutes, Jake's thighs had grown as numb as rocks from plowing through defiant drifts. His ankle, however, refused to do the same—reminding him with every footfall how utterly witless it was to throw oneself from a moving train onto frozen ground. He glanced aside at Gus to find him similarly limping like a spent racehorse.

"How you holdin' up?" he asked between gasps of air.

"Right fine." Gus inhaled a stuttering breath of his own. "Gonna need to get fitted for a new knee after this. Maybe some extra brains while I'm at it."

Despite the grim nature of their march and the violence awaiting them at the end, Jake smiled. He could use an extra dose of cranial matter himself. And a new ankle.

Jake focused his eyes again on the trail ahead, wondering if they'd be able to cover the final few hundred yards before the thieves showed up. A flash of brown and white five seconds later provided a disappointing answer. One by one, men on horses rode into view from behind the rise, following the path they'd beaten when approaching the railroad tracks. Jake unslung his Henry and picked up his shambling pace. He covered another twenty steps before the bandits noticed they had company. A scatter of rifle shots sent Jake and Gus to the ground as lead splintered the snow around them.

"Well, that ain't no good," said Gus.

"Not even a little."

Jake wormed forward to find cover behind a rocky protrusion and let fly three shots. They all missed, given the distance and the tremor of his heaving lungs. Another volley of bullets dug up snow, sage, and earth around him. He put his head down against his rifle and willed his lungs to still. As his breathing finally slowed, he ejected a spent cartridge and cocked the hammer.

"One. Two. Three."

He lurched to his knees, brought the rifle to his shoulder, and squeezed. More shots chased him back to the earth, but not before he watched a rider twist sideways off his horse. He cut his eyes at Gus to find him watching.

"My turn, Paynter."

Gus emulated Jake's maneuver, springing up to fling a shot from his Spencer toward the crowd of men. Before he could drop prone, though, he yanked backward as if hammer struck, collapsing to his back. Jake watched in horror as liquid spread along Gus's exposed shirt at an alarming rate. He rolled the Henry into the crooks of his elbows and wriggled toward Gus with abandon, a snake in flight. He and Gus had survived a dozen pitched battles together. They'd even seen each other shot up more than once. But he'd never witnessed his old friend lying so still on the battlefield before.

"Gus! Gus!" He closed the final feet between them. "Where were you shot?"

Gus rolled his face toward Jake, a pained grimace plastering his normal amiable features. He emitted a grunt. "In the canteen. Knocked the wind right outta me."

Jake shoved a hand onto Gus's shirt and pulled it away wet. But not bloody. "The canteen?"

"Yep."

"That's unfortunate."

Gus's frown grew deeper. "Unfortunate that the canteen took a bullet instead a' me?"

Jake shook his head. "No. But ask me again this time tomorrow."

Gus flung away the useless container with a curse, and Jake helped him roll again to his belly. The opposing bullets had ceased flying, so they crawled up to a thick tuft of sage and burrowed through it enough to spot the thieves. The outlaws were loading two men onto the wagon, both dead or badly wounded.

"You musta got one," he said to Gus.

"'Course I did. Can't let you be the hero all the time."

"I ain't no hero."

"True. True. But you are right stupid. And stupidity that

survives has a peculiar way of gettin' mistaken for heroism. I figure history's full of stupid men who just happened to be the last ones standin' after everything went to hell."

"Maybe. But I'd remind you that we ain't exactly standin' at the moment." He shuffled to his knees and chambered a new round. "But if you think I'm stupid now, just wait around. You ain't seen nothin' yet."

Jake peered through the cover of the uncaring sage to find the riders and wagon rolling out, soon to leave them behind. After pinning his gaze on the rearmost rider, he pinched his eyes shut to preserve the image and shouldered the Henry.

"One. Two. Three."

He popped above the sage, opened his eyes, and squeezed. The targeted rider spun violently in his saddle and tumbled from his mount as the horse bolted north for parts unknown, free at last. Jake ignored the spray of shots erupting from the bandits and continued popping lead in their direction until the Henry's chamber came up empty. Gus took over the job, sending the wagon driver into a slump with his third shot. The other wagon driver took over the reins and hightailed it away with the riders before Jake could finish reloading. Jake rose up to watch the departing outlaws. He spat forth his frustration with a single bellowing breath and rose to his feet. Gus stood and joined him.

"What now?"

Jake rocked into motion toward the now-empty trail. "Maybe the dead man has a canteen."

Gus huffed a short laugh. "Let's hope so. Never know when you might need one to stop a bullet."

They trudged together through the chill air toward the fallen rider, reloading rifles as they went. The man's earthy brown coat covered most of his unmoving form while his hat lay belly-up a few feet beyond. His stillness lulled Jake into the complacency reserved for the dead, though he should've known better. The encroaching serenity fled when the bandit leaped to his feet and began to run. Gus and Jake hurled half a dozen bullets into the ground near the man's feet before he slid to a halt and raised one hand above his head.

"Lift your other hand," Jake said while continuing to close the distance.

"Can't."

"Why?"

"You fellas shot my arm."

Jake limped to within ten feet of the outlaw, acutely aware the man might be harboring a revolver instead of a bullet wound. He maintained pressure against the Henry's trigger as a hedge against that possibility.

"Turn around, slow. You so much as flinch and I'll liberate your brains."

As the outlaw complied with the order, Jake saw blood soaking the arm hanging uselessly at his side. The man was tall and rail thin, his weather-beaten face all edges and lines like a collection of used knives. Jake pulled a bandanna from his coat pocket and extended it to the injured man.

"Tie it off to stop the bleeding."

The outlaw frowned and narrowed his eyes before gingerly accepting the offering. He set about tying the bandanna around his upper arm using one hand and yellowed teeth. Gus interrupted the procedure with a question.

"You got a canteen anywhere?"

The outlaw pulled the knot tight with his teeth. "No."

"A pity, that."

Jake coughed phlegm from his throat and heaved it into the trampled snow at his feet before wiping his mouth. He drew his brow down at the bandit, who still seemed confused that he wasn't yet dead.

"Who do you work for, mister?" said Jake.

The outlaw's bushy eyebrows rose a quarter inch and he blinked once. "Ain't tellin'."

Jake lifted the drifting barrel of the Henry to point at the man's determined face. "Come again."

The outlaw stared down the barrel for ten seconds before his brows lowered to their former position, nearly swallowing his eyes. "I. Ain't. Tellin'. You may as well just shoot me."

Gus choked a guffaw while Jake swallowed a sigh. He didn't know if the bandit was of the stupid or heroic variety, but it didn't much matter. He believed the man's claim. "Suit yourself. But we're all gonna take a long walk."

"And if I refuse to go?"

Three long strides brought Jake to the surprised outlaw. He stabbed his thumb into the bullet hole in the man's sleeve until he elicited a howl of pain. "I can pull you along this way if you prefer."

"I'll come! I'll come! Leave it be already!"

Jake pulled his hand away and wiped the blood on his coat. "A prudent choice. Now start walkin'."

He waved toward the distant railroad tracks. Gus smiled and lifted his chin at the man. "Look on the bright side, mister."

"What's that?"

"It's a beautiful day and you ain't dead yet. Might as well go for a stroll."

The bandit exhaled a short breath, and the lines of his mouth softened in what was likely his best version of a grin. "I suppose. Ain't got nothin' else to do just now, anyways."

He leaned into motion toward the railbed and started walking with loping, bowlegged strides. Jake and Gus fell in behind him, rifles at the ready.

CHAPTER THREE

AFTER INITIALLY ADMIRING THE FIRST FINE SUIT HE'D owned in his life, Gus moved quickly down the path of cursing it to the depths of Hades. While appropriate for courtrooms and train coaches, the suit was a haberdashery disaster of epic proportions against the droning winter winds of southern Wyoming. At least he'd had the good sense to wear his wool-lined boots. He pulled his useless coat tighter against his frame and prodded the faltering outlaw with the barrel of the Spencer.

"Keep movin', mister. The slow become dead right fast out here."

The bandit picked up his loping pace after wading through a knee-deep drift. It had taken Gus and Paynter two hours to coax five more words from the man. Otherwise, he appeared intent on imitating the Egyptian Sphinx, a wordless face of stone. They'd doubled back to the railroad tracks and had been following the railbed ever since. The wind had picked up, blowing frozen powder like fleeing spirits across the bleached ground broken only by tufts of determined sagebrush. The scatter of hills and distant mountains had disappeared in a wind-whipped haze, enclosing the traveling party in a bubble of white, cutting them off from the world like a pack of wolves culling out a weak member of the herd.

When Paynter fell a few steps behind, Gus glanced over a shoulder to find him scanning the horizon at their backs. After a few seconds, Paynter high-stepped through the snow to catch up with Gus.

"Don't think they're comin'," he said.

"And that bothers you, right?"

"It does. You too?"

"Yep." Gus nodded to the north. "Lettin' us walk away seems too much like a plan. Anybody that could liberate a Wells Fargo safe from a moving train in the middle a' nowhere is too clever to just let us mosey on to Fort Steele without some form of reprisal."

The prisoner peeked back at Gus. The set of his countenance indicated agreement with Gus's theory. His lips parted as if he was about to weigh in on the matter, but he instead turned away and continued his frozen trudge. The diffuse light of the meager sun began to fade, marking the coming of night and a further drop in temperature. However, they couldn't afford to stop walking or they'd risk freezing.

"By Harry, it's cold out here," Gus huffed finally.

Paynter chuckled. "What's a matter? Too much Alabama in you still? I thought a couple of winters at Fort Bridger woulda toughened you up."

"Oh, they did. But at least I had gloves and an army-issue overcoat. I miss that blessed overcoat."

"And a horse."

"That too. Havin' twelve hundred pounds of stallion

beneath you is like travelin' with your personal potbelly stove. But yes, Alabama never prepared me for this tomfoolery. A light frost was enough to make me holler for heat back then. If only I'd known what was comin', I mighta run to Mexico instead of Kansas."

Paynter nodded beside him as they continued their relentless march into the dusk. "The Texas coast was no better. I barely wore shoes most of the year. But I'd take this over the midsummer heat. The kind where water hangs in the air and your lungs close as you gulp it in. The kind where you sweat through your shirt before breakfast."

"I know the kind. I didn't mind it so much. When it was hottest, the overseers would set themselves in the shade and mostly leave us alone. I'd like about five minutes of that right now."

"I wouldn't turn it down," said Paynter. "But at least this is better'n that ice storm in '63 that froze us into our trenches in Missouri."

Gus laughed. "Darn right. Took us a half hour to chip our gear outta the muck, all while Johnny Reb was taking potshots at us because they had the sense to camp under the trees."

They lapsed into silence as the sun outran them. When darkness had nearly enclosed the world, Paynter called a halt. "We should pile up some sage and make a windbreak. You still carryin' some lucifers?"

"Always do."

"Right." He faced the prisoner. "What's your name, anyway?"

"What's it matter?" the man said.

"If we're gonna freeze to death in each other's arms, I might as well know your name."

The hard set of the outlaw's jaw softened. "I suppose it can't hurt. Call me Greely."

"And you can call me Marshal." He tossed his head at Gus. "Greely and me will round up sagebrush. See if you can gather enough fuel for a fire."

"Amen to that. And a couple a' hallelujahs."

Greely remained wordless as he attempted to collect sagebrush with Paynter. His injured arm conspired against him, but he made a game effort of it. Meanwhile, Gus collected oil-soaked chips from a splintered railroad tie and some reasonably dry stems of bald sage plants—hopefully enough for a flame. They'd have to burn what Paynter and Greely were collecting to keep it going through the night. The three of them shoved the gathered sage into a low spot beneath the tracks and constructed a porous fortress that at least slowed the wind to a brisk crawl. Gus retrieved his matchbox from his coat and gave it a shake. Four, maybe five sticks. After building a pyramid of the chaff he'd collected, he fired one of the matches, only to lose it within seconds.

"Well, horsefeathers."

He glanced up to find the shadowed faces of Paynter and Greely watching his efforts with the scrutiny of an investor. He huddled closer to the chaff, enclosing it with his body, and lit a second match. Some gentle coaxing followed by a round of swearing convinced the small flame to struggle to life. With practiced patience, he added debris to the fire in ever-increasing sizes until the heat began penetrating his gloves. He dodged away from the thick, black smoke as Paynter squatted across from him, palms held toward the flame.

"We're gonna need more sage. It burns hot but too fast." He turned to Greely. "Let's go."

Gus nursed the fire into a reasonable incendiary while Paynter and the outlaw doubled the wall of sage. When they'd finished, Paynter settled next to the fire, effectively blocking Greely from approaching the flame. The bandit's narrow frame grew narrower still as he rubbed his injured arm and eyed the fire with a desperate hunger. The enticement of warmth appeared to unthaw his silence.

"Might I sit beside the fire with ya?"

Paynter kept his back squarely to the man. "Tell us who you work for."

Silence. Then, "I won't."

"Won't?"

Greely shifted his weight from foot to foot. "Can't."

"Why?"

"'Cause if I breathe a word about it, I'm a dead man."

Paynter turned his cheek to Greely. "Without a fire, you might soon be dead anyway."

The outlaw continued shifting his weight and rubbing his arm. After a minute, he shoved aside snow with his boot and settled to the ground where he was. "I just can't."

Gus believed him. Worse, he felt a little sorry for the outlaw, which annoyed him to no end. A few hours ago, Greely had tried to kill him. He deserved no empathy. Gus assumed Paynter felt the same, but he couldn't have been more wrong. Paynter slid over and patted the frozen ground next to the fire.

"Come on over."

Greely blinked in seeming surprise but quickly occupied the offered spot. Gus shook his head in disbelief. Old Paynter from the war would've held no room for mercy to his enemies. He'd changed the past couple of years, and for the better. After Greely had soaked up the flame for a few minutes, Paynter waved a hand at him.

"At least tell us where you're from. Someplace cold I reckon, given your lack of complaint thus far."

Greely cut narrowed eyes at Paynter, frowned, and then nodded. "Minnesota. Cold as hell."

Gus realized Paynter wanted the outlaw to talk. As it happened, conversation was near the top of Gus's list of skills. He leaped at the opening.

"How'd you end up in Minnesota? Your accent seems more southern."

Greely swayed back and forth, probably warring with himself over answering the question. Disclosure won out. "My family was from Kentucky, but Pa drug us north when I was knee high to help build Fort Snelling. After that, we just stuck. He cut wood and timber for the fort and then for the mills when they began openin' in '39. He tried to make me a woodcutter like him, but I wasn't so keen on settlin' in one spot. So I shook his hand and kissed my ma and started headin' west. Been doin' that for more'n twenty years now. Headin' west, workin' as I go."

Gus leaned closer. "What kind of work?"

Greely's eyes narrowed again. "Cattle drovin'. Buildin' fences and barns and such. Even woodcutting, which would make my pa shake his head."

"Not gunslinging? Or thievin'?"

Greely looked down into the flames. Paynter tossed in some more sagebrush and skewered the outlaw with an iron gaze. "We already know the answer to that question. Who do you work for now? You know, gunslingin' and thievin' and all."

The man shook his head. "I can't tell you."

"Suit yourself."

———

In the depths of the night, Greely decided to run. Paynter had taken first watch but must've fallen into a stupor. Next thing Gus knew, his old friend was shaking him awake.

"The old boy lit out. We gotta go get him."

Gus threw more brush on the dwindling fire, grabbed his rifle, and followed Paynter into the enfolding darkness. They tracked Greely down ten minutes later. Paynter threw the outlaw to the ground and pressed the man's face into the snow for a few minutes to communicate his displeasure over Greely's poor decision-making. By the time they dragged him back to the fire, the outlaw was half-frozen. Paynter shoved him down beside the flames.

"Well?"

Greely looked up at Paynter woefully. "Just let me go or shoot me dead. Please."

"Tell me why."

Perhaps Greely's frigid condition muddled his brain. Maybe he was just tired of playing cat and mouse. Whatever the reason, he broke.

"Because!" he shouted, his voice tremoring with grief. "Van Zandt says that anyone left behind is as good as dead. If I stay a prisoner, he'll find a way to spring me or kill me."

Gus arched his eyebrows. Dutch van Zandt! The outlaw boss who'd sent men to try burning out miners and lynching Paynter a year earlier.

"So," said Paynter with an exaggerated Texas drawl. "Van Zandt is behind the robbery. But what about his partner, Lucien Ashley? He part of this as well?"

"I..." Greely sucked a breath. "I don't know any Ashley. And I'm done talkin'."

The outlaw rolled into a ball on the ground and pulled his hat over his face. Across the fire, Paynter locked eyes with Gus, clearly thinking similar thoughts. Dutch van Zandt's reputation for calculated violence was already legendary in the territory. If Greely was right, they'd be seeing the outlaw boss soon. And the meeting would prove far from pleasant.

CHAPTER FOUR

WHEN DESPERATION SETS IN, SEEMINGLY SMALL INDIGNI-
ties become mountains of hostile offense. The staccato chug
of a train approaching from the west shortly after sunup
drew Jake's attention from his already-trudging footsteps.
The iron horse bore toward them at a steady clip, swallowing track like so much fodder. Still half-frozen, Jake and Gus
began waving their arms and hollering to flag down the train.
Even Greely contributed to the effort by stabbing his good
arm skyward and shouting, "Hey! Hey!" repeatedly. Not
only did the engine fail to stop, but the engineer had the
audacity to blow his steam whistle twice as he barreled by.
The wind of displaced air that followed the train's passing
burrowed through Jake's defenseless suit and drove ice into
his flesh. Gus threw down his hat with impressive violence
and a blurted epithet.

"Well, if that ain't the most unchristian conduct I seen in
a month a' Sundays!"

Jake swallowed his indignation and expelled a stream of
frosted breath. He retrieved Gus's hat, brushed snow from
it, and offered it to his friend. "Worse than robbing a train?"

Gus yanked the hat from his hand and jammed it onto his
head. "Damn right. Van Zandt's crew knew they was doin'

wrong when they did it. That engineer left us to freeze but probably congratulated himself for giving us a friendly wave. Wrong done in blind ignorance is just as bad as wrongdoing without remorse."

Jake nodded. He'd witnessed a hundred times the way Gus had been slighted, overlooked, diminished, and dismissed by "good" folks who seemed unaware of the hurt they caused. Gus seemed to prefer direct hostility to that. At least then he could punch the offender's chops in good conscience.

"Preach it, Reverend Rivers," Jake said. They moved on, without choice in the matter. Every hundred steps carried them nearer Fort Steele and reprieve from the biting wind. Jake's feet had become unfeeling blocks of wood when he spied riders on the horizon, sweeping down from the north. The Henry was at his shoulder before he could decide to raise it.

"Company comin'," he said.

Greely choked a cough. "Oh God."

After a few seconds, Gus exhaled a breath. "It ain't God. The Almighty don't wear a blue overcoat so far as I know."

The line of riders congealed into twenty or so U.S. cavalrymen bearing directly toward them. The contingent fanned out as they reached the track. Gus shot the lieutenant a sharp salute and smiled. "Are we ever glad to see you boys."

The officer ignored the salute and turned his attention to Jake. Another dismissal to add to Gus's ever-growing list.

"You Marshal Paynter?"

Jake glared and let the question hang for three seconds, just for spite. "I am. What can I do for you?"

Seemingly unaware of Jake's message, the lieutenant pushed his hat back on his forehead. "After the train arrived at Fort Steele yesterday, we set out in search of the robbers. By nightfall, we tracked 'em to the Medicine Bow River. We found a blown safe, a burnt wagon, and horse tracks leadin' in six different directions across the river."

"So you turned back?" Jake meant it as a challenge, and the officer finally heard him. He pulled his hat forward again and set his jaw.

"Lucky for you. Or we could just leave you to freeze in this waste."

Jake had a mind to tell the lieutenant just where to put his suggestion. Gus's grip on Jake's forearm stopped the words in his mouth. He set them aside and found new ones. "We'd be pleased to accept your aid, Lieutenant. We captured one of the train robbers and are eager to bring him in."

"Very well," said the officer. He tossed his head toward the riders at his side. "Mount up these fine gentlemen with you. If they cause any trouble, throw 'em back in the snow."

Gus rolled his eyes at Jake. "Still makin' friends, I see."

"As always."

———

Jake was pleased to discover they'd covered more than half of the twenty-five miles to Fort Steele on foot. On horseback, they finished the journey in under three hours, and mostly in silence. The lieutenant had apparently lost interest in conversation with his wards, though the troopers maintained a light banter the entire time. Jake just listened. He'd spent most of his adult life in similar company—men of war waiting for the next battle. He didn't miss the crushing boredom, the sometimes-hellish conditions, and the horror of armed conflict. But he did miss the sacred camaraderie that filled all the gaps in between. Even though he hadn't been one for much conversation, Jake had come to realize how the mere presence of others sharing the same heavy burden fed his spirit. Men walking shoulder to shoulder transformed into something greater than the sum of men walking alone.

Upon arriving at Fort Steele, the lieutenant deposited Jake, Gus, and Greely in the mess kitchen so they could unthaw by the stove. The company cook scowled at them but otherwise continued slopping together whatever passed for the midday meal at the fort. Within minutes, a stranger wearing a three-piece suit entered the cramped space, drawing the cook's frown down nearly past his chin. The newcomer removed his hat and extended a hand to Jake.

"Barney Smithson with the Union Pacific. I heard you'd arrived."

Jake shook the man's hand. "Yep. Minutes ago."

Smithson extended his hand to Gus. "And you are the deputy marshal?"

"Yes, sir." Gus shook the man's hand.

"You have my thanks."

When Smithson offered a hand to Greely, Jake pushed the hand down. "This is Mr. Greely. He is in the employ of Dutch van Zandt and helped rob the train. We managed to claw him back before the others lit out."

Smithson nodded and twisted his mustache to one side. "Van Zandt, you say. Disturbing news."

"You know of him?"

"Indeed." The railroad agent spun his hat in his hands. "He's become quite the thorn in our sides, what with extorting railway workers and blocking water access. But he's never robbed one of our trains before. Wells Fargo is already pitching camp up my backside, insisting we make every effort to retrieve what was stolen."

Jake considered the man's words for a moment as he spread his hands over the hot stove in an attempt to restore his fingers to life. "You may need to involve the army, then. Van Zandt's got at least two dozen men on his payroll, operating out of Wind River Canyon and Hole-in-the-Wall. A few local marshals aren't up to the task of bringing him to justice."

When Greely snorted a laugh, Gus peered daggers at him. "You got somethin' to say?"

The outlaw looked up from the stove. "Forget going after van Zandt. You better have a lotta rifles and a good lockup here at Fort Steele. 'Cause if I'm still here in a couple a' days, he'll come to spring me. And if he can't bust me out, he'll burn the place down with me in it."

Smithson cocked an eyebrow. "But this is a military fort, garrisoned by a hundred men. Surely not."

A wry tobacco-stained smile spread across Greely's face. "You don't know van Zandt, then."

The agent's eyes went hollow. "I see. Well, Colonel Taylor has asked me to fetch you to his office. Perhaps he'll have something to say about this."

Jake and Gus marched Greely between them as Smithson led the parade to the colonel's office—a whitewashed square with a tin roof. The fort commander did not rise when they entered but instead pinned Jake with a glare of cultivated hostility.

"Mr. Paynter, I presume." His voice was as flat as the high desert.

"Yes. Sir."

"What do you want?"

The colonel's demeanor told Jake everything he needed to know. He knew who Jake was and clearly disagreed with Jake's presidential pardon for killing a superior officer, regardless of the reason. Jake suppressed a sigh, already weary of the man.

"We captured one of the men who robbed the Union Pacific express car yesterday. As this is not our jurisdiction, we figure you'd have a place for him in the stockade."

The colonel leaned back in his chair and steepled his fingers. "I believe our stockade is full just now. And neither is this my jurisdiction. Let the railroad handle it."

Smithson began to offer disagreement, but Jake silenced him. He met the colonel's gaze, careful to maintain cool nonchalance. "Understood. We have a cell for him in South Pass City. If you'll have your company surgeon fix up Mr. Greely's arm and lend us a spare horse, we will lighten your burden of responsibility first thing in the morning."

The colonel appeared ready to counter Jake's proposal but instead flipped a hand at him. "Very well. But I want you gone before breakfast. Am I clear?"

"As crystal."

After they exited the office, Smithson stopped them, concern dripping from his features. "Although I greatly appreciate your continued help, Marshal, if Mr. Greely is to be believed, Dutch van Zandt will soon pay a visit to South Pass City. Can you fend him off?"

Jake contemplated the valid question. Could they? Then he remembered what the townsfolk had done for him the previous summer. How when Lucien Ashley and a dozen of van Zandt's men had come to hang him, the good people of South Pass City had risked their lives to rally to his aid. He smiled.

"I don't know if we can fend him off. But we don't lack the courage to try. And the courage to try makes all things possible."

CHAPTER FIVE

THE TIME FOR COURAGE DECIDED NOT TO WAIT UNTIL some vague future date at South Pass City. It did bide its time a little, though. The first three days of travel progressed smoothly, owing to a warm spell that began clearing the muddy trail of lingering snow. Swaddled in their proper overcoats and mounted on warm-blooded engines, Jake, Gus, and the outlaw found the biting Wyoming wind less punishing. Jake's mare had seemed happy to see him when he showed up at the Fort Steele stables. Then she must've remembered her general animosity toward him and had attempted to remove his right ear. He hadn't much minded, though. When the world was arrayed against you, anger was a useful tool.

Greely hadn't said much as they rode, nursing his slung arm during the day and choosing to turn his back to the fire at night rather than risk conversation before sleep. Each morning had provided fresh evidence of his mounting concern, though. His eyes grew progressively hollower as he appeared to confront the lurking monsters of his imagination. The third day of riding ended as had the others. They pitched camp in a dusky glen just a half-day's ride from South Pass City and conjured up a smoky fire. After grub, Jake gripped the outlaw's shoulder before he could turn away again.

"You plannin' on dying, Greely?"

The man stared with those hollow eyes, twin beacons of miserable confirmation. "No plannin' necessary. Van Zandt's gonna kill me for certain. I been your prisoner far too long. He'll guess I told you something important and expect my life in exchange."

"You sure about that?"

"I am." His eyes found the dirt. "I seen him do it before. But it's what we signed up for. A regular payday knowing each one might be the last. Knowin' that failure or capture means a bullet."

Jake released Greely's shoulder and allowed the outlaw to roll again into a ball with his back to the fire. He hoped the man was mistaken but knew in his gut that he was not.

———

Two hours into the following day, Greely's dark prophecy came true with biblical certainty and consequence. Gus was the first to see it coming.

"Riders that a' way." He raised a finger to the northeast. A dozen mounted men galloped along a parallel but converging track with the clear intention of running down Jake, Gus, and Greely. Not one wore any shade of blue.

"I told you so." Greely's pronouncement stung only a little, owing to Jake's belief in the outlaw's dire claim.

Jake leaned forward and dug his heels into the mare's side. "Let's fly!"

The three horses bolted into a dead run. As he had the

most to lose, Greely led the way along the trail. Meanwhile, Jake and Gus pulled their respective rifles from saddle slings and laid them across their thighs. As the gap narrowed, Jake realized that van Zandt's men had chosen well the place of intercept. The trail cut between a pair of rocky rises, funneling their quarry into a point of no escape and no return. Jake let his mind tumble ahead to what would come, calculating trajectory and collision. He found no miracle waiting. They had to do something unexpected. Something unorthodox.

"Dismount!" he shouted while slinging his Henry over a shoulder.

Gus and Greely stared with astonishment at the command but obeyed. They slowed their horses and slipped to the muddy earth.

"We gonna fight it out right here?" said Gus.

Jake shook his head and pointed up the steep, rock-strewn hillside. "Nope. We're gonna drag our horses over the top. Then we'll circle back and go home by another track."

"You're loco," said Greely.

"I don't deny it. Now let's git."

Gus and Greely followed Jake as he yanked the mare up the hillside. She rolled her eyes, perhaps recalling the last time he had pulled her unwillingly up a mountain. Regardless, she climbed. Gus's magnificent buckskin and the hardy army loaner seemed to take heart from the mare's mad scramble and lurched ahead after her. Men and horses mounted the hillside, the former sometimes putting hands to the ground and the latter stumbling and recovering from the carpet of uncertain rock. Bullets began pinging the hillside around them before they reached the summit. Jake thrust the mare's reins into Gus's free hand.

"Get up and over."

"What you gonna do, Paynter?"

"What I always do."

Without looking back at Gus, Jake found a shallow crevice and belly-flopped into it. He let loose the first slug before taking a breath, levered out the shell, and squeezed off another shot. The second bullet clipped a rider and flipped him from his horse. The remaining riders veered abruptly north. Jake took down a second rider as they widened the gap between them and him. Their change of course was no accident of panic, though. It would carry them through the narrow cut leading to South Pass City. They clearly believed their prey would resume a northwesterly course toward the mining town after crossing the hill. Jake hiked the remaining distance to the summit, breathing hard.

"Now what?" said Greely. The tremor of his question betrayed rampaging alarm.

"We wait a minute."

"Wait! Why'n the hell?"

Gus winked at Jake with understanding of the plan and clasped a hand on Greely's shoulder. "Look at your friends. They'll be through the cut and outta sight right quick. Then we go back down the way we came, circle north, and come in from the east. Before they figure what happened, we'll be ghosts."

Greely blinked three times. "Oh."

Their little band did just as Gus described, more or less.

The horses resisted the descent much more than the climb. Half-ton animals don't particularly appreciate giving themselves over to the pull of gravity and the capriciousness of loose rock. However, they arrived back at the road without mishap and circled away behind the opposite hill to get lost in the sagebrush and rolls of earth. Their circuitous detour added three hours to the journey, bringing them to the cusp of South Pass City from the east over rough, mostly trackless terrain. Jake was beginning to congratulate himself on the brilliance of his plan when a shot rang out from his left. His darting eyes found a mass of riders angling toward them with speed and murderous intention.

"It's a footrace, gents!"

As one, he, Gus, and Greely spurred their mounts into a life-and-death sprint. Smoky haze from the town marked its location ahead, just beyond reach. Jake leaned closer to the mare's neck and urged her to grow wings. The race would be close. But quitting the competition was an option only for dead men.

CHAPTER SIX

STACY BLUE'S THREE-WEEK STINT AS TOWN MARSHAL OF South Pass City had fallen well below her fever-dream expectations. She had figured that while she and Gus were busy playing deputy, Paynter was fielding all manner of intriguing problems as marshal. Now she knew otherwise. The job entailed days on end of crushing boredom shot through with flecks of annoyance and a smatter of actual marshaling.

All that changed as she walked a patrol to the south end of Main Street for the hundredth time. Her ancient Lefaucheux twelve-gauge, carried lazily in the crook of her elbow, popped to her hip when she spotted a trio of riders racing down from the top of a rise a mile from town. The distinctive buckskin informed her who the riders were. Their breakneck pace alerted her deepest instincts to a dire situation. She pinned down her hat and ran for the nearby tack store.

"Moretti! Moretti!" she shouted while bursting through the door. "Round up men and guns and send 'em to the creek, pronto! We got a situation!"

The startled shopkeeper hesitated a couple of seconds before retrieving a rifle from the wall and hurtling past her down the street, apron flapping. She bolted away from the store across mostly vacant ground occupied by a few scattered tents. A clutch of wide-eyed men stood as she flew by.

"Grab your pieces!" she hollered. "There's gonna be a fight!"

All it took was the raising of her eyes to the high ground to prove her instincts correct. Coming like proverbial bats out of metaphorical hell, a larger band of riders was descending the rise on a course to intercept Gus, Paynter, and a third man. As she plowed through the thigh-deep Willow Creek to the far bank, the pursuers began popping shots at the pursued. Gus clenched his buckskin between his knees, twisted in his saddle, and fired three shots in quick succession at the larger party. A horse tumbled to the ground, dumping the rider into a violent collision with rocky soil. Stacy threw herself against the far bank, using it as a natural palisade, and brought the Lefaucheux to bear. *Hellfire,* she thought. *Too far for a scatter gun.* As Paynter and Gus neared the creek, other bodies threw themselves against the bank beside Stacy after splashing up behind her. An array of long barrels appeared over the top of the bank on either side.

"Hold!" she shouted. A shadow falling over Stacy drew her attention. Glen Dunbar, the Scottish blacksmith whose family she had plucked from the wilderness two years earlier, loomed next to her wielding his biggest hammer. She furrowed her brow. "You gonna throw it at 'em?"

"No," he said with mild affront. "But if they try crossing this creek, I'll make sure they fail spectacularly."

"Fine. Get ready."

She returned her attention to the oncoming cavalcade.

When Paynter's mare flashed past her into the creek, the sight line to the larger party cleared. She inhaled and stretched her neck.

"Fire! Fire!"

The line of long guns opened up in quick succession as answering bullets kicked up soil before them. However, the pursuers veered sharply away and returned up the rise. At least two of them appeared to slump in their saddles. The man who'd fallen rallied his wounded horse and dragged it upward behind his retreating comrades. Upon reaching the top of the rise, three of the men turned to survey the town and its defenders below before spinning away to join the others.

When the last of the attackers had disappeared from view, Stacy pried her bloodless fingers from the shotgun and turned slowly toward the creek. Paynter, Gus, and a stranger watched her from atop their mounts on the far bank as if nothing of importance had just occurred. Gus even had the audacity to grin at her. She slogged through the water with mounting pique and stomped up the bank.

"What the heck just happened, Paynter?"

One side of his mouth lifted with amusement. "Easy, little sister. You did good."

The compliment bled away most of her irritation. But not all. "Fine. But you got some explainin' to do, *Marshal*."

"Fair enough." He raised a hand and lifted his chin toward the men behind Stacy. "You all did good. We owe you our lives."

Stacy turned to find the men doffing hats and caps at Paynter as if he were a visiting prince, offering words of thanks and self-deprecation to the conquering hero. She shook her head in disbelief. How a man so resistant to human relationships managed to draw such devotion from others, she'd never know for sure. Paynter turned away with Gus and the stranger. Dunbar strolled after them with his hammer over a shoulder, whistling a jaunty tune, leaving no one with whom Stacy could argue further. She sighed and fell in behind the horses while blowing cruft from the barrels of her shotgun.

———

The lanky stranger with a slung arm was called Greely, and he worked for Dutch van Zandt. That much Stacy gathered while Gus deposited the man in one of the two jail cells. Greely promptly reclined on the bunk and pulled his hat over his eyes. She remained by the door, still armed. As Gus pulled up a chair by the already-seated Paynter, he waved her in.

"Sit a spell, Miss Blue."

"As long as it involves you explainin' stuff."

"Of course."

She propped her weapon beside the doorframe, straddled a chair, and rested her arms over the back of it. "Well. Let's hear it. This better be a good story."

Gus laughed. "It is a right fine tale. Startin' with the train robbery."

She'd already heard that much via the telegraph sent to Esther Morris from Fort Steele three days earlier, but she decided to humor them. "You got my attention."

Paynter described his mounting suspicion that day of

four men riding the coach from Laramie to parts west and how he and Gus had followed them when they moved forward through the baggage car. Gus described the ensuing gun battle, the exit from the train of the safe and the robbers, and his finding the wounded Wells Fargo agent.

"Forty thousand!" she whistled. "That's a fortune. And I'm guessing by your prisoner there, you decided to go after 'em."

"We did," said Gus.

"How?"

"We grabbed our rifles and jumped."

She frowned and lifted a finger. "Did you remember to take your overcoats?"

Paynter and Gus exchanged an amused grimace. Gus rolled his eyes. "No. That was Paynter's fault."

"The hell it was."

"Either way, it was stupid," she said.

"Duly noted," said Paynter. "Do you want the rest of the story, or'd you rather just tell us everything we did wrong?"

"Why can't we do both?"

Paynter shook his head and continued the telling. He and Gus had exchanged fire with the train robbers, Gus may or may not have been shot in the canteen—whatever that meant—and they'd knocked down Greely before losing the rest of the party. They'd walked back along the tracks, nearly frozen overnight, and eventually encountered the cavalry out looking for them.

"Bet you wish you had them overcoats," Stacy said. She had cultivated a well-earned reputation for poking bears and didn't want to disappoint anyone now.

"Anyhow," said Gus as he spoke over the top of her jab. "We ran into van Zandt's men this mornin' and again later just outside town. That's when you came in."

"And lucky I did," she said. "You'd be passing sunlight through your body otherwise."

Gus squared on her, lifted his chin, and motioned to her. "What of *you*, Miss Blue? Maybe you should tell us what *you* did in our absence."

"So you can mock me?"

"You know it."

She leaned back and folded her arms. "Fine, then. I caught a runaway horse and two runaway kids. Widow Wilson's boys got loose again. I broke up a fight between two painted ladies down at the brothel but got scratched up for my thankless efforts. And Josiah Boedecker got flaming drunk and started firing his revolver in the middle a' Main Street again."

Paynter's eyes narrowed. "He hurt anyone?"

"No. I knocked him down before he did any real damage."

"You coulda been shot, Stacy."

She frowned. "Goshdarnit, Paynter, ya jackass. I'm not a child. I waited until he was reloadin'."

"You put him in jail, then?"

Her frown faded. "No. Sent him home with Mrs. Boedecker, and she was fit to be tied. That's a sight worse'n jail."

Her remark coaxed the appearance of the rarest of creatures from Paynter—a grin. "I reckon it is worse. Like I said before. You did good."

"Thanks. But you can keep yer job. I ain't interested."

Paynter sighed with seeming disappointment. He stood

and pressed the chair beneath his desk. "Right, then. Gus, can you go fetch Maddie to look after Greely's arm? I trust her more than that drunken surgeon at Fort Steele. Meantime, I'll head over to give the particulars of the prisoner to the new justice of the peace."

Without invitation, Stacy fell into step with Paynter as he walked toward the courthouse. He cut his eyes at her sidelong but said nothing. Upon arriving, he opened the door and motioned for her to pass. "After you."

"Jackasses first."

He exhaled a breath and stepped inside ahead of her. They approached the closed door of the tiny office belonging to the justice of the peace. Paynter rapped at it with his knuckles.

"Enter," came a familiar voice from inside. He opened the door to reveal a stone-faced Esther Morris. However, her eyes lit when she saw her visitors. She stood to unfurl every inch of her six feet of frame. "You're back. And still breathing, I see."

"Barely," he said. "I brought in a prisoner and a report."

"I heard you may have fallen into some trouble. I received a telegraph from Fort Steele three days ago. But let's hear the details."

She sat and scribbled notes while Paynter recounted again the story. She raised her eyes briefly at the mention of van Zandt but said nothing. When Paynter had finished the tale, he tossed his chin toward her.

"So, Mrs. Morris. What's it like being the first woman justice of the peace in the entire United States of America?"

Stacy liked the question. Ever since Judge Kingman had convinced Mrs. Morris to take the role a month earlier, Stacy had been dying to hear the answer. The gray-haired woman grew a hard but wry smile.

"I've had better jobs. This one is often aggravating, mostly engrossing, and always challenging."

"Sounds like my job," said Paynter.

She nodded and steepled her fingers on the desktop. "Speaking of your job, Marshal, what's your plan for the prisoner?"

"Simple," said Paynter. "Keep him alive until Judge Kingman comes. Do you know when that'll be?"

"At least a week. Do you expect trouble?"

"I do."

Stacy rubbed her hands together, a nervous habit. They'd turned away ten of van Zandt's men at the creek. But he had at least twice that many under his thumb. If the outlaw boss decided to cause trouble, there could be hell to pay for everyone.

CHAPTER SEVEN

As Rosalyn Ashley released her twenty-three students from school, her thoughts drifted from the demands of the day to her favorite recurring subject. Jake Paynter. The kids had been abuzz with the news of his return beneath a hail of bullets the previous day. To hear Lisbet Emshoff tell it, the entirety of the Roman legions had been hot on his trail, but he managed to vanquish them. Vincent Moretti, one of the older boys, gave a more accurate description of the arrival as told by his father, including Stacy Blue's rallying of a defense against the oncoming riders.

Lisbet wouldn't have it, though. She had folded her arms and refused to believe any other version of the story. Rosalyn understood. Paynter's exploits over the past two years had become legendary across the territory. And legends had an odd way of feeding on their own significance until growing far out of proportion.

Such was Rosalyn's state of mind when the object of her musings turned up the street toward the school, on foot. She immediately forgot the students filing past her out the schoolhouse door. She smoothed her dress, tucked a loose lock of hair behind her ear, and clasped her hands at the waist, waiting. However, the Emshoff children intercepted Paynter twenty steps short of the schoolhouse steps.

"Mr. Paynter! Mr. Paynter!" Otto, Dora, and Lisbet huddled around him, yanking his shirt and seizing his hands. He froze for a few seconds under the assault, his eyes wide like a deer encountering a predator in an open field. Rosalyn saw him draw a deep breath and smile. His hands lifted to muss Otto's hair and squeeze Dora's shoulder. Lisbet, now seven, had other ideas. She captured his right hand with both of hers and began dragging him toward the steps.

"Come, Mr. Paynter! I want to show you what I drew."

Rosalyn stepped aside as Lisbet swept past with her quarry in tow. Paynter grinned apologetically at her as he slipped by. She followed as Lisbet tugged Paynter to the bench and table she claimed as her own. The little girl finally released the marshal's hand to dig out her prize from beneath the desk—a hand-drawn sketch on a book-size rectangle of paper. Rosalyn wrung her fingers as she watched Paynter view the familiar drawing. He dropped a forefinger to run along a line of tiny wagons pulled by blobby oxen beside what seemed to be a river.

"This us?"

"Yes." Lisbet appeared immensely pleased that he recognized the context of the drawing—their shared journey along the Oregon Trail from Missouri two years prior.

"Which one's yours?"

She tapped the end of the line. "The last one, of course. You knew that."

"Yep. Just wanted to make sure."

He moved his eyes to the right and the mass of figures emerging from the edge of the paper—riders and men eating into the small gap between them and the wagon train. "And what about these people?"

She folded her arms. "The bad men who shot my leg and killed Mrs. Janssen."

Rosalyn leaned forward involuntarily as Paynter seemingly forced his eyes on the figure between the wagons and the "bad men." A man on a horse, riding toward the attackers. His finger moved to underline the solitary figure. "And this is?"

"It's you, Mr. Paynter. Going to kill the bad men."

He pulled his finger away from the paper as if retreating from a hot stove. After a few seconds of silence, he cut his eyes toward the little girl. "And what do you think about that?"

She unfolded her arms and spread her hands. "It had to be done. Everybody knows that."

He nodded slowly. "I suppose it did."

She lifted the paper gently and held it to him. "I made it for you."

He froze again, for perhaps a heartbeat, before accepting the drawing. "It's a fine picture, Lisbet. And you made me a good likeness. I'm proud of you."

Lisbet was beaming when her brother and sister bid Paynter good day and hauled her out the door. The hint of smile on his lips faded when the door closed behind the departing children. His eyes met Rosalyn's over the tabletop separating them. He removed his distinctive tasseled hat, showing its age after seven years of hard wear.

"How goes the teaching, Miss Ashley?"

"Proceeding well, I think. I'm learning along with the children. Sometimes, I'm just one day ahead of them in mastering a subject. I'm good with grammar and math but having to relearn my history a day at a time. The older students help the younger, and I think at least two of them will make fine teachers someday."

"That's good to hear. We need good teachers."

A few seconds of silence fell between them. She lifted her chin, wondering why she'd tucked it in the first place. "And you? How goes the marshaling business?"

He rocked his head side to side and examined the ceiling. "Oh, you know. Quiet most days. A little tedious at times. But I like it all right." His eyes returned to catch hers. "There's good people here, and that's enough for now."

She blinked twice before allowing her clasped hands to roam freely. "Look, I heard what happened on your return trip from Laramie. I'm pleased to see that you are unharmed, other than that limp."

"That pleases me too."

He didn't seem pleased, though. A shadow hung over his eyes, a specter of dire events past or future. She wondered if he might stand all day without speaking and decided to help him along.

"Something's on your mind."

It was a statement, not a question. He ground his jaw back and forth and dipped his forehead in acknowledgment. "I have to ask you a question."

She strongly suspected the nature of his question, given the events he'd just experienced. "I'm listening."

"Do you know if your brother and Dutch van Zandt are in business together?"

She dropped her gaze and ran a finger in a lazy circle near the edge of the table. "Not for certain. Lucien hasn't spoken a word to me since I left the ranch last year."

"But?"

"But Mrs. Guilfoyle slips me information from time to time when she comes into town for supplies. She says van Zandt's men are regular visitors at the ranch, sometimes bringing, sometimes taking."

"Bringing and taking what?"

She shrugged. "Cattle. Ammunition boxes. Crates containing who knows what."

Paynter rubbed his chin as his eyes stared into the vacant distance. "Sounds like a business partnership to me. But what kind of business?"

"I don't know. But I have an idea."

He met her eyes, his face as grim as a marble statue. "What's that?"

She folded her arms as a sudden chill gripped her. "Lucien wants to be a big man in this territory. He wants to dominate every landscape, to own it. He intends to run for the state legislature, and then governor after that. To accomplish those goals, it would be useful for him to have an army at his disposal. One that doesn't much worry about laws and rules."

"And Dutch van Zandt has an army that doesn't much worry about laws and rules."

"Exactly."

Paynter nodded slowly, seemingly accepting easily what he'd already expected. "Then I'm sorry."

"Sorry for what?"

"For what might happen next. I don't want to…" His statement faded into the floor.

"I understand," she said. "Do what you must. I trust you to do what's right."

He placed his hat back on his head and rolled up Lisbet's drawing. "I'll try not to disappoint you."

"You can never disappoint me."

In the silent pause that followed, Rosalyn wondered for the thousandth time if Paynter would ever see himself as a good and decent man. She did. Others did. But the harshest critic of Jake Paynter continued to be Jake Paynter. He touched the brim of his hat and half turned to leave.

"By the way," he said, almost as if an afterthought, "is Blackburn still on Lucien's payroll?"

She should have expected that question as well. "He was when last I spoke with Mrs. Guilfoyle two weeks ago. And Sweeney too. I'm sorry for that."

Paynter heaved a weary sigh. "Not your fault. Good day, Miss Ashley."

He departed quickly but left behind the specter of inevitable violence to come. Rosalyn whispered a brief prayer for him, knowing it would not be nearly enough.

———————

As Jake left the schoolhouse behind, he tallied his many enemies in his head. Dutch van Zandt, the nebulous outlaw boss seemingly intent on burning down Jake's corner of the Wyoming Territory. Rosalyn's brother, Lucien Ashley, who had spared no effort to see Jake hang before a presidential pardon and a marshal's badge had put Jake beyond his reach. Sweeney, the leader of a Philadelphia street gang Jake had systematically slaughtered when they had come for the significant price on his head a year earlier. Then his thoughts settled on Ambrose Blackburn. Always Blackburn.

When Jake had joined the war in '61 as a naive seventeen-year-old, Captain Blackburn had quickly become a stand-in for the nurturing father he'd never had. For six months, he had molded the clay of that guileless boy into a vessel of pure death, hardened by fire and flame. In a moment of harrowing insight that had cost him his soul, Jake had abandoned Blackburn and his raiders, eventually landing with the First Kansas Colored Volunteers on the other side of the conflict. However, Blackburn was like the hot winds of summer—returning like clockwork to wilt Jake in the heat of his fiery mission.

Six years. Jake had been free from the man for half a dozen years before the withering wind had come again. As he turned onto Main Street, the memory of that foul reunion slipped into his thoughts, a lifetime ago and yesterday.

"Rider comin'. Wearing army colors."

The announcement from Sergeant Rivers drew Jake, lieutenant of the Tenth Cavalry K Troop posted at Fort Bridger, through the open front gates of the fort. Curiosity gripped him. Jake's former first sergeant had mustered out only a week earlier. Jake hadn't expected a replacement for another week yet. He shaded his eyes from the noonday sun to peer at the oncoming rider, squinting for recognition. As the man approached, the skin of Jake's forehead went cold with erupting perspiration. He knew the form, the swagger, the carriage in the saddle before he recognized the face.

Captain Blackburn.

The devil himself.

Jake lowered his hand to rest it against his revolver. Blackburn seemed to take great delight in the expression on Jake's face, for he smiled broadly as he reined his mount to a stop. Gray peppered the red flame of his beard, a testament to the passage of years.

"As I live and breathe," he drawled. "If it ain't young Jake Paynter, all grown up and wearing army stripes."

"That's Lieutenant Paynter to you," growled Gus at his side.

Blackburn shot Gus a look of pure darkness and touched the stripes on his shoulder. "You'll speak when spoken to, boy."

Jake remained motionless, his jaw locked from the cascade of bleak memories rampaging through his skull. Blackburn swung down from his saddle and produced a casual salute.

"First Sergeant Blackburn, reporting for duty."

In that moment, Jake became again the malleable kid who'd initially seen Blackburn as the second coming of the angel Gabriel before learning that the man fought for the camp of a different angel, fallen far from heaven. All Jake's hard-won efforts at redemption began to fade before his eyes. His breathing grew shallow. His pulse quickened to thrum in his ears. Gus's grip on his shoulder arrested Jake's slide into darkness.

"Lieutenant."

Jake ingested the single word and used it to fortify his faltering confidence. He stretched his frame but maintained fingertip contact with his Kerr. "How in God's name did the army see fit to give you a uniform?"

Blackburn produced a mock frown. "What? No friendly words of reunion?"

"I asked you a question."

Blackburn let his smile fade, no doubt a calculated maneuver. "Fine, then. It seems the army is hard up for white officers to ride herd on these black soldiers. The uniform I wore two years ago don't seem to matter much to them now. Hell, they even gave me a signing bonus. But you know what?"

Jake refused to swallow the bait. He continued glaring at Blackburn, his lips a thin line of disregard. His old captain, however, didn't wait for Jake's acknowledgment.

"When they gave me a choice of posts, and I heard you were here, I jumped at the chance. And I'd trade the whole wad of money they gave me for the look on your face right now." He spat in the dirt. "Lieuuu-tenant."

Jake was on Blackburn before he could consider what he was doing. He flung the surprised man to the hard-packed dirt of the gate entry, straddled him, and leaned near enough to see the fine hairs around Blackburn's eyes.

"If you ever," he rumbled, "disrespect me in front of the men again, I will take your hide inch by bloody inch. Understood?"

Blackburn's wide eyes narrowed and he lifted one side of his lip. "Understood."

Jake rose to his feet. "Sergeant Rivers."

"Sir?"

"See our new first sergeant to his quarters."

"Yes, sir."

As Blackburn stood to replace his hat and brush dirt from his uniform, he gave Jake a grim-eyed glare. I will kill you one day, it said. Jake nodded confirmation. The devil had come again, and they'd not part until one of them was dead.

As Jake stepped up to the door of the marshal's office, he rubbed his face to banish the searing recollection of Blackburn's reemergence. He inhaled a deep breath and considered how his life had changed since that day nearly three years earlier. He'd survived the noose. He'd made lifelong allies. The finest woman he'd ever known held him in some regard, much to his bewilderment. And the best friends a man could ask for waited just beyond the door, wearing deputy's badges. They were the reason he hadn't succumbed to darkness. They were the flames lighting his path toward a better way. It was for them that he wore the mantle of marshal, to do what he could while he could. As he clutched Lisbet's drawing in one hand and turned the door handle with the other, Jake reminded himself of all these truths. They were mostly enough.

CHAPTER EIGHT

"What'll it be, Gus? The goat or paperwork?"

Gus never broke eye contact as he sat across from Jake inside the marshal's office. "That ain't even hard. I'll take the goat."

"You sure?"

"Darn sure."

Jake heaved a sigh. "All right, then. But take Stacy with you to cover your back. Disputes over molehills have a way of blowin' up into mountains when livestock's on the line."

"Will do. Be back in a few hours. And by the way, that's a nice sketch." Gus pointed to Lisbet's drawing, now pinned to the wall beside Jake's desk. "A wagon train, is it?"

"Yep."

"Where'd you get it?"

"From a friend."

Gus rose, retrieved his Spencer from the wall rack, and nodded at the old man standing by the door. "Let's go, Mr. Epps, before that goat gets skinned, cooked, and digested."

"Thank you kindly," said Mr. Epps. When the two men stepped through the door, silence fell again in the jail and Jake dug into the cursed paperwork. Greely waited ten minutes before interrupting from his cell.

"They don't got no law at Atlantic City?"

"No," said Jake. "They've been lookin' for a peace officer since New Year's, but nobody wants the job. Meantime, me and the deputies handle those chores whenever the need arises."

Jake withheld his annoyance in the reply, but Greely must've seen through it. "And you don't mind?"

"I do mind, as a matter of fact. Mostly, though, they handle their own business. But this time it's a goat. You don't mess with a man's goat. They're like family."

Greely chuckled. "Like my family, anyways."

They fell again into a mutual wordless state while Jake wrestled the paperwork into submission. Most territory justices would accept just a wink and a nod from local lawmen concerning the prosecution of their duties and not ask too many questions, but Judge Kingman wasn't most territory justices. He took his job seriously. Sacredly.

"By the book," he'd told Jake in Laramie. "Accountability inspires trust, and paperwork is the anchor for the accountability chain."

Jake agreed with the judge's point but despised the paperwork nonetheless. Anytime he tried to pawn it off on Stacy or Gus, they'd find something else to do in a hurry. But such was the burden of the town marshal's badge, and he knew the judge would hold him accountable to his lofty standards. Jake gritted his teeth and dug deeper into the job. Upon finishing, perhaps a half hour later, he dropped the pencil to the desktop and clenched his fingers several times to relieve the persistent cramp. He stood and donned his hat.

"Greely."

"Marshal?"

"I'm steppin' out for some air. You need anything before I go?"

"Some air."

"Except that."

"Nope."

Jake nodded and slipped out onto the creaking boardwalk. He stretched his back while surveying Main Street, now a quagmire of muck from melting snow and endless horse and wagon traffic. He grew a half smile. It looked like hell, but it was *his* hell.

"Marshal Paynter?"

Jake turned to his right to find a strange beast who seemed to have escaped recently from genteel captivity. The tall man wore a finely tailored three-piece suit and shiny black boots. His neatly trimmed brown beard and mustache framed aristocratic angular features that in most places would mark him as mayor, governor, or soon to be either. He rested a gloved hand on the ivory head of a shiny cane, holding it casually as if for effect instead of support. His only nod to frontier life was the wearing of a wide-brimmed gambler's hat in place of a bowler or top hat. If the man had fallen from the sky, Jake couldn't have been more surprised by his appearance in the mewling midst of South Pass City mayhem.

"You seem out of place, mister," he said.

The stranger grinned nonchalantly. "Oh? How so?"

"You look like a New York City lawyer who lost his way and ended up tripping into Hades."

The man laughed—a deep, smooth chuckle that echoed in the expanse of his chest. "Very good, Marshal. In reality, I *was* a New York City lawyer for a time after graduating from Harvard. You might say I did lose my way."

Jake scanned the street for additional strangers. Finding none, he stepped closer to the man with suspicion. "What brings you to South Pass City?"

"Harrison's the name." The man extended a hand, but Jake ignored it. He lowered the hand and nodded slowly. "Judge Kingman sent me ahead to sort out the Union Pacific situation. He will be along in short order."

Jake returned the nod but nursed his skepticism. He'd been with Kingman for most of the previous month and had never laid eyes on the newcomer. He inched closer to the lawyer and motioned to the muck of the street. "Well, I can't imagine South Pass City compares to by-God New York City."

"What place does?" Harrison said. "But my life there was consuming me from the inside out. Feasting on me alive. One fine winter morning when frost blanketed the streets and a deep chill consumed the air, I was struck by a notion to try something new. Something out of the ordinary. Something bold. So I resigned from my firm, bequeathed most of my worldly possessions to my sisters, and headed west. And now here I stand, applying my Ivy League education in service of a greater purpose. Who knows? I might even hang out a shingle here."

Jake's eyes swept the newcomer again, from expensive boots to impeccable hat, as thoughts of Rosalyn rumbled through his brain. Harrison seemed precisely the type of gentleman far more suited for Rosalyn than he was. A surprising surge of jealousy drove him nearer the man. "May I be frank?"

"Indeed," said Harrison with a cool smile. "I prize frankness."

Jake straightened, trying but failing to match the lawyer's impressive height. "The big mines began playing out last year, and the placer miners have been comin' up more and more empty-handed. I reckon we lost a thousand people over the winter, movin' on to greener pastures and more agreeable climes. If you're lookin' for boom, I'm afraid you've stumbled into a bust instead. There ain't much greater purpose left here now."

Harrison accepted the information with a disappointed nod. "Ah, that's a pity for everyone." He gestured toward Jake's badge. "However, it warms my soul to see that the town has maintained its dedication to preserving law and order. Civic pride is a wonder to behold, no matter where it's found."

"I don't disagree," said Jake. "But you'd be better off serving in Laramie or Cheyenne. Or maybe south in Denver, far from here."

The man touched the brim of his hat. "Thank you for the neighborly advice, Marshal. But I wonder. What keeps *you* here, then, in a dying town? It seems a man of your reputation could maintain the law in any of those cities you just mentioned. Why, even New York City would be fortunate to engage your services."

Despite his creeping dislike for the lawyer, Jake frowned in thought. It was a good question. In fact, it was likely *the* question. Why had he remained? Why had he accepted a job he never sought nor ever wanted? Why not just move on like many of the others? He didn't need to reach very deep to find the answer.

"Loyalty."

"Loyalty? How so?"

"I've people here who call me friend, and I owe them more than I can hold in my head. I stay for them. I don't suppose you'd know much about that."

The stranger grew a wide smile. "As a matter of fact, I do. Men are at their finest when fiercely loyal to one another. I commend you, sir."

"Thank you," mumbled Jake as he absently touched his Kerr. "Next stage out of town is tomorrow. In the meantime, the Idaho House offers clean rooms and decent fare. Be careful of your boots when you cross the street."

The lawyer lifted his cane into the crook of an elbow and clapped his gloved hands together. "Or you can hand over that fine revolver."

The muzzles of two weapons, one pressed against the base of Jake's neck and the other lodged beneath his ribs, froze him. After a few heartbeats, he pulled his hand away from the holstered Kerr and extended it to shoulder level. The lawyer retrieved the revolver, and the unseen gunmen dragged Jake into the marshal's office. He made eye contact with Greely to find the prisoner saucer-eyed on the edge of his bunk. Understanding flooded Jake. He faced the four gunmen first and then the lawyer as the man shut the office door behind him.

"Wise choice," said Harrison. "But look at my poor manners. I don't believe I fully introduced myself. Care to guess?"

The horror he'd seen in Greely's eyes told Jake not to speak the name "van Zandt" lest he admit that Greely had talked. "I'm not much of a guesser. I have no idea who you are."

The man laughed. "Let me illuminate your benighted condition, then. Harrison van Zandt's the name, but my friends and enemies call me Dutch. I wonder, which one will you be?"

"I think you know."

"True, but no harm in asking. Now, on to business. You have one of my men in your custody. I'll take him now and be on my way."

Greely surged to his feet in the cell. "I didn't say nothin', Dutch! Not a word."

Van Zandt hummed. "Does he tell the truth, Marshal?"

Jake met Greely's pleading eyes, nodded, and lied again. "Bastard gave us squat. Even when we tortured him."

"Very good. Very good. Riesling!"

"Sir?" said one of the gunmen.

"Retrieve the keys and liberate our compatriot Mr. Greely."

A young man with a face that looked like it had been folded in half one too many times stepped around Jake, grabbed the keys from the wall, and opened the cell door. Greely inched out tentatively, gripping his slung arm protectively beneath the other.

"Step outside, Mr. Greely," said van Zandt.

As Greely slipped past, he spared a glance for Jake, one filled with all manner of demons. Gratitude, uncertainty, terror. Then he was gone from Jake's vision.

"You gonna kill him?" asked Jake.

"Oh," hummed van Zandt, "likely not. He's a good hand and knows to keep his mouth shut."

"So now what? You gonna murder a marshal in his own office?"

Van Zandt laughed. "That would make quite a headline, but no. I'd prefer to give you time to come around to my way of thinking. So if you would, deposit yourself in that newly vacated cell."

Jake turned as if in compliance but took only one step before wheeling on his new nemesis. Van Zandt must have known what was coming because he'd stepped back such that Jake's fist found only empty air. The gunmen collapsed onto Jake, including the hatchet-faced Riesling. Jake's darkest demons, which had long been dormant, flared to life. This time, however, the coming of the rage proved too little too late. The men piled atop him and beat him mercilessly until blackness pushed away the red haze.

CHAPTER NINE

IN THE BEGINNING, DARKNESS WAS ACROSS THE FACE OF the deep. And then there was light. The light revealed the blurry face of Stacy Blue floating over Jake, riddled with angry concern. He squeezed his eyes shut and reopened them to a squint.

"Paynter!" she said. "Wake up."

He did in an instant, flailing to fight off his attackers. She planted a hand on his chest and pushed him back into the bunk. "Easy. Easy. They ain't here anymore. Just me and Gus."

Jake cut his eyes to find Gus filling the cell door, his features as rife with concern as those of Stacy. He shuffled one step nearer to the cot. "What in heaven's name happened here?"

"Let me up," Jake replied. He guided Stacy's hand away from his chest and struggled to a sitting position. The aches of a dozen wounds assaulted his senses, temporarily stealing his breath. Stacy steadied him with a hand to his shoulder.

"Can you stand?" said Gus.

"Mostly, I think."

Gus leaned forward to help Jake to his feet and held him while his head stopped spinning. Gus let him catch a breath before drilling down further.

"Again, what happened to you after we left? And where's Greely?"

"Dutch van Zandt. That's what happened."

Jake moved stiffly from the cell, gingerly touching the swelling along and below his left eye. His jaw ached. His nose might be broken. His ribs didn't want to function properly. And someone had kicked him square in the kneecap. He found his Kerr abandoned on the floor and set about loading it. Stacy appeared before him with arms folded tightly.

"C'mon, Paynter. You gotta give us more than that."

"Fine."

While he loaded his revolver and the Henry rifle, he explained the surprising encounter with a former New York City lawyer who also happened to be the outlaw king of Wyoming. Gus and Stacy listened with similar surprise.

"It's my own fault," Jake concluded. "I knew van Zandt was comin'. I felt it the moment I saw him but ignored my gut."

He didn't tell the rest—of how thoughts of Rosalyn and the distraction of jealousy had held his suspicions at bay long enough for van Zandt to take him down. He was not proud of that.

Gus eyed him with speculation. "So what'll you do now?"

"Stacy," he said.

"Yes?"

"Go fetch the mare."

Gus laid a hand on Jake's arm. "You ain't goin' after van Zandt right now, are you?"

"Nope. I'm aimin' to have a chat with Lucien Ashley at his ranch. Now, Stacy, about my mare."

She unfolded her arms, eyes alight. "Fine. But we're goin' with you."

Jake shook his head. "You will not. You will remain here and watch out for van Zandt or any of his men returnin' to raise a ruckus. Hear me?"

"But why? And tell me the truth."

Jake heaved a sigh. "Okay. If I end up killing Ashley, then you don't have to lie on my behalf. I won't saddle you with that moral dilemma."

"At least let Maddie Dunbar have a look at those cuts."

"Ain't got time. Now, go fetch my horse from the stables."

Stacy's eyes flashed with indignation as she strode out of the office. Gus impaled Jake with a hardened stare. "You sure this is a good idea?"

"Nope. Not at all. Just help me find my hat."

———

Two things happened as Jake made the three-hour ride out to Lucien Ashley's lair at Flaming Rocks Ranch. One, his general anger and hostility narrowed considerably into a white-hot focus, like a glass lens against a heap of dry grass. Two, Gus and Stacy followed him at a distance as he had assumed they would. He could tell they were trying to evade his notice, but the open expanse of mostly treeless hills and trail failed to conceal much. Three times he nearly turned around to send them back, but he pushed aside the notion each time. He knew they had long ago appointed themselves his official caretakers and keepers and wouldn't listen to reason if they thought he was riding into danger. Which he most certainly was.

The nature of the danger became manifest when he descended from high ground into the crimson-red canyon that gave the ranch its name. The slopes above the canyon, which would become a carpet of green in a couple of months, slumbered beneath a mantle of snow. Cattle pawed for dead grass beneath while grazing the long upsweep, unconcerned about Jake's passage. The five men riding out to greet him, though, seemed of a different mind. They lifted an array of long guns at his approach. Two he recognized well. Blackburn and Sweeney.

"What's your business, Paynter?" shouted Sweeney. Jake swept aside his coat to reveal the marshal's badge. He wanted them to view it clearly and to think twice about attacking a lawman unprovoked. After all, killing a peace officer was still a hanging offense in every state and territory. Sweeney spat in the dirt and reached into the coat pocket where Paynter knew he kept a loaded pistol for the purpose of intimate killing.

"I owe you a bullet for what you did to my boys."

"Stay your hand, my Philadelphia friend," said Blackburn with magnanimous gravity. He swung his regard to Jake and allowed a smile to spread slowly across his face. "We've time and opportunity on our side. Patience is a virtue."

Jake stared a hole through Blackburn. "You know where I live. When you've grown a sack, come see me. For now, stand aside. I got official business with your boss."

Blackburn's smile faded, but he doffed his hat and bowed

in his saddle with a mocking flourish. "As you wish, *Marshal*. Wouldn't want to keep a peace officer from the execution of his duties."

The knot of horses parted and Jake rode into their midst without incident. His greeting party turned their mounts, flanked Jake on three sides, and followed him into the canyon with rifles at the ready. Along the way, Sweeney maintained a steady stream of conversation with the man to his left about the many ways he might kill Paynter when the time came.

Lucien clearly saw them approaching. As Jake rode up to the main ranch house, his nemesis stood planted on the overhung porch. He lifted a finger to impale Jake from thirty feet.

"We have nothing to discuss. You'd best swing around and return the way you came."

With his wishes spoken, Lucien disappeared into the house as if his words were a decree from the mountaintop and the mouth of the Almighty. Jake swung from his saddle and found himself surrounded by a dozen dismounted men with barrels leveled and nervous trigger fingers. He spun in a slow circle so they could all see the badge.

"Official business. Don't be stupid, now. If I don't kill you, the law will."

Some of the fight bled from the ranch hands, and they parted as Jake waded through them and onto the porch. He didn't bother knocking. When he swung the door open, Lucien stood facing him with a revolver in hand and a scowl on his face.

"I should have killed you when I had the chance."

Jake glared back, estimating how long it would take him

to draw if Lucien abandoned his normally well-maintained but duplicitous reason. "But you didn't kill me, Ashley. You didn't even try. And you and your sister are alive now because of that prudent decision."

Lucien kept Jake in his gaze while slowly returning his revolver to its holster. The hard edges of his features melted into wryness as he scanned Jake's battered face. "You are correct that I didn't try to kill you. But it seems as if someone else did try and fell just short."

"Can't argue that."

"It wasn't my men. So why the visit?"

Jake stepped nearer, raising a flinch from Lucien. He became aware that Blackburn and Sweeney had crowded through the door behind him, menacing his flank like a pair of malignant shadows. He shrugged them off and nodded at Lucien. "I'm not so sure about that."

"How so?"

"It was van Zandt and his boys who jumped me. He strolled up to the jail in South Pass City, all spit and polish. I thought he was just a misplaced dandy until too late. He took my prisoner and left me with a few mementos of our first meeting."

Sweeney belted out a loud guffaw at Jake's back. A mile-long smile split Lucien's face, and his eyes widened with mirth. "What? You fell for the smooth rhetoric of a man wearing a fine suit? Dutch van Zandt got the better of the great Jake Paynter? Well, I am rightly amused. You're no better than any other impressionable yokel in this backwater territory."

Jake flattened Lucien with an uppercut to the jaw.

Blackburn, Sweeney, and others wrestled Jake to the floor from behind, though he landed some elbows that would surely leave lasting marks. From beneath the crush of four or five bodies, he peered up to find Lucien rising slowly while working his jaw back and forth and holding a hand beneath it as if it might suddenly detach and fall to the floor.

"Let me kill him," said Sweeney. "Please."

"You can claim self-defense," added Blackburn into Jake's left ear. "We all saw him hit you. He's a killer, and I should know. I taught him myself."

Jake swung his head toward Blackburn in an attempt to break the man's teeth, but his old captain dodged him with a snorting laugh. With no other choice, Jake waited for Lucien to nod and give the order that would end him. However, the volcanic anger of Lucien's eyes cooled slowly to a hardened magma crust, predatory in its single-minded focus on Jake.

"Judge Kingman would be sorely displeased if we killed his marshal, so let him up. But hold his weapon for the remainder of this very brief conversation."

Someone lifted the Kerr from its holster, and the bodies peeled from Jake's back. He retrieved his hat, stood, and brushed dust from his jacket. Before Lucien could capture the remaining narrative, Jake lifted a finger that nearly brushed the man's nose.

"You're in league with van Zandt. You have been since they tried to burn out the miners last year. And now you run cattle and ammunition between here and wherever he's hiding. I want to know where that is."

Lucien's eyes flickered briefly with alarm, but he rushed

to conceal it behind a mocking smile. "What fool told you that lie? Was it van Zandt himself?"

"No."

"Then our business is finished. Get the hell off my land, Paynter, or I will see you out in a pine box."

Jake swayed in silence before nodding slowly. "Right, then. But give it time, Ashley. There will be a great reckoning between us before this is over."

"I am counting on it. In the meantime, you better be staying well away from my sister."

"Like she's stayin' away from you?"

"Get out! Never come here again!"

Jake turned to push his way past a disappointed Sweeney and through a horde of men, snatching his Kerr from a startled hand as he passed by. Upon reaching the mare, he faced the ranch hands, now numbering fifteen or more. He swept an arm toward them.

"Most of you seem like decent, God-fearin', law-abidin' fellas. Don't let your boss drag you into a noose. I'd hate that for you."

Sweeney stalked away in anger, but Blackburn leaned against the doorframe with folded arms and smiled. "I'll see you again real soon, boy, and you won't see me coming."

"I expect nothing less," Jake said.

As he mounted the mare, one of the hands that had trailed him into the canyon mounted alongside Jake and nodded to Blackburn. "I'll make sure he quits the area."

"See that you do. Ride at his back with scattergun leveled. Shoot him if he turns back this way."

"Yes, sir."

The escort trailed a few lengths behind with his shotgun at the ready as Jake rode out of the canyon. Gus and Stacy sat mounted on the ridge, having given up their clandestine ruse. Jake just shook his head. When he neared his deputies, the ranch hand closed the distance to ride alongside Jake.

"Marshal?"

"What?"

"Was that true what you said? That if Mr. Ashley is breakin' the law, we could all hang?"

"It's possible. If nothing else, Judge Kingman will grant you a long holiday in a drafty cell. He's a principled man, but I wouldn't test his mercy."

The rider spurred his horse ahead and turned it back toward the ranch. Jake halted the mare on a hunch. A war of attrition behind the ranch hand's eyes finally broke when he leaned toward Jake. "Van Zandt has a compound in the guts of Wind River Canyon, about halfway down from the entrance beside a bend of the river. If somethin' happens with Mr. Ashley, just remember that I tried to help you. Name's Harper."

"Thanks, Harper. I will."

The ranch hand dropped his eyes before raising them to Jake once more. "You know you're ridin' into a buzz saw if you go into that canyon after van Zandt. You'll never find 'em before they find you first. You don't know that hellscape like they do."

Jake nudged the mare forward. "True. I don't know the place. But I know a man who does."

CHAPTER TEN

OF ALL THE GIFTS THAT CAME WITH AGE, BEAH NOOKI counted contentment as the finest. As a young man, he'd rarely been content. Thoughts of the next hunt, the next fight, or the next woman drew him inexorably through his youth in a rush of moons and seasons. No longer. After seventy winters, he could crouch beside the river and consider thoughts both grand and mundane with equal pleasure. Some of those thoughts sent him forward to wonder what would become of his people. Other thoughts considered the present, reveling in the experience of the day. Many, though, took him backward to the day he laid eyes on white men for the first time, and them in the company of a long-absent Shoshone woman no less.

Captain Lewis and Lieutenant Clark had seemed like creatures from the spirit world to a five-year-old Beah Nooki, so strange were their mannerisms, appearance, and speech. He'd wondered if they were men at all or just clever beasts. Sacajawea, however, appeared to consider them harmless and perhaps even tolerable. Then had come the wars with the Crow, the Blackfeet, the Cheyenne, strung out over decades for control of the rich hunting grounds of the Wind River Valley. Beah Nooki had risen in stature among his people as much for his survival as for his courage. When each battle had ended, he had found himself upright to bid farewell to the dead. This had always amused him. The heroic dead occupied the stories of legend. Those who lived crafted the future. He was content to occupy the latter camp a while longer.

His thoughts turned toward the puzzle of the white men who had recently begun overrunning the plains and mountains like a swarm of locusts, seemingly unstoppable and without end. Chief Washakie had fashioned a treaty with the white man's government to preserve the valley for the Shoshone. Would the treaty hold? Few treaties had, invariably broken by the oncoming locusts. His study of Jake Paynter had proven hopeful, though. Formerly plagued by violence and regret, the man had learned to live in peace with Beah Nooki's people for a time. Perhaps others could as well.

With his thoughts on Paynter, Beah Nooki was not surprised to find the man approaching along the river in the company of others. Some days, the Spirit perfectly prepared him for what came next. Beah Nooki stood from the rock on which he'd been resting and cupped a hand above his eyes. He recognized the buffalo soldier, Gus Rivers, and the granddaughter of Many Horses, Stacy Blue. The other four men were strangers to his eyes. A disturbance from his periphery drew his attention to the village a few hundred steps away. Young warriors armed with bows, spears, and rifles were massing beyond the boundary of the lodges, clearly preparing for a skirmish with the unwelcome intruders. He lifted his chin to shout at them.

"Be still! Paynter comes!"

His words settled the flurry of activity. Satisfied, Beah Nooki began walking to meet the advancing party. They came together in an expanse of ankle-deep snow unmarred by the relentless sagebrush. Beah Nooki held up a hand.

"Paynter. Stacy Blue. Gus Rivers. What brings you here?"

He knew on sight that the reason must be compelling. Paynter's eyes were cold. Beah Nooki had seen those same eyes when Paynter had first arrived unexpectedly three winters earlier, sent by Beah Nooki's grandson to seek shelter after killing an important white soldier. The return of those eyes caused him concern. Paynter dismounted and strode forward to clasp Beah Nooki's forearm. The other riders swung from their saddles into the snow, but only Stacy and Gus joined Paynter. Stacy greeted Beah Nooki warmly in the Shoshone language while Gus silently touched his hat. Without answering Beah Nooki's question, Paynter gestured to the four other riders.

"These men are Aguilar, Emshoff, Roberson, and Jackson."

Beah Nooki greeted them in English. "Pleased to make your acquaintance. You are my guests."

The men smiled and nodded, and the one called Emshoff even bowed to Beah Nooki. He remembered that name from Paynter's stories when he'd returned for a second winter with his people. Emshoff had shown Paynter kindness, he recalled, and had given him bread. In Beah Nooki's view, kindness and bread were as gifts from the Creator. Beah Nooki turned his eyes on Paynter and studied the young man's face.

"You seem on a trail of intention," he said. "Perhaps we might talk of it."

Paynter nodded as seeming relief softened his features. "That would please me."

Beah Nooki cleared a space in the snow with his foot and sat. Paynter joined him while the others clustered around the parlay. Beah Nooki dipped his forehead. "What troubles you?"

"We are going to war against a fierce enemy, but first we must scout his territory."

Beah Nooki listened in silence as Paynter described an outlaw gang and their raids against people, trains, and towns alike. Beah Nooki grunted recognition. "We know of these men. They make us unwelcome in the canyon of the Wind River when we try to hunt and fish."

Paynter seemed surprised. "You know where they are? Why did you not ask me for help?"

"We mount a thousand warriors on horseback. We do not need anyone's help."

"Right," said Paynter with a chuckle. "I don't suppose you do. But might you be willing to help us?"

"I am listening."

"We ride from here to the Wind River Canyon to find these men, to study their defenses, to fight if we must. Might you tell me the turns of the canyon, where we might be ambushed, how best to approach the enemy?"

Beah Nooki glanced at the assembled company. Six men and a woman against three or four times that number in unfamiliar country. It seemed the journey of those wishing to meet an early death. He leveled his eyes at Paynter.

"I will not tell you the path." When Paynter's frown grew deep, Beah Nooki held up a hand. "I will *show* you the path."

A grin crawled across the young man's face. "I was hopin' you'd say that."

Beah Nooki stood, his old knees popping as he straightened them. Another gift of old age—knees that sang. "Wait here. I will fetch a few others and speak with Washakie. We will return to ride with you."

Paynter held up a hand in protest. "You don't need to endanger anyone else."

Beah Nooki nodded. It was a noble sentiment. But also wrong. "We must learn to ride together," he said, "instead of always apart. One way is life, the other death. You know this already."

Paynter blinked softly. "I do."

"Good. Let us choose life today."

Stacy blurted a laugh. "You might as well be askin' a rock to grow into a tree."

Beah Nooki just smiled at her. "Fire opens even the hardest of seeds."

"That's my prayer," said Paynter.

"Keep praying, then."

As Beah Nooki walked away from the scouting party toward the village, he felt a spring in his step that hadn't been present earlier. He was once again going into battle, and as a gray-hair. Nothing had ever filled him with life more than the prospect of losing it.

CHAPTER ELEVEN

JAKE LED A PARTY OF THIRTEEN AWAY FROM THE Shoshone village with the blessing of Chief Washakie and the well wishes of a nomadic nation. The unlucky number might have bothered many, but Jake had sworn off superstition long ago. In his experience, truth demanded evidence. So-called truth without confirmation was merely wishful thinking. Thus far, he'd witnessed no evidence to convince him that numbers were unlucky, crossed fingers brought good fortune, or fates were written in the stars. He did, however, believe in the Roman proverb that "fortune favors the bold." Courage alone could never guarantee success, but it was always a good starting point. The twelve riders in his wake were nothing if not bold.

Beah Nooki had brought along five men—Darwin Follows the Wind, Big Elk, and three eager youths who hadn't offered their names—with repeating rifles all around. Follows the Wind, Beah Nooki's grandson, had scouted for the army under Jake's command three years earlier. He was present that fateful day above the Green River basin when Jake's shooting of his captain had altered forever the trajectory of his life. Big Elk was a broadly built man who a year earlier had violently finished off the bounty hunters who'd come for Jake's head. The man was anxious to dislodge the outlaws from the canyon and had brought a panoply of weapons should it come to that. Jake smiled to himself. If his expedition found itself in a desperate fight with van Zandt's men, he trusted Follows the Wind and Big Elk implicitly.

The traveling party left behind the Little Wind River and the shadow of the mountains after midday and forged northeast across the flats. By nightfall, they'd found the Wind River proper and crossed it before setting camp. Big Elk and the young men appeared ready to separate themselves from the rest of the group, but quiet counsel by Beah Nooki convinced them otherwise. Francisco Aguilar motioned for Big Elk to sit beside him while Emshoff began digging out a seemingly endless supply of rye bread from his overstuffed saddle pack. Within an hour, the entire party was exchanging bread and jerky around a roaring fire and generally engaging in civil communication. Jake shook his head with wonder. How had he, a man who'd ridden with the worst of men and performed the foulest of deeds, found himself in the company of such noble people? It remained a pleasant mystery. He pulled Beah Nooki aside.

"Thank you," he said.

The elder just smiled. "I did nothing."

The second day of travel progressed much the same as the first, except for Stacy and one of the young warriors. Shortly after they'd departed camp at sunup, the young man had pulled his horse alongside Stacy's calico and began conversing with her in the Shoshone language. Stacy seemed more than willing to engage. Jake heard little of it and understood even less, but he recognized flirting when he saw it. Meanwhile, Gus followed behind the two, growing grimmer and grimmer as the exchange and laughter between them stretched into the afternoon. Finally, he appeared to reach a breaking point.

"I'm scouting ahead," he told Jake flatly. His standard good humor had fled completely.

"Whatever you like. Find us a camp short of the canyon."

Gus rode off without a word. Jake glanced at Stacy to find her watching Gus ride away, her forehead creased with confusion. "Why's he ridin' off in such a huff?"

Jake shook his head. "That's between you two. Do your own dancin.'"

He ignored her insistence that he clarify his remarks and instead concentrated on the landscape unfolding before them. The snow-dusted red and yellow rocks of the Owl Creek Mountains swept east and west with seemingly no end, like a mottled snake of nearly infinite length intent on circling the world to swallow its tail. A smudge of shadow in the smack middle of the range marked the yawning entrance of Wind River Canyon. An hour on, they found Gus some two or three miles from the canyon gate nursing a fire to life. Jake addressed the group.

"We'll camp here for the night. Riding into that hole in darkness is a death wish." He motioned to Beah Nooki. "He leads from here. We do as Beah Nooki says."

The elder's eyes beamed with mirth. "Now, you have made me important. This is no favor."

"Welcome to my life," Jake said.

Emshoff appeared to share Beah Nooki's amusement. "Consider the advantages," he said to Jake. "If we had not made you important, you would have died and us with you."

"If only," Jake replied.

As the band settled into camp, Stacy dragged Gus out into the brush where they held an animated conversation muffled by distance. When Jake turned away, it seemed as though they might go twenty-five rounds with bare knuckles. When he glanced back a few minutes later, he found them in a tight clench with Gus's mouth near Stacy's ear. He couldn't help but smile. Someone ought to be happy in this world. Since it couldn't be him, then why not his closest friends?

Jake's scouting expedition pressed onward ahead of the sun and entered the top end of the canyon just as the first rays of dawn caressed the entrance. They progressed carefully through hellish terrain littered with tumbled rock and clinging shrubbery. Bighorn sheep treading the canyon walls above watched them with casual interest, secure in their lofty fortress. Rising birdsong echoed across the rocks, punctuated by the periodic aria of a lone meadowlark hidden from view. Fat trout repeatedly punctured the surface of the river to feast on mosquitoes that strayed too near the water.

The rising sun soon began filling the gash of earth with soft light, illuminating walls of pink and black rock seemingly heaved from the belly of the world to swell heavenward as the river knifed through the gap. When sunlight touched the water, Beah Nooki halted them at a place where the river ran wide and easy, a false prophet of the mayhem in store downriver. Just ahead, the sloping canyon walls tipped toward the river and raised up like a rearing horse.

"We rest for a moment and talk of what comes after."

The party dismounted and gathered around the elder. Beah Nooki gazed down the canyon for a time, wisps of gray hair waving in the light breeze. Finally, he motioned toward the bend of the river perhaps a half mile distant.

"When I was young and my head was empty, we rode that way with one hundred warriors to meet the Blackfeet in battle. Fish swarm this river like flies on curing meat. The Blackfeet did not wish to share. We did not either."

Everyone craned their necks toward Beah Nooki's soft-voiced telling while Darwin Follows the Wind translated quietly for Big Elk and the youths.

"Beyond that turn of the river, the way becomes narrow for a time. The only path is by water or a trail like the edge of a knife. We left our horses and walked. Our enemies met us there. They ran down from high ground with cries and hatchets. We fought until the river ran red with the blood of both peoples. The Blackfeet left after a time and the fish were ours. But we traded nine men for those fish."

He fell silent, his gaze never leaving the river ahead. No one dared interrupt him. After a minute, he stood to face the party. "He who holds the narrow places holds the canyon. For now, they belong to the outlaws. We must move on foot above the water. One of us must climb higher and follow the high ground until the walls cannot be passed. This person will warn of ambush."

Roberson lifted a hand. "Why don't we all follow the high ground?"

The elder nodded, but Jake could tell he saw it as the question of a child. "Because," said Beah Nooki, "death stalks the high ground. A loose rock and a man stumbles. To stumble is to fall into the pit. And the way requires hands and feet. A man cannot continue that way and fire a weapon at the same time. If the enemy sees you, then you are already dead."

Jake understood Beah Nooki's meaning and hoped everyone else did as well. Whoever volunteered to become the eyes of the party from above put his life in mortal danger. He couldn't ask that of anyone. He didn't need to.

"I'll do it," said Gus.

Jake narrowed his eyes at his friend. "You don't have to."

"I know. Nevertheless."

Big Elk appeared at Gus's side and spoke to Beah Nooki. The elder nodded and a grim smile captured his lips.

"Big Elk will join you. He says two are better, for a man might help a man."

Gus dipped his forehead to Big Elk. They slung rifles and ammunition over their shoulders and began mounting the high ground, ascending like minor gods toward Olympus.

"Don't you fall, Gus Rivers," Stacy said. "Or I will surely kill you."

"I'll do my best, Miss Blue. You stay alive."

She rubbed her face and turned to Beah Nooki. "What now?"

"We walk. But you remain with the horses so they do not run."

Her eyes flashed. "But I want to go with you. I *need* to go with you."

The elder placed hands on each of her shoulders. "Stacy Blue. I promised your grandfather, Many Horses, to protect you always. I will do so now."

The hard set of his gaze brooked no disagreement. Stacy glanced up the canyon wall toward the retreating Gus, swallowed hard, and nodded. "Okay. But I don't like it."

Beah Nooki released her shoulders and grinned. "The words of a true warrior."

"Set a picket," Jake told Stacy. "Keep your shotgun handy. We may be comin' out hot, so have the horses ready to ride."

"I'll have 'em ready. Don't you worry."

"I wasn't worried."

Jake turned to find Beah Nooki already traversing the ground above the river with the other eight men single file in his wake. He caught up with the procession to walk behind Jim Jackson. The young man, no more than eighteen by now, seemed particularly fraught with nerves. That didn't surprise Jake. The boy was young and inexperienced in the ways of violence. When Jake had been held captive by Lucien Ashley and his hired gang the previous summer, it was Jim who'd been assigned to guard him. And it was Jim whom he'd spared when escaping. The young man had insisted on joining the expedition when Jake had recruited the others. Jake hoped the eagerness to join wasn't a misguided sense of guilt or gratitude, but he feared it was. When Jim faded back toward him, Jake got his answer.

"We might die today," said the boy. "Do we really have to go in there after them? Not just wait 'em out?"

It was a reasonable question, but Jake held the answer deep in his gut. He stared ahead for a half minute before responding. "Gus and I served together with the First Kansas Colored during the war. I guess you know that."

"I'd heard. It musta been glorious."

Jake shook his head. "It was long stretches of boredom, deprivation, and hunger between days of pure hell. Never glorious. But I learned a thing or two about momentum and morale in the process."

"Momentum?" said Jim.

"And morale." When Jim cocked his head, Jake heaved a sigh. "I'll tell you a story, then, so you'll know."

"That would be much appreciated, sir."

"Right." Jake closed his eyes briefly to stir up a particular memory. "On the borderlands between the Cherokee and Creek Nations, July of '63. The Confederates had massed at Honey Springs, intent on drivin' the federals from the territory for good. General Blunt caught wind of the plan and decided to attack before the rebels could join up their forces. Long story short, First Kansas found itself in the center of the line during the thick of the fight and was ordered to capture the artillery battery supporting the Texas cavalry units."

Jake could still hear in his head Colonel Williams's words from that fateful day. *No quarter will be given you by our adversary if you are captured. Do not falter. Do not fail.*

"So we fixed bayonets to our Springfields and marched forward, exchanging volleys with the Texans, a call and answer of thunder and smoke. Colonel Williams went down, and Gus pulled him out of the fight. In between volleys, we were dodging bullets and pulling our wounded from the open field to the safety of a berm. Next thing I knew, the Confederates were charging us a thousand men strong. We stood our ground with our dead and wounded at our feet and stopped them not twenty-five paces from our line when the Confederate color-bearer fell. Another man picked up the colors, and we shot him down too. A third tried, and we leveled him with a hundred pieces of lead. After that, the Texans stalled, then fell back, and we slowly took the field. Only the final stand of their Choctaw and Chickasaw Regiment kept us from routing the retreat."

Jim was wide-eyed. "It *sounds* glorious."

"No, I told you, it was pure hell. We lost a lot of men that day. But that's not the point. You listenin', kid?"

Jim nodded. "Yes, sir."

"Good. Then hear this and treasure it in your heart. When we took down the Confederate colors three times, it shook them. Even though they outnumbered us two to one, it cost 'em their momentum and bled away their morale." Jake motioned toward the canyon ahead. "Dutch's stronghold ahead is his banner. His emblems. His flag. As long as he holds it uncontested, he remains invincible. We need to take it from him. We need to bring down his colors, whatever the cost."

Jim stared blankly ahead for a minute, unspeaking. Jake

felt for him. The prospect of losing one's life tended to extinguish the need for conversation. He dropped a palm onto Jim's shoulder and gave a gentle squeeze. "Fighting's not for everyone. You can remain with Stacy and keep the horses if you like. I won't think any less of you."

Jake watched with fascination as the angst in Jim's eyes slowly congealed into resolve. The young man exhaled a determined breath.

"I believe I will continue onward, if you don't mind."

Jake did mind. Jim's death would become as much his fault as that of any man he'd shot directly. But he knew that every soul must beat its chosen path through the world.

"I don't mind," he lied. "And besides, if we're gonna die today, this canyon is at least a beautiful place to rest."

CHAPTER TWELVE

GUS HARBORED NO INTENTION OF DYING FROM A FALL. Gravity had other ideas on the matter. As he angled up the steepening slope behind Big Elk, every step became more precarious than the last. After rising perhaps two hundred feet above the tumbling river, the way became impassable using feet alone. He followed his companion's example and gripped outcroppings of rock and clinging tufts of grass to support his weight against the inexorable pull toward oblivion. After ten minutes of traversing the slope upward and into the canyon, he was regretting his eagerness to volunteer for the hazardous duty. However, the elevated vantage allowed him to understand the method to Beah Nooki's madness. From the higher slope, they would be able to see over the rocky rise that forced the bend in the river ahead. Any ambush beyond would be revealed.

As he moved along the wall, Gus ventured a downward glance to the river far below. The rest of the party moved along just above the waterline, a disjointed snake burrowing relentlessly into a deadly hole. He reached for a new grip while turning his eyes back to the work at hand but found nothing but empty air. His shifting body tipped forward as he groped in vain for another handhold, and his trailing foot lost purchase. The counter movements began to release the tension of his body against the wall, surrendering to the pull of gravity for a stretching second during which Gus recalled a dozen memories in a curious flash of remembrance. None of them offered a solution for preventing his imminent death.

As his forward foot slid free of its perch, he began to fall, only to stop short. He lifted his eyes from the river below to find Big Elk's fingers wrapped around his wrist, the man's other hand jammed into a rocky crevice. Gus scrambled to reset his feet as Big Elk heaved him upward by the wrist until Gus's panicked fingers found new purchase. Gus laid his cheek against the cool stone, embracing it like a long-lost lover. Both men breathed heavily for a few seconds to allow the exertions of the moment to settle. When Gus finally looked at Big Elk, the man was shaking his head. He put a finger to his eye and then pointed at Gus's feet. Gus understood the message. *Watch the hell where you're going.* Good advice that he intended to heed. He dipped his forehead to Big Elk with gratitude. The big man cracked a slight smile and continued moving along the wall.

A few minutes onward, Big Elk discovered a narrow ledge of earth wedged into a seam of rock that moved laterally along the canyon wall. Droppings marked it as a path forged by the bighorn sheep that cavorted in the high places. Though razor thin, the path allowed them to move at a walking pace as they approached the bend. As the space behind the turn revealed itself over the course of minutes, Gus breathed a drawn-out sigh of relief. The potential ambush point was devoid of outlaws, horses, or anything else more threatening than loose boulders. He lifted his eyes to the canyon beyond, which stretched a couple of miles more or less straight. Still no sign of bad intentions.

Big Elk had seemingly come to the same conclusion. He spoke Shoshone words to Gus that he couldn't translate, but the meaning was clear. No ambush. Not here, anyway. Gus peered below to find Beah Nooki with the rest of the party stacked up behind him, waiting for a signal. Gus swept an arm overhead to indicate "all clear" and then made a chopping motion down the canyon to indicate that they should continue. Beah Nooki sat motionless for ten seconds before motioning to Gus that he and Big Elk should return to the river bottom to rejoin the others. Gus was happy to leave the canyon wall behind. The bighorns could have their blasted high ground, with his blessing.

Jake moved to the front of the line as Gus and Big Elk intercepted them above the river. He patted Gus's back with more relief than he'd expected. "Welcome back to earth. Thought we lost ya there for a moment."

"I thought the same. For a moment, anyhow."

"It's a good thing Big Elk seems to like you. I mighta just let you fall."

"And I woulda pulled you down with me, just for spite."

They chuckled together, each understanding the fabrication beneath their claims. They'd already shown ample evidence of a willingness to lay down their lives for each other.

And if there was any sentiment grander in the universe, Jake surely wasn't aware of it.

Meanwhile, Big Elk made his report to Beah Nooki. The elder nodded and leaned again into motion. "We go forward. The river twists but runs straight for five thousand steps. We will see the enemy coming."

The guidance held true as the scouting party struggled for nearly two hours along the river bottom, sometimes clambering over rock falls, often walking along the wash beside the river, and other times plowing through waist-deep snowdrifts in the hollows. Jake led the way to spare Beah Nooki the indignity of stepping into a snow-covered hole or stumbling on loose rock. However, it was Follows the River who spotted the smoke. He tapped Jake's shoulder from behind and pointed.

"Look there."

Jake stopped, cupped a hand over his eyes, and found a thin wisp of smoke rising above an abutment of rock perhaps a mile ahead, nearly imperceptible against the camouflage of a rocky backdrop. The smoke displayed a signature unique in all creation.

"Stovepipe," he said. Beah Nooki was suddenly beside him.

"Yes. It rises above the place I would choose for a camp."

"How so?"

"See that rock, like a buffalo's head?"

"Yep."

The elder made a sweeping motion. "The river bends around it. Flat ground lies between the river and cliffs beyond. Enough for tents and horses. The cliffs are steep. Easy to defend. Hard to attack."

"You think that's van Zandt's camp, then?"

"Yes."

Jake rubbed his chin. "Still, I'd like to be certain. I'd like to know what we're up against."

Beah Nooki whispered to Big Elk, and the big man responded. The elder swept his hand up. "Big Elk agrees. We go until we see the outlaws or they see us."

"You sure about that?" said Gus. "This whole canyon is a choke point. They open up on us, we got a mountain a' trouble."

Jake harbored the same doubts but didn't want to come so far without learning what they needed to know. "I understand, Gus. But if we come back later with more men, every detail might save a life."

"Okay, then. I'm with you."

The party lapsed into silence and moved onward, everyone acutely aware of how voices carried along a funnel of rock. The rock abutment marking the bend of the river grew nearer until it loomed overhead. The scent of smoke joined the sight of it. Behind Jake, Roberson chuckled softly.

"I wonder," he whispered, "if there's even anybody home?"

Two seconds later, a trio of shots rang out from the cliffs above. Jake dove against the rocks to his right, crouching low. Another round of shots kicked up dirt and chips of gravel. He whipped his head around to find everyone similarly huddled against cover. Except one. Roberson lay sprawled on the rocks, his lifeless eyes studying the sky. Blood pooled from a wound in the center of his chest. Jake spat a curse. The man had survived repeated attacks of raiders along the

Oregon Trail only to fall while volunteering at Jake's request. Jake thought of Roberson's family and briefly wondered if the man's teenage sons could shoulder the burden to come. He shoved aside the maddening guilt and surveyed the situation. Pulling the Henry to his shoulder, he leaned away from the rock to find a firing line. Instead, a lead ball pinged the rocks a yard from his feet. *Dammit,* he thought. *Pinned down.*

Before Jake could assemble a reasonable plan, the sound of clambering feet drew his attention. He looked back over a shoulder to find Big Elk disappearing up the rock slope with the three youths at his heels. With no other recourse, Jake shouted instructions to those remaining.

"Pop and fire! Cover 'em!"

He sprang up from cover, fired a blind shot, and returned to a crouch. He crawled four feet forward while ejecting the shell and repeated the maneuver. Sporadic rifle fire from behind told him the others were following his command. After half a minute, a cascade of shots rang out above him, followed by another volley. When he popped up to fire again, he found an outlaw sprawled over a rock and the other two absent, no doubt seeking shelter from the Shoshone guns.

"Let's go! Let's go!" he shouted. He thrust the Henry at Emshoff, heaved Roberson over his shoulders as he would a deer carcass, and retreated while Big Elk's cadre maintained a steady drumbeat of fire against the outlaws. Then the big man shouted a Shoshone phrase Jake recognized.

More men coming.

Jake kept moving, gasping for air with Roberson's dead body doubling his weight. He pinned his eyes on Jim

Jackson's boots ahead of him, and the trail became a narrow tunnel, a pinpoint of escape. Burning rage rose within to lend him strength. How long he continued that way, he couldn't say, but Gus practically tackled him to bring him to a halt. When two pairs of hands relieved Jake of Roberson's body, he dropped to his knees and coughed up his lungs with a series of heaving barks. After a minute, he wiped his mouth and peered up at Gus.

"They didn't follow," said Gus. "We just need to keep walkin' now."

Jake nodded understanding, stood, and accepted his rifle from Emshoff. The German held his gaze. "Are you good, Herr Paynter?"

He nodded again, even though he wasn't. Roberson was dead because of him, and nothing could change that. Movement from above drew his attention to find Big Elk and his men rejoining the trail. One of the youths—the one who had conversed with Stacy—was holding a bloody hand just beneath his ribs and staring vacantly ahead as he walked. Jake turned away to find Beah Nooki studying him. The old man bore a cut on his knee but otherwise appeared unharmed. However, the hollow of his gaze told Jake that he understood the burden of leadership—that every death of those in your command took a piece of your soul with them.

———

The sun had crawled nearly to midday when Stacy heard the first shots echoing faintly up the canyon. They were distant, to be sure, but absolutely unwelcome. This was supposed to be a scouting expedition, not a fight. The sound of gunfire meant the mission had gone horribly wrong. She checked the horses once again before steering her riveted attention downriver to where the others had gone. She worried over Gus, and Paynter, and Emshoff, and Beah Nooki—all of them. When the shooting stopped, she considered the scenarios. Her friends were all dead. The outlaws were all dead. And the vast landscape of possibilities that spread between the two extremes. It was that preoccupation with what-ifs that allowed the stranger to slip up behind her.

"Don't move a muscle."

The fetid, tobacco-heavy breath sounded into her left ear as a blade pressed against the side of her neck. An arm encircled her waist, bracing the attacker for a potential killing stroke. She lifted her empty hands, painfully aware of her shotgun leaning against a boulder ten feet away and well out of reach.

"I'm not armed, mister."

The biting blade loosened against her throat and the stranger froze. After a few yammering beats of her heart, the man spun her away to face him. His eyes grew as wide as his squint would allow. He pointed a six-inch hunting knife at her face, nearly touching her chin.

"Yer a dang woman!"

Stacy kept her hands wide and raised. "I been called worse."

A half grin grew on his tanned and beaten features as he surveyed the length of her body while waving the knife in a casual circle. "Did Dutch invite you here maybe? For some fun?"

"Hell, no."

"More for me, then."

When she hurled a gob of mucus onto his cheek, he swiped it away, sheathed the knife, and circled her throat with his hands. "I like it rough anyways."

He pressed Stacy to the cold earth and flung himself atop her. For an instant, she panicked—before remembering who she was. The granddaughter of Many Horses. The daughter of Cornelius Blue. The friend of Jake Paynter. The sweetheart of Gus Rivers. And every one of their voices invaded her head and told her what must be done. While the man struggled to loosen his belt, she calmly pulled his knife from its sheath and plunged it into the middle of his back. He leaped away while attempting to turn his head backward and reach to find what was biting him.

"Damn you!" he shouted. "What'd you do ta' me?"

By the time he spun to face her, she was glaring at him down the barrel of her Lefaucheux. When he went for her, she unloaded a barrel into his chest. He sailed backward to land atop the knife, driving it through his chest. He stared without understanding at the iron tip protruding from his shirt as blood spilled from the creases of his lips. Stacy kept the shotgun leveled at him until he stopped wheezing and lay motionless. She backed away, still aiming, and watched the dead man for a while just in case. Then, she doubled over and vomited the remains of breakfast into the trampled snow. When her father's wagon train had been attacked on the Oregon Trail, she may have killed a man or two while shooting at shadows in the darkness. She couldn't be certain. But this time, she'd watched the man's face as he surrendered his ghost. After retching a second time, she wiped her mouth and straightened.

"By the Lord Harry," she said. "Get ahold of yourself, Anastasia Blue."

She steeled her spine and cast another glare at the dead man. He'd tried to rape her, and maybe worse. Now he was dead. It had to be done. She turned away, fetched powder and shot from the calico's saddlebag, and reloaded the empty barrel. Again ready, she settled atop a small boulder and waited to learn what had happened in the canyon. The sun was falling toward the horizon when the scouting party returned carrying two bodies. She popped to her feet, barely breathing until she spied Gus bringing up the rear. When Paynter arrived, his eyes fell on the dead outlaw before searching her face.

"You all right?"

She nodded resolutely. He returned the gesture, a hint of sadness in his eyes.

"Who'd they get?" she said.

"Roberson. And that young man you were talkin' to."

She turned away to hide the solitary tear. "I'm sorry about that."

"We all are, little sister. We all are."

CHAPTER THIRTEEN

THE MEETING OF THE WIND RIVER AND THE LITTLE Wind River proved the parting of the ways for the battered scouting band. Few words had been spoken in any language since they'd emerged from the canyon the previous afternoon. The presence of two dead men strapped to horses had cast a pall over the living, a stifling shroud that muffled conversation and enthusiasm. Jake remained particularly glum about the outcome, and everyone appeared to notice. They had given him a wide berth and had avoided any form of meaningful interaction. Sentenced to occupy his bubble of regret, he had fixed his gaze forward and let the mare find the trail southward.

Upon arriving at the joining of the rivers, Big Elk and the surviving Shoshone youths began angling west toward home without a word of parting, leading the horse carrying their fallen comrade. Spontaneously, Jake rode after them. He pulled alongside Big Elk and mustered up his best Shoshone, which was still rudimentary.

"Big Elk. I am sorry."

The man initiated prolonged eye contact with Jake. "Such is the way of war. Old men start fights but the young die first."

Without further comment, he nudged his horse into a

trot and the others kicked after him. Jake halted the mare and watched them ride away until a roll of the earth swallowed them from sight. When he returned to the others, Beah Nooki was still among the group. Jake drew the mare alongside the elder's black-and-white stallion to find the old man watching him carefully. Jake tossed his head in the direction the Shoshone had ridden.

"You will not go with Big Elk?"

"No."

"Why?"

"Big Elk will return to the canyon with two hundred men during the blooming moon. As you call it, 'May.'"

"Thirty, maybe forty days from now? And you agreed to this?"

Beah Nooki laughed. "Big Elk cannot be told what to do. He wished to return in a few days. I told him to wait."

"Why?"

"Because." He pointed to the middle of Jake's chest. "These are your outlaws. My people should not die to fix your lodge."

Jake nodded firmly. "I agree."

"Good. You have thirty days. I will go with you to help." The elder chuckled. "Besides, I decided to learn more of the white man's ways. Then I can give Washakie better advice. This path has been in my thoughts for many years now. A whisper that does not leave. Today, I will listen."

The grim set of Jake's jaw softened. Beah Nooki's quiet resolve to travel to South Pass City pleased him. He liked the old man and looked forward to having his easy presence during the trying days to come. However, he knew Beah Nooki likely withheld some of the truth. He had little doubt that the elder was tagging along to keep an eye on him. Lord knew, he needed all the help he could get.

Jake gave himself over to silent consideration for the remainder of the day, emerging from his isolation only when everyone had gathered around the campfire for the night. Conversation among the others remained light. Still, the sound of Jake unexpectedly speaking had the effect of sudden cannon fire.

"I have a plan."

Voices fell silent and every eye flickered in the firelight, regarding him with deep interest. Gus dipped his chin at Jake, a tacit gesture of support. Jake inhaled a breath and exhaled slowly.

"When we return to South Pass City tomorrow, we bury our friend Roberson and then make sure his family has all the support we can lend. The sons are old enough to take over the hard work, but they are still just boys. This country grinds up even the hardest of men. We can't leave those boys to fend for themselves."

"We will help, of course," said Emshoff. "My partnership with Herr Roberson remains intact. We will share in the profits of our claims as planned. We will continue to raise funds for homesteads. Ours and theirs."

Jake dipped his forehead. "Thank you. I had no doubt you would hold to the agreement."

"And I will make sure no one goes hungry," said Stacy. "Me and Gus will. Right?"

Gus reached aside to squeeze her hand. "As you say."

Jake trusted that the Roberson family would not suffer too greatly beyond the anguish of losing their father, thanks to the determined charity of their friends. He counted himself fortunate to be welcomed by a circle of such fine people, despite the many sins of his past. However, he wasn't finished explaining his intentions.

"Just as important as caring for Roberson's family, we need to make sure his death was not in vain."

"How can we do that?" said Aguilar. "You saw the outlaw camp. It seems unbreakable."

"Agreed. It does seem that way. Attacking van Zandt in his stronghold could cause a bloodbath for both sides. For that reason, we should try to weaken him first. Maybe even draw the enemy out to fight on level ground, like we did during the war."

Gus nodded. "I expect you got a plan to do just that?"

"It's comin' along," he said. "We know Lucien Ashley's in cahoots with van Zandt. I'm pretty sure he's supplying the outlaws in exchange for, well, I don't exactly know yet. Regardless, we need to disrupt their operation. We got maybe twenty-five days to make it happen. Either way, we're gonna need more guns."

Stacy cocked her head. "Are you sayin' we should recruit more of the townsfolk?"

"As many as we can. Gus, you can drill 'em. Figure out who should shoot and who should load shot. Like you drilled the men at Fort Bridger, and before that during the war."

Gus nodded. "I can do that. But where do we start, then,

in forcing van Zandt into the open? I know you got somethin'. I can hear it in your voice."

Jake smiled. This was why he'd never play poker with Gus. He could never bluff the man. "I do have somethin'. I need to make a little side trip in the morning but will meet you back in town."

A grin crawled across Stacy's face. "You gonna go start trouble, then?"

"You know me, Stacy. It's what I do best."

CHAPTER FOURTEEN

AFTER MONTHS OF PERSISTENT THOUGH PLEASANT COM-pany, sudden separation from humanity perversely lifted Jake's spirits. And he hated that it did. Isolation to a loner was like gin to an alcoholic. It satisfied the deep cravings while promising to kill him slowly.

As the others of his party veered south to avoid Red Canyon, Jake set the place in his sights. He waited until dusk to make his final approach, knowing the encroaching dark-ness would cast a mantle of shadow over him and the mare. After setting a cold camp on the back side of the eastern ridge overlooking the sprawling valley, he staked the mare to the rocky earth.

"Stay put," he told her. She rolled a mocking eye at him, tossed her mane, and proceeded to forage the short grass at her feet. Satisfied, Jake mounted the ridgeline with his Henry in hand. Night had fallen with no moon, drenching the ranch in obscurity. However, lantern light leaking from the main house, bunkhouse, and outbuildings marked the presence of many people—most of whom were cowhands but armed nonetheless. Jake maintained the watch for several hours until he was certain that Lucien had not begun running night patrols. Lucien's lack of vigilance didn't surprise him, though.

The man's confidant bravado was his greatest strength, but it made him careless. If Lucien knew a storied killer was surveilling his spread, he might've thought twice about his certainty. Jake withdrew from the ridge to his camp, bundled up against the chill, and fell quickly into sleep.

The following day, he repeated the ritual but started right after breakfast. From his perch, he watched the ranch below shimmy to life in fits and starts. Men emerged from the bunkhouse. A woman who could be none other than Mrs. Guilfoyle brought breakfast in platters to a long table outside the kitchen and the cowhands tucked in. Jake swore he could smell the bacon across the distance but credited that to his imagination. Afterward, the men set about their respective chores, some running an immense number of cattle up the grassy slopes leading away from the canyon, others working an army of horses, and some enlarging the second corral. Around midday, an empty wagon and two riders made the circuitous climb from the canyon to meet the road bound for South Pass City. A supply run, most likely.

The day passed with no one else arriving or leaving. Lucien appeared several times, easily identified by his long coat the color of rust. Jake followed the man's movements but found in them nothing of interest. Lucien was as much a part of the ranch's daily workings as any man in his employ. When night fell again, Jake descended the ridge early. The mare waited for him with mild animosity, no doubt having taken umbrage to his daylong absence. She took a swipe at his hat as he stepped around her.

"Easy, girl," he said. "I ain't cheatin' on ya. Besides, no

other horse would have me." He removed her tether from the stake and began leading her away from the ridge. "Let's go fetch some water."

He found the trickle of snowmelt he'd crossed on the way in and refilled his canteen and water pouch while the mare drank her fill. By the time they returned to camp, the coyotes were calling to one another. Jake wished for the thousandth time that he knew what they were saying. Was it just friendly greeting? Or commiseration? Maybe they were talking about him and the mare and wondering how they'd taste. Resigned to not knowing the answer, he instead counted shooting stars until sleep overtook him again.

Perhaps it was the isolation. Maybe it was his nearness to an enemy. Whatever the reason, he clawed at the earth while his dreams yanked him back to the battlefields of Missouri, Arkansas, and the Cherokee Nation. Men who'd fallen dead years before rose from unmarked graves to call on him. To ask why he lived while they'd become food for worms. To wonder aloud why he hadn't saved them from enemy bullets, misplaced artillery, or bowels that leaked until they'd died. He had no answer for them. His continued presence among the living astonished him every morning. The Reaper should have taken him long before but hadn't for reasons he could not fathom. Jake finally roused early to escape the dreams and a night of fitful sleep. If not for that good fortune, he might've missed the outbound rider.

The muffled clatter of trotting hooves in the predawn gloom drew his attention because of its trajectory—north rather than south toward town. North toward Wind River

Canyon. He marked the location of the sound while gathering up his camp with the urgency of a runaway cart. The mare complained at his hurried attempts to saddle her, initially refusing to exhale so he could tighten the saddle girth. She finally relented, but the delay put Jake at a disadvantage. The sound of hooves had dwindled into the ether. He trotted the mare north until well after the sun had cleared the horizon before spotting the rider in the distance—two miles, maybe three—and on a familiar line. He settled into his discreet pursuit through the rolling terrain that was the connective tissue holding mountain range to mountain range, maintaining the gap and hoping the man wouldn't study the trail at his back with too much scrutiny. When the rider stopped, he stopped. When the rider rode on, he followed again. When the sun set, he mentally marked the distance and direction of the rider, dismounted, and continued leading the mare on foot. A half hour later, he was rewarded with a blaze of light that marked the rider's camp.

After tying the mare to the grandaddy of all sagebrush plants, Jake rolled out his blankets and sat down on them. With the Henry in his lap and the Kerr at his side, he settled into a nightlong vigil. His upright posture allowed for snatches of sleep but never surrendered him to the arms of deep slumber. When stars began to fade in the eastern sky, he slipped away on foot until finding a tuft of juniper some fifty feet from the sleeping cowhand and crouched to wait. After a time, the man stirred. Jake waited for him to rise and rebuild his fire before announcing his presence.

"City marshal."

Hearing such a phrase might startle anyone. The innocent, however, wouldn't lunge for a rifle. Jake's shot ricocheting off the rifle's stock brought the cowhand to a frozen halt. He carefully raised his hands overhead and turned. Jake didn't recognize him.

"Now, why," said Jake while closing the gap with his rifle barrel leveled at the man's chest, "would you shoot at a city marshal?"

The cowhand's furtive glance at the overstuffed saddlebags splayed over a rock told much of the tale. He was carrying something of importance. The man shook his head.

"Just surprised me, that's all."

Jake halted ten feet away, still in full aim. "Let's say I might believe you. But let's also say you should have a seat and keep your hands in plain view while we have a little chat. Savvy?"

"Yes, Marshal."

"Good." He waved the Henry's barrel toward the saddlebags. "Whatcha got there, my friend?"

"Nothin'."

"I see. Since it's nothin', then you won't mind if I take a look?"

The stranger swallowed hard but held Jake's gaze. "Suit yourself."

Jake kept the man at the end of his rifle barrel as he sidestepped to the bag. After opening a side one-handed, he shuffled his hand inside without taking his eyes off the rider. A shirt maybe. Jerky for sure. A few loose paper cartridges and a box likely holding more of the same. The man eyed Jake's progress, his uplifted hands beginning to tremble.

When Jake rifled through the other side, he immediately hit pay dirt. He withdrew a bundle that he knew to be bills without looking at them.

"How much you carrying?"

"It ain't yer business, Marshal."

Jake tried to smile but feared he produced more of a feral scowl. "You made a move on me. Everything about you is now my business, including this money. How much?"

The cowhand exhaled. "Five hunnerd."

Jake whistled. "That's a lot a' scratch. What's it for?"

"Can't say."

"I bet you can." Jake stood and stepped to the campfire to catch its warmth. "But let me guess first. I'll lay ten dollars that this is bound for one Dutch van Zandt, resident of Wind River Canyon. Am I right?"

The cowhand's eyes widened briefly. "I can't say. It ain't mine."

"No?" Jake shoved the bundle under his armpit and pulled the top bill. A ten. "Then you won't mind if I stoke the fire a bit with this kindling."

The stranger rocked forward when Jake tossed the bill into the fire but settled back again. "No."

"Fire's warmin' up already. Let's add some more."

Jake tossed two more ten-dollar bills into the flames before the cowhand broke. "Stop, for God's sake!"

"Why? Why should I stop?"

The man inhaled sharply. "'Cause van Zandt will nail my hide to a barn door if I show up without the money. And if he don't, Mr. Ashley will."

Jake set the bundle aside and squatted to bring himself level with the man. "What's your name?"

"Clay."

"No last name?"

"Just Clay."

"All right, just Clay." He let the Henry's barrel drift toward the cold earth, a gesture of goodwill. "Now, I know you're just followin' Ashley's orders, and I don't hold you to blame for that much. But Dutch van Zandt is a wanted outlaw. Anyone providing material aid to an outlaw is himself an outlaw. Are you an outlaw, just Clay? Is that who you are?"

The cowhand straightened his spine. "No, sir. I'm a God-fearin' man just tryin' to make a living. I ain't no criminal."

"Didn't think so." Jake opened his coat to tap his badge. "But in the eyes of the law—that's me—you are taking criminal action by helping a criminal." When Clay's eyes widened in alarm, Jake raised a hand. "However, my judgment would change substantially if you'd tell me what you know. All of it."

Clay held his posture for ten seconds before deflating like a crashed balloon. "All right. All right. But you promise not to hold me responsible for any of this."

"You have my word. You can lower your hands."

Relieved of his duty to Lucien and the upholding of his hands, Clay spilled the details in all their morbid glory. Lucien and van Zandt held the same aspiration—to become cattle barons with enough wealth and influence to control a significant piece of the map. Van Zandt stole or extorted money and precious goods of various kinds and funneled them to Lucien, who converted the goods, pooled the proceeds with the extorted money, and purchased cattle out of Cheyenne at the end of the Goodnight-Loving Trail. Meanwhile, van Zandt's men threatened sellers to ensure that Lucien paid below-market prices. Then Lucien moved the cattle to his ranch to graze until such future time as the two men divided the herd before van Zandt lit out for parts unknown with his spoils. Throughout this process, Lucien supplied enough ammunition, explosives, and weapons to van Zandt to keep the outlaw in business.

"Why this money, then?" Jake asked after Clay's explanation.

"Stolen bills can be traced by serial numbers, so they tell me. This here's clean money straight from a bank. All legitimate-like."

Jake touched the brim of his hat, collected the bundle of bills, and stood. "You have my thanks. I consider you blameless in this affair, but only if you turn aside."

Clay squinted up at him. "Turn aside? How so?"

Jake stripped one hundred dollars from the wad of bills and dropped them at Clay's feet. "Take this money and quit the territory. The railroad is three days south. I suggest you find passage to another place for your health. Or you can go back and tell your boss how you lost five hundred dollars. But who am I to demand?"

As Jake stood watch, Clay the cowhand collected the hundred dollars and his belongings, saddled his horse, and spurred it south at an energetic pace. Jake smiled as he watched the man ride away. He carefully lowered the hammer of the Henry, contemplating the redemptive nature of unspent bullets.

CHAPTER FIFTEEN

WHATEVER TROUBLE PAYNTER HAD STARTED, IT HADN'T killed him. Not yet, anyway. Stacy glanced up from her desk at the marshal's office to find him filling the doorframe, rifle in hand and no apparent signs of blood. The casual set of his features told a deeper truth—that he hadn't killed anyone during his side venture. The crease that inhabited the center of his forehead after acts of violence was wholly absent. She exhaled a brief sigh on his behalf.

"You gonna tell us about your mysterious business these past three days?" The "us" of which she spoke included Gus, who sat with feet propped on his desk while cleaning his Colt .44, and Beah Nooki, who reclined on a cot in an open and empty cell with hands clasped behind his head. Paynter cut his eyes at the Shoshone elder and lifted one brow. Beah Nooki returned the gesture.

"This bed is soft," he said. "It pleases my old bones."

Paynter shrugged. "It should. We paid Mrs. Mulroney six dollars to restuff the mattress. Glad you're gettin' our money's worth."

He closed the door, racked his rifle, and pulled up the empty chair. Stacy continued to pin him with her best burning stare. "Well? About your little side trip?"

"Easy," said Gus in low tones. "Let the man assemble his thoughts. You know he can't talk until he lines it all up in his head."

"I'll give him ten seconds."

Paynter shook his head at her while a half grin dragged aside one cheek. He pushed his hat back and rubbed his temples, treading perilously near Stacy's ten-second deadline.

"First things first," he said just before the bell. "Tell me about Jed Roberson."

Of course, he didn't know the details. He'd just ridden into town. "We brung Roberson to his missus. She held her grief tight with both hands, for the sake of the young'uns, I think. Then Gus took him to Moretti for prep."

"Moretti? The tack store owner?"

"Yup," said Gus. He slapped the chamber shut and set aside his revolver. "His grandfather was a mortician in Italy, and he learned the trade. For them who's willin' to pay for his services, he'll prepare a body for burial."

Stacy nodded acknowledgment. Mostly, folks just put bodies in a blanket or pine box, buried them deep, and stacked rocks over the grave to keep out the animals long enough for the juices to leak into the earth. Burial services were an extravagance few people could afford in a declining mining town. Paynter clearly knew this.

"Who paid?"

Gus motioned to Stacy. "We did. And you pitched in five dollars, Marshal. I'll take that in cash at your convenience."

"A kind gesture." He withdrew a handful of coins from his pocket, sifted through them, and pitched the entire lot onto

Gus's desk. "That's three dollars and thirty cents. I'll make up the difference later."

"I know you're good for it."

"Anyhow," said Stacy, knifing back into the conversation. "We held a wake two nights ago and toasted him into the afterlife. Buried him the next mornin' out on the hillside overlookin' the vale."

"And his family?"

"Hurtin', for sure. But they're tough folks. And they got us. For now, anyway, until Mrs. Roberson decides what to do next."

Paynter's eyes found the floor between his boots as his elbows met his knees. He hung over his entwined fingers for a few moments, almost as if in prayer. She didn't know if he was a religious man, but most folks who rode with Death at least learned to pray. When he lifted his eyes, his countenance was as grim as a tombstone. He might've continued to inhabit his silence for hours if Beah Nooki hadn't risen from the bunk to sit at its edge.

"What did you learn?" asked the elder.

Paynter's gaze flickered to the old man, and he seemed to regain some sense of awareness. "Most of what I'd hoped."

Gus removed his boots from the desk and leaned forward. "We're all ears."

Paynter straightened in his chair and unfolded the events of the past days with an economy of words. Of how he'd watched the ranch before trailing a courier. Of how he'd run the man down and interrogated him. When he explained what the cowhand had told him of Lucien's and van Zandt's partnership, Stacy drifted somewhere between mild surprise and smug confirmation. Nothing of the arrangement seemed particularly astonishing, given the oily natures of both men. She might've nailed most of the details if anyone had pressed her for a guess. When Paynter finished explaining, Stacy tapped her fingers on her desk in thought.

"So what now?" she said finally. "Big Elk's thirty-day clock is countin' down right fast."

Paynter nodded agreement. "It is. So we can't waste a day or an hour. We need to work."

"Doin' what, exactly?" asked Gus.

Paynter stood from his chair to pace. "We gotta harass their little operation. We need to throw a boxload of spanners into the works and grind 'em down until they decide to come out to fight. That's what we'll do."

Though light on details, Paynter's explanation seemed to Stacy like a promising start. She plopped her palm on the desktop. "I'm in. Any plan that calls for annoyin' the hell outta someone has my support. I could agitate Ol' Scratch himself given enough time and opportunity."

Gus laughed. "Don't I know it."

She swung a finger at him without the benefit of her gaze. "Watch your tongue, Augustus, or I'll have it for supper." She rose from her chair and collected her forage cap. "When do we start?"

"Today," said Paynter. "But first we gotta run an errand."

"We?"

"Come along, little sister."

He walked out the door without a backward glance. Beah

Nooki chuckled softly while settling back onto the cot. "The hunter waits for no one. I will take a nap."

Stacy hurried out to catch Paynter as he strode up Main Street. Within seconds, she knew where he was headed. She followed him without conversation as they breached the border of town and dove into the low folds of earth that spread like ripples to the east. They arrived at the Robersons' camp a few minutes later. The family had constructed a pair of permanent tents—wooden frames stretched with canvas for walls and roof. Mrs. Roberson must've heard their approach, for she emerged from the tent with her youngest daughter in tow. Paynter stopped five feet away and removed his hat.

"Mrs. Roberson."

"Mr. Paynter."

He gripped the brim of his hat until the edge began to crumple into the shape of his bloodless fingers. Stacy nudged his back with her shoulder to loosen his tongue. It worked.

"I'm sorry," he said. "Jed was a good man. The best of men."

Mrs. Roberson rubbed away a tear that abruptly leaked from one eye. "He was."

Paynter swayed back and forth for a few seconds. "And I'm sorry that I dragged him into a fight. I shoulda known…"

Mrs. Roberson closed the gap between them and placed a hand on his wrist. "Do not, Mr. Paynter. Do not carry the blame for what happened to my husband. He wanted to help. He was determined to go. An infantry battalion couldn't have kept him away." She released his wrist. "That is not your burden."

Paynter nodded once, twice. "What'll you do now?"

The woman's eyes drifted up to blink at the sky. "I don't know just yet. The boys want to work the claim until we've saved enough for a homestead. My sister and her husband just set up a business in Cheyenne, and she'd be happy to have us there." She returned her gaze to Paynter. "I'll need to decide in the days to come."

Paynter shoved an urgent hand inside his coat and withdrew a small bundle wrapped in newspaper. He pressed it into her hands. "Maybe this will help."

Curious, Stacy stepped around Paynter to eye the bundle. Mrs. Roberson peeled back the paper to show a flash of familiar color. She glanced up sharply with narrowed eyes. "What's this?"

"Three hundred and seventy dollars."

The amount stole Stacy's breath as surely as it did Mrs. Roberson's. That sum of money was a year of decent wages. It would more than pay for a homestead, with enough to build on the land. Or enough to throw in with her sister's business. Enough to open up options from a narrow window. The woman blinked several times in disbelief.

"Where'd you get this?"

Stacy swore a grin tried to form on Paynter's lips.

"From the widows and orphans fund," he said. "We recently experienced the good fortune of a very generous donor."

Mrs. Roberson began extending the money toward him. "I can't…"

He pushed the bundle back to her waist. "You can. And you will. For Jed. For the kids." He paused. "For me. He's dead on account of me."

Mrs. Roberson's eyes flashed with fire. "No, sir. He is not. In fact, we'd all have been two years in our graves if not for you, Mr. Paynter. I still have my life and the lives of my children because of you. And there's nothing you can do to change that."

He dipped his chin. "I reckon not."

She nodded firmly, once, settling the matter. But she wasn't quite finished. "Just do me one favor."

"Anything," he said.

"Make sure you find the men responsible for my husband's death and kill them all."

He slowly settled his hat back on his head. "That I can do, Mrs. Roberson. That I can do."

Stacy knew he was telling the truth. In the violent harvest of souls, Jake Paynter always managed to find himself holding the scythe. He was good at the profession, despite the plain fact that he'd rather not be. She was just happy to be on his side. She didn't relish the notion of standing against a man who held death so close while trying to find his bearings.

CHAPTER SIXTEEN

NOTHING FUELS TRIVIAL CONVERSATION LIKE THE lurking specter of disaster. In this case, the specter was a probable exchange of gunfire. Distraction took the form of whispered conversation about meaningless things.

"Paynter."

Jake glanced up from the rifle in his hands to find Gus in a similar prone position below the edge of the road, ready to unload his carbine on what was coming. "Yah?"

"What's the best meal you ever had? The one that your memory dredges up every time your stomach growls?"

Jake frowned in thought. His best meal? He recalled his grandmother's cooking as having tasted like the southwest corner of heaven, but he was only six when she passed. What could a six-year-old know? Another memory came to him, though, from the war when he served with the First Kansas Colored. "That hog we roasted in a pit outside a' Fayetteville when we were iced over for a week. I swore it couldn't feed a hundred soldiers but it did. Couldn't feel my fingers from the cold but that pork warmed my belly like nothin' I'd ever eaten before."

Gus chuckled fondly. "I remember that. Akins tried for a second helping before everyone got a share. We made him carry the grenades for a month after that and didn't let him march too close."

"Yah. Akins. I liked him. Too bad he didn't make it." Jake shoved the dead soldier back into the trench from which he was trying to rise. "What about you? Best meal you've ever had?"

"Easy," Gus said. "Yam and bean stew with pork belly and catfish, collard greens, and corn bread with redeye gravy in Cairo, Illinois, fourth of May, 1861."

Jake cut his eyes at his oldest friend. The date preceded their acquaintance by nearly a year. "That's mighty specific. What was the occasion?"

"My first meal as a free man. I crossed the Mississippi on a lick-and-promise raft upriver of Wickliffe, Kentucky, the night before. I was dryin' out my clothes in the bramble near the river when a man out fishin' for breakfast caught *me* instead. He figured me for a runaway, and rightly so. He'd done the same ten years before. Invited me to his house to rest awhile. When his wife cooked us up some lunch, it wasn't no different than food I'd eaten practically every day of my life." Gus paused to study his hand beneath the barrel of his rifle, his eyes unmoving. "But I haven't savored a better meal before or since."

"I don't imagine so," Jake said. "I *can't* imagine so. But I'm glad you made it out. Otherwise, I'd surely have died in the war, what without you there to keep me from doin' something stupid."

Gus laughed softly again. "Oh, no. I never could rein in your stupidity. I only managed to keep it from killin' you a time or two."

A smile stole across Jake's face. "Thanks for that. Just

remember—your job ain't finished. I got a few gallons of stupid left in me."

"Don't I know."

Francisco Aguilar's sudden appearance over the lip of the road brought the conversation to an abrupt halt. He slid to the ground beside Jake, breathing hard from a long run.

"They comin'?"

"Yep. Half a mile upriver beyond the rise. Three riders and a wagon."

"Sounds like our target. Get ready."

Jake scrambled up the incline, made sure the road was clear, and dashed across to the other side into dense brush. Stacy jumped and jerked her shotgun toward him.

"Careful," he said. "And kindly lower that scattergun."

She blanched and lowered the weapon. "Don't go sneakin' up on us, then. My trigger finger's jumpy as a trout."

Emshoff emitted a low chuckle and shook his head. Beah Nooki simply watched in silence, his weather-beaten features arranged in a diorama of unconcern. However, he caressed the stock of his carbine as if calming a spooked horse.

"We're gonna need that jumpy trigger finger," said Jake. "Three riders and a wagon approaching. Stay under cover, though. We want 'em thinking there's twenty of us instead of six."

Stacy expelled a huff. "We shoulda brought Jim Jackson up here, then."

"Somebody had to watch the horses, and you made it clear you didn't want the job this time."

She rocked her head back and forth. "You're right."

"Didn't quite hear that. What'd you say?"

"You heard me, Paynter. Now, don't get shot."

"I'll try not to."

He departed the brush and moved up the road a hundred feet to the outcrop of rock and sagebrush he'd found an hour earlier when they'd chosen the spot for an ambush. The confluence of the Wind River and Little Wind River where they'd parted with Big Elk lay a few hundred yards downriver. He turned his back to it, watched the road from behind the natural barricade, and waited. Perhaps a minute later, the traveling party rolled into view as it emerged from behind the rise. Jake lifted the Henry to peer down the sight. He blinked and rubbed his eyes with the back of one hand as the men drew nearer.

"I'll be damned."

Two of the riders were Blackburn and Sweeney. Nobody in the world wanted Jake dead more than those two soldiers of misfortune. Given their importance to Lucien as hired guns, he hadn't expected them to be Lucien's errand boys. Especially not Blackburn, given his disdain for anyone's leadership but his own. The party approached, confident and unaware of the deadly snare into which they'd blundered. Jake waited until they had come alongside the five rifles pointed at them before showing himself. He stood from the brush with the Henry aimed at Blackburn's forehead. The riders went for their holstered weapons but Jake froze them.

"Hold there. You've twenty rifles drawing beads on you."

Blackburn's widened eyes narrowed and a grin stretched across his face, creasing the two scars Jake had given him during their previous two meetings. "Well, if it ain't Jake Paynter. Imagine that."

Sweeney pulled his pistol from the pocket of his black tailored suit while muttering epithets at Jake, culminating in *scurrilous bastard*.

Blackburn reached aside to stay the easterner's hand. "Easy, friend. You'll be in the devil's parlor before you touch the trigger."

Sweeney cursed again and returned the pistol to his pocket.

Blackburn scanned the sides of the road, finally noticing the barrels pointed at them. Then he fixed Jake with a hard stare. "I keep hopin' to hear a report of your demise. But here you are again, and so soon."

Jake continued to glare down his barrel, his hands steady as stone. "I been tryin' to get killed for a while now, but no such luck."

"I'd be happy to oblige you now," said Sweeney. "You killed my boys after all."

"Not true. The Tenth Cavalry got a few. I just mopped up."

Sweeney's jaw flexed as he appeared to grind his upper molars into his jawbone. "Me and those boys grew up on the streets together. They were my crew and I their captain until you had at them. I owe you seven deaths, Paynter, and I plan to pay up with interest."

Jake shifted his aim toward Sweeney's forehead. "Your *precious boys* tried to burn up women and children. I don't abide killin' innocents."

Sweeney's eyes hardened further, if such was possible. "I still can't believe you killed Bollinger. You must've had help."

Jake could barely believe it himself. Bollinger had been a mountain of muscle that scraped seven feet, and he'd killed the man with his bare hands. But he knew how he'd done it. "No help. Just me and the red haze."

"The red haze?"

Blackburn let loose a mocking laugh. "That's what he calls it when he's in a rage. Used to blame it on a wolf. I remember when he gets that way, though. There ain't no talkin' to him then. He almost forgets he's human." The man cocked his head and squinted one eye. "But I think maybe he's goin' soft now. Too many friends. Not like before."

Jake returned his aim to Blackburn. "I've had you in my sights twice now and let you live, even though you were trying to put me below dirt. I'll not make that mistake a third time." He touched the trigger with gentle pressure. Subtle fear rippled over Blackburn's features before he steeled them again. Jake let him stew for the space of several heartbeats. "Turn around, Blackburn. Leave the wagon and scurry back to your hole."

Blackburn apparently knew Jake well enough to understand the imminent danger. Though his cheeks reddened with mounting anger, the man began to turn his horse in the road.

Sweeney proved more naive. "This is petty theft!" he shouted, a bit too indignantly for a man who'd stolen every dollar he'd ever held. "You're naught but a highwayman, no better than the rest of us!"

Jake didn't disagree completely. Sweeney had a point, but he failed to grasp the larger picture. "A man can't steal what's already been stolen. Any good capitalist knows as much. Now, leave the wagon and move along."

"Come on, Sweeney," said Blackburn. Rage clouded his words. "Now ain't the moment. But soon enough."

As the wagon driver abandoned his post to climb up with the third rider, Sweeney doffed his bowler at Jake. "I will kill you, Paynter."

"I'll be waiting with bells on." Jake lifted his chin at the departing Blackburn. "Be sure to tell Lucien that it was me who took his cargo."

Blackburn lifted the back of a hand. "Oh, we will, you son of a bitch."

Jake didn't lower his rifle until Lucien's men had retreated from sight around the rise. The others emerged from cover to assemble on the road. Stacy slapped Jake's back, raising a sting. "That was a mite tense. How'd you know they wouldn't just open up on you?"

"I didn't."

"We'd a got 'em first, though."

"I figured as much." Jake stepped to Gus and grasped his shoulder. "You willin' to go back up into the canyon? Get the lay of van Zandt's camp? The cadence of his patrols?"

Gus smiled. "I am. Deputy marshaling can wait a few days."

"I will go too."

Jake cut his eyes at Beah Nooki. "You don't have to."

The elder simply turned and began making his way east to where Jim was holding the horses. Gus grinned at Jake.

"Well, that's been decided. I better catch up before he leaves me behind."

"He'll wait. He loves a good project."

"You sayin' I'm a project?"

Jake lifted half his lip. "Just like me. But unlike with me, Beah Nooki might do you some good."

CHAPTER SEVENTEEN

GUS DECIDED HE PREFERRED THE SHOULDERS OF THE world to its gullet. At Beah Nooki's insistence, they had eschewed following the river into the bowels of Wind River Canyon, instead treading the eastern rim that left the river deep in shadow. Unlike the prison of rocky cliffs below, the highlands spoke of liberation, of options, of unencumbered vision. With the patience of an artist, Beah Nooki led them along a serpentine route, threading a path through the chaotic ripples of shattered earth that formed the rising rim. Every time Gus became certain they'd need to backtrack, the Shoshone elder would find a cut, a gully, or a ledge to pass their horses through to the next obstacle. It was just such a passage that brought them abruptly face-to-face with strangers. Gus raised his eyes from the rocky trail at his feet to find Beah Nooki's upstretched hand.

"*Wuhr*!" he said sharply. "Stop."

Gus reined his buckskin to a skidding halt even as his eyes found the six men blocking their path. Most carried bows, but one leveled a rifle at Gus with steady hands. Gus let his arms drift aside to show lack of animosity and hoped the decision wouldn't put him in an unmarked grave. After a stretching anxious moment, Beah Nooki casually dismounted, walked to the man with the rifle, and pressed the barrel earthward with a feathery touch. He spoke a few words Gus failed to understand except for possibly one. *Friend.* Most of the tension bled from every face, and one man even nodded. Beah Nooki motioned to Gus.

"Come down. These are Bannock men. Allies."

Gus followed the suggestion even as the band turned away. When Beah Nooki began pulling his horse after the Bannock, Gus followed. He had little choice but to trust the elder's strategy. After a short distance, the collective group climbed an angling seam of rock that deposited them on a broad bowl of earth rimmed by rock walls and thin air. Signs of many campfires dotted the area, marking it as a favored camping spot for those who dared wander the edge of the deep. The youngest of the Bannock retrieved a stick to begin stirring to life a dormant fire inside a ring of stones. When the others settled on the ground around the ring, Beah Nooki released his horse and joined them. Gus swayed side to side, uncertain. He hadn't felt so awkward since his ma caught him swimming naked in the creek bottom when he was nine. Beah Nooki rescued him with a word.

"Come," he said while pulling his hand toward himself as if scooping earth. "They promise not to kill you."

Gus must have betrayed his alarm, because the elder smiled as if he'd been joking. Maybe. With no alternative, Gus dropped the reins and pulled up a circle of dirt beside Beah Nooki. The Bannock watched him with hooded eyes, particularly the man wearing a fresh scar that spanned the length of his bicep. Gus performed his best impersonation of a forest fawn, hoping the manufactured serenity might explain his disinterest in fighting. However, the men continued watching him even when Beah Nooki began to speak. The man with the rifle responded at length, as if asked a question. The exchange continued for some time as others offered comment. Gus picked up a word here, a word there, but was unable to determine any meaningful context from it. After a bit, every head dipped nearly simultaneously and thin smiles formed, mostly free of suspicion. Knowing something had changed, Gus removed his hat and inclined his head toward the Bannock.

"What'd you say?" he whispered sidelong to Beah Nooki.

"I said you are the buffalo soldier who rides with Niineeni' howouuyooniit. They are pleased by this."

Gus snorted a laugh. Of course. The mention of Paynter's name given him by the Arapaho seemed to have a way of opening the stiffest of doors. "You spent three minutes just saying that?"

"No," said Beah Nooki as if correcting a child. "We spoke of more."

"Such as?"

The elder brushed a streak of dirt from his leggings. "Your outlaws chased these men from the canyon when they went to catch fish. The white men killed one and hurt two others. Now, these men wait and talk. Some wish to return to fight. Others wish to bring more men but need more guns. They cannot decide."

"Can they tell us about van Zandt's camp?"

"No. They did not go so near."

"Too bad." Gus swept his eyes from face to face. "Will they stop us from doing that?"

"Let us see." Beah Nooki addressed the group with a combination of Shoshone, Bannock, and sign language. Expressions of enthusiastic approval crossed each face. The rifleman spoke warmly to the elder.

"Well?" said Gus.

"I told them of our plan. You see their hearts on the matter. They have offered to share meat and a warm fire for the night. I accepted."

Gus breathed a sigh. "Thank 'em for me, or tell me how to."

Given that Beah Nooki was first a teacher, he chose the latter.

———————

After two days and a night clambering on foot through the canyon, Gus was missing his horse like a week of meals. He had faith that the Bannock would take good care of the animal in his absence, but his weary soles yearned for relief from the punishing rock. Beah Nooki seemed tireless, though, moving at the pace of a wide river, not rushing but never still. Fortunately, his relentless maneuvering had borne reasonable fruit. They'd located the trail used by the outlaws to descend on foot from the rim to their camp alongside the river. They'd watched men ride horses along the river, some north toward the Bighorns and some south toward South Pass City. They'd located the nests of the sentries—three in all. Two flanked the abutment that bent the river and sheltered the outlaw camp on a flat wash north of the bend. The other perched high up the far wall. Anyone approaching the gate of the outlaw domain would be pinned down by a triangle of fire. Such information might have satisfied Gus, but not Beah Nooki. Gus reminded the elder of his oft-stated opinion.

"This ain't such a good idea."

"Still, it is necessary," said Beah Nooki. Again.

"So you've said."

Gus continued behind the elder as they descended in near darkness down the perilous slope before them, invisible to watchful eyes above but wary of sending loose rock cascading downward in alarm. Their progress brought them to within a hundred feet of the camp just behind the four riders that had been approaching from the south since late afternoon. Gus perched near Beah Nooki in a pocket of rock, unable to breathe. The shadow of a tall man appeared from the large canvas tent that housed a stove, given the steady puff of woodsmoke leaking from a pipe above it.

"Gentlemen. What have you to report?"

In the dim glow of a large fire, the riders dismounted to face the asker, shifting from foot to foot. One rubbed the back of his neck and ducked his head. "We found squat, Mr. van Zandt. The ammo boxes weren't where they was supposed ta' be."

"You certain of that, Mr. Boggins?"

"Yes, sir."

Van Zandt began pacing slowly back and forth along a ten-foot line. "Your news greatly disappoints me. In fact, it leaves me terribly disgruntled."

Boggins, the unfortunate bearer of the bad news, winced. "I'm sorry, sir. We looked hard for 'em."

He appeared ready for a backhand, but van Zandt instead unfolded his arms and let them drop. "I'm certain you did. Were there signs of theft, perhaps?"

"None we could tell."

"I see." Van Zandt paced the line once more. "Damn that Ashley and his rotten soul. I knew he'd stab us eventually. We will wait another five days to see if he makes amends. If he chooses otherwise, I will be sure to send a party of armed visitors to call on him. Besides, that Union Pacific money does us no good boxed up in this canyon. Perhaps the sight of forty thousand will remind that weasel of our agreement."

Gus agreed with van Zandt's descriptive sentiments regarding Lucien and briefly imagined a scenario where the two men eliminated each other from the fight. He brushed the notion aside, though. Wishful thinking was too often the enemy of truth. Gus drew Beah Nooki's attention with a shoulder tap and led the way up into the yawning darkness. He'd heard enough. If the climb up the canyon in pitch-blackness failed to kill him, he'd need to tell Paynter about the storm that might be coming and the moving of the money. They'd either need to weather the storm or meet it head-on. He'd known Paynter long enough to guess which he'd choose.

CHAPTER EIGHTEEN

JAKE'S MIDAFTERNOON PATROL OF SOUTH PASS CITY AND its immediate surrounds usually proved as mundane as week-old bread with no butter or jam. This day proved no different. No quarrels. No drunks. No bodies. No busted windows. Just an elderly widow who needed her door fixed, which Jake managed with a few minutes of labor and a mashed thumb. Nope. Just another day, serene and routine.

Until he approached his combination office, armory, and jailhouse on Main Street.

Even from a distance, he spied Lucien Ashley stalking the porch in front of the door like a vulture assessing a freshly dead carcass, head down and muttering, planning how to extract the meat. Jake nearly rode up on the man without notice, keenly aware of the revolver at Lucien's hip.

"Afternoon, Mr. Ashley."

Lucien's head jerked up and he delivered the mother of all scowls that transformed his face, considered handsome by the ladies, into a skin-stretched skull. Jake dismounted casually and tied the mare to a post before returning the heated glare with an amiable grin.

"What can I do for ya? Cattle rustlers? Busted fence? Confession?"

Lucien's face clouded further, impossibly. "Inside. *Marshal.*"

"I'm here to serve, citizen."

Jake ambled past him and unlocked the door with deliberate slowness, never letting his hand stray too far from his Kerr. As he stepped into the jailhouse, Lucien poured inside after him, all kinetic agitation and pent-up rage. Jake kept his eyes pinned on the pacing man while he tossed the door shut behind him. Before he could pose his question again, Lucien lurched toward him and planted an index finger in the middle of Jake's chest.

"What'd you do with it?"

Of course, he knew what Lucien meant. However, he continued to take perverse pleasure in the man's rattled state and wanted to keep him wound up tight as a spring a little longer. He pushed the finger away from his chest, giving it a little twist as he did, and met the glare with manufactured ignorance. "Do with what? I need details if I'm to help you."

Lucien stalked to one end of the office and back, a brief but intentional journey lasting no more than five seconds. He pressed near Jake again on his return but had the good sense to keep that index finger firmly ensconced in his fist. He appeared to will away the sharp edges from his anger, tempering it to deep indignation.

"It would seem," he said, "that I am missing a courier."

"You don't say. What was he carrying?"

"Five hundred dollars belonging to me."

Jake whistled surprise. "Five hundred. That's quite a sum. Are you certain your courier didn't decide to keep the money and head for parts unknown, richer and more liberated than when he left your place?"

Lucien shook his head adamantly. "Not Clay. He didn't have a thieving bone in his body. Unlike you."

Jake cocked his head with mock affront. "You callin' me a thief?"

"Are you claiming you aren't?"

"I ain't a thief, Ashley. But it just so happens a mysterious soul made a large anonymous donation to the Greater South Pass City Widows and Orphans Fund. Still tryin' to sort out who that was."

For a half second, Lucien's hand began drifting toward his revolver. Jake unholstered his Kerr before the man could finish the move, aiming it at Lucien's left knee. "That," he said in low tones, "would be a mistake."

Lucien eyed the Kerr, startled, before folding his arms and recapturing the fading scowl. He locked eyes with Jake, the picture of almighty defiance. Jake had to give him credit. Upon first encountering Lucien two years earlier, he had taken him for a spineless dandy, a con man with important connections, deep pockets, and ruthless ambitions. While most of his first impression had held true, he no longer considered Lucien a coward. The man had demonstrated an unrelenting resistance to fear too many times, sometimes to his detriment. For that reason, Jake had long ago decided to never lower his guard around the man. As if to paint a picture of Jake's musings, Lucien lifted his chin, his blue eyes glinting like the steel of twin sabers.

"You also stole a horse, wagon, and three hundred pounds

of ammunition, black powder, and shot. I demand their imme-diate return as you took them without a warrant or cause."

Jake lifted his chin to match that of his adversary. "Oh, I had cause. But I'll gladly return the horse and rig."

"And the munitions?"

"Tell you what, Ashley. I will also return the ammo." When triumph began to crown Lucien's features, Jake froze them with an upraised finger. "On one condition. That you draft a letter to the territory governor explaining how you obtained the munitions and who you obtained them for. Then they're yours."

Lucien faded back a step, as if to launch himself at Jake. Instead, he inhaled a pair of seething breaths before relaxing the clench of his fists and exhaling. "Fine. Keep the ammuni-tion. But I will have my horse and wagon."

"You may collect those at the stables just down the street. And the Greater South Pass City Citizens' Armory thanks you for the kind donation of ammunition, black powder, and shot."

Instead of flying into a rage as Jake suspected he might, Lucien's scowl faded into a hard smile. "Enjoy your little vic-tory while you can, Paynter. It won't last long."

"That so? Care to enlighten me?"

Lucien straightened his tall frame in a clear attempt to loom. It might have intimidated others, but Jake had been fighting giants his entire life, laying them low with a relent-less forward motion that mowed down those who stood violently against him. Kings and convicts were of the same height when lying on the flats of their backs, and the dust took them all eventually. Lucien seemingly did not notice Jake's failure to be impressed.

"It is about time you know," he said. "Everyone will soon hear. Come the next election, I am throwing my hat in the ring for territory legislature. I will win, of course. In no time, I'll have the governor and his lieutenants in my pocket." His thin smile widened. "And then, I will make your life hell."

Jake couldn't help but grin. "My, my. That there's a right ambitious plan. Except for one thing."

"And that is?"

"You've already been makin' my life hell."

Lucien shook his head, eyes glinting with burgeoning mockery. "Perhaps you misunderstand. Dutch van Zandt is a supremely dangerous man. That he allowed you to live when he confiscated your prisoner is a minor miracle for which you ought to be praising all the saints. In meddling with my business, you have caused him great consternation. He does not abide those who cause him consternation of any sort. He will not hesitate to destroy you and yours, nor give it a second thought."

Jake frowned and nodded. "Thanks for the warning. But then again, most everyone who's tried to kill me is rotting in a hole somewhere. I wish him the best of luck."

Lucien's triumphant smile gave way to disdain. He pushed past Jake to yank open the door. "Good day, Paynter. Or go to hell. Whichever you prefer."

Jake floated out the door in Lucien's wake, hoping to enjoy every last drop of the man's flustered annoyance. "Ain't you gonna tell me to stay away from your sister, like you always do?"

"It won't matter anymore," Lucien blurted while mounting his horse. Then his eyes flashed regret before recovering. "She has lost interest in you."

Jake stood rooted to the porch and gave a casual wave as Lucien spun his horse away toward the road out of town. When he was sure Lucien wouldn't cast a backward glance, Jake bolted into the office, grabbed the Henry, and dashed back out the door. He untied the mare with one hand, leaped aboard, and kicked her toward the schoolhouse on the hill. Lucien had given warning, no matter how inadvertently. He would not have made such a claim unless he had Rosalyn again under his thumb. Jake dug his heels into the mare's sides, hoping he wasn't too late.

CHAPTER NINETEEN

FOR ROSALYN, THE WORK OF A TEACHER WAS NOT UNLIKE that of a soldier—some days she conquered, and others she retreated to lick her wounds. Most days fell into the vast middle, a chaotic brew of success, failure, almost, and not enough. She had just completed one of those middling efforts and was turning out her students one by one as they filed through the door.

"Goodbye, Caroline. Be sure to repeat your alphabet three times to your mother before bed time."

"Yes, Miss Ashley."

"A good evening to you, James. Your algebra is improving. Keep practicing."

"Yes, ma'am."

And so it went, individual farewells to the twenty-three students in her care, ages six through fifteen. After the last three departed, the Emshoff siblings, Rosalyn closed the door to set her sights on the morrow. She was shuffling papers on her desk when the creak of the door reached her ears. Certain one of her students had forgotten some item, she glanced up with an anticipatory smile. The smile snuffed like a candle in a hurricane when she saw two familiar men entering. She lurched to her feet in alarm.

"Mr. Blackburn. Mr. Sweeney. Why are you here?"

Sweeney tipped his bowler. "Why, Miss Ashley. Your tone sounds right unneighborly."

"As if you're not happy to see us," said Blackburn.

She backed away from her desk as they approached. "Did my brother send you? What does he want?"

Blackburn circled the desk to one side while Sweeney closed around the other. Blackburn laughed. "He wants you home."

As she tried to dart around Sweeney, he caught her long hair and slung her to the wooden floor. She came to rest against a student's desk, banging her shoulder painfully into the oaken leg.

"Easy," said Blackburn as he came up behind her. "Ashley's particular about the treatment of his sister."

Sweeney grabbed her wrists to pin them behind her back. "How so?"

Blackburn secured her ankles with a quick twist of rope. "Says she's a lady and should be treated as such."

When Rosalyn began to scream, Sweeney turned her wrists over to Blackburn and strung a gag around her mouth, pulling it tight until she thought the corners of her lips might tear into her cheeks. Sweeney shoved her face to the floor and leaned near one ear.

"When 'ladies' come to my neighborhood, we treat 'em same as the whores, and the screams only make it better for us. Say the word, Miss Ashley, and I'll show you."

She fell quiet. Sweeney and Blackburn exchanged chuckles.

"That's how it's done," said Blackburn. "Shall we, sir?"

"Indeed."

Two pairs of hands roped her elbows together behind her back, drawing them tight until the sockets of her shoulder complained. Before she could test the strength of the bonds, Rosalyn flew from the floor as Sweeney hoisted her to a shoulder.

"Remember," he said. "Quiet now."

As he hauled her tail first out the door, she raised her tear-streaked face to find Blackburn following. He tossed her a chivalric smile, as if he'd just helped her down from a carriage. "We'll have you back to the ranch by sunset, unless you give us reason to stop along the way. Which'll it be?" When she remained silent, he shrugged. "A pity."

Sweeney dumped her in the bed of a buckboard and joined Blackburn on the bench. When she tried to wriggle to a sitting position, Blackburn shoved her down again. "Lie still, Miss Ashley. Wouldn't want anyone trying to become the hero to save you. I haven't killed anyone in a while, but I ain't above makin' up for lost time."

She nearly resisted as thoughts of Paynter leaped into her brain. If gunplay ensued, she had little doubt about which man would lie dead at the hand of the other. However, what if someone else attempted a rescue? One of the shopkeepers, or miners, or Stacy Blue? Someone would end up dead at Blackburn's feet because she had refused to lie still. She couldn't live with that. Instead, she became like stone and glared murder at Blackburn. A wide smile split his face.

"Good girl. That's the way I like my women. Compliant and tied up."

He turned around to share guffaws of hilarity with Sweeney. Rosalyn rolled to her side to keep from crushing her bound hands and waited as the wagon bounced along the rough road. She visualized leaping from the bed. But where would she go? The rope constraining her ankles had already begun leaching feeling from her toes, and her shoulders cried for relief. Abandoning that plan, she instead imagined what might happen when Paynter caught up to them. Then she realized the unlikelihood of such a scenario. He would be making his rounds, then go for supper. She'd be back at Flaming Rocks Ranch before anyone noticed her absence. Her heart leapt, though, at the sound of fast-approaching hooves. She struggled again to a sitting position, hoping to find Paynter riding up from behind. A groan escaped her when she spied her brother reining his horse to match the wagon's speed. He took one long look over a shoulder before catching Rosalyn in his gaze. Her forehead drew into a crease as she narrowed malefic eyes at him. He shook his head.

"Come, now, Sister. Don't look at me with such venom. This is for your own good."

She tried to disagree, but the gag rendered her fiery speech a string of sounds more reminiscent of a mewling cat.

"Remove her gag," said Lucien.

"But she was screaming like a banshee, Boss," said Sweeney.

"She'll behave. Won't you, Rosalyn?"

She glared in silence while Sweeney hopped into the bed and reached around her shoulders to loosen the knot. He withheld suggestive remarks but exhaled one soft breath into her ear, a nearly inaudible moan. She recoiled from it, yanking away as the gag came free. Sweeney shot her a wink and resumed the bench. She whipped her head aside to find Lucien riding the road beside her.

"Lucien! Why…"

He shot out a hand to strike the back of her head. His features went cool, devoid of any emotion. "Civil, now. Or the gag returns."

She inhaled a hot breath, gathered her raging gumption into a neat ball, and tried again. "Lucien. Why have you taken me? You know I've no wish to see you again, let alone share the same house."

His face remained blank. "Let us explore that assertion. You left without telling me. I am your only brother, your only kin west of the Mississippi. You may have disowned me, but at least I deserve an explanation. Why did you run like a thief in the night?"

She had assumed he knew. And likely, he did. Regardless, she wanted him to hear the reason directly from her own lips. She owed it to herself to muster up at least that much courage.

"I left because you intended to lynch Mr. Paynter. I'd hoped to warn him but failed. Thankfully, neither did you succeed."

Lucien's face clouded, the promise of an angry outburst. However, he seemed to bite his tongue as the redness faded from his cheeks and neck. Then he smiled. Of his many smiles, some genuine and some manipulative, this was the one she hated most—and feared most. It calculated, the way the spider might as the fly circled nearer and nearer the web.

"Tell me, Sister." His voice had become honey smooth and deep. "Why Paynter? What hold can a man of his violent reputation possibly have on one as finely bred as you?"

She flared her nostrils but managed to level her emotions for an appropriate response. "*Hold.* That is the word you use, but you could not be more wrong. Mr. Paynter has no *hold* on me, unlike every other man of my family or acquaintance, all of whom wish to possess me in some manner. He, on the other hand, flatly refuses to claim any possession of me—any *hold* on me whatsoever. For that reason, I trust him as I have trusted no other man. And because he sacrifices his desires for my safety, for my best interest—that is why I care for him, Lucien. I might feel even more than that."

The clouds returned to Lucien's face. "More? You admit it?"

"Yes."

"I cannot abide that. I will not. When we arrive home, I will…"

The ping of a bullet on the road followed by the crack of a rifle stopped the words unsaid in his mouth. As the wagon ground to a halt, Rosalyn spun to follow the wide-eyed hatred of Lucien's gaze to the road ahead. Paynter stood at the edge of the track, perhaps a hundred feet ahead, his rifle aimed at her brother.

"Miss Ashley," he called without moving a muscle. "Do you travel with these men of your own free will?"

She lifted her chin to call back. "No. I do not."

"Shut up, Sister, or…"

Paynter interrupted him. "Release Miss Ashley immediately, or face charges of kidnapping. Or take a bullet to the forehead."

Lucien had the nerve to respond. "She is my sister. My responsibility. My property. I own her."

"Not according to the law. I'm leanin' heavily toward the bullet just now."

Rosalyn saw that Blackburn and Sweeney were apparently considering a gun battle, with hands drifting toward their respective weapons. She braced her body, ready to throw herself flat during the coming melee, while considering the unthinkable. Either Lucien would die or Paynter would die. She'd lose her brother or the man she cared for. A shout from Lucien froze her.

"Damn you, Paynter." He motioned to Sweeney. "Cut her loose."

"Boss?"

"Just do as I say."

Sweeney obeyed. The instant he removed the second bond, Rosalyn scrambled from the wagon and began stumbling on numb feet toward Paynter. He waved her to one side.

"Into the brush, Miss Ashley. You'll find my horse in the draw. I'll join you presently."

She left the road, trying not to look back. The sooner she removed herself from the situation, the less likely that bullets would fly. When she reached the mare, she finally ventured a backward glance. Paynter was hurrying to catch up, shuffling in sidesteps to keep his weapon trained on the road.

"I *will* kill you, Paynter!" shouted Sweeney, now unseen from Rosalyn's position in the draw. "For my boys!"

"After I kill you first, turncoat!" added Blackburn.

Lucien shouted no promises but had long ago made

clear his intention to see Paynter dead. Paynter continued his careful retreat and didn't lower the rifle barrel until he reached the mare. He held a palm to her while craning his neck toward the road, listening to the sound of the rig moving on. When the clattering of wheels had diminished, Paynter cut worried eyes at Rosalyn. He reached toward the side of her lip where the gag had pulled so tightly.

"Did they hurt you?"

She turned her head aside before his hand could fall. She wanted nothing more than to feel the touch of his fingers on her cheek, but she feared what would come of it. Feared that in doing so, he might run again. She forced a smile. "No. Just a scratch."

He lowered the hand, all expression draining from his face. "Good. I'm glad."

Her body swayed in place a moment, heavy. "Please don't kill my brother."

"I'll try not to."

She exhaled a pent breath and changed the subject. "What happens now, with van Zandt?"

"We'll see what Gus and Beah Nooki report first. They're due back anytime." He grabbed the mare's reins and held a hand to her. "You should ride. It's a bit of a walk in those shoes."

She mounted with his help, and he turned to lead the horse back toward town. Not a word escaped his lips for the entirety of the return trip, and she knew it was her fault.

CHAPTER TWENTY

"Dang it, Stacy. Just promise me."

Jake folded his arms to make his point. Stacy stopped running the brush along her calico's flank and matched his posture, including the frown. She lasted three seconds before letting slip an amused smirk. "I'm just bustin' your chops, Paynter. "Of course I'll keep an eye on Rosalyn for ya when I ain't workin'. But if you mount a posse, don't dare leave me behind."

"As if I could," he said.

Stacy let her arms drop and her amusement faded. "You *really* think Lucien will come back for her?"

"Don't know why he wouldn't. I'm just hopin' he'll give up eventually if he knows kidnapping his sister will drop him into the worst tangle of his miserable life."

"And do you really believe Rosalyn will let me move into her extra room? I mean, I ain't exactly genteel company."

Jake grinned. "Hadn't noticed. But yes, she will. She likes you. Truth be told, I think it's *because* you ain't genteel. You are who you are and never pretend to be anything other. I think she prizes that."

Stacy lifted one eyebrow. "That why she likes you?"

Jake cut his eyes to the manure pile beyond his boots and

picked at his shirt. He had not the murkiest notion of what Rosalyn saw in him. He lay awake some nights just wondering about it. "She just feels sorry for me, like she might a stray dog."

"Right," Stacy drawled, dragging out the word. "I'm sure that's it."

Jake's neck grew suddenly warm. "We done here?"

"You tell me."

"We're done. See ya."

"Later."

Jake beat a path from the stables as if fleeing an angry grizzly. He'd barely stepped onto Main Street when he spied a familiar pair of riders approaching up the road. He lifted a hand. Gus waved back, while Beah Nooki simply dipped his forehead. Townsfolk stopped to watch them pass, staring just short of rude. While they'd grown used to Gus, the appearance of a Shoshone warrior in the middle of town proved a novelty. Jake arrived at the marshal's office as the men tied their horses to the hitching post.

"You aren't dead," he said.

Gus cocked his eyebrow. "Thanks for the vote of confidence."

"Anytime."

Beah Nooki swept his eyes between Jake and Gus, frowned, and entered the marshal's office. Jake followed, feeling well reprimanded, and Gus trailed him inside. Beah Nooki entered the open cell and settled on the cot with his hands behind his head.

"I missed this bed."

Gus pulled up a chair while Jake leaned against his desk. He spread his hands. "Well. Let's have it."

Beah Nooki exhaled a sigh. "I will listen."

"Right, then," said Gus. "We scouted the canyon for a couple of days with some help from a Bannock hunting party."

Jake put his fist beneath his chin and stared at the floor as Gus described the expedition. How they'd found a foot trail that descended from the rim to the river near the camp. How they'd located three sniper's nests. How the outlaw camp was arranged behind the rock abutment at the bend of the river. How men came and went, following a precarious path along the river. However, it was the last part that speared his attention.

"You got close enough to hear van Zandt talkin'?"

"Yep." Gus seemed proud, though Beah Nooki appeared to remain unimpressed by the accomplishment.

"What'd you learn?"

"He seemed rightly annoyed by the missing ammo shipment and blamed Lucien for it. It's clear he don't trust Ashley."

"Well, van Zandt *is* an intelligent man."

"Anyway," said Gus, "he still has the money from the Wells Fargo safe they took from the train. Even mentioned the amount."

Without glancing at Jake, Beah Nooki held up four fingers. "Forty thousand dollars."

Gus nodded. "Yep. And he means to bring it out to Ashley."

"So Lucien can clean up the money for him," said Jake.

"Seems like."

Jake tapped his foot while considering the information.

He dropped his fist from his chin. "I have legal questions. We need to go see Mrs. Morris. She's been studying the law nonstop since she became the JP."

"Right behind you," said Gus.

"I will stay here and think," said Beah Nooki.

Jake laughed. "Someone needs to."

Jake and Gus made the short trip to the courthouse and entered. They found Esther Morris with several law books spread across the top of her desk. She lifted gray eyes and smiled.

"Gentlemen. What can I do for you?"

"I have a question," said Jake.

"Professional or personal?"

"The former."

"I'm all ears, then."

He leaned against the doorframe of her office and folded his arms. "If we were to acquire a large sum of money from Dutch van Zandt during the course of our duties, what would happen to it?"

Mrs. Morris drummed her fingers atop a legal volume that could probably sink a paddle steamer. "Given that we know Mr. van Zandt stole forty thousand dollars from a Wells Fargo agent aboard a Union Pacific train, any amount up to that point should be returned to Wells Fargo, unless other claimants emerge."

"Seems reasonable. But if the money in question was bound for Lucien Ashley, could he lay claim to it?"

Her eyes widened in surprise, counter to her unflappable nature. "Is that a material fact?"

"Assume it is."

She pursed her lips in thought for half a minute. "No. Otherwise, he would directly and immediately implicate himself in the robbery. I do not know Mr. Ashley well, but I don't believe him the kind of man to risk his neck in a noose so needlessly."

Jake disagreed—mostly. Though Lucien was careful, his greed was bound to trap him eventually. Maybe this was a honey pot into which he would fall. "And if he does claim the money? If he does implicate himself?"

She appeared to anticipate the question. "Then you, as town marshal with jurisdiction over this financial district, may arrest him for accepting stolen funds."

A thin smile took hold of his lips. Her opinion was exactly the one for which he'd hoped. He touched the brim of his hat. "Thank you, Mrs. Morris. You've been mighty helpful."

She smiled, her eyes alight. "Good luck, Mr. Paynter. Mr. Rivers. And Godspeed."

"Ma'am."

Gus caught up to Jake's elbow after they'd left the courthouse. "Alert the posse?"

"Yep. We'll leave at first light and wait five miles past Red Canyon. Tell 'em to pack the heavy hardware."

"Is there any other kind?"

"I reckon not. This is Wyoming, after all."

CHAPTER TWENTY-ONE

OVER THE PREVIOUS TWO YEARS, JAKE HAD LEARNED TO again inhabit the world of men and to even enjoy the company of people. However, he still required intervals of solitude in the same way he needed the next breath of air. After two days in the same spot sharing the same campfire with five others, a stroll into the brush seemed the only means to preserve his hard-won humanity. From his vantage point two hundred steps distant, he watched his posse mill around the campfire, stirring coals while choking down coffee so thick it might start expressing opinions.

Snatches of conversation drifted his way, sometimes a laugh. Gus and Stacy appeared to be sniping at each other as usual. Emshoff was apparently telling a story to rapt Aguilar and Jackson. The scene brought a smile to Jake's lips. For the first time in his life, he had more friends than he could count on one hand. Though he sometimes needed to stand apart from them, he'd not hesitate to march through the gates of hell for any one of them.

With camaraderie on his mind, he turned his attention toward Wind River Canyon, unseen in the distance. Beah Nooki had departed alone two days earlier to watch the entrance for the emergence of outlaws, malevolent moths bursting from a cocoon. If van Zandt held to his timeline, that emergence was already overdue. Jake surveyed the area again, still pleased with the location—far enough from the outlaw hideout to prevent pursuit, distant enough from Lucien's ranch to muffle gunshots that might otherwise draw Lucien's men, and with plenty of cover on either side of the trail. He lifted his eyes toward the far Wind River Mountains, still blanketed in white during the middling days of spring beneath a spotless sky the color of his grandmother's eyes.

The expanse of plain, broken only by resistant sandy hills, beckoned him toward mountainous solitude—to lose himself there for a time. He pushed away the notion. He'd run too much already, and now was not the time. Still, he spent a while traversing the high country in his head before a call drew him back to reality. He looked toward the north to find Beah Nooki approaching on his black-and-white stallion at a determined clip. Jake rose from his resting place and trotted to camp to intercept the Shoshone elder. As Beah Nooki dismounted, the others clustered around him with earnest expectation. The gravity of his features told Jake the time had come.

"How many men?" asked Jake.

"Six," said the elder. "Well armed. Two horses carrying packs. The man called Boggins leads them. He wears his beard long on the sides, bare on his chin."

"And van Zandt?"

"Not with them."

Jake couldn't decide if he was relieved or disappointed by the outlaw leader's absence. "All right, then. Time to go to work. Stacy, Emshoff, Aguilar—take the east side. Gus, Jim, Beah Nooki—the west. And for God's sake, don't shoot one another across the trail."

Stacy planted herself before him, hands on hips. "And what about you?"

"I'm gonna wait in the road."

She stared at him as if he'd lost his mind, which he likely had to some degree, but too long ago to repair the damage.

He shook his head. "Just leave me be, little sister. If I die, you can have my badge."

"Don't want it." She stomped off the road into the brush. "Try not to get shot."

Jake left her behind and led Beah Nooki's stallion to the river where they'd stashed the other horses beneath the flood bank. As he untied his mare, she went for his hat. He ducked reflexively and took no offense. He'd come to learn that hostility was her love language, just as tacit reservation was his. He dragged her up the bank, mounted, and patted her neck.

"Things might get a little hot. If they kill me, just run. I won't think ill of you."

He nudged her toward the road and, upon arrival, took up position just south of the ambush—the same strategy he'd used with Lucien's men. Brief concern nagged him. Should he change the scenario? Switch it up a bit? He decided to let it ride, given Gus's report indicating that van Zandt remained in the dark about what had happened to the lost ammo shipment. He pulled the Henry from its sheath and lay it across his lap to wait.

Perhaps a quarter hour passed before he heard the approach of riders and another five minutes until he laid eyes on them. The lead rider halted his mount briefly upon spying Jake but then pressed forward as if determined to ride through him. When they'd closed to within thirty yards, Jake showed his badge.

"City marshal," he called.

The cavalcade came to a halt—smack in the middle of the kill zone. So intent were they on Jake that they missed the impending death lying in the weeds on either side of the road.

"Whadda ya want?" asked the lead rider. He wore long sideburns with no hair on his chin. Boggins, Jake assumed.

"I know you're haulin' a fortune belonging to Wells Fargo. I'll give you thirty seconds to surrender it."

Boggins laughed. "Or what? You'll gun us down all by your lonesome?"

Jake let the question hang in the crisp air between them for a few seconds. "Never said I was alone."

The outlaw scanned the sides of the road, but perhaps his eyesight was poor. He faced Jake again. "You seem alone."

Jake shrugged. "Nevertheless, you got fifteen seconds left."

Boggins leaned forward in his saddle, his arms crossed casually over the base of his horse's neck. "Why don't you come and get it. *Marshal.*"

"Have it your way."

Jake kicked the mare into motion, squeezed her belly with his knees, and lifted the Henry to his shoulder. The man beside Boggins reached for his revolver in apparent panic, so Jake put a bullet through his chest. Before the man's body became one with the dust of the road, further shots rang out from the margins. Two more outlaws fell from their saddles, while a third slumped forward, clutching his belly with a loud groan. Boggins's certainty and the fact that he was tethered to a pack-horse likely saved him. He hadn't even reached for his weapon. His eyes widened as he came to grips with the carnage and the pair of unattended horses ambling back the way they'd come.

His frozen indecision broke, culminating in the poor choice to flee with the packhorse. Jake caught him before he'd finished his arc and belted the man from his saddle. Meanwhile, the sixth outlaw stretched both hands emphatically skyward, indicating his disinterest in receiving a bullet. Jake dismounted and planted a boot on Boggins's jaw as the man went for his revolver. A spray of blood spewed from the outlaw's mouth and he tumbled into a facedown heap. Jake touched the base of Boggins's spine with his rifle.

"Rest a moment while we talk."

Boggins growled but remained motionless. Jake retreated two steps, sparing a glance at Gus and Emshoff pulling the other mounted men from their saddles. He lifted his chin, striking an officious pose.

"In the name of the territory law, I hereby confiscate these packhorses and all financial instruments they carry on the suspicion of it having been taken illegally from a moving train. Now, stand up."

Boggins complied, pushing to his feet and facing Jake with hands outspread. The man's expression was a wonder of conflicting emotions. Anger. Surprise. Hatred. Dread. Jake waited for him to stop swaying.

"Now, go tell your boss what happened."

The twist of the outlaw's face gave over firmly to dread. He shook his head slowly. "Mr. van Zandt ain't gonna like this. Not one little bit."

"I don't expect he will. But can you do me one favor?"

Boggins's brow creased. "Favor?"

"Tell van Zandt it was Jake Paynter who took the money. And tell him I'm comin' for him next, and right soon."

The outlaw stared almost without comprehension before nodding. "I'll do that. But he's gonna kill you for this."

"Every man's gotta die of something."

"And he'll come after the ones you care for too. I seen him do it."

The words landed like a punch. Jake hadn't given much thought to the ramifications of his war against van Zandt. But he'd waded too far into the pond to stop treading water now. "Take what's left of your men and git. If you so much as peek back over a shoulder, I'll liberate what little brain matter you possess from your skull."

Boggins didn't need to be told twice. He clambered astride his horse, stripped the packhorse's tether, and rode north. Gus shoved the wounded man back onto his mount and sent the horse away with a slap to the flank. Jake watched the three survivors make quick work of eating up the trail before disappearing from view.

"Collect the horses," he said. "Let's head home."

Stacy stood before him again, her eyes narrow with question. "What about the dead men?"

Jake surveyed the bodies, sprawled unceremoniously in

awkward heaps beside the road. The right and respectful behavior would be to bury the men to keep the bodies from coyotes and carrion birds. However, van Zandt needed to know what he was up against.

"Leave 'em where they lie."

Stacy continued to eye him, perhaps waiting for a change of heart.

He set a hand on her shoulder. "Van Zandt is a heartless bastard. He doesn't understand any language but power and violence. We leave these men as a message to him. And they're too dead to hold a grudge."

She rocked her head side to side. "I suppose. But what if van Zandt comes for you like Boggins said?"

"I expect he will. I hope he will. This was the plan—to draw him out of his stronghold. We just need to be ready."

"And the money?"

"We'll stow it in the vault at the bank. Should prove an enticing honey pot for van Zandt."

"All right." She didn't seem convinced of the plan but had surrendered the argument.

Jake mounted the mare and brought up the rear as his posse returned to the river for their horses. Stacy's questions kept ringing through his head. What came next? And could his people take on a determined and cutthroat van Zandt? He resolved the dilemma by doing what came naturally— not thinking about it. The demons within him cried for blood, and Jake was certain he'd soon have it.

CHAPTER TWENTY-TWO

Usually, the scent of smoke precedes the fire. Sometimes, though, fire explodes unannounced. The sixth day after Jake's posse had returned with the recovered money got very hot, and quick. It began with the sound of footsteps thumping along the boardwalk to the door of the marshal's office and said door flying open with such force that it jarred a picture loose from the wall.

"Marshal Paynter!" A familiar young man, still shy of twenty, began to explain his explosive arrival but doubled over when his breath failed. Jake surged from his chair to catch the stranger before he fell over and pushed him into his now-vacant seat.

"Easy, boy. Catch your breath a second."

The young man—Thaddeus something, he recalled—gasped his lungs full a few times before trying again between breaths. "There's shootin'. Over at Atlantic City. Men on horseback. With lots of guns."

Jake was already in motion toward the rack to retrieve his rifle and a bag of .44-caliber cartridges. Thoughts of Dutch van Zandt stampeded through his head. "Did you run all this way?"

"No, sir. Two of 'em followed me and shot down my horse. I made the last two miles through the brush."

"We got spare horses. Come on."

The flush-faced youth rose from the chair and followed as Jake quick-stepped to the stables. Gus, Stacy, and Beah Nooki glanced up startled when he burst through the stable doors.

"We got trouble in Atlantic City."

Gus dropped a horse brush and grabbed his hat. "Van Zandt?"

"Maybe. But I need you to stay here."

"But, Paynter..."

"I need you here, Gus. If they're hittin' the mining camp, South Pass City might be next. Ring the church bell to bring everyone in. Organize a defense. Get Glen Dunbar to help."

Stacy was already walking toward him with Beah Nooki close on her heels. "What about..."

"Grab your scattergun. You're coming with me." He locked eyes with Beah Nooki. "I'd love to have you, but it's your choice."

The Shoshone elder nodded. "I believe I will ride."

He grabbed a horsehair bridle, and his stallion immediately left his stall to follow as Beah Nooki walked outside. Jake retrieved the mare, who protested the abandonment of her bucket of oats, and joined Beah Nooki and Stacy. He found Thaddeus pacing, eyes wide with shock. Jake stepped to the youth and gently punched his jaw. The boy stumbled backward, cupping his jaw with one hand.

"Why'd you do that?"

"You awake now, Thaddeus?"

"Uh, yah. I suppose."

"Good. Then go with Mr. Rivers and do what he says. Understand?"

"Yes, Marshal."

Jake swung into his saddle and found Gus. "I'll find you on the other side."

Gus nodded solemnly. "If I don't find you first."

Jake kicked the mare into motion, never doubting the promise. If, someday, he found himself alongside the ferryman crossing the River Styx, he'd no doubt that Gus would be there to meet him. And he was all right with that.

———————

"Just up there," said Stacy. She pointed ahead to the clutch of tents, large and small, permeated by a scatter of wooden structures. The mining camp clung to the crease between two hills, cozy and confined at the same time. At least three columns of smoke rose from the cluster. Jake, Stacy, and Beah Nooki pushed their horses like whirlwinds the final distance to arrive in the aftermath of chaos. A weeping woman lay sprawled over a dead man in the middle of the road. Another woman sat in the dust, her hair and face caked with blood, while two men tried to stanch the flow. Men, women, and children had formed a bucket brigade to extinguish a flaming building, but the structure seemed doomed to fall.

The all-consuming activity allowed Jake and his associates to gallop into the midst practically unnoticed. Jake jumped from his horse and corralled a pudgy man he recognized from the miner's union—Tom Epson. The man's frantic eyes lit with hope when he realized who'd stopped him. Jake grimaced, bearing the weight of unrealistic expectations once again.

"Marshal Paynter! You came!"

The mention of his name had the effect of rotting apples on fruit flies. Those who'd been milling aimlessly descended on him, grasping, clutching, demanding. Stacy saved him by pushing through the throng and creating a buffer between Jake and his petitioners.

"Shut the hell up, people!" she shouted. The crowd quieted until only the sound of the burning building filled the silence. Stacy waved a hand to Jake. "It's all yours."

He leveled a solemn gaze at the expectant citizens. "Tell me what happened. One at a time." He pointed to Epson. "You start."

Epson wrung his meaty hands together. "Men came riding in. Fifteen. Maybe twenty. Shooting, breaking, burning."

"They take anything?"

"No, sir."

"They demand anything?"

"No, sir."

The woman to his left edged nearer. "They wanted nothin'. Just violence. Just mayhem. Just to hurt."

Her eyes flickered over Jake's shoulder and she melted back, matching the space others had suddenly given Jake. He glanced aside to find that Beah Nooki had joined him, rifle in hand, jawline like a granite outcrop. Jake hadn't particularly thought of the elder as intimidating, but now he reconsidered his opinion. Beah Nooki seemed suddenly like the edge of a knife. He peered at Jake, deep into his soul.

"These men did not come to steal. They came to break spirits. Among my people, we send such men away until they show great sorrow or die. I fear these men have no sorrow."

His words chilled Jake but echoed his guess. "I agree."

"Does anyone know who they were?" said Stacy. "Anyone recognize them?"

The crowd exchanged befuddled glances, maybe hoping that somebody knew something. Anything. Instead, they received headshakes, shrugs, and upturned hands. Jake lifted his eyes past those nearest to find a young woman clutching her torn dress, pinning it to her shoulder. The haunt of her features drew him instinctively through the press of bodies, and she waited. Three deep scratches laced her bare upper arm, and a knot had formed on one cheek. Jake removed his hat.

"Miss? You know somethin'?"

She began to nod, hesitated, then finished the gesture.

"It's all right. I'm here to help. What can you tell us?"

She swiped tears from her eyes with her free hand. "I was over there..." She flicked a wrist toward the burning building, which was in the process of collapsing. "I ran out. These men. They laid hands on me. They threw me in the street, kneeled on me. They did..." Words failed her, but she motioned to the ripped fabric of her dress. Stacy slipped up beside the woman and circled an arm around her.

"There, there," she said. "I got ya. Did they...hurt you?"

The young woman shook her head. "No. I thought they would, but this man came. A tall stranger. Dressed in a suit—the kind with a vest and pocket-watch chain. He made them stop. They listened to him. I think they were afraid of him."

She inhaled a stuttering breath while Stacy kept her propped up. "Then he helped me up and said he had a message."

Jake drew his brow down. "A message? For who?"

"For you, Marshal."

The red haze began rising in Jake, one that might send him howling after van Zandt in a rage that would likely get him killed. He drew a deep breath to tamp it down, to silence the howls. "What was the message?"

She turned her eyes up and to the right, recalling. "He said...he said, 'Tell Paynter he can't be everywhere at once. Tell Paynter he can't protect everyone. Tell him he will be forced to choose. Tell him that we can go where we like, when we like, and do what we like, and there's nothing he can do to stand against us.'"

Again, the thought of Jake's friends crowded his thoughts. The Emshoffs. The Dunbars. The Aguilars. Gus and Stacy. And, of course, Rosalyn. What van Zandt promised was not an idle threat. Jake lost track of the moment, folding in on himself. The girl drew him out after five seconds, or maybe five minutes. He couldn't be certain.

"That's not all, Marshal."

Jake blinked twice. "Oh? What else did this man tell you?"

"He said, 'Tell Paynter to return our money and sweeten the pot, and maybe we will spare his friends.'"

The pronouncement was every bit as bad as he'd expected. Van Zandt had declared war on Jake personally and meant to demolish him by first destroying those he called friends. The dandy lawyer from New York City turned outlaw had rounded a very dark corner. He'd crossed the Rubicon from train robbery into daylight murder in the presence of scores of witnesses. Left unchecked, van Zandt would drag the citizens of the territory into a hell of his making, stepping over the corpses of Jake's friends along the way. Jake Paynter of old might've taken on the storm alone, hoping to bring down as many of the enemy as possible before falling dead. But if the previous two years had taught him anything, it was that two men together were ten times stronger than two men alone.

"Thank you," he told the woman. "Deputy Blue will help you." He swept his eyes across the devastated crowd. "As for the rest of you. Care for your wounded. House your burnt-out neighbors. Bury your dead. But know this. I won't rest until these men lie cold. You have my word."

He turned away to find his mare and mounted. As he started back toward South Pass City, Beah Nooki appeared at his side. When he looked up, the elder was again piercing his soul.

"How will you keep such a promise?" asked Beah Nooki.

Jake looked straight ahead, unable to bear the old man's scrutiny. He wasn't sure he could, but he'd die trying. In the meantime, his call for help was long past due.

"We need professionals," he said.

Beah Nooki frowned in consideration. "Professionals? Soldiers, perhaps?"

"Yep. And I happen to know a mob of 'em just south of here a few days."

"Your Tenth Cavalry K-Troop?"

"The very same. I need to send a telegraph to Fort Bridger."

Beah Nooki nodded understanding. He'd heard the story. K-Troop had shown their mettle the previous year when rescuing several dozen mining families from certain death during a prairie fire. More importantly, they had scattered the outlaws and Philadelphia gang who'd started the blaze, killing several in the process. The trust the soldiers had gained from the people of South Pass City couldn't be duplicated by another unit.

"Do you believe they will answer your call?" asked Beah Nooki.

"Yes," said Jake. "They always do."

CHAPTER TWENTY-THREE

FOR THE FIRST TIME IN DAYS, ROSALYN WALKED HOME alone after locking up the schoolhouse. Since Stacy Blue had moved into the spare room of Rosalyn's log-walled cabin at the edge of town, she'd insisted on accompanying Rosalyn to and from the schoolhouse every day with a shotgun cradled in her elbow and a knife at her hip. Stacy had claimed all of it was her idea, but she was a poor liar. Paynter was clearly the impetus behind Stacy's nonchalant request to rent a room and then escort Rosalyn everywhere while armed to the teeth.

Rosalyn welcomed the company, though. Stacy filled up the tiny cabin with her outsized personality and did a yeoman's work cooking, cleaning, and patching leaks. Regardless, Rosalyn worried over the unspoken reason for Paynter's maneuver. Her brother had attempted one kidnapping, and despite dire threats from Paynter in his capacity as a marshal, he might try again.

Stacy had left early that morning to look after those in Atlantic City affected by the recent raid, and Rosalyn didn't expect her to return until nightfall. Without her personal bodyguard, Rosalyn found her feet moving quicker along the muddy streets toward her house. As she rounded a huddle of wood-framed canvas huts, her cabin came into view. She froze in her tracks upon spotting a man lingering by the cabin door. One of Lucien's men? She was preparing to turn away, to find help, when vague recognition halted her. As she peered closely at the man, he noticed her and made eye contact. The view of his face marked him as a clerk at the Idaho House hotel on Main Street. Duff, or Duffy, or something like that. He leaned in to motion to meet her half-way, doffing his hat as he walked.

"Miss Ashley," he called.

"Sir?"

He stopped several feet away, his hat at his belt. "I've been sent to fetch you to the Idaho House. There's a gentleman awaiting your presence."

A gentleman? That word failed to describe Lucien's men, and surely the clerk would have mentioned her brother by name. "A gentleman, you say? Who is he?"

"Don't know. He paid in cash and refused to sign the guest ledger. But he's an older fella. Gray hair and wearing a fine suit. You know, one of them kind you can't buy around these parts."

Suspicious but intrigued, she walked with the clerk as they angled back toward the center of town. "Did he say where he was from, perhaps?"

"No, ma'am. Came in on the stage from Laramie yester-day and took our best room. About a half hour ago, he sent me to find you and said, 'Don't come back without her.' So I been waitin' for you ever since. Didn't seem like the kind of fella who abides disappointment."

The fine hairs on Rosalyn's neck stood like tiny sentinels scouring the horizon. A flicker of unease briefly plagued her, but she swept it aside as unlikely. But who was this stranger? So deep was her consideration of the question that she'd rounded the corner before raising her eyes to the hotel. She thudded to a halt. A half block ahead, her brother, Lucien, was roping his horse to the hitching rail in front of the hotel. As he swiveled his gaze toward her, she prepared to run to the marshal's office across the street or the Dunbars' smithy nearby. The befuddled expression that crossed his face delayed her plan. His eyes narrowed and he called out.

"What are you doing here?"

"I'd ask the same of you," she said. "You're a long way from the ranch."

He failed to reply but waited while she cautiously closed the distance between them. His posture seemed anything but threatening—only baffled.

She stopped out of arm's reach, just in case. "Well?"

He cocked his head. "Did you receive an invitation from a mysterious stranger to come here?"

The question startled her. "I did, just minutes ago. And you?"

"A messenger arrived at the ranch around noon. Said to present myself promptly at five o'clock at the Idaho House hotel and said it would be worth my while. I nearly declined, but curiosity got the better of me."

"Are you expecting a visitor?"

"Nobody." He motioned toward the door. "After you?"

She folded her arms and shook her head. "No. I'd rather keep you in front of me, thank you."

Mild guilt appeared to ripple across his features. He grunted. "Come now, Sister. I was only looking out for your best interest."

"By sending the worst of men to hog-tie me, throw me in a wagon bed, and haul me away against my will? How is that in my best interest?"

He frowned deeply. "Look. They were rougher than I would have preferred, and I'm sorry for that. However, that doesn't erase the fact that you'd be safer and happier with me at the ranch instead of playing schoolmarm and chasing after Jake Paynter."

"I'm not playing schoolmarm!" Rosalyn stamped her foot into the muck for effect, splattering her shoe. "I love my work. And I'm not chasing after Jake Paynter. You can't catch what can't be caught."

Lucien's brow drew down into a glare. "We will simply disagree on this, then. But suit yourself."

He spun away to shove open the door of the Idaho House. The cowed clerk at least retained the wherewithal to hold the door for Rosalyn. She followed in Lucien's wake, but he stopped to turn on the clerk.

"Just where is this stranger?" he growled with impatience.

The clerk stammered and began waving energetically toward the middle of the hallway. "In…in…in the guest parlor. Just there."

The man retreated around the counter to place the barrier between him and Lucien. Rosalyn understood his reaction.

Her brother could charm a person in one breath and terrify them in the next. She didn't know which behavior was real, which was an act, or if he was simply a chaotic blend of the two—an unsavory pot of stew that might boil over at any time. Lucien shifted his offended glare from the clerk to Rosalyn. She refused to cower. If nothing else, Paynter had taught her how to handle bullies—lean in and never show fear. The strategy worked. Lucien closed his eyes, reached up to pinch the bridge of his nose, and exhaled a slow breath. When he opened his eyes, the charm had returned. Mostly.

"We should find out what this is all about," he said.

"On that we agree. After you."

He led the way down the hall before pushing through a double door on his left. When she entered behind him, his halted form blocked her view of the room. She stepped gingerly around him to find the stranger casually arranged on a sofa, one arm spread across the top of it. His mop of gray hair cascaded to his shoulders, framing extensive mutton chops that met above his lip in a spectacular mustache. Eyes the color of raindrops peered from beneath bushy brows, like unholy beacons in the night. His impeccable suit topped a pair of brown leather boots that she had polished a hundred times in another life. She collected her slack jaw.

"Father." The word emerged half choked. "What are you doing here?"

"My question exactly," said Lucien by her side.

The senator from Missouri grew a look of mild affront and spread his hands. "Such a churlish question, children. You cut me to the quick. Can a devoted father not see to the well-being of his only offspring without facing prosecution?"

Though very convincing to the untrained eye, Rosalyn knew her father's display to be an act, a theatrical production for the benefit of setting his audience on its heels. As with Lucien's masquerades, she'd seen too many to believe even one iota of it. Their father wouldn't have traveled from Missouri to Wyoming, even by train, unless he wished to share bad news or derive some personal benefit. Given his presence despite the availability of the telegraph, she suspected the latter. They'd parted on poor terms two years prior, with Rosalyn practically fleeing west after resisting her father's wishes for her to remain in St. Louis and marry for money. She felt her face becoming granite, like a statue of the ancients. She clutched her arms tightly around her waist.

"Come now, Father. You may dispense with the dramatic oratory. Your little displays may fool others, but Lucien and I know you too well. Anything further would simply be a misuse of our time."

"Hear, hear," said Lucien.

Her father's eyes softened briefly before he caught himself. He shook a finger at Rosalyn. "You've changed, my girl. The proper young woman has allowed this frontier hovel to roughen her once-pleasant demeanor. I must say, I am saddened by that. You had such potential, should you have stayed in Missouri. But alas."

She wilted, sagging into herself. Her father always seemed to know just where to land the blow that it might hurt the most. Lucien's hand on her arm caused her to jump.

"Don't listen to him, Rosalyn. You know better."

The senator's eyes flashed with indignation. "Now you take her side? Where is your mettle, boy? I did not send you west to cry on behalf of a set of frilly skirts."

Lucien dropped the hand from her arm and gritted his jaw. "Again, why have you come here?"

"No small talk?" the man said. "Well, so be it."

He rose, unwinding his six-and-a-half-foot frame to loom over them, and evaporated the space between them until Rosalyn was forced to crane her neck. Despite knowing it was yet another tactic of political intimidation, she couldn't help but shudder. He peered down at his son.

"It has come to my attention," her father said in tones so low that the windowpanes buzzed from the sound, "that you have made poor choices regarding your selection of enemies and friends."

She glanced at Lucien to find his brow creasing. "Explain, please."

Her father clasped his hands together at his waist. "Let us begin with your enemies. Word has reached me of a condemned killer turned marshal who has stymied you at every turn. His repeated successes make you look weak, Son. Spineless. Inept." When Lucien began to sputter, the senator raised a finger to silence him. "However, your more pressing problem is your association with a prominent outlaw who runs roughshod over all common decency. You must cease any such association immediately."

Lucien stood taller. "Is that so? Or what?"

Rosalyn's father snatched Lucien's lapel and pulled her

brother close to his chest. His cheeks flushed red. "Or you will ruin everything you've worked for! All our best-laid plans. All my efforts to send you west with a fortune. Your association with this van Zandt character will cost you a seat in the territory legislature. Without that influence, you will remain just another *little man*, scrabbling for the crumbs falling from the table of the powerful."

As Rosalyn watched Lucien, the fight seemed to drain from him as his features went slack with realization and a pinch of fear. The senator seemingly approved of the reaction. He nodded, released Lucien's lapel, and patted it flat.

"I'm pleased you understand. You must win a seat at all costs. Once in the halls of power, you may do as you please. You have the resources and charisma to dominate them all. A governorship will soon follow."

Even as Rosalyn blanched upon realizing the extent of Lucien's and her father's mad plan, her brother straightened again. A smile drifted across his face. "Very well, Father. I will do as you say."

"There's a good lad."

Bile rose up in Rosalyn's throat. She had witnessed her father's political maneuvering for a lifetime and had even learned from it. Only in her separation from him, though, did she perceive the reptilian nature of his scheming. And Lucien was cut from the same cloth. She began to lean away from the men, repulsed by their shared lust for power.

"One problem," said Lucien. "What about the cattle I've amassed for van Zandt?"

"Is his ownership captured in a legal document?"

"No."

"Then keep them. All the better for you."

Lucien narrowed his eyes. "But van Zandt is formidable and runs twenty or more hired guns."

Rosalyn's father turned aside and settled again on the sofa. He waved a hand. "I was told that the cavalry is coming to bring the outlaws to heel. And isn't your marshal leading them into the fight?"

"That is true."

"Then tell this Paynter what you know so that he might succeed in destroying van Zandt's operation. And who knows? Perhaps the whole affair will turn into a bloodbath and will solve both your problems. No more outlaw friends. No more Paynter."

A flare of rage burned a path from the pit of Rosalyn's stomach to knot the muscles of her jaw. Before she could muster rational speech, her father coolly shifted his attention to her.

"Rosalyn. I've heard a rumor that you teach illiterate yokel youths. Is this true?"

She bit her tongue and nodded.

He rolled his eyes. "I raised you to be better. I cannot sufficiently express my disappointment in what you've become. Perhaps I should have expected as much, given your origin."

Rosalyn clenched her fists into tight knots of fury but leveled her voice. "How long will you be staying, Father?"

He flipped a hand. "Not long. I leave on tomorrow's stage."

She stretched her spine until it popped. "Wonderful. I hope they reserve a warm spot in hell for the both of you."

She spun on her heel and stalked from the hotel, disregarding the demands for her return. Outside, she stopped and inhaled a deep, shuddering breath. In the open air of Main Street, she felt as if she might take flight.

CHAPTER TWENTY-FOUR

Gus passed the afternoon by digging a grave. He'd dug many graves over the course of his life, the first for his father at age nine. The others that followed were mostly final acts of tragic plays—friends who'd fallen beneath the whip of a taskmaster, comrades in arms slaughtered on the field of battle or cut down by disease, newcomers frozen by the harsh Wyoming winter. The list grew longer year by year. This particular grave, however, belonged to a much shorter ledger of those who'd lived long lives and passed from the world in their sleep surrounded by loved ones. Mr. Caroche had seen ninety-seven winters and died with a smile on his lips. Gus envied him and prayed for a similar ending. However, eight solid years of making a living with a gun seemed to stack the deck against him.

After interring Mr. Caroche on the hill overlooking town and mounding the now-occupied hole with excess dirt, he leaned against his spade, wiped his brow, and pulled a long draught from his canteen. In the near silence, he heard the distinct rumble of many hooves. A short walk over the hip of the hill revealed the source of the sound. A line of mounted soldiers rode trotting horses along the creek bottom toward town, blue overcoats flapping in the breeze. He called back over a shoulder.

"I'll be going to meet the Tenth now. A good day to you."

"Same to you, Deputy," called Caroche's eldest son, himself seventy-five at least and too infirm to dig a hole.

Gus descended the hill to intercept his old troopmates as they set up camp beside the creek marking the town border. He counted as he went, so his first words were a question as he slipped up on the group.

"Is this all?"

Sergeant Stubbs turned and a grin split his face. "Sergeant Rivers, you old dog. Still here, I see."

"And up to my neck in this mess." Gus waved to the other twenty soldiers. "Where's the rest of the troop?"

Stubbs's smile faded and he shook his head. "Afraid it's just us. The lion's share of the troop went south with Lieutenant Stallings to deal with trouble along the border. Twenty is all the colonel would spare, and only for a time."

Gus surveyed the buffalo soldiers again and found not a white face among them. "They put you in charge?"

Stubbs tapped the sleeve of his uniform. "New stripes. I'm first sergeant now. The colonel wanted to send along a white officer, but Stallings talked him out of it."

"Why do you suppose he did that?"

Stubbs lifted his palms. "Don't know for sure. But I think he's tryin' to make a point with the commander. Whatever the reason, I'm glad for it. The effect on morale has been a couple ounces shy of miraculous."

"Sergeant Gus dadgum Rivers!"

Corporal Jefferson mobbed Gus from behind and nearly took them both to the ground. Gus pushed the young man away. "Jefferson. Good to see you too."

Stubbs belted out a laugh. "See what I mean about morale?"

"I believe I do."

They spent a few minutes catching up with one another until Paynter and Beah Nooki strolled up. Stubbs saluted Paynter smartly.

"Lieutenant."

Paynter waved away the salute. "I ain't that no more. You don't have to salute every time you see me. Just shake my hand."

"I can do that." They shook.

Paynter motioned to Beah Nooki, who was standing just off his shoulder. "Sergeant Stubbs...or should I say, First Sergeant Stubbs, this is the grandfather of Darwin Follows the Wind, Beah Nooki. Beah Nooki, Sergeant Stubbs."

The two men shook hands. Beah Nooki smiled wryly. "Paynter and Gus speak well of you."

Stubbs laughed. "Because they're addled."

"This I know."

Meanwhile, Paynter performed a head count just like Gus had. "This it? Twenty?"

Stubbs repeated his explanation, and Paynter nodded. "Well, I'm glad to have you nonetheless. Twenty trained and mounted guns are better than anything we can dig up around here."

While the soldiers pitched tents, Gus, Paynter, Stubbs,

and Beah Nooki settled to talk logistics and strategy on a patch of grass just stirring to life after the long winter. Paynter explained the situation with the outlaw stronghold and their recent activities while Gus and Beah Nooki offered details about what they'd determined on their scouting expedition. Stubbs whistled when he learned of the raid on Atlantic City and the message van Zandt had sent to Paynter.

"Sounds like a first-rate jackass, this van Zandt. But a jackass with crates of ammo and too much attitude. To attack a town in broad daylight like that. What gall."

"Which is why we gotta take 'em down right quick," said Gus.

"I agree. Whatcha got in mind? Split forces? Two angles of attack?"

A thin smile softened Paynter's stony countenance. "Just what I was thinkin'. With twenty troopers and the seven of us, we can split three ways and hit 'em all at once. Pin them down with triangular fire, maybe take the fight out of 'em."

Gus looked sidelong at Paynter. "You really think van Zandt's the kind to surrender?"

"No. Him, we'll have to kill. But maybe the rest won't be so eager to die."

Gus nodded, but he worried over the force size. At best, they'd outnumber van Zandt's crew by a few men. He kept his concerns private, though. Paynter seemed certain, Beah Nooki remained silent, and Stubbs was still in his oats. Expressing doubt didn't seem particularly helpful at the moment. However, he couldn't help but think of Stacy. There was no way in Hades they'd be able to stop her from coming along. If he got shot up, so be it. Wouldn't be the first time. But not Stacy. The thought of losing her came close enough to killing him as it was. Mired in such thoughts, he drifted in and out of the conversation. Meanwhile, K-Troop finished setting camp and began drifting over to the circle, joining the conversation, as spirited as dancing kites.

After a few minutes, motion from the footbridge over the creek caught Gus's eye. Miss Ashley and Mrs. Morris were approaching with full hands, and many others trailed behind them, similarly laden. When he rose to his feet, the raucous conversation dwindled as everyone turned their regard to the oncoming parade. Paynter met the advancing party.

"Miss Ashley," he said. "What's the occasion?"

She flashed a warm smile at him, wide as the Wyoming sky, likely meant only for Paynter but apparent to all. "We've come to feed the men of K-Troop. We owe them at least that much after what they did for us last year."

"I think that's a right fine idea," said Paynter.

As the townsfolk arranged their shared suppers on the ground and pulled back covers to reveal a riot of savory scents, the hungry soldiers clustered around them, marking out their favorites. Esther Morris set down a Dutch oven, unraveled her lanky frame, and held up her hands.

"Gentlemen," she said. "Welcome back to South Pass City. Now, let's say grace and break bread together."

They did. Soldiers and townsfolk alike heaped plates with food and gathered around a fire set by Corporal Jefferson that had become a determined blaze. They chatted, laughed, and shared the meal as if long-lost family. After half an hour, one of the soldiers retrieved a guitar and began strumming popular tunes. Everyone joined in, singing in the night under a sea of hopeful stars. After a while, Paynter leaned near to Gus.

"Can you believe this?"

Gus grunted. "Barely. I'd a' never thought…" His voice failed.

Paynter squeezed his shoulder. "I know. I know. I been fightin' for most of my life, not always knowing why, not always knowing what for. Not knowing if the cause was worthy." He nodded toward the circle of people. "But this. This is worth fighting for."

Gus agreed. He'd rush a thousand palisades, fight ten thousand men, face a hundred thousand bullets—if only to experience a handful of moments like this one.

CHAPTER TWENTY-FIVE

How many times had he ridden toward the crack in the world called Wind River Canyon to shed blood or die? *Too many*, thought Beah Nooki. *And now, once more.*

Paynter had just divided the advancing force into three parties with instructions for the predawn attack still a half a day in the future. Gus led Aguilar, Emshoff, and three soldiers up the west rim. Sergeant Stubbs, Stacy, young Jim, and twelve troopers dove into the belly of the bear, following the river into the canyon's shadowy abyss. Beah Nooki, Paynter, and four troopers had begun mounting the eastern rim, following a path the elder knew well from half a hundred ascents scattered across a lifetime. As the river fell away to his left, flashes of recollection stirred his mind. Of fishing the tumbling waters for speckled trout and large-finned grayling. Of flushing deer along the river into the arrows of waiting hunters. Of nestling among the rocks beneath the stars in the crisp autumn air.

Mostly, though, he recalled those moments of conflict that had both shaped him and scarred him. A memory came to him of Proud Nose, his closest friend from childhood, as he lay dying in Beah Nooki's arms in the shallows, felled by a Blackfoot arrow to his chest. Blood streaming from the wound trailed over Beah Nooki's hands in a steady stream that fed the river while he tried in vain to will his friend back to life. Afterward, the Shoshone hunting party had returned to the village with a thousand fish, two dozen deer, and nine dead men. Though the loss was nearly too much to bear, Beah Nooki had taken heart from the fact that the sacrifice ensured the survival of his people through a hard winter when the snows had piled waist-deep and the wind had blown insistent death from the mountains.

"You seem far away."

Paynter's statement as they rode together shook Beah Nooki from the sticky web of recollection. "I am."

"Worry?"

"Yes. And memory."

Paynter would understand. He was a man of few words who walked vast worlds of dark remembrance. Beah Nooki had seen him collapse many times into the shadowy hollow of past events, living them again and again while his spirit faded in turn.

"This place haunts you," said Paynter.

"Yes. But I have learned from this canyon what matters."

"And what matters?"

Beah Nooki set his gaze on the young marshal. "That some fights you must win, or you will lose everything. If you defeat these outlaws, all benefit with you. If you fail, all lose with you. You give over power to your enemy to rule as he pleases." He paused. "You must not lose. This time, you must not retreat, no matter the cost."

Paynter nodded, his face grim with difficult

understanding. "You are remembering the fight here with the Blackfeet when you were young? For hunting rights?"

"Yes. But that victory lasted only a few seasons. Other victories last for all time."

Paynter blinked slowly as he studied Beah Nooki's face. "What kind of victories?"

He had expected the question. Other memories crowded his thoughts, like a rush of buffalo through a narrow valley. Perhaps his expression betrayed him.

"Crowheart."

Paynter's eyes widened. "You've never spoken of it before, even though others in the village could not stop talking about it."

"That is true." Beah Nooki drew a deep breath and blew it slowly into the ether. "But now is the time to tell it."

Paynter drew his horse nearer, intent.

Beah Nooki faced ahead. "The white government gave our land, the Valley of the Warm Winds, to the Crow twenty years ago by treaty. My people had hunted the valley for longer than the memory of the eldest, so this disappointed us. Five years ago, Chief Washakie explained this to the government and asked for a new treaty. They did not listen. The next summer, the Crow came to the valley to hunt, led by Chief Big Robber. He was a bear of a man, a strong warrior. The Crow sang songs of his bravery by their cook fires. But the Crow were not our enemy. They only wanted to feed their people, just like the Shoshone."

"So what happened was an accident?" said Paynter. "A twist of fate?"

"Fate, perhaps. Accident, no. When Washakie asked the Crow to leave, Big Robber said no. Washakie led us into battle, along with Bannock allies, to fight the Crow. For many days, we fought them between the flat-top mountain and the black mountain. The grass and sage filled with blood as many warriors died, Crow, Shoshone, Bannock. But the Crow could not win and my people could not win. We could only keep killing one other. On the fifth day, Washakie called the eldest warriors together and spoke a plan."

Though four years had passed since the battle, the smell of it still filled Beah Nooki's nostrils. Dust. Blood. Death. He closed his eyes to tell what had happened, living it again as he spoke.

"Tell us your plan, Shoots-on-the-Run," said Beah Nooki with arms folded. He and Washakie were of nearly the same generation. They had hunted together, gambled against each other with the gourd and stones a thousand times, and fought countless battles side by side. As a result, he could show direct challenge to Washakie in a manner the younger men could not.

Washakie understood and took no offense. He produced a grim smile, indicating as much. "The battle cannot be won by the Shoshone, nor by the Crow. If we continue to fight, more young men will die, and for nothing. But I know how to end this today."

Dread crept over Beah Nooki. He recognized the glint of Washakie's eyes, determined and final. It was the look of a man ready to gamble his very life. Beah Nooki flared his nostrils. "Tell us, then. We are listening."

"I have already challenged Big Robber to mounted combat,

man against man, to the death. The people of the winner remain. The people of the loser must leave the valley."

Beah Nooki shook his head. "But you are an old man, a white hair. Should we not choose another?"

"No, my friend. It must be me." Washakie pointed aside. "See. Even now, Big Robber comes."

Beah Nooki watched as the Crow chief approached with a knot of warriors at his side. The man was legendary among the tribes, a fierce fighter who overwhelmed his enemy with size, strength, and determination. The dread mounted in Beah Nooki as he considered the loss of his old friend and the tragedy of surrendering their ancestral valley to another people.

"I come to fight you, old man," called Big Robber.

Washakie rode to him and pointed to a rise in the distance. "We fight there, alone. All others remain where they are. One dies, one returns."

"I agree. You will die, I will return."

Washakie straightened on his horse and cast a glare that might set dry grass ablaze. "Big Robber. I will kill you and cut out your heart this day."

Big Robber smiled. "Let us ride together, Shoots-on-the-Run."

The two chiefs kicked their horses into motion and raced for the rise as if already in competition. Beah Nooki could only watch and grip the reins with knuckles drained of blood. When the combatants reached the high ground, they squared their horses against each another, raised war lances, and charged. They struck out with the lances but passed aside without one spearing the other. The action kicked up a cloud of dust that scattered against a setting sun and began to obscure the distant conflict. The dust only grew thicker as the chiefs made pass after pass at each other and circled for advantage. Soon, Beah Nooki could not tell which shadow was which in the cloud. His heart hammered in his chest as the fate of his people lay in the balance.

After what seemed a very long time, the shadows stopped moving in the dust. One man was down and the other over him. Then the victor mounted his horse and emerged from the dust on a line toward the tense watchers. Within moments, Beah Nooki spied the flowing white hair of the rider and expelled an explosive breath of relief. Washakie reached him with lance held high and the heart of Big Robber impaled on its point. A line of blood along Washakie's side showed how near the Crow chief had come to killing him.

"Big Robber fought bravely," said Washakie. "A true warrior. I honor his death by taking his heart."

The Shoshone lifted cries of victory while the collective chins of the Crow fell to their chests. The eldest of the Crow nudged his horse toward Washakie.

"Shoots-on-the-Run. You have defeated Big Robber fairly. You have shown yourself to be the greater warrior this day. We will honor the agreement and leave the valley at sunrise."

Paynter's eyes never strayed from Beah Nooki as he told the story of Crowheart. "So the Crow left Wind River Valley as promised?" he asked.

"They did and gifted Washakie with a Crow woman as a sign of respect. I expected them to return eventually. A few years maybe, and we would fight again."

"And did they return?"

"No. Two years after the battle, Washakie convinced the

government to grant the valley to the Shoshone people by treaty. He made his victory that day a victory for all time." Beah Nooki peered at Paynter. "Every victory makes possible a future victory. Every defeat makes a future defeat more likely. So do you understand now?"

Paynter stared ahead and nodded. "Yes. If we lose this fight, van Zandt and other lawless men will rule this land for years."

"True," said Beah Nooki. "And so you must win. Learn this wisdom from an old man."

Paynter nodded but said nothing, instead pinning his attention on the ground ahead, the battle ahead. Beah Nooki grunted with satisfaction. The young man was ready.

CHAPTER TWENTY-SIX

IN THE FULL LIGHT OF DAY, THE STEEP SIDES OF THE canyon were a minefield of ankle-snapping obstacles. In pitch-darkness, they became a death trap. Having left the horses at the rim with one of the buffalo soldiers, Jake had no alternative but to trust Beah Nooki's memory of the treacherous descent above the outlaw stronghold. With three soldiers at his back, including an uncharacteristically quiet Corporal Jefferson, they moved downward in increments, every inch of ground hard won. Any heavy grunt, any kicked stone, any expulsion of breath could alert the sentry as they slipped down on the man. Beah Nooki reached him first and silenced him with a steady hand and a long knife.

As they neared the river, its flow began to occupy the background, muffling the sound of horses and snoring men below. The scudding and sporadic clouds veiling a half-moon revealed fleeting glimpses of the outlaw camp a hundred yards upriver of their position. The large tent puffing smoke from a stovepipe. A dozen smaller tents, no doubt housing two men apiece. A makeshift corral that pinned a herd of horses against a wall of rock mere feet from the river. The river itself, a chaotic tumble through most of the canyon, grew wider and shallower as it swept around the massive rock abutment that loomed over the camp. When Beah Nooki halted their progress, Jake turned to Jefferson.

"Find cover," he whispered. "Settle in. Pass it along."

Jake heeded his own advice and found a crease of rock where he could lie at an angle for cover or lean forward to fire into the camp. There, he waited. If all went according to plan, Gus's unit should have moved down from the west rim to occupy ground opposite the camp above the river, maintaining a downward shooting angle. Meanwhile, Stubbs should have pushed his larger troop to within a half mile of the abutment to await the sound of first shots—the signal to rush the camp. Jake thought of Stacy and prayed that Stubbs would keep her from taking too many risks. However, Stacy tended to do as she pleased, so his prayer was likely moot.

Perhaps an hour passed before the star field above began to fade and the vanguard of dawn lessened the blackness. The sun rising behind them cast the camp into sharper relief, and outlaws began stirring from their tents to rekindle the central fire and relieve their whiskey-washed bladders. Within minutes, the western rim lit with gold fire as the sun's rays caressed the pinkish rocks, and a line of gold began descending with a cascading massage of light. The moment of conflict had come. Jake lifted his eyes to the still-dark ground on the opposite side of the river and held his breath. Seconds later, his anticipation was answered. Muzzle flashes from Gus's band sparked briefly and bullets pinged the rocks above the corral. The scatter of gunshots had two immediate effects, both according to plan. The horses stirred to life in the corral and began pushing at the log-fence barricade in unease bordering on panic. Meanwhile, the outlaws in the open began diving for cover while those still abed erupted half-dressed from tents.

"Over there," shouted a couple. In short order, an array of outlaw rifles began sending volleys of shots at Gus's position, throwing lead in the general direction of the unseen attackers. Van Zandt exploded from the larger tent.

"Join the firing line, dammit!" he shouted. The rest of the milling outlaws scurried to comply and soon were raining bullets on the canyon slope beyond the river. Jake hoped that Gus and his men had found suitable holes in which to hide. He leaned forward gingerly from the rocky crease and began counting the enemy. He lost count at thirty-one and bit off a muffled curse. More men than he'd expected. A lot more.

While a few of van Zandt's men peeled away to calm the horses, the others kept up a steady drumbeat of fire and hurled taunts and promises of murder at the unseen foe. Meanwhile, the sun's rays continued their steady descent into the void of the canyon, illuminating it layer by rocky layer. Within minutes, Gus and his men would become exposed and the potshots would transform into a proper turkey shoot. Not to be outdone by the bandits, though, Gus responded to the vicious chatter with insults of his own.

"You missed again," he shouted from the distant darkness. "My aunt shoots better than that, and she died ten years ago."

As Jake had anticipated, several outlaws slipped downriver, likely hoping to ford the water and flank the shooters. As the outlaws passed by on foot, blithely unaware of the mortal danger, Jake lifted his Henry and put a bullet in the lead man's head. The others fell within a heartbeat, taken down by the soldiers and the Shoshone elder. As he knew it would, this fundamentally altered the nature of the outlaw defense.

"Take cover! Take cover!"

The shout erupted from several men, including van Zandt. Bullets began ricocheting off the rocky extrusions protecting Jake and his crew. For the next few minutes, the battle continued with the outlaws concentrating fire on the far canyon wall and Jake's entrenched position downriver. Unable to get off more than a passing shot, the pinned-down posse was forced to weather the storm that raged around them. However, the action accomplished the intended purpose of putting the backs of the outlaws to the trail upriver. As a result, Stubbs's unmounted men began raining fire into the outlaw camp before they noticed the flank attack. Outlaws fell left and right, pinned down on three sides. For an instant, Jake basked in the glory of a perfectly executed plan and waited for van Zandt's men to wilt. Not for the first time in his life, though, he was gravely disappointed by what happened next.

Van Zandt shouted heated and hurried instructions to his men. As one, they swiftly fell back to the corral. The corral's sheltering rock blocked the firing sight line for Stubbs and his soldiers, giving the outlaws reprieve from the withering triangle. From there, van Zandt divided his men. While half redoubled their efforts in pinning down Gus's and Jake's bands and preventing Stubbs from pressing closer, the others began saddling horses. Several times, Jake lunged forward to squeeze off a hurried shot, only to be met with a hail of bullets striking rock inches from his head and body. His sniper's nest had become a prison, offering no retreat and no advance.

"Rally! Rally! Rally!"

Van Zandt's shout was followed within seconds by the thunder of hooves pounding toward Jake's position. He pressed his body into the crease, braced the Henry with his left hand, and pulled his Kerr with the right. He drew a deep breath, savoring the manner in which it filled his lungs—because it might be his last. Three heartbeats later, van Zandt's mounted men began barreling past, shooting indiscriminately at Jake's squad. He fired the Henry as riders flashed by, dropped the rifle, and managed two more shots from the revolver before the stampede dissipated. He clambered from his rocky crypt with the Kerr cocked, but the last of the riders was dodging behind a boulder that obstructed the retreating outlaws from gunfire. Jake leaned over with hands on knees, the revolver still clutched in his fingers, to catch his breath and curse again. How'd he let this happen?

When he stood again, his eyes found Corporal Jefferson with a hand pressed against his thigh, blood oozing past his fingers. He was leaning over a trooper—a young private called Rice. The soldier lay unmoving, his face a mask of blood from a wound to his forehead. Jefferson cut woeful eyes at Jake and shook his head grimly. Jake pinched the bridge of his nose and sighed. When he dropped his hand, he found Beah Nooki at his elbow, seemingly unhurt.

"We cannot give chase without horses," said the elder. "See to the wounded and the dead."

"Right." Jake waved to Gus across the canyon as his band

emerged from the rocks and began a descent. Then he went looking for Stacy. She met him at the outlaw camp with Sergeant Stubbs, clutching her shotgun in both hands. Her eyes were wide from the heat of battle and the shock of its abrupt ending. He knew the feeling. The rampaging emotions of brutal conflict did not easily dissipate and sometimes lingered for days. Much to his surprise, he stepped in toward her and pulled her head to his shoulder.

"I'm glad you're not shot."

"Me too," she choked.

He released Stacy and shook Stubbs's hand. "Well done. That last bit was my fault. I shoulda planned for it. Any casualties?"

"One shot, but he'll live. And you?"

"Jefferson's hit in the leg. Rice didn't make it."

Desolation swept through the sergeant's eyes before they grew steady again. "We'll see to his body."

"My condolences."

Unable to linger in the moment, Jake began assessing the effects of the raid. He counted eleven outlaw dead. None of the wounded had been left behind. And from what he could determine, van Zandt had abandoned all supplies, opting for a hasty retreat rather than a well-provisioned one. He watched Gus and his uninjured unit ford the river at the wide shallow, trudging thigh-deep through the chill water. Gus waved his carbine.

"What's the tally?"

Jake shared his assessment with Gus, who listened with a stony demeanor. Stacy, who'd been rooting through the larger tent, emerged with a heavy saddlebag draped over one shoulder. Upon spying Gus, she hurried toward him with a smile wider than the river. She jerked sideways and sprawled to the dirt as a rifle cracked above them.

"Down!" shouted ten men at once. One pointed at a puff of smoke dissipating in the rocks above. "There!"

Gus spun with carbine at his shoulder, flipped up the sight, and fired as the sniper edged up for a second shot. The shooter's hat flew back as the bullet impacted his skull, and he slumped from sight behind a rock. Gus bounded to Stacy's prone body and began a frantic search for the wound. Jake knelt beside him to assist but found nothing obvious.

"Help me turn her over," said Gus. When they began the procedure, Stacy cracked open one eye.

"Why're you puttin' hands on me?"

"Lookin' for the bullet that knocked you down."

Stacy frowned. "Is that what happened? Holy Hades."

They surveyed her back and found nothing. Jake's eye drifted to the saddlebag still draped askance across her shoulder. He pressed his finger through the fresh bullet hole until striking unyielding metal. Nudging Gus aside, he yanked the bag away and dumped the contents. Seven bars of gold marked with the letters "CSA" fell to the dirt, along with a mangled slug of lead. One bar bore a dent that penetrated half the depth but no further. Gus expelled an exploding breath and leaned against his knees, overcome.

Stacy sat up and began laughing. She punched Gus in the shoulder. "Will you look at that?" she said with hilarity. "Saved by Lucien Ashley's stolen Confederate gold."

Gus gathered her into a bear hug. "Same thing happened to me with a canteen, but I was lucky. I thought I'd lost you, Anastasia Blue."

She returned the embrace, still chuckling. "Your luck's run out, then, Augustus Rivers. I'm stickier than sorghum syrup."

He choked a laugh. "That you are."

She pushed him away as a narrow crease formed in the center of her forehead. "What about the man who shot me?"

"I got him."

The crease disappeared and she grinned. "Good man. I knew you weren't just all talk and no deed."

"I do my best."

When they'd lifted Stacy to her feet, Jake became aware that Sergeant Stubbs, Beah Nooki, and most of the buffalo soldiers had gathered around. Stubbs was the first to intervene.

"What of the other outlaws? I expect twenty rode out of here."

Jake pursed his lips, chewing on the question. Van Zandt didn't seem the kind of man who'd let one loss finish him. And if Beah Nooki was right, finishing van Zandt was the only path to the greater good.

"We haven't seen the last of them," he said. "This ain't over by any stretch."

CHAPTER TWENTY-SEVEN

They buried Private Rice on a grassy rise four miles outside the mouth of Wind River Canyon. From the crest of the knoll, rolling plains stretched out in three directions in endless waves of earth, obstructed only to the north by the Owl Creek mountains through which the Wind River chiseled its frenetic course. Knots of antelope dotted the plain, ready to run forever at a moment's notice if threatened. The Wind River range rose as a distant fortress wall to the southeast, merely hinting at the immensity of the skyscraping peaks within its ranks. The river wandered lazily below the rise, gathering itself for the harrowing plunge through the canyon. All in all, it was exactly the kind of final resting place Jake would choose if the choice was his. He hoped Private Rice might've felt the same. At minimum, it was far better than the mass grave in which they'd dumped the dead outlaws.

Gus led the burial ceremony, calling on the oratorial spirit of his preacher grandfather to usher the young soldier into the afterlife, quoting poetic scripture that Jake vaguely recalled. Jake found his heart thudding and eyes pricking as his friend seemed to invite heaven itself to witness the humble interment of a fallen soldier. After the speech, one of the troopers blew taps on a bugle, and seven of his comrades sent their mate off with a twenty-one-gun salute. When the crack of the final volley had echoed across the plain to be swallowed by the distance of the immeasurable, Jake replaced his hat on his head. On turning away from the mound of fresh earth, he found Beah Nooki watching him. The old man stepped to his side.

"A fine ceremony. Is this the way white men bury all their dead?"

"No," Jake said. "Only those fallen in battle or great warriors who die of old age. You would receive such a burial if you were a government soldier."

Beah Nooki nodded, stroking his chin and staring into the distance. "Such a burial would not offend me, I think." He faced Jake. "May I sing the young man into the next life?"

Jake nodded, not bothering to suppress a smile. "Private Rice would be honored, I imagine."

Beah Nooki began singing, low and mournful at first. His song swelled both in volume and determination until it occupied the stretching emptiness of the wilderness, like a church bell calling the faithful. When his song had faded into the breath of silence, Jake lifted his head, only then realizing that he'd bowed it.

"Amen," he whispered.

The old man slipped to his horse without another word and mounted the black-and-white stallion. Everyone else followed his lead, though Corporal Jefferson required assistance, what with the hole in his leg and all. As the party moved toward distant South Pass City, the restraint of the hallowed ceremony faded with each mile, and lighter conversation arose among the soldiers and the posse. After a few miles, Emshoff rode up on Jake's left side.

"Herr Paynter," he said. "What shall we do now? Do you believe this is finished?"

"I been wonderin' the same," said a voice on his left.

Jake found that Gus and Stacy had ridden up. He stared ahead for a bit, letting the question settle, gathering his thoughts. "Way I see it," he said finally, "is that we tried to burn the hornets' nest, but instead, we just knocked it down and kicked it around for a while. Van Zandt is probably madder'n hell and not inclined to quit the territory."

"You think he'll regroup?" asked Stacy.

"I'd wager money on it."

Emshoff nodded in agreement. "I have seen men like him before. Men who grasp power so tightly they cannot let go even as it drags them beneath the waves. Such men sent my country to war against other such men. Such men conscripted me to fight and die for them without giving in return. Such men raided my farm for supplies and tried to rape my wife. I left those men behind, some of them dead by my hand, and dragged my family across an ocean for a new life. But I have learned that such men live in every place, and you must oppose them or they will grind you to dust for their own ends."

Jake could not have said it better. "By my count, he has twenty-five men in his outlaw band, less the ones who died from bullet wounds after riding out of the canyon. In these parts, that's still an army. And we have Lucien Ashley to consider as well, wonderin' what he'll do to wreak havoc. A war on two fronts, the way I see it."

"And van Zandt's smarter than Sally was," said Gus. "He won't make the same mistake of underestimating a bunch of farmers and city dwellers."

Jake agreed. Sally's mistake had been to believe that common folk wouldn't be willing to risk all—to even die—for what they cherished. Jake and a band of settlers had made him pay dearly for that misconception. Van Zandt, on the other hand, appeared to take no such chances. He planned his strikes to his advantage, not at the whim of his arrogance. If he regrouped and retaliated, the people of South Pass City likely wouldn't see him coming until the hammer was already falling. But like Sally, van Zandt was the kind of man Emshoff described—willing to use other men as cogs in his machine and discard them when they broke.

"Maybe the Tenth can help," said Stacy. "I don't imagine van Zandt would want to tangle with 'em again."

Gus shook his head. "That's the bad news. Their colonel gave them strict orders to return to Fort Bridger as soon as possible. They can't stay more than a day or two, and then we're on our own."

"Just because we lose the soldiers," said Emshoff, "doesn't mean we shouldn't operate like an army."

Jake had been thinking the same for a while. "Gus has already been drillin' folks into a militia. We have Lucien's ammo shipment and plenty of long guns. We can set up over-lapping patrols, make sure we got eyes on every approach at all times. At least until van Zandt tries somethin' or moves on to easier prey."

Everyone agreed with varying degrees of enthusiasm. It seemed the least they could do, given the looming threat. But Jake knew better than to elevate hope to high ground. If van Zandt was determined to exact a price for his defeat in the canyon, he'd succeed in some measure. A citizen militia could only hope to mitigate the damage. Jake shook his head while considering the irony of his situation. Two years earlier, he was a man alone and comfortable with the prospect of imminent death and, therefore, feared nothing. Now that he was responsible for two thousand souls who looked to him for salvation from evil men, Jake's heart brimmed with fear. Fear that he couldn't protect everyone. Fear that he'd let some die. Fear that he'd slip away in the night to escape the unwanted responsibility and become again the shell of a man he was trying to leave in the past.

Left unchecked, fear could kill a man as surely as a bullet to the heart.

CHAPTER TWENTY-EIGHT

JAKE'S MILITARY FORCE PARTED WAYS IN THE FALLING dusk at the west end of Main Street, the alliance of posse and soldier crumbling under the auspices of having done all it could. First Sergeant Stubbs led his troopers across Willow Creek to reestablish a camp. They'd spare a day before heading south to Fort Bridger and the border beyond to join the trouble brewing there. The posse members splintered just as readily, beating a path for their respective domiciles with the suppressed euphoria of having met the enemy and survived. Barely a word of "good day" was exchanged, for each of them knew the conflict with van Zandt's band wasn't finished.

The mare needed no guiding. She knew where to find the stables, a brush down, and a bucket of oats. Beah Nooki's stallion had already learned the same lesson, and he practically raced the mare into the barn. Jake turned the mare over to the boy watching the horses and pressed two bits into his hand.

"Brush her out good," he said. "She's earned it."

"Yes, Marshal."

He watched the old man lead his stallion into a stall. "Beah Nooki?"

"I will attend to my horse and exchange tales with the boy. See you soon."

Jake nodded and stepped from the stables onto Main Street to make his way to the marshal's office where he kept a cot. In nearly a year as marshal, he hadn't bothered to rent a room anywhere. The jail was as good a place as any and a far sight better than most places where he'd slept during the previous decade. Beah Nooki's recent presence had become a welcome reprieve from solitude, though. The old man knew just when something needed saying and when to shut up. In his musings, Jake got caught watching his feet trudge through the muck of the road. When he stepped up onto the porch of the office, he nearly collided with a figure standing by the door. He threw a hand against the rail to keep from stumbling onto his backside in the road.

"Miss Ashley," he said. "I almost didn't see you there in the dark."

She pulled her arms tighter about her waist and offered an apologetic smile. "I'm sorry, Mr. Paynter. I shouldn't have been lurking so."

"No need for concern. You caught me napping, that's all."

She cocked her head, studying his face in what little light the adjacent buildings offered. "You seem weary."

He grunted a chuckle. "I reckon I am." He opened a palm toward her. "You need something?"

"Just to talk. I have information that should interest you."

"You been waitin' long?"

"Oh, maybe three hours."

"Is that so?" He frowned with speculation. "Must be mighty interesting information, then."

"It is. First, though, I need to know what happened in the

canyon. My information might have been rendered useless by certain outcomes."

Jake pursed his lips in consideration of the request. He'd never learned to talk about violent days to those who hadn't been present. When he tried to speak of the terror, the rage, and the beast within him that served death to the living, words failed him. But he knew he must try. She'd been with him on the Oregon Trail two years earlier. She'd witnessed the worst that men could do to one another. Most of all, she'd seen the darkness within him rain hell on his enemies and yet still deigned to keep his company and treat him kindly. If nothing else, he owed her an attempt at words.

"Very well. But let me walk you home. We'll talk along the way."

Without knowing quite why, he offered her an elbow. He didn't know where the gesture originated. No one had encouraged him to gentility along the way, but somewhere, he'd apparently absorbed at least some notion of what a gentleman might do. She stared at his elbow for several seconds until he was certain she'd decline the offer. However, she slipped her hand through the crook of his elbow and edged up beside him.

"That would be fine, Mr. Paynter."

As they stepped from the porch, Jake began to describe the events of the expedition. She trembled when he spoke of the three-pronged descent upon the outlaw camp. When he described the ensuing battle at dawn and the outlaws' escape, her grip on the crook of his elbow became a vise, as if she might save his life in hindsight. The clench loosened when he recounted the losses on both sides and Stacy's brush with death.

"I tried to convince her to remain here," said Rosalyn of Stacy. "But she refused to listen, to the point of covering her ears as she left the house."

Jake chuckled lightly. "I gave up tryin' to tell her what to do. You'd rest easier by followin' my lead."

"I'm learning as much." The lilt of her voice faded into silence as she stared ahead. "Will the soldiers stay?"

"No. They leave day after tomorrow."

She inhaled a deep breath. "I see."

The response was clipped. Coiled tight and only partially surrendered. The tenor of it informed Jake that whatever she meant to tell him would likely raise the level of angst. When she fell silent, he squeezed her hand with his elbow.

"You can tell me, Miss Ashley. I won't hold the information against you."

"Right," she breathed. She cut her eyes up at him. "My father arrived from Missouri before you left."

Jake lifted an eyebrow. "That so? He still here?"

"No. He stayed barely a day. Long enough to set Lucien straight and set me down."

Her reply leaked pain from every corner. Jake understood it intimately. No repudiation burned a wider swath through the soul than the rejection of family.

"I'm sorry he did that to you."

"Thank you. I am over it now. But about Lucien. There is something you should know."

Jake listened intently as she explained her brother's

intended betrayal of Dutch van Zandt, outlaw king of the Wyoming Territory, and suppressed a shudder. Surely Lucien wasn't bold enough—man enough—to take such a stand. However, Rosalyn seemed certain he would. The potential benefits to Lucien far outweighed any short-term danger.

"He will do what Father asks," she concluded. "Of that, I am certain. In fact, he means to use you as the tool of Mr. van Zandt's destruction and hopes for your demise in the process."

Jake shook his head, not in disbelief but with realization. A betrayal made sense. Two birds with one stone, if Lucien was lucky. Such a Judas kiss would change the equation dramatically. Jake could only imagine what van Zandt might do, stripped of his expected assets and now facing two enemies instead of one. A man of his intelligence, determination, and cunning might try anything. Rosalyn seemed to guess Jake's thoughts. Maybe they were that plain on his face.

"Surely," she said, "Mr. van Zandt's resolve will be broken, what with his defeat in the canyon and my brother's duplicity."

Skeptical hope tinged her declaration. Jake hated to disappoint her. "Men like van Zandt are never broken by defeat, only motivated by it. He's a thinker, a schemer. His only path past defeat is a more audacious scheme."

She sighed heavily. "I was afraid of that."

With those words, they arrived at the door of the cabin. Stacy's calico was tied up outside and a light burned within. Jake released Rosalyn's hand.

"Well. Here we are."

"Yes. Here we are. Good evening, Marshal."

"Good evening, Miss Ashley."

As she reached for the door, he laid a hand on her forearm to pause her. "Do you still own that shotgun?"

"I do. A Smith Brothers' fowling piece, fourteen gauge."

"Good. Take it with you to school every day and keep both barrels loaded. Make sure Stacy's with you when you're out. And bar the schoolhouse door when you're in."

In the glow of lamplight leaking through the window, her eyes grew wide, inscrutable. "I will."

She slipped inside the door and closed it behind her. In her wake, Jake placed a palm against the planks of the door, mumbled a few words even he didn't know, and turned away to walk into the night.

CHAPTER TWENTY-NINE

"I WILL RIDE NOW," ANNOUNCED BEAH NOOKI. THE ELDER had risen from his favorite cot—the one in the jail cell nearest the door—after his midday nap and gathered his rifle.

Jake stopped his working meeting and raised his brows at the statement. "To hunt?"

"Perhaps. And to think. And to pray. I think and pray best on rocks or horseback. So I will ride and find some rocks."

Jake envied Beah Nooki just then. He almost joined the old man but only watched as he walked out the door of the marshal's office. Jake had responsibilities. Duties. Promises to keep.

It was hell.

He shifted his chair to again face Stacy and Gus, who watched him with half smiles.

"Thought you'd leave for sure," said Gus.

"Think you still might," added Stacy.

Jake sighed. "If only. Now, where were we?"

"Organizing the town into companies."

"Right." He retrieved his pencil and continued compiling names. Four days had passed since they'd returned from fighting van Zandt's outlaws in Wind River Canyon. He had put off organizing the citizenry long enough. For the next hour, Jake and his deputies grouped families into units of ten based on proximity to one another, the probable number of folks who could wield a gun, and general military experience. Most of it proved guesswork, which was military planning at its finest. Take a best guess at a plan, execute the plan with swagger, and then change it entirely on the fly when everything fell apart. Eventually, though, they managed to identify twenty-nine companies. Jake tapped the stack of papers scrawled with family names.

"We need to distribute the extra ammunition based on what weapons everyone carries. Any ideas about logistics?"

Stacy raised a hand. "We should have each company send a representative with a list of needs and then sort it out among those people all at once."

Gus glanced sidelong at her. "That's actually a decent idea."

Stacy sneered. "What? Did ya think I was a simpleton? Without a thought in my head?"

He held a palm of restraint up to her. "I'd never think that. In fact, I lie awake some nights wonderin' what you might be concocting."

"Wouldn't you like to know?"

"Fine," said Jake, wading into the igniting banter before it burned out of hand. "We'll do that. But first, we should inventory the ammo and spare firearms."

"Sounds fun," said Stacy deadpan, making clear her opinion that counting cartridges and caps fell well short of amusement. As it happened, she was saved from that fate by a worse one. The office door flew open and banged hard against the wall. Jake had his revolver drawn and aimed before the vaguely familiar intruder took a second step into the office. The man froze as he stared down the barrel of the gun and raised his hands.

"Shouldn't oughta barge in like that," said Jake. "It could end you."

"Sorry?" said the man.

Jake holstered his Kerr. "Lower your hands. What's this about?"

The man kept his hands raised. "I work for Mr. Ashley punchin' cattle. Dutch van Zandt and his boys hit the ranch this mornin'. Killed a couple a' men. Took some things, bullets mostly, and horses."

The ranch hand suddenly had Jake's undivided attention. "And Ashley?"

"Not hurt, last I saw. He's the one what sent me here to tell you."

Jake immediately wondered if this was just a ploy by Lucien. A charade. But for what purpose? To get at Rosalyn again? But the ranch hand seemed too rattled, too earnest. Men who worked cattle tended to make terrible liars. Otherwise, they'd have become lawyers or politicians.

"Does Ashley want my help?"

"No, sir. He just wanted you to know the outlaws are headed this way. I followed a different track, dodged 'em most of the way here. Lost 'em round about Atlantic City. I'm surprised they ain't here yet."

"Put your hands down, dang it." Jake retrieved his rifle from the wall and began filling a saddlebag with cartridges.

"Gus, Stacy—go warn folks. Tell anyone with a gun and sufficient gumption to stand ready to fight. Tell the rest to hole up."

"On it," said Gus. He and Stacy sailed out the door to rally the town. Meanwhile, the ranch hand had lowered his hands. Jake threw the bag over his shoulder.

"Now, which way did you say…"

An explosion rattled the windows. Jake hit the floor, driven prone by every instinct learned the hard way during wartime mortar bombardments. Silence fell, followed by cries of panic from the street. He leaped up and raced outside to find Gus pointing toward the big mine on the hill. Smoke drifted from it, clear even from a mile away. He ran for the stables while waving to Gus and Stacy.

"Let's have a look!"

His deputies raced Jake to the stables. The mare was none too pleased to be yanked from her stall and frantically saddled. She went for his left ear but failed. He pulled the girth tight with an aggressive tug as warning that this wasn't the moment for her to make a point. She whinnied her opinion anyway but followed as he dragged her outside and climbed aboard. Glen Dunbar was waiting with an expression of alarm. Jake leveled a finger at him.

"Rally the town. Take up arms and hole up. Van Zandt's on the march." When Glen nodded, Jake dug his heels into the mare's sides. "Git on!"

She did, with Gus's buckskin and Stacy's calico on her flank. They cut through the alleyway and over the lump of earth that backed the stables, providing an unobstructed view of the mine. A group of men appeared to be loading bags on horses at the mine office. Jake and his deputies had covered half the distance before the bandits fled—eight men. As Jake flashed by the mine, he slowed to shout at the mine clerk, who stood in lost disarray near the office.

"Who did this?"

The man blinked rapidly. "That…that outlaw."

"Van Zandt?"

"That's the one."

Jake grimaced. Van Zandt had promised chaos, and now he was delivering. He glanced back at the town below, which had become a flurry of activity. He hoped they were up to the challenge if worst came to worst. He and Gus and Stacy raced on, sweeping around the hip of the hill to find that the outlaws had split up, four and four, veering away from one another in an ever-widening sweep. One set seemed headed toward Lucien's ranch, the other toward Atlantic City. Jake pointed toward the latter quartet.

"Gus! Take Stacy and trail them. Don't let 'em turn on you. Just find out where they're going."

"Will do." Their horses curved away as Jake maintained his sights on the other four riders. The men cast backward glances as he slowly closed the distance. He readied his Henry while wondering about the number. Eight men. Where were the rest of van Zandt's people? Advancing on South Pass City? Headed for the mountains? Most likely, he thought, they were leading him into an ambush, driven by van Zandt's personal vendetta against Jake. His eyes lifted to the high ground the outlaws were passing. There, maybe? He scanned the hill for signs of men with rifles but saw none. Gritting his jaw, he plunged ahead, narrowing the gap further. The minutes and miles passed by until he'd drawn within three hundred yards of his quarry. Not quite close enough for a decent shot. Then, without warning, the four men split again and spurred their mounts into a dead run, coaxing from the animals whatever remained of their equine resolve. Jake shifted his attention between the two pairs, trying to decide which to follow. And then he began to listen to what his instincts had been shouting for the past fifteen minutes. He tugged on the mare's reins until she ground to a halt and he watched the fading pairs of riders for a few seconds.

"Oh hell," he breathed. He kicked the mare and spun her back toward South Pass City as the answer to his earlier question became obvious. The town was, in fact, the target. As if in confirmation, the sound of a distant blast echoed through the hills, originating somewhere near town. Faces flashed before him. The Emshoffs. The Dunbars and Aguilars. And Rosalyn Ashley.

He drove the little horse hard, and she responded.

CHAPTER THIRTY

WHEN ROSALYN SPOKE OF TOWERING HISTORICAL figures—emperors, generals, scientists, artists—her students listened politely and sometimes scribbled notes about the subject. But when she shared stories of the lesser, the obscure, the forgotten, the children set down their pencils and leaned forward in fascination. She often wondered about the meaning of the phenomenon. As the children of miners, farmers, and laborers, perhaps her students identified more with the common man than the conqueror. On this day, she gave them Sempronius Densus, centurion of the Roman Praetorian Guard, bodyguard to Emperor Galba.

"When the usurper Otho gave the order," she said, "renegade Praetorian Guards attacked the emperor's litter as it was carried through the streets of Rome. They fell as fire from Mount Olympus on the emperor's outnumbered bodyguard. The defenders immediately fled or changed loyalties…" She paused, relishing the collective held breaths in the perfect silence. "Except one. Though he did not much care for Emperor Galba, centurion Sempronius Densus drew his sword to defend his charge. After failing to convince the attackers to leave, he fought them all single-handedly and cut down those before him."

She swept her eyes over the rapt students before spreading her hands.

"What do you think is the lesson of Sempronius's story?"

One lad, Robert Waverly, seemingly enamored by the glory of battle, shot a hand skyward. She dipped her chin to him. He stood from his desk, one arm behind his back and the other gripping the seam of his shirt.

"The lesson," he said, "is if we stand fast against our enemies, we will surely triumph." He sat down, sure of his understanding.

Rosalyn nodded. "Perhaps. Perhaps. But in this case, not accurate. For you see, Sempronius died at the hands of the attackers, who then killed the emperor, hacked his body to pieces, and displayed his head on a pike. Triumph, then, was sorely lacking."

The boy frowned. "Then what is the lesson, miss?"

She clasped her hands at her waist and peered at *her* charges. "It is more heroic to stand on principle and lose than to stand for nothing and triumph." She again paused while her words settled into the young hearts and minds, perhaps to simmer until a later time. "When Roman historians wrote of that rebellion, they said of Sempronius that his was the only heroic deed done that dark and miserable day. He is remembered. Those who killed him are not."

Of course, Rosalyn couldn't help but think of Jake Paynter—a man who considered himself without a soul but who poured himself out for others as if a patron saint of impossible causes. She shook her head, smiled to the students, and clapped her hands together. "All right, then. Enough of history. On to mathematics."

The collective groan over numbers and equations never failed to amuse her. She began returning to the chalkboard when the sound of an explosion echoed from the big hill opposite town. On instinct, she lunged for the shotgun behind her desk, earning saucer eyes from the students, and rushed to the door. She pressed against the plank barring the door to test it. It held steady.

"Otto," she called over a shoulder. "Get everyone down."

She had watched Otto Emshoff calm other children while their wagon train was under assault on the Oregon Trail. She could count on him now. Chairs shuffled behind her as the boy directed everyone to the floor. Rosalyn maintained a grit-jawed vigil for ten minutes, running her thumb over both hammers obsessively. She nearly jumped through the ceiling when heavy pounding rattled the door.

"I have a loaded shotgun!" she shouted.

"It's me," cried a familiar voice. "Mr. Ellison from the sundry store! Let me in, for God's sake!"

Hesitation seized her. Dare she open for him? The notion that perhaps Paynter had sent Mr. Ellison to help shoved aside her suspicions. She leaned the shotgun against the wall and pulled the plank from its moorings. No sooner had she stepped back than Ellison burst inside and slammed the door behind him. He leaned against it, seemingly intent on holding it closed.

"Outlaws just robbed the big mine," he announced like a town crier. "The marshal and his deputies rode off after them. But now more outlaws have showed up."

Rosalyn blinked rapidly. "Have you come to protect us, then?"

Ellison cut baffled eyes at her. "Protect? No. I figure even Dutch van Zandt wouldn't hurt children."

She grimaced. He hadn't come to help but to hide. She shook her head viciously. "You may have figured wrong." She lifted the plank to again bar the door. "My brother just betrayed Mr. van Zandt. He may send men *here* to find me."

Ellison's eyes flew wide. In one spastic motion, he stripped the plank from the door, flung it aside, and bolted outside. Rosalyn raced to retrieve the discarded door bar. No sooner had she started again for the door when three strangers burst through. She managed to belt one with the plank before he hammered her to her knees.

"You shouldn't oughta do that, Miss Ashley." He yanked her from the floor, tossed her over a shoulder like a laundry bag, and hollered to his accomplices. "Grab some a' the little ones! Let's git!"

When she pounded her fists against his back in defiance, he rammed an elbow into her temple, sending a shower of stars across her vision. She blinked away the fuzz and lifted her head to find the other intruders following with a pair of children apiece, one under each arm. Polly Waverly. Herbie McGee. Ann Sislak. And Lisbet Emshoff. Otto Emshoff was giving chase, but her abductor waved him off with a revolver and a deadly curse.

"Stay back, Otto!" Rosalyn shouted. "Run to the mine, and fetch your pa."

That earned her another elbow, this one to the cheek. Regardless, she continued to struggle until the man dumped her in the middle of Main Street. Before she could rise, she found the barrel of a gun pressed beneath her chin. Her kidnapper kneeled in her face.

"The lives a' these kids are in your hands, schoolmarm. You keep fightin', and they won't see their next birthday."

A tremor spasmed through her body, leaving a chill in its wake. She collected her rebellion and held it close. "I understand."

"Good girl."

Rosalyn motioned to the children, who'd been deposited in the mud beside her. "Gather around. Stay by me, and don't resist."

The kids, none older than seven, scampered to her side. Lisbet Emshoff leaned into Rosalyn's ear to whisper. "When do we run away?"

"Not yet," she whispered back. "Keep the others calm."

"Yes, ma'am."

Rosalyn lifted her eyes to find a band of armed men swarming the street, firing indiscriminately at windows and buildings to cow the townsfolk into compliance. The strategy was working as the citizens of South Pass City hunkered under cover. With the miners mostly at their claims this time of day, the assembled guns proved too few to challenge the mob of bandits. A man lay wounded and moaning in the street—one of the clerks at Ellison's store. She swiveled her head in all directions, searching. Where was Paynter? He'd have something to say about this. A tall man wearing a three-piece suit and a gambler hat caught her eyes. As if sensing her scrutiny, he shifted his attention toward her. A smile crawled across his face, and he began striding in her direction.

"Here comes Dutch," said one of the abductors.

Rosalyn blinked in disbelief. Dutch van Zandt? Jake had told her that he looked like a lawyer, but she'd counted his description as hyperbole. However, the man looked every bit the New York City socialite, dapper, pleasant to look at, intelligent eyes, a warm smile. For an instant, she wondered if he might call off his men, set everything right, apologize, and leave. But for only an instant. Van Zandt paused his progress long enough to blithely draw his revolver and put a bullet through the moaning clerk, stilling him forever. As he casually returned the revolver to its holster, Rosalyn saw through his charade to the reality beneath. Van Zandt was every bit the soulless killer his reputation dictated, and perhaps worse. With new perspective, she saw that the intelligence in his eyes was predatory, like that of a tiger on the hunt, thirsting for the kill. She winced when he squatted before her while flashing a smile worthy of a stage actor. Instead of addressing her, though, he spoke aside to the man who'd hauled Rosalyn from the schoolhouse.

"Mr. Boggins. Do you know who this lovely creature is?"

"Yes, sir," said Boggins. "Lucien Ashley's sister."

"Indeed. And what is our opinion of Lucien Ashley at this time?"

Boggins drew a thumb across his bearded throat.

Van Zandt chuckled. "Precisely."

Rosalyn bowed her spine, met van Zandt's gaze, and dared not look away lest he leap for her throat. "Do what you will with me, but in the name of decency, release the children."

Van Zandt belted out a laugh. "Decency? I tried that for a while, but it only put me at a disadvantage. So I decline your suggestion. And never fear—I *will* do as I please with you, Miss Ashley. Until then, I suggest you cover your ears."

She blinked rapidly at the outlaw, trying to assimilate his measured threats and odd instructions. The ensuing blast rattled her eardrums, replacing half her hearing with a resonating ringing. She stretched her jaw while holding her ears.

Van Zandt laughed again as he stood. "Too late now, but let us learn from our mistake. When I give instruction, you best abide or face unforeseen and accelerating consequences."

Rosalyn yanked her eyes from his Greek pose to peer up the street in search of the blast's source—and found it. The bank. Several men emerged from billowing dust carrying heavy bags—gold, no doubt—and piled them onto packhorses. Seconds later, Boggins yanked her upright again while the other abductors scooped up the children. They dragged the five captives to a knot of four waiting horsemen and tossed one child to each. As Rosalyn reached for Lisbet, a hand seized her arm from behind and began dragging her toward a fifth horse. Dutch van Zandt flung her onto the horse and mounted behind her. He circled her waist with one long arm and leaned intimately over her shoulder.

"For each mistake you make, Miss Ashley, one child dies. I insist you aspire to perfection, then, for the sake of the little ones. Do I have your understanding?"

She nodded, powerless to stop the unfolding nightmare.

Van Zandt straightened. "Excellent."

He snapped the reins, and his horse bolted forward down

Main Street. Twenty-odd men and half a dozen packhorses pounded the dirt in his wake, like the rumble of a flash flood sweeping away everything in its path.

CHAPTER THIRTY-ONE

MOST OF LIFE'S MOMENTS ONLY HAPPEN ONCE, BUT THE best and worst are lived a thousand times. During Jake's dash toward South Pass City, the latter kind resurrected and stormed forth from the grave of memory. The staccato reports of gunshots echoing in the distance and a plume of dust and smoke rising from the unseen town dragged Jake through a series of personal hells featuring burning hulks and exploding shells before entrenching him in the moment when he had nearly abandoned his faith in humanity.

"Keep yer blam-jam peckers in the mud!" shouted Sergeant Winton. "Stay down like yer mama's watchin'!"

The men of Kansas First Colored heeded the command, pressing deeper into the muck as the fury of Confederate and Union mortar shells pummeled their position. Except for Winton, who paced over the top of the prone men repeating his instructions with an ever-increasing velocity of swearing. Shells whistled nearer, and bullets flew.

"Winton!" Jake shouted. "Get down!"

He rose to his knees to retrieve his sergeant, but the catapulted residue of a shell impact ripped the man in half. His blue-pantalooned legs and lower torso remained in place for an impossibly long time, like the base of a neglected Egyptian monument liberated from the sand, before teetering into the muck among those he'd tried to save.

"Dammit all to hell!" spat Gus Rivers at Jake's side. "He knew better."

Though he disguised his statement as judgment, Gus's deep and immediate pain infused his words with a strangling thickness that emerged as more of a wail. Jake bit his tongue with bitter understanding. Winton had been Gus's first protégé to rise to the rank of officer. Now the young sergeant was dead, a man divided. The blast of another shell just yards away swept aside all sorrow, all regret, all recollection, filling the void with utter terror. Jake's head went soft, as if someone had scooped out his brains and stuffed his skull with cotton. Gus was shouting at him, but he heard nothing except the aftermath of a bell mired in mid-ring.

With no other choice, Jake did what anyone would do in the presence of the Almighty or an aerial bombardment—planted his face in the muck, pressed his hands over the back of his head, and counted seconds like small, fleeting lifetimes. A stillness fell over him, aided by his still-impaired hearing. How had this happened? One moment, his men had overrun a Confederate position strewn with bandaged and bleeding men tended by three women—a field hospital—and the next, both sides were raining hell on the point of contact. Who had given the orders? Why shell the wounded or your own people? It made no sense.

He remained floundering in the well of confusion for an indeterminate period as the ground rolled with the thud of repeated impacts flung in anger by two armies toward a mass of faceless men. It was Gus's hand that finally plucked him from the morass.

Jake lifted his head to find the sergeant peering at him, splattered with mud and gore, and motioning for him to get up.

"It's over. They stopped."

The words came through muffled, but Jake mounted his feet. When he dared to survey the forty troops who'd charged the enemy with him, he found most of them still alive. But not all. The living stood as husks of men, though, staring at him. When he realized they were in reality staring past him, he turned to find the aftermath of a minor Armageddon. The field hospital had been obliterated. The line of wounded men had all but disappeared, replaced by a chaos of fabric, appendages, and exploded meat. A skirt marked what remained of a nurse, which wasn't much.

A boy of no more than fifteen sat amid the carnage, staring blankly at the absence of his arm beneath the elbow. Jake climbed over the slaughter to reach the boy. Without a word, he slipped off his bandanna and tied it over the stump to stanch the flow of blood. The boy watched with wide, questioning eyes until Jake finished and then raised the revolver Jake hadn't seen. A bullet from one of Jake's men shattered the boy's head before he could pull the trigger to kill his benefactor. Jake rose slowly from the body with fists clenched, rage rising like the swell of a hurricane tide. The fury crested in a howling cry of unadulterated wrath.

"Grab your guns and ammo!" he screamed to his men. "We got more killin' to do!"

Without waiting, he hurled himself toward the next enemy entrenchment, the vanguard of violent destruction. He was death…determined death…incessant death…

Jake pounded the side of his head with a fist three times to will away the dismal recollection before it dragged him deeper into the abyss. He needed to have his wits about him, to be fully engaged in the present and not wandering a wasteland of regretful memory. The town limits had slipped into view. The mare was still hurtling toward it but gasping air with great heaves of her flexing ribs.

"A little more, old girl! One final sprint."

Whether or not she heard his encouragement, the little horse continued pressing toward the goal with angry determination. As she entered the outskirts proper, Gus and Stacy appeared as if from nowhere, their mounts similarly huffing and spraying mucus. Jake slowed the mare to a trot.

"What happened?"

"They split up on us," said a breathless Stacy. "We figured it was a trap or a trick, so we turned back."

"I figured the same."

They rode into town together, one horseman short of an apocalypse. Upon spotting their lawmen, frantic townsfolk descended on them with chaotic reports that perfectly drowned out understanding and reason. Jake reined the mare to a halt and fired his Kerr skyward.

"Quiet! For God's sake." The chaos stilled, frozen on wide-eyed and anguished faces. He waited for Aguilar to reach him. "Francisco. Talk to me."

The miner was leaking blood from a bullet to his shoulder but seemed to hold the wound and his dangling arm in temporary disregard. "Van Zandt showed up with a dozen more men after you left. They cleaned out the bank—Wells Fargo money and all. They took everything. Every cent." He seemed apologetic for having failed to stop the assault.

"They were armed with enough weapons to flatten a brigade. I don't know where they found it all."

"I do," said Jake. Lucien had clearly amassed quite a cache before van Zandt had relieved him of it. Glen Dunbar arrived just then with his hammer in one hand and Mr. Ellison in the other. The store owner sported a welt under one eye and appeared as if he wished to crawl into a prairie-dog hole. Glen hauled him up before Jake.

"Tell him, Ellison, or I'll strike you again."

"All right! All right!"

When Ellison lifted his eyes, Jake's blood ran cold. Instinct whispered that the world was about to shift on its axis.

Ellison lifted his hand imploringly to Jake. "I tried to stop them. But they were too many."

Jake's heart began to hammer as his hands formed a vise clench on the reins. "Them? Them who?"

"The men who attacked the school. The ones who took Miss Ashley and four kids, including the little Emshoff girl." He pointed east, past the far end of Main Street. "And went that way."

The red haze descended with a startling immediacy, and his primal instincts, barely restrained until then, burst forth as if shot from a cannon. A visceral growl ripped from Jake's throat, and he kicked the mare again into motion. She was flying down the street as his rage swirled into a maelstrom of murderous desire. He wanted to break Ellison in half for bringing such bad news. He wanted to bolt into the wilderness, catch van Zandt's men, and kill them one by one with his bare hands. He wanted blood, and now.

"Go!" cried the demons. "Ride! Seek! Destroy!"

He listened to the whispers as buildings flashed past, until another voice shouted over the one in his head.

"Paynter! Stop!"

He yanked his eyes aside to find Stacy giving chase, driving her calico to within inches of the barreling mare. She was waving frantically.

"Stop, Paynter! He's got twenty men. You'll be dead and Rosalyn and the kids with you."

He tried to ignore her, but the tears streaming down her cheeks to be snatched away by the wind spoke to him in a voice far more expressive than the sound of mere words.

"Please, Jake. Stop."

The sound of his Christian name, the cry of pain so reminiscent of Gus's when he lost Sergeant Winton, the flow of tears—these broke through the haze and gave him the wherewithal to beat back the darkness. He let the mare drift to a halt and hung his head. His breathing slowed as he restrained the demons within, locking them away until a more suitable time. He looked up to find Stacy wiping away the vestiges of tears. When he extended a hand to her, she grasped it.

"Thanks, little sister. I needed that." He wheeled the mare around to return toward the knot of townsfolk milling about the street.

Stacy galloped her calico beside him. "What should we do?"

In the absence of snarling rage, reason had returned. Cold and cunning, but reason nonetheless. "The only thing we can do. Assemble a posse, load up with ammo and enough supplies for a long haul, and go after van Zandt within the hour."

"You think we can catch him?"

Jake nearly smiled when she said "we." "I don't *think* nothin'. I *will* catch up to Dutch van Zandt and send him to the devil even if I have to escort him myself."

However, for all his bravado, for all his determination, it was all Jake could do to hold at bay dark visions of Rosalyn and Lisbet dead on a trail, with him as the reason.

CHAPTER THIRTY-TWO

GUILT IS A HEARTLESS TASKMASTER, ADDING BURDEN upon burden without concern for the sagging of shoulders or buckling of knees. Stacy's knees were atremble as she rued having let Dutch van Zandt and his band of thugs waltz through her town and strip it bare as a swarm of locusts would. She should've guessed the ruse quicker. She should've stayed behind. Perhaps then she could've...done what? Stood down a dozen men? Laced a few with her scattergun? Gotten her head blown off for her efforts?

No.

Maybe it was best she hadn't been in town when the hammer fell. At least her absence had given her a chance for redemption. Keeping Paynter from hightailing alone after van Zandt was probably the most valuable act she'd performed during her brief stint as deputy marshal. Sure, she'd seen Paynter perform unbelievable feats worthy of myth, legend, and folk songs. But running up behind twenty armed desperados holding the leverage of five captives would have certainly been his end. As a result of her convincing, he was still in the game. His pile of chips was diminished, but he still held a winning hand.

By the time she and Paynter returned to the gathering of citizens, Glen and Maddie Dunbar were already seeing to the wounded—Maddie the doctor and Glen her enormous assistant. Esther Morris was talking to folks, scribbling notes about what had been taken from them. Paynter dismounted and surveyed the aftermath before stepping onto the porch in front of Moretti's tack shop.

"Listen up!"

A hundred pairs of eyes turned his way. He paced three steps along the porch before returning to address the throng.

"I'm going after van Zandt. I'll take a few with me, those I can trust in a fight. The rest must stay behind to set up a defense in case the outlaws circle back or have others waiting in reserve for us to leave. The only truth of van Zandt is that he's unpredictable and capable of most any atrocity. Band together, neighbor to neighbor. Keep the children hunkered down. And if the men who attacked you dare to return, give 'em all the lead plums you got. Understand?"

Heads bobbed as resolve settled on the collected faces. Mr. Ellison, on the other hand, cringed. "What about the Tenth Cavalry? Shouldn't chasing after outlaws be their job?"

Dunbar pushed Ellison to his knees. "Don't be a fool. They're a week south of here. By the time they arrived, van Zandt could be in Canada."

Paynter glared at the storekeeper before pacing again and pointing. "Gus Rivers. Stacy Blue. Jim Jackson. You're with me."

Stacy breathed a sigh of relief even as her stomach fell into her britches with a thud. He was inviting her on his ride toward the devil, and she'd all but asked for the ticket.

"I'm with you too," said Aguilar, even while Maddie fished for the bullet in his shoulder.

Paynter shook his head. "No, my friend. You're wounded and I need you here. You and Glen and Mrs. Morris. I appoint you as deputies in my place to organize the militia and lock down the town boundary."

"But, Marshal..."

"It's done, Francisco. Hold the fort."

Aguilar nodded, much to his wife's relief. "I will."

"Mrs. Morris?"

The tall woman stood taller still. "We'll button this place up like a kettledrum."

"And you, Glen?"

The big Scotsman thumped his hammer into his palm. "'Twould be my honor."

"Good. Your first assignment is to requisition from Mr. Ellison enough supplies for two weeks on the trail while Gus rounds up enough ammunition to stop an infantry charge."

"With pleasure."

Glen yanked up Ellison by the collar and marched him toward the sundry shop. As Stacy watched them walk away, motion from up the street drew her eyes. Mr. Emshoff was riding toward them at a dead gallop, musket in hand and a bag thrown over one shoulder. His normally warm eyes had gone cold, hard, lifeless. The amiable planes of his face seemed suddenly cast in concrete, unflinching and resolute. She'd heard the story of how he'd killed the Prussian soldiers who tried to rape his wife. Now she knew how he might've looked when he did it. Emshoff reined his horse to a halt and flung himself to the dirt to stand before Paynter.

"If you're giving chase," he said, "then I am going with you. Otherwise, I go alone." He clipped the words, his German accent never more pronounced.

Paynter simply nodded once. "Have Gus lend you a carbine. Leave the musket for Otto. We light out as soon as we provision." As Emshoff turned away, Paynter stepped from the porch to place a hand on the man's shoulder. The two men locked eyes and spoke epics with no words. In that exchange, Stacy saw clearly how this would end. Paynter and Emshoff would die a thousand times before giving up the chase. They'd kill their enemies and retrieve their loved ones or lie cold in the soil. All middle ground had shrunk to an infinitesimal point where no man could stand without falling to one side or the other. Emshoff dipped his forehead and walked away to find Gus. When Stacy looked back to Paynter, she found herself inside the narrow focus of his calculating gaze.

"We're gonna need two packhorses."

"On it."

She trotted several blocks to the stables and picked out two of Gus's best horses—a big roan and a sturdy black mustang. She paused only long enough to collect her extra saddlebag, stuff in a spare shirt, and grab the long leather coat that had been hanging ownerless in the stables for six months. As she led the horses down the street, the flurry of activity in front of the sundry mimicked a kicked-over anthill. Townsfolk were making a pile of supplies in the street while Gus, Emshoff, and Aguilar inspected extra rifles and measured out cartridges, powder, shot, and caps. Maddie was wiping down her bullet forceps, having removed the ball from Aguilar's shoulder. She pressed the instrument into her black bag and hurried up the street, holding her skirt above the slosh of mud. Stacy frowned but continued toward the growing pile.

She handed over the tethers to a couple of young girls and began helping Jim Jackson and Glen pack the horses. Jerky, hard biscuits, salted ham, a tin of lard, cook pans, drinking tins, canteens, rope, rolls of canvas, blankets—the pile shifted from the street onto horseback item by item. Mr. Ellison's face fell in the process as he appeared to count his loss of profits. Stacy failed to muster much sympathy for the man. He'd made a fortune gouging folks with exorbitant prices. Civic duty was precious when freely offered but just as valuable when coerced.

After she cinched down the last of the leather straps holding the supplies in place, Stacy found Maddie standing beside her. The woman had exchanged her dress for britches, a cotton shirt, an oversized coat, and a weathered hat. Her hand clenched the tether of her horse, which loomed over her shoulder. Stacy squinted.

"Mrs. Dunbar?"

"I'm going with you."

A shadow fell across them, cast by Glen. He stared at his wife with incredulity. "Maddie? What the devil?"

"I'm going with them." Her tone was cast in iron, like the products of her husband's forge. "They'll need a doctor at some point but will have to settle for me."

"But..." Glen swallowed. "But you're no gunfighter. You've never killed a man."

She stepped in toward him and gently poked his chest with her finger. "I don't plan to kill anyone, you big ox. But I might save a life. So I'm going. I'll be back. Take good care of Lily."

When her voice broke, Glen gathered her into an enveloping embrace. He whispered something Stacy couldn't hear, but his terror and pride were on full display. Maddie nodded twice, kissed him from toe tips, and spun away. Glen's woeful eyes locked with Stacy's. She dipped her chin.

"I'll bring her back or I won't come back. You have my word."

His nostrils flared, but he gave her a nod. "Your word is as good as gold, Miss Blue. Godspeed."

She mounted her calico, adjusted her cap, and fell in behind Paynter as he kicked his mare into motion. With a sparsity of called farewells, the band of six headed east along Main Street in the direction van Zandt's men had traveled an hour earlier. They'd only just cleared the outlying buildings when Beah Nooki met them. The elder rode up alongside Paynter, his rifle across his lap.

"I tracked them for a time. I know where they ride."

"Where?" said Paynter.

"The broken red hills at the mouth of the Bighorns. I traveled there many times in my youth."

"Hole-in-the-Wall?"

"So white men call it."

Stacy had heard of the place—a pass into the Bighorn Mountains with a thousand blind corners in which to hide or lay an ambush. If van Zandt beat them there, he'd be difficult to track. Paynter's thoughts must have aligned with hers.

"Then we've got to hurry. Can you describe to us the landmarks along the way?"

"No. I will show you."

Paynter shook his head. "I can't ask you to go. This is our fight."

Beah Nooki urged his horse ahead of Paynter's and swept an arm forward. "I will show you."

Stacy drew alongside Paynter. "Give it up. When a Shoshone elder says, 'This is what I will do,' then he by God means 'This is what I will do.' You're better off convincing a stone to bleed than to change his mind."

"I know. But I had to try."

"'Course you did. But I'm glad he's with us."

Paynter flexed his jaw. "Me too."

CHAPTER THIRTY-THREE

RISING WELL BEFORE SUNRISE WOULD PROVE SIMPLE FOR Jake, for he barely slept that night, wrapped in his blanket and his feet still shod in boots. Every time his eyelids drooped and he slipped over the borderlands of sleep, strident dreams descended on him, trapping him in a crushing cycle of anxiety, incapacity, and trepidation until he jerked awake to cradle his revolver closer to his chest. After countless rounds of the fitful sleep, his body began whispering that dawn was near, not understanding that it hadn't really slept.

He listened, though, and sat up to survey his companions. They lay scattered about a sandy clearing in a field of sagebrush, mostly curled tight against the chill air of midspring. They'd ridden until cloud cover had buried the sliver of moon and plunged the world into inky darkness. He didn't begrudge his friends their sleep, but he envied them nonetheless. In his solitary musing, he decided that if anyone ever invented spectacles that could see in darkness, he'd stand first in line to buy a pair. After all, the prospect of an enemy possessing them instead was unthinkable. He chuckled to himself. Surely, such a device was not possible.

"*Tuc, tuc, tuc.*"

The mimicked sound of a night bird drew his eyes to find

Beah Nooki watching him. The old man rose, stretched his bones with a symphony of popping joints, and came to sit by Jake.

"It is time to go," Beah Nooki said.

"Just what I was thinking."

"Are you prepared to die today?"

"I am."

"Good. Dead men fight without fear."

"Don't I know. I've been dead for years."

Their conversation, though muffled, had the effect of stirring the others. Gus sat up and scratched the stubble of his short beard. "The grown-ups are talkin'. Must be time to rise and shine." He slapped Stacy's backside. "Get up, Miss Blue."

"I'm gittin'," she grumbled. "Stop layin' hands on me before I break 'em."

"Yes, ma'am. Can't ride a lick with broken fingers."

Ten minutes later, the intrepid company rode out like the seven stars of the Little Bear, moving through the twilight on a predictable course.

Emshoff pushed his horse alongside Jake's. "We left early. Do you hope to catch van Zandt sleeping?"

The German's question dripped with wind-driven anxiety. He seemed a moving bullet, a fired projectile on a relentless path to punish those who dared steal his daughter. Of all people, Jake understood. The thought of Rosalyn in such peril slingshotted him through the night with similar frenetic intent. But he was also beginning to understand van Zandt.

"No," he said. "I don't think we will catch him sleeping. Not ever again after the way we waylaid him in the canyon.

I figure he's pushin' hard for Hole-in-the-Wall and is willing to lose a few horses or men along the way. I imagine they marched in darkness longer than they should've and started earlier than we did."

Emshoff glanced away, mildly distraught. "Then how will we catch them?"

"By never giving up. Van Zandt will need to stop eventually. Maybe at Hole-in-the-Wall. Maybe the Bighorns. Maybe Alaska, for all I know. But when he does, I'll be thirty seconds behind to make him regret his pause."

Emshoff nodded. "And I with you."

"Damn right."

"*Verdammt richtig.*"

Beah Nooki picked up the outlaw trail at the dawning of light and followed with help from young Jim. The kid was already an accomplished tracker, but he devoured Beah Nooki's steady stream of instruction about signs of passage. With them intent on the trail, an hour ticked by before they noticed the others. It was Maddie Dunbar who saw them first.

"Look there."

Jake glanced in the direction of her pointed arm to find a line of riders in the distance, probably three miles out. Everyone studied the strangers for a couple of minutes before Stacy broke the silence.

"They ain't comin' for us. Who do ya suppose they are? More of van Zandt's boys catchin' up to him?"

Jake had considered that question himself. Were they some of the riders who'd led Jake, Gus, and Stacy away from town? Likely not, he decided. Those men would've been able to circle back to meet up with their boss while Jake was still assembling his posse. Gus must've thought the same, for he spoke Jake's mind.

"I doubt it. But they're for sure headed in the same direction as us. Hole-in-the-Wall or bust."

"Who are they, then?" said Emshoff.

Jake wasn't certain but considered the possibility of… no. He shook away the notion. "Not sure. Other outlaws. Cowhands lookin' for strays. Lost travelers. The president and his cabinet. Could be anybody."

Jake's company pressed onward, keeping one eye on the trail and the other on the riders. After about an hour, the gap between the groups narrowed enough to awaken Jake's dismissed suspicion. Two hours on, he was certain.

"Lucien," he spat.

"What's that?" said Gus. "Lucien Ashley?"

"Pretty sure. I recognize his horse. And I can smell the stench of Ambrose Blackburn from here."

Gus rubbed his neck while squinting into the distance. "Six of 'em and one packhorse. They ain't out for a stroll."

"Doesn't seem like."

"They're after Rosalyn," Stacy blurted out as she barreled into the conversation. "Only question is whether they're with van Zandt or against him."

Her line of questioning intrigued Jake. "How do you mean?"

"I mean, Lucien tried to steal away his sister not so long ago. What if, what if…" She stared skyward while collecting her thoughts. "What if this whole thing is a ruse cooked up between Lucien and van Zandt to get the Union Pacific money and Rosalyn in the process. Seems like a good outcome for both. And if we've learned anything about Ashley, it's this. He'll stoop low enough to crawl beneath a snake's belly to put his hands on a few dollars."

Jake wanted to dismiss her logic but couldn't find the wherewithal to do so. A duplicitous agreement between Lucien and van Zandt seemed well within the foul wheelhouse of each. If that was their plan, they'd avoid intersecting Jake's path until rejoining the outlaw band.

"Maybe," he said. "Let's see what they do."

They rode on at an energetic clip, and Lucien's crew kept pace on an increasingly parallel course. However, the others seemed clearly uninterested in drawing nearer to Jake's posse. This raised his suspicions further that Stacy was right. By the time the sun dipped below the horizon, he was almost convinced of it.

"Whadda ya think now?" asked Stacy as they struggled to make progress in the rapidly fading light.

"We're gonna have to fight 'em," Jake said bluntly. "We need to pick them off now before they hook up with van Zandt."

"You sure?"

"Don't see another way around it."

Having made his decision, Jake wasted no time when grinding darkness drew them to a halt. He pulled Beah Nooki aside. "You think you can find their camp?"

"On foot, yes."

Jake waved to Gus. "Beah Nooki and I are goin' for a walk. Settle everyone in with rifles at the ready. An owl's call will tell you it's us returning."

Gus patted his carbine. "Will do. Take care, Paynter."

"Don't I always?"

"Decidedly not."

"Duly noted."

He and Beah Nooki slipped away from the cold camp in the general direction of Lucien's men, a two-mile plunge into pitch-darkness in search of six needles in a boundless haystack. They marked contours of the horizon to allow a return trip. Otherwise, they might wander all night trying to find their own camp. Jake harbored serious doubts that they'd locate Lucien's camp, so certain was he that his nemesis would practice a similar level of stealth. He couldn't have been more wrong. A glow in the darkness told him that Lucien had committed the cardinal sin of pursuit. He'd lit a campfire, announcing to the world his precise location. Beah Nooki whispered a sharp phrase in Shoshone.

"What's that mean?" Jake asked.

"He who grazes his horse on salty ground." He paused. "I think the white man's phrase is 'mindless fool.'"

"It's a good saying."

Jake and Beah Nooki approached the camp obliquely and with care not to spook the horses. When they drew near enough to overhear conversation, they stopped to listen. Sweeney told a story, then Blackburn relived his glory days in morbid detail. One of the other men recounted his recent visit to a flophouse in Cheyenne where he met and fell in love with a painted lady called Maybelline who refused his offer of marriage but took his money instead. Nothing of interest. After the flophouse story, Lucien turned away and rolled into a blanket. This effectively killed the conversation, and the camp ground into silence as the men bedded down by the fire. Jake tugged at Beah Nooki and they slipped away as silently as they'd arrived. When they'd put a mile behind them on the return journey, Jake finally spoke his revolving thoughts.

"We need to drop in on 'em well before dawn. Catch them with their britches down."

"It's a good plan," said the elder.

Jake continued after Beah Nooki, wondering if this was the day when he'd finally face down Lucien Ashley until one or both of them lay dead. Either way, he was ready.

CHAPTER THIRTY-FOUR

THE STARS STILL RULED THE NIGHT WHEN JAKE AND HIS team walked out of camp with horses on the tether. It had to be this way. With two miles of night-soaked brush to cover, they'd need to arrive and set up a perimeter before Lucien's men began to stir. Every member of the posse knew the blunt but simple plan. Leave the horses a few hundred yards out. Surround Lucien's camp. Threaten him into divulging his intent. If worst came to worst, they'd be in position to win a gun battle or force Lucien and his men to turn back.

The silence of the walk and the still of the night provided Jake ample time to envision a myriad of possible scenarios and consider logistics. How they should spread out to cover the sleepers without shooting one another in a cross fire. Who should train weapons on whom. Which of them would slip up on Lucien's horses to prevent a breakaway. By the time they'd approached within a quarter mile of the unseen camp, Jake had worked out the details to military precision, which was to say he had only the vaguest idea of what he was doing. He stopped behind a cluster of junipers that hugged an unseen but insubstantial creek.

"We leave the horses here," he whispered to the assembled

party. "Maddie, you stay with them. If we call for you, come runnin' with your bag. Got it?"

"Got it." Her voice trembled, and no wonder. Maddie had survived a front-row seat at several bloody battles during the war and had lived through the violent attacks along the Oregon Trail. To be thrust back into peril after a two-year respite would shake anyone.

"You sure you don't want a gun, Maddie?"

She ducked her head in silence for a few seconds. "Maybe this once."

Gus pressed a spare Colt revolver into her hands. "Know how to use it?"

"Yes."

"And reload?"

"Yes. But if I have to reload, I'm probably dead anyway."

Gus snorted quietly. "Good point."

"Stay safe," said Stacy after punching Gus's shoulder. "We'll be back before you know it. Promise."

"Godspeed," Maddie said.

Like restless unchained spirits, the party crept quietly from there. On the cusp of the campsite, Jake motioned for Emshoff to cover Lucien's horses while Gus and Jim set up a firing angle to the left. Stacy and Beah Nooki went right to establish a cross fire. Jake stayed put and counted to two hundred and fifteen. Upon reaching that arbitrary number, he rose from his crouch to close the final hundred feet to the cluster of bushes from where he and Beah Nooki had reconnoitered the camp earlier. The fire had gone cold, but he counted six vague forms strung around its remains. The two shadows on the far side of the ring gave him pause. Was that two men, or just one and baggage? He shook his head. Had to be two. He pulled back the hammer of his Henry, inhaled a slow, deep breath, and expelled it with a call.

"Lucien Ashley! We got you covered! Don't none of you start reachin.'"

The bundled forms reacted as he'd expected, bodies propelled upward from sleep to claw at the air, claw for weapons, claw for reason. Jake's shot exploding the ashes of the fire froze them all. Three of them extended their hands. But not the one he knew to be Lucien. The man stood instead.

"Paynter? Is that you?"

"The one and only. Tell your men to stand down."

Before Lucien could give the order, if he even intended to, a low chuckle sounded from not thirty feet to Jake's blind side. The fine hairs of his neck stood on end, but he kept his rifle trained on Lucien and waited for the other shoe to drop.

"How about *you* stand down, *Marshal.*"

Jake suppressed a groan. Ambrose Blackburn.

Jake maintained his position. "What's your move, Ambrose?"

Blackburn laughed, louder this time. "I figured you'd come for a visit. I figured you couldn't stay away long. Been waitin' half the night for you to show up with your little posse, and my finger's a mite itchy. If I could scratch it against the trigger just a little bit…"

"Do that," said Jake, "and most of us will never leave this place."

"Stay your hand, Blackburn." The order from Lucien

carried entitled authority. Jake knew Blackburn hated authority, entitled or otherwise. He expected a bullet to the back of his head any second.

"Ambrose," he called. "How much is Lucien paying you anyway?"

"None of your business."

"Maybe so, but is he paying you enough for Gus Rivers to put a hole in your head?"

In the pause, Jake heard shifting in the brush. A single shot from one restless hand would instigate a bloodbath with all the guilty dead or dying. Maybe that wasn't such a bad outcome after all. Sweeney broke the silence.

"Come on, Blackburn. Just shoot him and be done with it."

"Do it," said Stacy from cover. "I'll shoot you first and still have a barrel left for your pet rat from Philly."

Jake would have required the sharpest of blades to cut through the ensuing tension. The moment stretched until he heard Blackburn reset his feet behind him.

"Keep talkin', Paynter. But even so much as a flinch will be your last."

"You heard the man," said Lucien to Jake. "State your grievance or get the hell away."

Jake couldn't resist such a poetic invitation to parley, and he appreciated the unabashed bravado. Lucien was nothing if not overconfident. "Here's the way I see it, Ashley. I figure you and van Zandt planned the whole fiasco back at South Pass City, and now you're ridin' to meet up with your friend to divide the spoils. One of the spoils being your sister. All the talk of you supposedly betraying van Zandt? Probably just a grand ruse intended to line your pockets and fetch Miss Ashley home where you can lock her down. That about right?"

Lucien's shadowy form swayed in place. "Not even close."

"Care to correct me, then?"

"Not particularly, but as I have no choice…" He put his hands on his hips, both of which appeared free of hardware. "I did double-cross van Zandt, on orders from my father. It wouldn't have been my preference left to my own devices. But my father's plans are often bold and rarely wrong, so I cut van Zandt loose. As you might have heard, he took offense. I didn't consider that he'd ever take Ros…"

Lucien's voice broke, which lessened the growing knot in Jake's throat as he peered down the rifle barrel. "How could you not? You know van Zandt. What he's willing to do to his allies, let alone to his adversaries."

Lucien's hands fell from his hips and he hung his head, expelling a sharp curse in the process. "That was my mistake. If I'd ever guessed this outcome, I'd have shot him on first sight a year ago. But make no mistake. If he harms a hair on Rosalyn's head, I'll slit his belly and pull his guts out while he watches."

Against his better instincts, Jake believed the man. Sure, Lucien was a scoundrel of the first order, a man who'd sell just about anybody for gold. But that greed did not extend to his sister. She was likely the only person in the world he'd be willing to die for. Besides, Jake had never before heard Lucien admit to making a mistake.

"Okay. Maybe you're not lying, at least this once."

"Don't do it," called Stacy from the darkness. "Don't let him into your confidence. He's a lyin' snake."

"I agree," said Gus. "I don't trust him as far as I can spit my tongue."

"He's lied to us before. Remember that." This from Emshoff.

Jake knew he should listen to his friends. They cared for him. They had his back—literally. They had never let him down. But his mind cycled again through an array of alternatives and led him back around to the best way forward—a shining door he couldn't resist opening.

"I've decided," he said. "And I have a proposal."

Lucien shuffled forward a step. "I'm listening."

"We all continue, but together. We join our forces, hunt down van Zandt, and take back the ones he stole. If you're lying, I can keep an eye on you. If you're tellin' the truth, then we double our numbers."

"You can't be serious." Lucien chuckled.

"I've never been more so. But it's your choice. We open up on one another right now, or we work together and settle our differences another time. For the children. For your sister."

Lucien lifted his hands to rub the top of his head, swaying back and forth in the throes of indecision. "Fine, then. We'll travel together. But only for Rosalyn's sake." Then he lifted an index finger to point at Jake's nose. "But she is not yours, Paynter. You will never have her. Never. I'll die before I let that happen."

Jake ground his teeth together, but not because Lucien was wrong. He knew better than anyone the gap between him and Rosalyn. "I believe that too."

"It's a bad idea," said Blackburn. "We'll end up killin' one other along the way."

Lucien turned away. "Maybe so. But it's the best bad idea we have. Start saddling up."

Jake lowered his Henry and cut his eyes to where Blackburn crouched in the darkness. "Another time, then, Ambrose."

"Same to you, Paynter."

"We'll be back in ten minutes. Don't start without us."

"Wouldn't dream of it."

As Jake and his band made their way back to the horses, Stacy sidled up to him. "C'mon, Paynter. Do you really trust Lucien Ashley to do what's right?"

"Not in the least."

"Then explain why we're gettin' in bed with him, right between the silk sheets."

"Because of the first rule of conflict," he said. "Some of the greatest generals in history have tried fighting a war on two fronts and lost. We can't do the same and hope to save Miss Ashley and the children. Instead, we fight the battle before us and save the next one for later."

"Okay," she said. "Maybe I buy that."

Jake didn't blame Stacy for her skepticism. He remained deeply suspicious of Lucien's motives, Sweeney's compliance, and Blackburn's restraint. Regardless, he vowed to know at all times where Sweeney and Blackburn were, understanding that the moment the alliance succeeded or failed, they would try to kill him.

CHAPTER THIRTY-FIVE

ROSALYN'S FATHER, A SELF-APPOINTED FOUNTAIN OF political wisdom, had always told her the best way to overcome an all-powerful enemy was to play opossum until the adversary became convinced of your weakness and then mount an assault with every weapon at your disposal. Though her disgust for her father had grown over the years, she still found much of his advice serviceable in most situations. The ruthless outlaw holding her and the children prisoner certainly constituted an all-powerful enemy. However, she possessed only one weapon with which to fight back—choosing the opportune moment for them to escape.

"Move it, you scat-tailed collection of mangy gumps!"

Van Zandt's prodding of his men sounded innocuous enough, but the outlaws redoubled their efforts at breaking camp an hour before dawn. In the short time she'd ridden with the outlaw band, she had learned the depth of the men's respect and fear for their leader—though mostly fear. What might generate such a reaction from those in his service, she could only imagine. Rosalyn figured she'd learn the reason soon enough. The outlaw king continued prodding his men.

"We don't know who might be on our trail. Could be that hopped-up marshal, or Ashley, or elements of the army.

Regardless, we'll not lounge around camp like pampered housewives to find out. Pack up as if your life depends on it, because it surely does."

Rosalyn hoped that all the aforementioned parties were tracking them. Did Paynter even know she'd been taken? Did Lucien? Paynter would come if he could—of that she was certain. But her brother? Would he leave well enough alone, having solved the embarrassing problem of his sister's rebellion? She shook away the dismal musings to attend to the four children. She offered them biscuits and jerky she'd begged from one of the scowling outlaws.

"Eat some now, put the rest in a pocket for later. Make sure you relieve yourself before we ride. They won't stop for our discomfort. Understand?"

The kids nodded. Lisbet pulled the only boy aside. "Especially you, Herbie. You know how small your bladder is."

Lisbet's earnest instruction nearly brought a grin to Rosalyn's lips. At age seven and the oldest of the four children, she had gathered the others under her wings that first night on the trail.

"I will," said Herbie.

Lisbet lifted five-year-old Ann's chin and peered into her eyes. "Don't be afraid now. I've been shot before, and though it wasn't much fun, I lived. We just have to hold on until Mr. Paynter comes for us."

"Is the marshal really coming to save us?" said Ann with tremulous hope.

Lisbet smiled. "He always does. Don't you worry now."

Though the girl's optimism was infectious, Rosalyn

harbored significant doubts about Paynter's ability to catch up in time to prevent tragedy. She lurched abruptly to one side as a looming figure shoved past her to face Lisbet.

"Girl. What you sayin' about that damned marshal?"

Lisbet raised her chin to the bearded outlaw. Boggins, van Zandt's right-hand man. "I said he's coming for us, and he'll kill you all if you try to stop him."

Boggins laughed and backhanded Lisbet across the cheek, sending her sprawling into the dirt. He flung an arm against Rosalyn to prevent her from intervening. Lisbet lay still a moment before pushing back to her feet. She folded her arms and faced the man again.

"He'll kill you first for doing that."

"Why, you little…" Boggins raised the back of his hand again but Rosalyn seized his wrist with both hands.

"If you must strike someone, strike me. But if you again lay a hand on one of these children, I will cut your throat in your sleep. I swear to God."

Boggins growled, pushed her down, and strode away. Lisbet and Polly helped Rosalyn regain her feet and brushed debris from the back of her skirt.

"Are you hurt?" asked little Polly.

"I am perfectly fine. Eat your biscuits now."

A renewed presence at Rosalyn's back sent her spinning with arms wide, preparing to protect the children from Boggins. She met the gaze of one of the others. The tall, angular man touched the brim of his hat. "Ma'am. The name's Greely. I was an unwillin' guest of your marshal at the jailhouse until Dutch broke me out." He kept his voice low and glanced over a shoulder at his milling comrades. "A word of advice. Threats like the one you just made will get you killed. If Boggins don't do it, the boss will. I'd settle your tongue, for the sake of the young'uns, and comply as best you can."

She glared up at Greely. "Will you be the one to kill me? The one to harm helpless children?"

He shifted from foot to foot and leaned nearer. "No, ma'am. I wouldn't. But plenty others here would without a second's remorse. Just heed my words."

He left without waiting for a response. In his absence, Rosalyn considered what Greely had said and her father's advice about overcoming an all-powerful enemy. Her situation could not be more dire. Van Zandt had saddled up nineteen men to ride with him. The first morning after the abduction, the outlaw had allocated three spare horses for her and the children. She rode alone with hands bound before her while the kids rode two by two. She'd argued in vain to leave the children's hands free in case they fell from the huge horses, but van Zandt would have none of it.

"The ties will keep them squarely focused on remaining astride, lest they learn a valuable lesson about the unpleasant results of inattention," he had said. "I am nothing if not a teacher of the young."

She gritted her jaw, calling back a curse at the remembered conversation. Van Zandt found her moments later, the damnable ties dangling from his fingers. He called back over a shoulder. "Greely."

"Sir?"

"As you are apparently on friendly terms with our guests, I will allow you the honor of securing their hands."

"Yes, sir."

"And, Greely?"

"Boss?"

"Make sure the bonds are tight. Any unfortunate incidents will surely earn my displeasure."

"Yes, sir."

As Greely began binding wrists, van Zandt stood watch over the proceedings, his head cocked to one side. He nodded with seeming satisfaction when Greely finished and left.

"There," he said to Rosalyn. "I hope you find neither the bonds nor general situation untenable. We've no reason for incivility between us, I hope."

Rosalyn noted Greely's warning and simply nodded. However, she knew the outlaw's definition of civility was as fluid as the Platte River, twisting, forking, and shifting with the terrain. He'd be civil until he chose not to be, and then, Lord help them all. She stretched her spine, hoping to close some of the gap between his stature and hers. "Then in the interest of civil conversation, might you share what you have in mind for the children and me?"

He scratched his jaw. "Honestly, I haven't yet decided. It depends greatly upon the actions of your brother and Jake Paynter."

"How so?"

"If they leave well enough alone, we will release you after we've secured our cargo and established a new stronghold. You have my word."

Of course, Rosalyn knew better. Van Zandt would keep her and the children until they were of no more value to him, which could be a very long time. When their value evaporated, she didn't figure he'd be inclined to spare her in any humane way.

"But," said the outlaw with a raised index finger, "if they pursue, I have no control over who lives, who dies. I wouldn't prefer that. Would you?"

She shook her head in silence. This threat she believed.

Van Zandt let loose a low chuckle dripping with darkness. "You've become awfully laconic since yesterday, Miss Ashley. If I knew no better, I'd believe you have come around to my way of thinking. However, I know better." He swept his eyes over the length of her body. "Be a good girl now. What a tragedy for you to fall from my good graces while in the company of such despicable men."

As he walked away, she was more convinced than ever of the truth. She couldn't blindly wait for help—from Paynter or otherwise. Her only certain salvation was to escape with the children. When? And how? These remained among the greatest secrets of the universe. A tugging of her skirt drew her attention to find Lisbet pressing conspiratorially near.

"I was wrong," said the girl.

"Oh? About what?"

"About Mr. Paynter killing Boggins first. I think he'll get Mr. van Zandt instead."

Rosalyn pulled Lisbet to her chest. "Let us hope so."

"Until then," said the girl, "we'll be like Sempronius."

"Sempronius?"

"Sempronius Densus, centurion of the Roman Praetorian Guard, like you told us. We will be heroic no matter what happens."

Rosalyn squeezed Lisbet tighter. "You inspire me, little one. Let's hope that heroics are enough."

CHAPTER THIRTY-SIX

WHEN BEAH NOOKI JUMPED ASTRIDE A HORSE, HE BECAME the best version of himself. Though he'd tried, he could not explain the particulars of the phenomenon, other than the extra height might put him nearer the Great Spirit. Regardless, as his body fell into rhythm with the flow of the horse, he began to lose track of where he ended and the animal began. The raw power of his mount flowed through his veins, carving channels of potential that caused his blood to sing.

More importantly, his mind settled into a sacred place of quiet he rarely found when not on horseback. Thoughts grew deeper, plumbing the depths of a bottomless well of the mind. Assessment became finer, sharper, a knife blade of consideration and decision. Future possibilities emerged from the fog as if he could touch them with the reach of a grasping hand. Three days into the chase, he had fallen into just such a well, at one with his mind.

"What do you think, Beah Nooki?"

Paynter's question lifted him slowly from the well, but he maintained a trailing hand in the depths that he might return later. "I think of many things, with not enough words to speak them."

Paynter smiled. "Let me be more specific, then. What is your assessment of our mission to catch van Zandt?"

"I have given that much thought," Beah Nooki said.

"I figured. Tell me, if you will."

Beah Nooki swept a hand toward the rough country ahead. "The place of the broken red hills lies a day from here. We will not catch the outlaws before then."

Each day, they had started as early as they had dared in darkness, risking wandering away from the outlaw trail before daylight. Each evening, they had traveled past sundown, again risking losing the trail. The day before, in fact, they had fallen off the trail and given up precious hours before finding it again. Though they had pushed the horses as hard as they dared, the outlaw leader had matched the posse's determination with a harder march. Beah Nooki had pushed forward the previous night in search of the outlaws but had returned without locating their camp. Based on the signs of the trail, he guessed the outlaws led the posse by a quarter day. Paynter's features grew grim with Beah Nooki's analysis and he nodded reluctantly.

"Trapping the bear will be much harder, then, if they reach Hole-in-the-Wall."

Beah Nooki agreed. He had considered the many possibilities of what might happen when the posse did close the gap. In his experience, the battle often went to the bear instead of the hunter. Though he considered the doubling of numbers helpful, he knew well how conflicts among grumbling allies could become the true enemy. Unless harnessed toward a common goal, rivalries would hollow out an attacking force and give the enemy an easy victory. He nudged his horse closer to Paynter's disagreeable mare.

"Do you trust Ashley in a fight?"

Paynter shrugged. "No. But I reckon we have little choice."

"We do not." Beah Nooki glanced at Stacy, who rode behind off his left shoulder. "I worry for the granddaughter of Many Horses. She owns the heart of a true warrior. But she is no killer."

"I share your concern."

As if knowing herself to be the subject of the conversation, Stacy pushed her calico up beside Beah Nooki's stallion and offered a Shoshone greeting. He leaned his forehead toward her in reply. She shifted her gaze from him to Paynter and back again.

"Stop worrying about me. Both of you."

"Who says we're worried?" said Paynter.

"I'd be offended if you weren't. But stop anyway."

Beah Nooki smiled thinly. "As you wish. Then talk of something else."

The young woman tilted her gaze skyward in apparent thought before pinning him with a gaze filled with curiosity. "Your name, Beah Nooki. I know it means 'Big Run.' I've always wondered how you came by it. Every time I ask, you change the subject. So if you want to talk of something else, start there and stick to the topic."

Beah Nooki turned his attention to the trail ahead, his mind falling backward to his youth and those dark days when he had earned his name. Though he rarely spoke of them, not a day passed that he did not revisit the sharp memories, clear as still water even after a lifetime. They still brought him acute pain. Perhaps it was his age. Maybe it was the stark reality of the looming conflict. Whatever the reason, Beah Nooki decided to tell the story, possibly for the last time.

"My name is as you say. But in the white man's tongue, a better phrase is 'Runs Far.'"

"You could run far?"

"I *did* run far," he corrected. He let the memories surround him, speak to him, and give him the words. "When I was twelve winters, I decided to take Touches the Fire as a wife when I came of age."

Stacy cocked her head. "I never met her."

"You did not. That is true." He gathered his surging emotion. "She was one winter older and to me like the stars in the sky. Beautiful. Untouchable. The medicine man's daughter. But she was kind to me, and when we passed, she looked at me through the tops of her eyes. One day, I gathered my courage and told her my plan to make her my wife. Her smile removed my doubt."

"Touches the Fire agreed to marry you when you came of age?" said Stacy.

"She did." He paused to gather further recollection. "During early spring, when snow was still deep on the mountains, two Crow warriors came to us for shelter from a storm. Their chief had cast them out for crimes against the Crow. In kindness, the medicine man gave them shelter and venison. The men left in the night and stole Touches the Fire. Her father was in a rage and called for men willing to go into the storm to find her. I joined the chase, even though the older men told me to stay in the village. We traveled through deep snow for two days but lost the trail. When the rest turned back, I went alone on foot."

"For many days, I walked through wind and snow, looking for signs of men and horses. Then I saw smoke from their fire rising from a place between two hills. Though I was nearly frozen, I waited for night. Then I entered their camp and found Touches the Fire there. I killed one warrior as he slept. The other rose up with a knife to fight me, but I killed him too. I took their horses and brought Touches the Fire to her father. That day, he looked into my eyes and called me 'Beah Nooki' for the first time."

Words failed him. He swallowed the rest and studied his hands, lined with years.

Stacy stared into the distance as he finished the story. "So you have loved her ever since?"

"I have."

"And you ran far to rescue her."

"I did." He let a smile capture his face. "And see, the medicine man named me well, for I am running far still."

"To again save a woman in danger," said Paynter, emerging from pensive silence.

Beah Nooki merely nodded in reply, not wanting Paynter to know how close he was to the awful truth.

CHAPTER THIRTY-SEVEN

As Hole-in-the-Wall rose into view half past sunrise on the fourth day, Jake briefly fancied himself a medieval knight preparing to lay siege to a citadel. A weathered wall of red rock above a steep incline remarkably resembled a construction of human hands, a crimson fortress built to withstand the assaults of marauding armies. And he without a catapult with which to pound the walls. The rolling terrain leading up to the natural castle was as the sea before the fortress, waves of brown and emerging green shot through with bands of snow like cresting waves. The creek running parallel to the natural barrier seemed more moat than anything. Jake scanned the crest of the cliffs, not so much expecting archers but outlaws with repeating rifles. He saw nothing but ample sky rising behind the summit. Beyond lay an open path to the Bighorn Mountains.

"There," said Beah Nooki as he motioned east. Jake's eyes followed the wall south to where it pinched against itself, creasing where opposing walls came together at something resembling a right angle. The joining of the walls gave way to a passage, a narrow gate into the wilderness beyond. Lucien spurred his horse past Jake, and his men followed at a loping gallop. Jake urged the mare forward to catch them.

"Ashley!" His call emerged harsher than he'd intended, though less acrid than he felt. "What the heck are you doing?"

Lucien narrowed his eyes and frowned but did not stop. "We need to get through the pass. That is where they certainly went."

Jake kicked the mare past him and wheeled her around, nearly unhorsing Lucien as he reined his mount to a skidding halt.

"What the heck are *you* doing, Paynter?"

"We can't just rush up there." Jake swept a hand along the line of cliffs. "It's a perfect place for an ambush. You could put twenty rifles along that rim, and we'd never see 'em until they buried us in cross fire as we rode in a line through the gap. It's a death trap."

"For some, maybe. But the outlaws would be on foot and we have twelve mounted shooters. If we sweep through with guns blazing, we'll put them on their heels. We might break them here and now."

Jake laughed long and low. "Right."

The rancher grew red-faced. "Why are you laughing? It's better than sitting down here waiting while they disappear into the wilds."

Jake shook his head. "You never heard of the three hundred Spartans at Thermopylae?"

"Of course I have."

"Then you'll recall they held a similar pass against tens of thousands for days. And you ain't never heard of Gettysburg?"

"Everyone's heard of Gettysburg," snapped Lucien. "What's your point?"

"The battle was won at Little Round Top because a few men held the high ground against a larger force. History is littered with examples of victors who held passes or high ground against greater numbers. Van Zandt has both, as well as the greater numbers. If we just gallivant up there, guns blazin', we'll be food for worms in ten minutes."

As Jake had been talking, Blackburn and Sweeney had closed on either side of him. The former lifted one side of his lip. "Whatsa matter, Paynter? Scared of a little fight?"

"You know I ain't."

Gus, Emshoff, and Jim closed behind Sweeney and Blackburn, forming a concentric ring of stretching tension. Sweeney appeared to take offense, and a pistol appeared in his grip. In the blink of an eye, guns filled every hand until everyone was in someone else's sights. Jake's Kerr drew a bead on the crease between Lucien's eyes.

"Put it down!" shouted Gus and Blackburn at each other as they squared off, Colt against Colt. Stacy began yelling threats from behind her shotgun. Sweeney expelled a colorful blend of curses and poison promises. The three ranch hands, Thompson, McPhail, and Svoboda, seemed on the cusp of exchanging bullets with Emshoff and Jim, shouting over one another in a perfect cacophony of panicked malice. In the midst of the mayhem, Beah Nooki sat astride his horse with his rifle still slung across his lap, shaking his head with disappointment.

The old man's surprising demeanor yanked Jake back

to '64, back to a day at Poison Springs, Arkansas. General Steele had sent Colonel Williams and his units, First Kansas Colored and Eighteenth Iowa, to forage for food as attrition and starvation gnawed at the larger force. Minutes into the march, hostilities had broken out between the black and white regiments.

Jake sat astride his horse surveying the oncoming columns. First Kansas Colored marched through the grass on the right side of the road, while the Eighteenth Iowa marched to the left. He tried to ignore the epithets flung from the left to the right and the responding calls. Even as he watched, though, one of the Kansas corporals appeared to reach his fill. He stepped onto the road shaking a fist. An Iowa private launched himself to meet the corporal, and they descended into a flurry of mutual haymakers. Instantly, both columns disintegrated as they formed a raucous ring around the combatants, pushing and shoving where the regiments pressed against each other. Some began gesturing with muskets and pulling bayonets. Alarmed by the unfolding disaster, Jake spurred his horse into the fray, only for a bubble ten bodies deep to block his progress.

Meanwhile, Sergeant Mecklenburg of the Eighteenth began plowing a path through the masses toward the combatants. Mecklenburg, a brawny Iowan with a buzz of red hair and one eye, was among the purest sons of bitches Jake had ever met, a fountain of profanity spraying every man in his path with a caustic rain of belittlement. If ever a brutish caveman had survived from antiquity, it was Mecklenburg. Jake left his horse to meet Mecklenburg in the middle, certain the sergeant would attack Jake's corporal. He had not quite reached the eye of the hurricane

*when the sergeant burst through the ring. Rather than assault-
ing the corporal before him, the sergeant stepped past him and
belted his own man hard enough to lay him out flat on the road.
Mecklenburg lifted his chin, his face crimson, and bellowed to his
men while gesturing toward the bulk of First Kansas.*

*"They ain't the enemy! Not today! Any man who don't fall in
line by the time I stop talkin' will get the flat end of my fist until
he ain't breathin'. Now, fall in!"*

*The press of bodies dispersed like chaff in the wind, black,
brown, and white alike, forming again two columns, one on
either side of the road. Jake stood in amazement, watching the
sergeant glare a thousand men into submission. When he caught
Jake staring, a hard smile crawled across his face.*

*"The only remedy for jackassery is to be a bigger jackass or
the better man. Ridin' the fence just gets you splintered."*

Jake emerged from the memory just as quickly as he'd
entered it, lurching back into the frenzy of shouting and
brandished weaponry. His mouth formed the same hard
smile Mecklenburg had worn that day. With a slow and
deliberate motion, he released the cocked hammer of his
Kerr and holstered it. As he crossed his arms to lean over
the saddle horn, Lucien blinked with surprise. Then, just as
carefully, Lucien lowered and holstered his revolver. One by
one, the assembled members of both parties retracted their
weapons until Sweeney alone remained poised to fire—at
Jake. Lucien glared at the Philly street thug.

"Put it away, Sweeney."

"I've been waiting a year for this!"

"There will be plenty of other opportunities after this is

over. But if my sister dies because you shot the help, then I'll be sure to kill you myself."

Sweeney growled but shoved his pistol back into his coat pocket. He glared at Jake. "Just you wait. You're gonna get it."

"Aren't we all," Jake said. Dismissing Sweeney, he swung his regard to Lucien. "Okay. We'll do it your way, but with a condition."

Lucien cocked his head, suspicion in his eyes. "And that is?"

"You and I go first. That way, if there's an ambush like I suspect, it'll be just us that die here today."

A smirk lifted the right side of Lucien's lip. "Fine. Let's go."

Jake cut a glance at Gus. "Wait 'til I call you. Then come on."

"Be careful, Paynter."

Jake pulled his Henry from its sheath. "You should know better by now."

They rode away to Gus shaking his head and laughing. Jake and Lucien crossed the winding creek, which held only a faint promise of water. As they drew near the rock wall, the ground tipped up into a steep grade strewn with loose rock that had chipped away from the cliffs over the millennia. Jake let the mare navigate the obstacle course while he kept his rifle trained on the rim. The broken terrain gave way to a cut between the intersection of walls, a rocky passage offering a gentler rise to the plateau above.

Every fiber of nerve buzzed in his body, waiting for a bullet to the head, the back, or the chest. He pressed ahead so resolutely that the breaching of the plateau caught him by surprise. He crouched low in the saddle and swung his rifle in a wide circle, eyes peeled for the enemy. He blinked three times. Not a soul in sight. Jake frowned deeply with confusion. The smart strategy would've been to lay an ambush at the rim, and van Zandt's intelligence was second to none. Why had he not?

"Well, Marshal Paynter." Lucien barely restrained his glee. "Seems one of us was right and the other mistaken. I wonder—which are you?"

Jake ignored Lucien's lording the small victory over him and trotted the mare to the rim. He waved the Henry back and forth twice, propelling the remainder of his party forward toward the Hole-in-the-Wall. From his vantage point, he spun the mare in a wide arc, understanding the appeal of the plateau. His line of sight was unobstructed for ten or more miles in every direction, save the crevices and folds tucked among the rising rolls of earth as the world marched toward the Bighorns to the north. Despite that, he'd need every tracking skill of Beah Nooki, Jim, and Blackburn to find the outlaw trail. They could be anywhere. More mysterious, though, was why van Zandt had let pass such a golden opportunity to lay waste to Jake's posse. The man was too cunning to have made the decision without a reason. Jake only wished he knew what that reason was. But then again, he'd never claimed to be a smart man.

CHAPTER THIRTY-EIGHT

GUS WAS FIRST THROUGH THE GAP AFTER PAYNTER AND Lucien, and he was nervous as a cat in a lightning storm. Despite Paynter's seeming calm, Gus kept his carbine at the shoulder as his buckskin clambered up the steep slope into the rocky pass. He didn't lower the weapon until reaching flat ground above the rise. On surveying the wide-open view with rising mountains to the north, he gave a long whistle.

"Gosh-a-mighty," he whispered to himself. He'd not be against staking out a plot of land and making a life in the very spot. He nudged his horse toward Paynter and Lucien, arriving with Beah Nooki and Blackburn.

"The outlaws rode north to the mountains," said the elder.

"I concur," said Blackburn. "There's lots a' tracks here, and they tried layin' down three trails, but they're all headed toward the Bighorns."

"Why three trails?" This from Stacy as she rode up, likely fearful of missing out on important intelligence.

"Three trails to divide us," said Beah Nooki.

"Yep," said Blackburn. "Divide and conquer. Just like we used to do, Paynter. Back in the day."

Paynter's face clouded. Gus knew how he felt about his

old captain. How he blamed the man for destroying his soul, for making him a killer. Maybe Blackburn had done those things, but Gus had seen his friend learn a thing or two since then, slowly unmaking what Blackburn had wrought. Paynter glared at the man for the space of several deep breaths before turning his attention to Gus.

"If you'd been van Zandt," he said, "what would you have done here?"

Gus surveyed the high ground again. "I'd have set a line of rifles on either side of the pass. I'd have waited until everyone moved into the gap. Then I'd have opened up on 'em. When they turned to run, I'd have chased them down from behind."

"Just what I woulda done. This shoulda been a trap. I don't like it."

Lucien let loose a laugh. "What's wrong with your head? We make it through the Hole-in-the-Wall without so much as a scratch and you are dissatisfied? Would you rather we'd all died?"

"I don't much care for unpredictability."

"Says the most unpredictable man I've ever encountered."

Paynter scowled. "Which is why I don't like it. Just like you don't much care for thievin' bastards."

Lucien's lips drew into a hard frown. "Are you calling me a thief?"

"Well, ain't ya?"

Gus prepared to intervene when Lucien flared his nostrils. However, he spun his horse north. "Come on. We still have a few hours of daylight, and van Zandt seems disinclined to wait for us."

Gus rode after Paynter as he pulled alongside Lucien. Lucien pinned Paynter with a glare. "What now? You want to set a picnic, maybe?"

Paynter refused the obvious bait. "We need to string out, ten yards between each horse. Bunchin' up makes us a fat target."

Lucien snorted. "You're too cautious. If we string out, then how can we fight?"

"Paynter's right," said Blackburn as he caught up. "For once. We gotta spread out in this broken country." He grinned at Paynter. "I'm pleased to see you remembered what I taught ya, back when."

Paynter drew his mare away in seeming disgust. "Gus, Beah Nooki. Take the rear guard. Watch our backs. Blackburn, you take front since I know you're eager to show off your trackin' skills. I'll be right behind you, locked and loaded. Just like you taught me."

Unease rippled across Blackburn's features before he repulsed it with a half grin. "Suit yourself. *Lieutenant.*"

They moved forward and the other riders settled into a line. Gus found Stacy and Maddie preparing to take a spot in the parade. "Maddie, you hang back with us. We'll cover you."

"All right."

"Stacy, you ride ahead of her and keep your eyes peeled."

Stacy smirked. "You the one givin' orders now, Augustus?"

"I am a sergeant. What's your rank?"

Her smirk spread into a smile. "I'm a by-God woman, which makes me a born general. But I'll allow your plan, just this once."

He returned the smile as she rode ahead, but it faded

as the gravity of the situation settled in. He should've tried harder to convince Stacy to remain in South Pass City. Not that it would've done any good.

━━━━━━━━

Gus settled into the rearmost position behind Beah Nooki. At least once every thirty strides of his horse, he swiveled in the saddle to study the ground they'd covered, looking for dust, reflected sunlight, forms on the horizon, movement of any kind. He only saw the latter two, and those in the form of curious antelope that watched the progression of horses and probably hoped they'd all leave. The line of thirteen riders and three packhorses made steady progress along the grassy plateau above the red wall before dipping into a vale and climbing an adjacent plateau. The cycle repeated twice more as the sun fell toward the horizon. Within the hour, they'd be traveling blind over treacherous ground.

When Blackburn's horse had crossed a dry creek bed and begun to climb from the third vale, the report of a rifle sent Gus's spine board-straight. Blackburn retreated, dove from his horse, and pressed against the lip of the waterless creek embankment. Paynter jumped in beside him as shots flew from attackers and attacked alike. One of Lucien's men tumbled from his horse and fell facedown in the vale. In a rush, the other riders flung themselves against the embankment, huddling beneath the shallow lip that spared them from bullets by inches. One by one, they began firing blindly above the embankment but otherwise remained pinned. Beah

Nooki, on the other hand, retreated and motioned to Gus to follow. When they'd circled away a hundred yards, the old man stopped to motion to the left.

"One behind those high rocks. The other that way." He swung his hand to the right.

Puffs of smoke from firing rifles confirmed the elder's observation. Two shooters on opposite ends of a rise, laying down cross fire. Why two? Gus scanned the trail at his back to find it still empty before peering at the trapped party. Realization struck. This wasn't an all-out assault. This was a delaying tactic meant to give the other outlaws more lead time. Gus faced Beah Nooki.

"If we backtrack and circle around from that last draw, you think we can come up on that one?" He pointed to the position occupied by the leftmost sniper.

"I do."

Without further conversation, Gus and Beah Nooki beat a retreat to the previous vale and followed the winding creek bed westward. After maybe a mile, they cut along the hip of the rise above the draw, following the curve of earth half-way between base and crest. The continued reports of sporadic gunfire led them back toward the fight. They crossed a second creek bed west of the gunfight to circle the adjacent rise. Twenty minutes had passed. Maybe more. Gus allowed himself a moment to fret about Stacy, Paynter, Emshoff… but dismissed it. Worry was a distraction. Distraction during battle was what got men killed. He put his head down and kept pushing his horse around the hill until Beah Nooki motioned for him to climb.

They dismounted below the crest of the rise and continued on foot. Upon crawling to the crest, a flash of red caught Gus's eye. A bandanna. Worn around the neck of a man behind a mound of rock firing into the valley below, maybe two hundred yards away. Beah Nooki patted Gus's carbine.

"Paynter says you shoot with eagle eyes. Show me."

Gus flipped up his sight and steadied his elbows. He drew a bead, exhaled slowly, and squeezed. The sniper spun in a circle and flopped to the grass. He squirmed for thirty seconds before falling still. Meanwhile, the second shooter's rifle had gone silent.

"He's runnin'," said Gus. He rose and loped to the crown of the hill to find a man on foot hurrying to mount a waiting horse at least four hundred yards distant. Gus stood tall, raised the carbine, and fired. He ejected the shell and fired again as the rider opened the distance. And again. The fourth shot nearly knocked the rider from his saddle, but the man hung on and disappeared from view. Gus spat in the dirt.

"Hellfire."

He looked up to find Beah Nooki at his side. The old man nodded approvingly and touched the corner of his eye. "Eagle eye."

"If you say so. Let's get the horses."

They hurried back to their waiting horses, mounted, and pressed them over the hill to the vale. In his mind's eye, Gus suffered horrible visions. Of Stacy lying in a pool of blood. Of Stacy dead in the creek bed. As he raced down the hill, he soon discovered her alive and well and nose to nose with that bastard Sweeney, their heated argument carrying across the distance.

"Paynter tried ta' tell you, didn't he! But no! You all had to do it your way, as if you knew squat about runnin' gun battles in the middle of nowhere!"

"I'll not have a half-breed woman call me into question! I ought to slap you down like the dog you are!"

"You'd like that, wouldn't ya? You ain't no kinda man, are ya?"

When Sweeney lashed her across the cheek with the back of his hand, Gus pressed his buckskin faster to save her. He needn't have bothered. A knife appeared in Stacy's hand, and she slashed it across Sweeney's chest, opening his shirt. Sweeney jumped back and fell to his backside. Lucien and Svoboda restrained him while Paynter captured Stacy and dragged her away from the point of attack. Gus leaped from his horse between Stacy and Sweeney, not knowing who to wrestle first. He turned to Stacy and folded her in his arms.

"Easy, easy. I got ya."

"He hit me," she said.

"I saw."

"And you went for me with a blade!" shouted Sweeney as he jerked away from Lucien. He held his hands to his boss. "I'm done. I'm done."

Lucien nodded. Sweeney retrieved his bowler from the creek bed and slapped off the dust. He flung Stacy a gaze of pure malice and lifted an index finger. "You're dead, girlie. Sooner or later."

She hocked up a retort, but Gus pressed a hand over her mouth and leaned into her ear. "Not now, Anastasia. Not now."

She bit back her words and nodded. He released her and tried to corral the chaos. "I took one down and winged the other. He got away, though." He pointed to the dead man, Thompson, lying a few feet from an equally expired pack-horse. "We should bury that one and unload the horse. The dead man on the hill left us a replacement."

Lucien stood over the fallen ranch hand, who stared at the sky as if deep in thought, and shook his head. "He was a decent fellow. What a shame. Who's got a spade?"

While Lucien and his men buried Thompson, Gus and Paynter transferred supplies to the dead outlaw's horse while the others fanned out to watch for signs of further ambush. After working in silence for a time, Gus leaned in to Paynter. "They're gonna kill you when this is over. And now maybe Stacy just for bein' Stacy. I can't allow that, you know."

Paynter gritted his jaw. "I know. I know. But we can only fight the battle in front of us. We'll fight that one later. When we do, I hope you unleash hell."

"That's my plan," said Gus. "I'm thinkin' Sweeney goes first."

CHAPTER THIRTY-NINE

Van Zandt's camp was just stirring in preparation for the day's travel when the dead man arrived. Rosalyn cocked her ear at the sound of urgently whispered calls from the trees west of camp. In an instant, ten outlaws had drawn weapons in response, prepared to shred the forest with a hail of lead.

"It's George," called the voice. "Hold fire. I'm alone."

Boggins stepped toward the approaching rider. "Where's Boots?"

"He ain't with me."

In the absence of light, the new arrival resolved into a shadowy creature, part horse, part man, with the man portion slumped deeply in the saddle. He half slid, half fell from the horse, losing a spur in the process. One of the other men propped him up and dragged him toward the feeble campfire that had been lit for coffee. Van Zandt met him there, looming like a column of the Parthenon. Rosalyn moved to better view the outlaw boss's face in the flickering firelight. He didn't seem pleased.

"Looks like you got shot."

"I did. And with all due respect," said George through a grunt of pain, "you ain't where you said you'd be. Been lookin' all night for you."

"Let's begin with that," said van Zandt. "You were supposed to *hold them* all night. What happened?"

George wheezed a wet cough, followed by a grunt of pain. "Can I sit?"

"By all means."

The wounded outlaw settled on a stone, bent nearly double while clutching his side. He peeked up at van Zandt, who continued to loom. "We set up the ambush, just like you said, Dutch. And they came in right where you said they would. We pinned 'em down right fast and got one or two at least."

Van Zandt rubbed his chin, his eyes hard as granite. "And yet here you are."

George dropped his head. "I don't know exactly what happened. Somebody broke loose from the creek or was maybe bringin' up the rear. Anyway, next thing I know, Boots goes down, and now I'm in the cross fire instead a' the other way around."

"So you ran."

George coughed again and groaned with pain. "No choice in the matter. Got pegged as I rode away. Don't know how they hit me from that distance. I rode to where you said you'd be and didn't find you. Been wandering the woods all night 'til I smelled fire smoke."

Van Zandt squatted before the wounded man, crossing his arms over his knees. "Look at me, George."

The man lifted his head, miserable. Van Zandt peered at him for the space of several seconds. In the gap, Rosalyn realized that every man in camp had frozen to watch the unfolding spectacle. Worse, the children were staring with saucer eyes, but she seemed rooted to the earth and unable to make them look away.

"You occupied the high ground," said van Zandt finally. "You had sufficient cover and enough ammunition to trap them for half a day and kill anyone who tried to advance. And yet you allowed one of them to slip up on you in what, half an hour, and unravel the entire plan. Do I assess the situation accurately?"

George dropped his eyes again. "I reckon."

"Were you followed?"

"Don't think so."

"The same way you didn't think anyone would come up on your blind side?"

George grunted with pain again. "I reckon that too."

Van Zandt shook his head. "You should have stayed, George, and done what you could. Instead, you ran, and now we must continue to press a hard march. Because of you."

George lifted his eyes. "I'm sorry, Dutch. Truly. But can I at least get some help? I been shot, right below my ribs."

The outlaw boss stood up. "I don't think so. You'll just slow us down. Wait here for Paynter to show up and finish the job I assigned you."

"They'll kill me for sure." George was practically weeping. "Don't care."

George struggled to his feet, angry resolve creeping into his features. "I won't do it. No, sir. And I will see to this gunshot."

A thin smile crawled across van Zandt's face. "Backbone.

I like it, George. I really do." He turned to his lieutenant. "Boggins."

"Boss?"

"Attend to the man's injury."

The subtle tenor of van Zandt's instructions broke the roots that had tied Rosalyn's feet to the soil. She spun to gather the children in a sweeping embrace. "Look away," she said urgently. "Cover your eyes."

The children were in various states of compliance when a shot rang out. Lisbet, who hadn't managed to look away, cried out in dismay. Rosalyn pulled the four children aside where they couldn't readily see the outlaw's body. Meanwhile, van Zandt lifted his voice to his men.

"You know the rules, boys. We don't slow down for the wounded, and we don't leave prisoners behind. You get shot, that's a problem. You get shot while being stupid, well, that's unforgivable. So endeavor not to get shot. Do you understand?"

A few mumbles sounded from the men.

"Louder," said van Zandt.

A chorus of "yes, sir" and "yes, Boss" rippled through the assembled party.

"That's better."

Rosalyn put a hand to Lisbet's cheek to turn her eyes away from the aftermath of the violence. As she peered into the children's tiny, distraught faces, fear for their safety nearly overcame her. If van Zandt would so cavalierly murder one of his loyal minions, what would he do to captive children when their value had evaporated? The concern must have been plain upon her face, for Lisbet's wide eyes narrowed. She put a hand to Rosalyn's cheek, much as Rosalyn had done to her.

"Don't worry, Miss Ashley," she said. "Mr. Paynter will make him pay for what he did. He will."

Rosalyn tried to force a smile but failed. Lisbet's expectations were likely too high, but she tried to humor the girl. "Perhaps he will."

"Of course he will. In the meantime, Sempronius."

This time, Rosalyn's frown did loosen. "Sempronius." The well of resolve within her began to rise, and she glanced over a shoulder. "Help the younger ones prepare to travel. I'll return in a moment."

She slipped away from the children to where the dead outlaw had fallen from his horse. After making sure van Zandt was turned away, she squatted to run her hand through the dirt until finding the object of her search. A spur. She stood quickly, hid the iron implement in a fold of her skirt, and headed back to the children. Lisbet eyed her carefully when she returned.

"What'd you get, Miss Ashley?"

"It doesn't matter."

Lisbet frowned with disappointment but thankfully didn't press. The less the girl knew about Rosalyn's intent to fashion the spur into a weapon, the better.

CHAPTER FORTY

AFTER LEAVING POOR THOMPSON BELOW DIRT AND THE unlucky packhorse for the coyotes, Jake's posse again picked up their quarry's trail and continued the hunt. The Bighorn Mountains ran roughly northward with a last-second curl to the west as if reaching to embrace distant Yellowstone. Given his angle of approach, van Zandt had two choices—follow the mountains along the forgiving eastern slopes toward the waiting Cheyenne or tackle the more treacherous western passage with a free run toward the Yellowstone country over the lands of the more amenable Crow. Van Zandt surprised Jake by choosing the former. The Cheyenne would certainly have an opinion about a train of outlaws showing up on their hunting grounds uninvited with the paint on the Treaty of Fort Laramie still wet.

As the posse trudged northward, Beah Nooki made estimates of the distance separating them from the pursued. As darkness fell on the second day after the ambush, he guessed maybe six hours. A half day. Too far to strike out in darkness without losing the trail. Although Jake considered employing the desperate move, reality reminded him once again why risky plans often produce disastrous results. Early on the third morning, they tracked the outlaw trail for perhaps an hour before coming upon the skeletal remains of Fort Phil Kearny. Officers from the fort had participated in Jake's mockery of a trial at Fort Bridger two years prior. Shortly afterward, the post had been abandoned in accordance with the Treaty of Fort Laramie. The Cheyenne celebrated the army's departure by putting the whole compound to the torch. As Jake surveyed the ruins, Beah Nooki chuckled beside him.

"Why so amused?" Jake asked.

Beah Nooki motioned to the devastation. "The Cheyenne called this place 'the hated post on Little Piney.' Up there"—he pointed away from the fort—"was where Crazy Horse led Lakota, Arapaho, and Cheyenne warriors against Fetterman."

Jake knew the story. The army was still sore over the vicious defeat, where Captain Fetterman and an entire troop of eighty-one had been killed to the man. "I remember hearing of it. The Fetterman Massacre."

The Shoshone elder cocked his head at Jake. "You call it a massacre. Crazy Horse called it 'the battle of one hundred slain.' If white soldiers had killed one hundred Lakota, Arapaho, and Cheyenne, the generals would have called it 'military victory.' Why is this different?"

Jake raised his eyebrows. Good question. "I suppose the word 'massacre' plays better for the newspapers, like insinuating maybe Crazy Horse cheated to win. Public opinion couldn't suffer the thought of the army losing to so-called uncivilized soldiers in a fair fight. Puts a big dent in the whole 'manifest destiny' claim, don't you think?"

Beah Nooki frowned in consideration. "Perhaps. I have much to learn about the way of the newspaper and your 'manifest destiny.' We will talk of it more another time. But not now."

He pointed to the ground ahead. Jake swung his attention to the outlaw trail to find it bending hard to the west, away from the remains of Fort Phil Kearny. He grunted surprise. If he had decided to pursue in darkness, he would've missed the turn and ended up facing the Cheyenne alone without ever catching up to van Zandt. Gus rode up beside him, similarly bewildered by the change of course.

"Now, why do you suppose they headed straight into the mountains? The snow's gonna be hip-deep in places."

Jake agreed. Though the spring had proven unusually warm, it took time for the hollows to clear of the snow that the peaks refused to surrender all summer. "Change of heart, maybe. If they make it across, though, they'll be in the Yellowstone country in three days. No law and a million places to hide."

"We have no alternative, then," said Lucien as he and Blackburn sailed past. "Where Rosalyn goes, there we go also."

"On at least that one topic," said Jake, "we are in fierce agreement."

The trail of the outlaws dove into the Bighorns on a direct line and was swallowed whole by a canyon that disgorged onto the plains a creek striving to become a proper river. The snowmelt tumbled through the canyon, white with froth and alarm. The carpet of pines occupying the lower slopes beckoned them forward, making promises they could not keep in the heights. By midday, drifts of snow began marking the passage of the pursued. However, the trail never meandered, never deviated, never backtracked from unforeseen obstacles but instead wove an intricate path that avoided long, steep climbs. Jake strongly suspected that one of van Zandt's men knew the mountains well and had traveled the same course before. Maybe that was the reason van Zandt had taken the harder route—to lose the pursuit like scraping mud from the sole of a boot. Jake vowed to remain sticky.

The posse moved deep into the Bighorns where air became thin and breathing more labored before night impaled them in place. Traveling in darkness across flat ground presented its hazards, but doing the same in mountain country was a sure recipe for sudden injury or death. Despite the air's chill, its stillness allowed for a passable if not comfortable sleep. Still, Jake found himself awake in the early morning hours counting the uncountable stars and wondering how near Rosalyn was. Speculating whether he could find her in the darkness if he rose and began walking. Knowing the foolishness of such a plan, he instead followed meteor trails across the vault of the night until the others began to stir.

"She's gonna be all right."

Jake turned his head to find Stacy watching him, her shadowy form propped on one elbow six feet away. "You can't know that."

"No. But you gotta hope that. Otherwise, what are we doin' here?"

"I suppose you're right."

"'Course I am. I've been tryin' to tell you that for two years." She laughed. "And I've been tryin' for that long to make you run after Rosalyn. I just never thought it'd go like this."

A grim smile stole over his face, and he rose from beneath his blanket. "We best be moving, then."

The second day proceeded much as the first had. Blackburn claimed they had closed the gap between them and the outlaws. Jake might not have believed him, but Jim nodded and Beah Nooki refused to disagree. As much as he reviled Blackburn and as wrong as the man had been on many important matters, Jake hoped that he was correct on this occasion. And as usual, no thoughts of hope went unrewarded with pain. As the sun moved toward the western reaches with promises of an early setting, a wall of clouds climbed over the peaks, slate gray with moisture.

A blast of wind announced the coming storm, followed by a spatter of cold rain. The riders pulled hats low and collars high as the temperature fell and the rain became sleet, unable to decide if snow should be its final form. Meanwhile, the drifts grew deeper, swallowing the horses nearly to their chests at times. The animals gamely plowed through the snow with vast expenditures of energy that would bring them to exhaustion by nightfall. The sleeting rain grew heavier and the wind more determined. Soon, every corner of Jake's physical and spiritual being was soaked to the bone, and his extremities were past numbness.

"We gotta hole up."

The announcement from Blackburn came as no surprise. The man was, above all, a survivor and, like a scorpion or a cockroach, hard to kill. Lucien appeared poised to disagree, but his frozen cheeks prevented him from saying more than "Fine."

Sweeney nearly whooped with relief and rode up with Blackburn to locate a suitable place to shelter. Emshoff appeared alongside Jake, just as bundled. Jake realized he was being watched.

"See here," said Emshoff. "In Europe, the armies that march through the cold gain the advantage. We could go on—you and I. We could find my Lisbet. She will certainly be suffering from the weather."

Similar thoughts had been echoing through Jake's head. Of turning the foul weather to his advantage. He worried about Rosalyn and the children. Were there blankets enough for them? Would van Zandt simply cast them aside when they froze beyond their ability to sit a horse? However, another increase in wind speed told him the truth. Nothing could travel in this weather—man, beast, or gods. Van Zandt would be forced to shelter or risk everyone, including himself.

"Thank you for believing that we can," he told Emshoff, "but we should take cover. We can't save anyone if we are frozen to the side of a mountain."

Emshoff looked away. "I hope you are right."

Jake hoped the same. He nudged the mare ahead to join the hunt for a place to shelter. They found it after maybe a quarter hour—a gash in the rock cut by a vacant stream, angled into the mountainside and lined with steep walls. Though the cold and a spray of rain persisted, the wind barely stirred in the cut. Within minutes, they'd stuffed twelve people and a herd of horses into the sacred citadel of relief. Under orders from Lucien and taunts from Sweeney, McPhail and Svoboda lurched back into the gale to find firewood.

"We should help those boys," said Gus.

Jake was thinking the same. As they left the shelter, Jake found Stacy at his elbow, pinning her hat to her head with one hand. "We got this," he said. "Go back."

"And let you two get lost? Not a chance."

As it happened, Stacy found a stand of pines tucked in an adjacent hollow. The five searchers snapped off low-hanging limbs and collected enough fallen timber from beneath the trees to fill up each set of arms and returned to the sheltering cut. Still, the sun set long before they were able to nurse two fires to life under Beah Nooki's expert guidance. In the meantime, Maddie, Jim, and Emshoff had been attending to the horses, stripping saddles and wringing out wet saddle blankets. Free of leather implements, the horses pressed together nose to tail for warmth. Jake envied them. He'd even huddle up with Blackburn if no other choice presented itself. As the traveling party clustered around the campfires in shared misery, it was Sweeney who asked the operable question.

"What now? Turn back?"

Lucien impaled the man with a hot glare. "Never. We move on."

Affront flared on Sweeney's face, but he corralled the emotion. "When would that be, Boss Man?"

Lucien seemed to ignore the sarcasm. "When the weather breaks."

"No," said Jake.

"Pardon?" Now it was Lucien's turn to express affront.

Jake poked the fire with a stick. "We go *before* the weather breaks. When it dies down enough for us to move. We have to make up ground, and the rain is washing out the trail." He swept his gaze around the adjacent circles. "If we let a little cold and rain keep us from saving Miss Ashley and the kids, then we're no better than cowards. So huddle up, best you can, and get some sleep."

Jake grabbed his damp blanket with the intention of taking his own advice. Emshoff settled beside him, again watching. Jake met his eyes.

"You're wonderin' what'll happen to the kids when we attack the outlaw camp."

Emshoff nodded. Jake pulled his blanket up higher.

"Me too."

Seemingly resigned, Emshoff rolled away and curled against the rock wall. Jake did the same while attempting to shove aside worry. But what could they do? The alternative was certain death for Rosalyn and the children. His mind turned to Beah Nooki's tale of determination. He had pursued his enemy against all odds, killed them, and recovered the girl he loved. Jake could afford to do no less and would accept no lesser outcome. Encouraged by the elder's long-ago success, Jake drifted off to sleep in the pattering rain.

CHAPTER FORTY-ONE

JAKE FOUND IT ODD THAT A MAN COULD SLEEP THROUGH a cacophony of noise but a sudden cessation of sound could bring him bolt upright from a dead sleep. Such was his reaction when the rain and droning wind outside the cut stopped. He rubbed his eyes to survey the sleeping camp, finding each person huddled against the rock for what little shelter it provided. He had no idea of the hour, but his numb senses told him that dawn remained far away. However, the calming of the storm had opened a window of opportunity to make up ground on van Zandt—assuming the outlaws didn't jump through the same window. He stood, rolled up his blanket, and nudged Emshoff with a toe.

"It's time," he said. Emshoff rose without a word and stirred the others while Jake began saddling horses. The rising sleepers joined him one by one. They exchanged few words, either from a general drowsy state or the brooding consideration of what lay ahead. Likely both. Sweeney, however, couldn't keep himself from jawing.

"This is an addle-headed plan, Paynter. I can't see three feet in front of me."

Jake grunted acknowledgment. "I agree. Walking through darkness is as dangerous as a gunfight. But it's the only plan we got. Me and Emshoff are committed to this course, hell or high water. The rest of you must decide if you're with us."

To punctuate the statement, Emshoff planted his hat on his head and began walking his horse from the cut. Beah Nooki already had his horse's tether in hand.

"The 'addle-headed' plan pleases me," he said before leaving the cut behind Emshoff. Jake retrieved the mare and followed. He resisted glancing back for some time. When he did, he saw a long line of horse-shaped shadows following behind him on the path above the rushing creek. He faced ahead again, suppressing a hard-won smile.

———————

For the next few hours, the posse followed the creek deeper into the mountains under the auspices of simple logic—all other routes meant climbing steep slopes. They doubted van Zandt would've done so under the best of conditions, but definitely not in the face of a howling assault of sleet and rain. Though the creek remained blanketed by darkness, its headlong rush toward the plains filled the narrow valley with a chaos of persistent noise, marking its nearness to the trail. Several times during the journey, a horse slipped and slid down the steep and muddy incline toward the creek, only to be pulled back by the herculean efforts of man and beast. After each such occurrence, Jake waited for Lucien to call a halt to wait for daylight. Each time they instead pressed onward, Jake reminded himself that Lucien was greedy, callous, and arrogant—but he was no coward.

And like Jake, he'd give anything to save Rosalyn, up to and including his life.

"Which way?"

Jake drew the mare alongside Emshoff. The clouds had cleared to reveal a patchwork of stars, throwing enough relief into the canyon to show a side stream joining the main creek from the right. Gaps between looming shadows indicated that both paths led toward possible escape routes. But which one did van Zandt's men follow? As he and Emshoff eyed the join in silence, the others bunched around him, whispering opinions. Jake found Maddie Dunbar standing off his shoulder in silence.

"What do you think, Maddie?"

She chuckled. "Why ask me? I'm no tracker."

"No, but you're smart. And treating wounded men on the battlefield has probably made you good at making life-and-death decisions."

"Is this life and death?"

"That's the way I see it."

She stood in silence for a moment, rocking forward and back. "I think they went right, along the lesser stream."

"Why do you think so?"

She shrugged. "Just a hunch."

"A hunch?" Blackburn laughed. "We gonna go right because some woman's got a hunch? Well, then. Why don't we just flip a coin? Or cast lots? Or perform some juju magic?"

Maddie turned slowly to face the man. "Mr. Blackburn. You are an expert tracker, or so I'm told. Which path would you choose? Left or right?"

Her question brought Blackburn into blessed silence. After several seconds, he said, "Right, dammit. I'd go right."

"Why?" said Maddie.

Blackburn grabbed his horse to begin following the joining stream. "I don't have to explain myself to anyone, least of all a pocket-sized Yankee woman."

Jake gave Maddie a squeeze of the shoulder and whispered, "If I'm shot and he's shot, promise you'll save me first."

She laughed. "I decided that long ago."

One by one, the posse formed a line along the smaller stream and followed the steady incline through another narrow valley, Blackburn in the lead. The clearing skies opened space for a concave moon to throw light on their path, making the way less treacherous than before. After maybe half an hour, Blackburn held his hand aloft to stop the train. Jake moved up beside him.

"Look there," said Blackburn. Jake lifted his eyes to find a hint of yellow sparkle on the hillside, barely distinct from the surrounding darkness. The reflection of a campfire against wet rock above. They'd found van Zandt. Jake stepped back along the train.

"Gus. Let's go have a look on foot. The rest of you stay here with the horses."

Emshoff grabbed Jake's arm. "Promise you won't start without me."

"I promise. I need you there when it begins."

Jake, Gus, and Blackburn trailed the stream toward the scatter of light, approaching from below. Within a few hundred yards, the forms of horses and a few people came into view. The camp was just beginning to stir. Jake motioned for a retreat. When they reached the others, Emshoff met him.

"What did you find?"

"Van Zandt's camp for sure. It was too dark to distinguish people. I saw no children, though, and no skirts." He clapped a hand on the back of the German's neck as the man's face fell. "That don't mean anything, though. Most of them were still sleepin'."

"We gotta hit 'em hard and now," Blackburn announced. "Charge up along the creek before they know what's comin'."

"That ain't no good," said Gus. "We wouldn't be able tell the kids from the outlaws. We need to slip past on the far side of the creek, high along the hillside, and wait for them to come to us in daylight. At least then we could see who we're shootin'."

Jake agreed with Gus's logic. He'd killed enough children for one lifetime, regardless of intent. Besides, van Zandt never set a camp without sentries, no matter how vulnerable it appeared. Blackburn had other thoughts.

"Hell, no. They'd see us for sure as we passed by. Then we'd be ducks on a pond. I say it's better we take our chances now."

Gus folded his arms. "I disagree."

Blackburn laughed derisively. "What does an ignorant boy from a cotton patch know about fighting in the mountains?"

"About as much as a rapist from the Texas swamps."

Blackburn lunged at Gus, and the two went down in a heap while hammering each other's ribs. Jake waded in to separate them. When he took a wayward blow to the jaw, the demons stirred. In a feat of fury, he yanked Blackburn from the earth and threw him at Lucien's feet. Blackburn rolled to his knees.

"That's the last time," said Blackburn. When he reached for his revolver, Lucien stooped to stay the killing hand.

"Not now, fool. A gunshot would tell them we're here sure as Gabriel blowing his golden horn." Lucien straightened and folded his arms. "However, I agree with Mr. Blackburn. We go now."

Jake was too busy caging the demons to offer reason. The momentum of the moment lurched forward before he could intercept it. Lucien's men mounted. Emshoff and Jim jumped astride their horses, clearly not wanting to be left behind.

Stacy shook her head at them. "Why must all men be so stupid?" However, she mounted her calico as Gus climbed aboard his buckskin. They were going to rush the camp whether Jake participated or not. He kicked the dirt.

"Well, hell."

If they were all going to die and get everyone they cared about killed, he should at least saddle up and lead the mayhem. After all, what was Death without his horse? He mounted the mare and nudged his way to the front with Blackburn before calling back to Maddie. "Maddie, stay to the rear and get your bag ready. Now, let's git."

Leading a horse through the mountains in near darkness was one thing. Riding one was another critter altogether. Jake should've known better, should've ordered an attack on foot. But he'd lost control of the strategy and would now pay the price. Unnerved by the unsteady footing, the horses began voicing their complaints. Within seconds of one particular vehement objection, shots from the expected sentries began pinging the rocks and soil ahead of them. Jake cursed, dove from the mare, and slapped her flank to send her downstream, hoping she wouldn't run all the way back to Missouri where he had inherited her. The others did the same, abandoning their mounts for cover. Bullets began crisscrossing between the posse's embedded position and the outlaw camp, with shouts rising from each.

"Don't fire without a target!" Jake shouted. "You'll shoot the kids!"

The sun chose that moment to announce its impending arrival as it began chasing stars from the sky with a slow sweep of purple. The growing light brought ever-increasing clarity to the gun battle. Van Zandt's men had taken cover behind stunted trees and scattered rocks along a bend of the creek, many prone, while Jake's posse leaned against the embankment of the hill behind whatever cover they could find. The distance—maybe a hundred and fifty yards—rendered most shooters inaccurate. Jake, however, was less interested in killing outlaws than in finding Rosalyn. He searched in vain from his position behind a vomit of rock for a minute, slowly coming to grips with her demise, when he spied her through the spray trees. She was crouching next to the hillside near the horses.

Even as he watched, one of the outlaws scrambled to Rosalyn, threw her to the ground, and put a gun to her head. Without making a conscious decision to do so, Jake exploded from cover, squeezed off a shot with his Henry that dropped the outlaw, and dove behind a shallow scrub of brush. Bullets chewed the earth around him. He lifted his head only to have a bullet whistle past his ear. He slapped the rocky earth and emitted a curse, trapped again like an animal in a pit. Condemned to his perilous position, Jake remained prone, unable even to shoot.

"Paynter!" shouted Emshoff. "I'm coming for you."

"No…"

A shot rang out. Jake craned his neck to find Emshoff stumbling back behind cover, clutching his hip.

"Stay put!" Jake shouted. "Don't nobody come for me. Keep shootin' at anything wearin' a hat."

As the exchange of gunfire continued, Jake began counting shots, reckoning the cadence of the battle. After a while, he determined that the outlaw fire had dissipated to a pair of rifles that kept up an alternating staccato of shots that pinned the pursuing party behind cover. They appeared to be taking advantage of the bend in the stream, with one to the far right against the rocky hillside and another farther back around the bend to the left, creating an efficient firing angle.

"Two left!" he shouted. "Can anybody lay eyes on 'em?"

"Yes." This from Lucien. "They're well protected, though, and have the superior sight line."

Jake frowned. Van Zandt had enacted the same strategy as before—using two men to pin down the posse while the rest opened up a lead. He craned his neck again. "Emshoff. You still with us?"

"Ya," came the reply. That single word carried with it a world of pain.

Jake redoubled his grip on the Henry, breathed in and out three times, and bolted for Emshoff 's position. Cross-fire bullets met his attempt, missing him by the width of good luck. He landed beside the German, breathing hard. "Let's take a look."

Emshoff pulled his hand away from the place below his pelvis where a bullet had entered. "It hit bone," he said.

"Okay. Maddie can help with that when the shooting stops. They gotta run out of bullets eventually. But for now, we need to stop the bleeding."

Jake pulled his bandanna and stuffed it into the wound to Emshoff 's grunts of discomfort. When the man settled back, his eyes were filled with pain. Jake suspected that the lion's share of it was not the bullet wound but the prospect that his daughter was slipping from his grasp. Jake gripped Emshoff 's hand.

"We're gonna get out from under this, and then we'll run 'em down and bring Lisbet home. There's no place on this cursed earth they can go to hide. Understand me?"

Emshoff nodded skeptically. "I understand."

"Good. Now rest."

Emshoff closed his eyes and clasped his hands at his belly, as if a dead man awaiting burial. Jake was glad to ease some of the man's anguish with promises of hope. He just wished he believed his own promises as much as everyone else seemed to.

CHAPTER FORTY-TWO

ROSALYN WAS PLOTTING TO KILL SOMEONE WHEN THE shooting started. After huddling with the children through the teeth of a windy, wet night, she grew tired of sleeping. The spur she'd taken from the dead outlaw dug into her hip, a reminder of her dire straits, crushing responsibility, and the mountains before her. She disentangled from the young ones and removed the spur from beneath her skirt. The iron implement had lost its rowel at some point and the former owner had not bothered to replace it. This left the long shank protruding from the band, dual extensions normally rounded at the end but growing progressively sharper through her efforts. She continued honing the shank against the flat rock beneath her while hoping the rush of the nearby stream would mask the sounds of her activity.

Already, a few of van Zandt's men were stirring. As Rosalyn continued the repetitive motion, she imagined how she might use the weapon. The shank was too short to penetrate deeply enough to stop a man. However, a sufficiently sharp edge could slice a throat, open a vein, slash an eye. She shivered involuntarily at the thought. How had a genteel young woman, the daughter of a United States senator, reached the point of deciding how best to kill a man in hand-to-hand combat? Her old friends from St. Louis would drop their jaws with shock and disgust if they knew how far she'd fallen.

However, Rosalyn's journey west had ripped her from that genteel reality to land in one far more visceral. In a reality where law was often but an unfulfilled, distant promise, where open warfare lay just beyond the horizon, where the land and weather and beasts conspired to consume the souls in their paths, it was the responsibility of every individual to stand and fight, even if that meant standing alone. This, then, was her solitary stand. When the fight came, she would stand for the children. She would stand for those who couldn't protect themselves, though her life might become forfeit. It was the way of the protector, the way of the martyr. Jake Paynter had taught her this, and she vowed to remain an apt pupil.

Her hand froze when a shot cracked from nearby.

"Riders! Riders!"

The sentry's call ignited the camp. Men leaped up as shots sounded from downstream and slugs pinged rocks and thudded into trees. She swept the children up the vale and shoved them into a hollow of rock.

"Remain here!" She grabbed Lisbet's chin. "Keep them down, no matter what! If I do not return, climb the hill and do not stop! Do you hear?"

"Yes, Miss Ashley."

Rosalyn crouched and hurried toward the strung line restraining the horses—with the intention of scattering them. The knot holding the line to a tree had become soaked with rain. Her fingers, which had warmed while she'd worked the spur, again grew numb. Nevertheless, she had nearly freed the knot when a blow to her back sent her sprawling. She rolled to find an outlaw looming over her.

"What the hell are you doing?" he shouted. She watched with disbelief as he leaned toward her with revolver barrel extended, aiming at her forehead. Her fingers wrapped around the spur in her pocket. Before she could act, though, the man lurched forward over her legs and fell still. She pushed frantically to free herself from the body but only did so when a second man yanked her loose. Van Zandt. He shoved her toward the children.

"Go to the children. If you stray from there again, I will kill them all, and you last."

He turned away without verifying her compliance with his order. However, Rosalyn knew the threat for what it was—a poison promise. She returned to the children, trembling.

"What is happening?" asked Herbie.

"Mr. Paynter is here," she said flatly.

"I knew it," said Lisbet. "Should we run now?"

"Not yet. Just stay down."

Within minutes, she regretted not running. Dutch's men managed to pin down the attackers in the narrow vale and began moving horses up the creek. The growing light revealed Dutch squatting before two wounded men not twenty feet from her location. One man was coughing up blood while the other pressed a hand to his belly as if attempting to hold in his intestines.

"You won't survive these wounds," he told them. "And we can't wait for you. I need you to relieve the snipers and hold this position for as long as you can."

The dying men exchanged miserable glances before one

peered at van Zandt. He was a young man with a distinctive hatchet face. "Why? Why should we do this? Why not ride on and see how far we get?"

Though Rosalyn prepared for the outlaw boss to simply shoot him dead, he instead dropped a hand on the wounded man's shoulder. "Because, Riesling, I know where your family lives." The tone was almost fatherly, if not for the vile threat beneath it. "If you perform your duty to my satisfaction, I'll make sure they receive a cut of the profits. If you abandon your post, I'll make sure they receive a cut of a different kind. So which will it be?"

The men again exchanged another glance before nodding. "We'll stay."

Van Zandt touched the brim of his hat and dipped his forehead. "Thank you, gentlemen. We owe you an enormous debt of gratitude. We will leave enough ammunition to last several hours. Maintain an alternating cadence of fire until you exhaust your cartridges or become unable to pull a trigger. Now, go relieve the snipers."

The men stumbled to their feet and did as van Zandt had instructed them. As Rosalyn watched them go, a cold wind knifed through her soul, colder than the gusts from the heights. Van Zandt seemed a man without conscience who moved men like chess pieces, sacrificing them without regret for the purpose of his greater good. She and the children were simply another rank of pawns to be thrown into the maw of conflict in the name of van Zandt's ultimate triumph. She wondered how a single unequipped woman from back east could stand in the face of such evil. Nevertheless, she continued to grip the spur in her numb fingers, steeling herself for what she must do.

CHAPTER FORTY-THREE

Over the course of three hours, two shooters became one, and then one became none. When several minutes elapsed after the last shot, Jake expelled a pent breath.

"Well, here goes."

Emshoff clutched Jake's arm. "Be careful."

"Too late for that."

He rose from behind the shallow cover with rifle planted against his shoulder and aimed at the source of the final shot. If a bullet tore through him, at least maybe he'd pick off the shooter to release the others. Nothing happened, though. He began pacing forward without lowering his weapon.

"Gus."

"Right behind you."

"Everyone else stay put while we reconnoiter."

They walked up the creek as if threading a path through a pride of sleeping lions, expecting that each step could be their last. However, no shots met them. Jake tossed his head to the right.

"Check that position. I'll go left."

While Gus trod carefully toward the location of one sniper, Jake converged on the other one farther up around the bend of the creek bed. He'd covered half the distance before freezing in his tracks. A rifle barrel protruded over a pile of rocks with the crown of a hat visible behind. Jake shifted aside, but neither the hat nor barrel moved so much as a hair's breadth. He maintained his aim while covering the remaining span. The closer he drew, the clearer it became that the shooter was dead. Jake stepped over the rocks, piled by defenders to form a firing position, and touched the body. It failed to flinch. He rolled the dead man over to find his entire torso sticky with drying blood that had exited from a wound to his lower abdomen. Jake scooped the pile of unspent cartridges into an adjacent leather bag and liberated the rifle from the corpse. The weapon was a Smith carbine, another refugee of the big war. He met Gus on the way back.

"My guy was dead. Gut shot and drained of blood."

Gus nodded. "The other took one in the lower ribs. Probably choked to death on his own blood. He still had ammunition."

"Mine too." Jake shook the leather bag and motioned to the carbine slung over his shoulder. "I'm pretty sure we didn't hit 'em after they pinned us down. What's your guess?"

Gus's natural smile drew into a hard frown. "I think van Zandt left 'em behind because they were dying and no good to him."

"That lines up with what Greely told us. About van Zandt leaving no prisoners and not haulin' those who'd slow his progress. Somehow, he convinced them to die by inches while pinning us down. That's some kind a' loyalty."

"Or some kind a' fear," said Gus.

"More likely."

The rest of the posse stood in the open, assembled for a report while Maddie inspected Emshoff's wound. Jake told them what they'd found.

"But we can move forward, right?" This question came from Lucien.

"As soon as we round up the horses."

Without a word, those standing spun away down the creek to retrieve the spooked animals. Jake could lay eyes on maybe eight or nine, which meant several had embarked on a longer retreat downstream. The mare, though, stood not twenty feet away, glaring at him with judging eyes, perhaps wondering why she kept pressing her into harm's way without so much as a by-your-leave. Jake didn't blame her. He wondered the same.

"Stay," he told her before leaning over Maddie's shoulder. She had Emshoff's pants pulled halfway down and was probing the bullet hole in his upper thigh with a finger. The German wore a permanent grimace but managed not to scream. Maddie glanced up at Jake.

"It's next to the hip socket, just above the femur. Don't think it broke anything. I can dig it out with forceps, given time to prepare and more time for Emshoff to wake up after he passes out."

Emshoff shoved her hand away and began pulling up his breeches. "No. Not now. We must continue."

"But, Mr. Emshoff…"

"No." He rocked to his knees, his face contorting, and struggled upright to stand one-legged. "We have lost hours. We cannot wait. When we stop for darkness, then you may operate."

"But you could die."

He cut pained eyes at Maddie. "If I cannot save my Lisbet, then I am better off dead."

Maddie peered up at Jake for support. He just shook his head and helped her stand. "If your little Lily was three hours westward in the hands of a vicious man, would you stop?"

She shook her head gently. "No. I wouldn't."

"Nor would any parent. Just keep an eye on Emshoff for now."

"I will."

———————

Sweeney and Svoboda were forced to backtrack nearly two miles to capture a runaway packhorse that seemed intent on returning to South Pass City. As a result, the posse lost another hour or more to van Zandt before resuming the chase. Beah Nooki and Blackburn took the lead, working in tandem to pick out the trail over rocky places with no mud or snow to indicate signs of passage. The partnership worked well as the pursuers began descending the far side of the Bighorns—until it didn't. With the sun already kissing the western horizon, the former raider and Shoshone elder came to an impasse atop an expanse of sedimentary rock wiped clear of mud and snow by wind and water. Jake rode up on the pair as they glared daggers at each other.

"What's the problem?"

Blackburn seemed eager to argue his case. "We lose the trail here. They went into one of those creeks." He pointed to indicate diverging streams, one on either side of the expanse.

"I say they took the one that turns north. The old man says it's the other."

Lucien and Sweeney had ridden up by that time. "What's your reasoning?" said Lucien.

Beah Nooki seemed content to cede the explanation, so Blackburn pressed his argument. "The northbound creek leads toward Montana, toward the Bozeman Trail. The other heads west toward Yellowstone."

"The Bozeman Trail?" said Lucien. "And on to the gold-fields of Helena and Butte?"

"Exactly."

"Then that's where van Zandt would go—to where the greatest money and opportunity lie. Yellowstone is empty wilderness with no fortune to be made." Without waiting for consensus, Lucien kicked his horse toward the northbound creek and the rest followed, drawn by sheer momentum.

Jake waited with Beah Nooki to bring up the end of the column. He frowned at the elder. "You think he's wrong."

"Yes."

"Are you certain?"

"Only a fool is certain. And I am no fool."

Jake heaved a sigh and fell in line. They covered maybe two more miles before darkness caught them. After setting camp, Jake, Stacy, and Jim helped Maddie attend to Emshoff while Gus and Beah Nooki kept an eye on Lucien's men. Maddie numbed Emshoff with a heavy dose of whiskey before plowing into his hip with bullet forceps every bit of ten inches long. As expected, the man howled under the hands of those who held him until he passed out from pain.

Maddie was forced to root around but eventually came away with the slug.

"It's out," she said. "He will be in considerable pain tomorrow. I don't know how he will sit a horse."

Jake shook his head. "He's experienced worse and survived. He'll find a way."

———————————

Two hours of travel the following morning proved Beah Nooki right. Though he, Blackburn, and Jim scoured the ground along both sides of the tumbling stream, they discovered no signs indicating the passage of horses. Lucien appeared determined to continue the course, but Jake finally reached his limit.

"Stop, for land's sake," he said after kicking the mare to the front of the column. "We're wasting time chasing ghosts. Van Zandt and his men went for Yellowstone, not Montana."

Lucien wheeled his horse to face Jake, perturbed. "Why are you so certain?"

Jake motioned to Beah Nooki as the old man rejoined the column. "Because he says so."

"That's not reason enough."

"It is for me."

Beah Nooki raised a hand to calm the brewing argument. Jake and Lucien gave him their attention until he lowered his hand. "When a man runs for his life," said the elder, "he forgets great plans. He remembers grand visions no more. He only knows escape, only survival. Van Zandt does not think of gold in Montana. He already has gold. He thinks of surviving to enjoy what he carries."

"Then what does that have to do with Yellowstone?" said Lucien.

Beah Nooki nodded, lending credence to the question. "Have you journeyed to Yellowstone?"

"No."

"I have, many times. In Yellowstone, the world broke itself into a thousand pieces and bleeds smoke and steam. Few white men enter there. Few can be tracked there. If I wished to be free of my enemies, to Yellowstone I would go."

Blackburn curled one lip. "He don't know what he's talkin' about, Mr. Ashley. We should continue north."

Lucien appeared ready to agree, but instead, he cocked his head at Blackburn. "Have you ever run for your life?"

Blackburn smiled. "Never. I'm always the one giving chase."

Lucien nodded. "Then we follow the old man. If he's right, we will find van Zandt. If he's wrong, I will kill him with my own hand."

Blackburn's smile turned sideways, and he exchanged a glance with Sweeney before facing Lucien again. "What if we all just turned back?"

"We all?" said Lucien as his brow drew down.

"Me, Sweeney, Svoboda, McPhail. We're just hired guns sent to get your sister, and I doubt she's on her way to the Yellowstone country. So way I see it, turning back is the prudent action." He cut his eyes at Jake and grinned. "Right, Paynter? You remember how to run away, don't ya?"

Under the spread of Blackburn's malevolent mirth, a vision

of memory washed through Jake like a caustic flood. Not of the day he had left Blackburn, for he harbored no regrets over that. No. For another day at Poison Springs, the darkest of them all. Regret for that one gnawed him to the bone.

"They're massing for another charge, and our ammunition boxes are empty."

Sergeant Rivers's casual observation failed to describe the dire peril in which the First Kansas had become mired. Confederate troops under General Cabell's command had blocked the path of their impromptu supply train, stretched out a mile along a deeply rutted road. When they'd turned to face the attack, troops under General Maxey had hit the column's flank, which was composed primarily of Jake's men. They had repulsed the first attack in minutes. The second assault had lasted an hour, with men falling on both sides like bloody rain, before First Kansas had managed to force another Confederate retreat. Now, a third attack loomed.

Jake scanned the road to either side, finding it littered with the dead and the dying. Though nearly numb from repetitive expenditure of fury, Jake strode along the road. "Take up what munitions you can from the fallen. We hold here with what we got left."

Sergeant Rivers scrambled to organize a line even as the third charge erupted across the expanse of field. The air filled with thunder and smoke as the clashing armies hurled death at one other, blood calling for blood. Jake emptied his Kerr into the advancing horde before attempting to reload. The shock of lead impacting his right thigh stole his support and drove him to the earth. As he rose, a second ball carved a path into his upper chest, flattening him. While he lay blinking at the sky in momentary confusion, hands grasped his arms and he was abruptly dragged away from the Confederate advance.

"Fall back! Fall back!"

He couldn't tell whose voice shouted the orders, but it carried the taint of restrained panic. When he slipped from the hands that gripped him, Jake rolled to find the empty Kerr still in his grip and Corporal Hammonds in his face.

"C'mon, Lieutenant! We gotta go!"

Jake rose to limp after the soldier as they abandoned the field. After a hundred yards, he became vaguely aware of Sergeant Rivers at his side, blood streaming from a head wound and welding his eyes shut. Jake threw an arm around Gus, and they carried each other into the relative safety of a line of trees. Only then did Jake turn to see what the god of war had wrought in his wake. The advancing enemy had swarmed the road and had begun to butcher the wounded.

No quarter given.

No prisoners.

No mercy.

Men with raised hands received bullets to the skull. Those who could not rise took bayonets to the chest, to the back, to the eye socket. The organized charge had descended into a frenzy of retribution and rage, bathed in the blood of defeated men. Jake rose to stand on his good leg and began stumbling toward the road, still grasping his empty revolver. A forest of hands pulled him back into the grove and again dragged him away from the mayhem.

"Retreat! Keep runnin'! Let's go!"

Jake's military brain knew this to be the right course of action. A languid retreat could turn a loss into a rout. His primal brain, though, had other plans. Save the wounded. Stop the carnage. Punish the guilty. Despite his best efforts, he found his weakening body being spirited farther and farther away from any opportunity to halt the unfolding slaughter.

He'd never felt so broken, body and soul, in his entire life.

Jake shook away the dark vision and inhaled a deep breath. He leveled a glare at Blackburn until the man blinked under its heat. Words rose from deep inside his chest, a restrained growl of unyielding pronouncement.

"Go back if you're afraid. I don't care. But there is no direction but forward for me."

He nudged the mare into motion and fell in behind Beah Nooki as the old man set a new course.

Blackburn shattered the silence in his wake. "You callin' me a coward?"

Jake ignored him.

"I ain't no coward, Paynter!"

Jake kept his eyes fixed on Beah Nooki ahead. Only after a half mile did he venture a glance over his shoulder to find the original party still intact and single file behind him. His eyes locked with Lucien's, and a flicker of agreement passed between them. Then Lucien turned his cheek as if regretting the brief overture. The gesture was enough to remind Jake of the truth. No matter the outcome of the mission, there would be a reckoning between Jake's people and Lucien's band, and both sides would suffer.

No quarter given.

No prisoners.

No mercy.

CHAPTER FORTY-FOUR

GUS BELIEVED THE OLD SAYING THAT PATIENCE IS A virtue. He had also figured correctly that Lucien Ashley was a less than virtuous man. True to his nature, Lucien began sowing doubt about the change of direction within hours as the posse failed to intercept meaningful horse tracks. Over the course of the day, his discontentment brewed, spewing a heady aroma of grandstanding and second-guessing. Sweeney, Blackburn, McPhail, and Svoboda all joined the chorus to curry favor with the boss or to revel in the failure of their rivals. As a result, the unified force broke into two camps for the night, each with their own campfire, coffee, and counsel.

"This ain't a good development," Gus said to Paynter.

His old friend stirred the fire. "Nope."

Stacy expelled a huff. "We've been foolin' ourselves thinkin' this so-called alliance could work. It's like makin' a treaty with a wildfire—all one-sided."

Gus waved a palm downward. "Not so loud. They'll hear you."

"I don't much care."

Paynter tapped her knee. "Probably best if we don't throw black powder on that wildfire. Be like young Jim there, and think the thoughts without saying the words."

Stacy cut her eyes at Jim. "So. Whatcha thinkin', Jim Jackson?"

Jim grinned. "About which a' them yahoos I'm gonna kill first if they pick a fight."

She laughed, too loud. "You're all right, kid."

"That's what my momma always said."

"That's a momma's job," said Maddie while patting the top of Jim's head. "If she won't love you, who will?"

Everyone chuckled before falling silent. Gus watched Emshoff at his side, reclining on the grass to keep his hip straight. "How you holdin' up?"

Emshoff winced as he shifted his injured hip. "I can still ride and I can still shoot. If I must run those men down on foot, I'll do that too. How much farther to Yellowstone?"

Beah Nooki, who'd remained characteristically quiet, raised a pair of fingers. "Two days. We must climb through the eastern door before walking into the land of healing waters."

"Healing water?" said Jim. He tried to laugh, but the warble of his voice betrayed disbelief.

"Hot water that springs from the earth. Steam, thick as clouds, but warm. Thunder from deep below the feet. Or as white men call it, geology."

"Geology?"

Beah Nooki chuckled. "I will explain later."

Gus smiled at the warmth around the campfire, of the log-fed kind and the human kind. It made him wonder about the other campfire perhaps a hundred feet away. What were they talking about? They seemed more a collection of predators than a band of soldiers, each fighting for his portion of the kill rather than for the man at his side. Gus wondered how long they could be counted on during the coming fight. Regardless, he knew one truth, pure and clear. The moment it became convenient to do so, Lucien and his men would turn from ally to adversary. When that happened, he'd kill them all without remorse. No man pities the snake that's biting him.

━━━━━━━

They rode hard the next day until evening before finding a trail. But not the right one. Beah Nooki and Blackburn studied the tracks while Gus tried not to loom over their shoulders.

"Unshod," said Blackburn. "Not van Zandt. Probably wild horses."

"Blackfeet," said Beah Nooki.

"How do you know?"

The old man swept his hand along the tracks through the muddy depression. "They ride in a tight line. Wild horses don't."

"Why Blackfeet?"

"A guess. The tracks turn north."

"The way we should've gone," groused Lucien. "Van Zandt will be in Montana by now while we chase wild geese to a fantasy realm."

"You tell 'em," said Sweeney. "We should never have taken instructions from an old man who lives in a tent. He's probably leading us into a trap. Mark my word."

"Is that what you're doin', *old man*?" asked Blackburn in a voice dripping mockery.

Gus's closely held anger broke through its wall of restraint. "Shut your trap, Blackburn. If you want to go north, then go the hell north." He extended a rigid arm. "It's thataway."

Blackburn shoved Gus hard to his backside. "Don't you be preachin' to me, boy. I know how to handle your kind just fine."

Before Gus could leap up and plant a fist in Blackburn's jaw, Paynter was off his mare and with his revolver pressed into the man's cheek. "Say that again, Ambrose. Just one more time."

Blackburn froze. Gus glanced around to find a dozen guns drawn. Another standoff. Blackburn slowly turned his head until the barrel touched the side of his nose. He peered coolly at Paynter and jerked a thumb at Gus.

"You willin' to die over him? Over that one?"

"As God is my witness," said Paynter. "I'm losing count of how many times Gus Rivers has saved my life. I owe him no less than mine in return."

Blackburn smiled and lifted his chin toward Stacy. Her shotgun was drawing a bead on his forehead. "But what about her? I see the way she follows Rivers around like a lost puppy, hopin' for a word from him so she might disagree."

Stacy laughed. "It ain't like that. I just don't like you. Never was fond of them who takes pleasure in killing."

While Blackburn glared at Stacy, Beah Nooki, who had remained mounted, slowly spun his mount toward the west. "I will go to Yellowstone to find the taken ones."

He rode away without another word, on a line for the

rising land to the west. Emshoff followed immediately. One by one, the others joined the exodus, even Blackburn, until only Gus, Paynter, and Lucien remained. Paynter finally holstered his weapon and went for his mare.

"I'm going to look for your sister."

Lucien clenched his fists. "You can never have her, Jake Paynter. She's too good for the likes of you."

"I know. Now, let's go find her."

The three of them saddled up in silence to join the line of horses crawling west toward an uncertain future.

———

With the bet now made and no chips remaining, the posse moved west for two days at an urgent but unsustainable pace. Gus rubbed down his horse each night, worried over the toll the hard journey was taking on the animal. All the horses appeared to be trending toward exhaustion, with the people faring not much better. But at least they had made good progress. After crossing high featureless plains, they had intercepted a substantial creek that poured out of the Yellowstone country in a rambling gush. A quick study of both sides found prints washed out by an overnight rain— tracks that might or might not belong to an outlaw gang. The morning of the third day, the walls of the world began rising around them, casting the creek in deep shadow beneath staggering bulwarks of weathered stone infused with swaths of stately pines and drifts of lingering snow.

The trail grew narrow, sometimes rising above the creek a

hundred feet or more, such that a single misstep would land horse and man broken in the creek bed far below. Vast herds of elk grazed the steep hillside below the walls, suspicious of the travelers but still lords of their alpine domain. Wolves lingered on the fringes of the herds, watching, waiting. Not unlike the posse in that way. Speckled trout crowded the pools of the creek in clouds of green and silver, just begging to be caught. Just when Gus thought he'd seen the roughest country, the way grew steeper, the walls taller and more forbidding. The thinning trees pressed against them, inundating the world with the sweet scent of their needles. If not for the urgency of the pursuit, Gus would've liked to set camp along the creek for the summer to hunt and fish.

The steep climb lasted several miles, forcing riders from their horses to mitigate the animals' burdens. Mud left by melting snow caked Gus's boots with residue, pulling him deeper into a shambling trudge. When he finally looked up from the trail after an hour, he found Beah Nooki and Paynter halted ahead. Beyond were a dozen men armed with lances and bows and seemingly ready for a fight. He pulled his Colt and moved forward.

"Who are they?"

"Mountain Crow," said Beah Nooki. "I will speak to them. Put your guns away."

When Paynter rocked forward behind the old man, Gus holstered his weapon and followed. The Crow eyed them warily but similarly kept their weapons in check. Beah Nooki raised a hand in greeting and began conversing with the Crow leader, a tall, broad man with a map of facial scars indicating a life of battle. The man listened briefly before flashing a wide smile at something Beah Nooki said. Gus liked him immediately. A kindred spirit. While the elders talked, two of the youngest Crow approached Gus, their eyes lit with curiosity, and touched his beard while whispering to each other. Gus raised his palm in greeting.

"Gus Rivers. Pleased to make your acquaintance."

The boys raised eyebrows at each other and retreated to their comrades. By that time, Beah Nooki had turned to Paynter and the newly arrived Lucien.

"What did they say?" asked Paynter. "Will they allow us to pass?"

Beah Nooki shrugged. "Depends. They want to know if we are with the other white men."

"The other white men?"

"The ones with a woman and four children."

Hope surged through Gus, and he saw the same relief on the faces of Paynter and Lucien.

"How long ago?" said Lucien.

"A half day."

"That long?"

"Yes."

Paynter shook his head. "Did you tell them we're chasing the others?"

"Yes. The Crow want to know what you will do when you catch them."

Paynter faced the Crow leader. "Tell them we will take our people back and kill as many as we must."

Beah Nooki repeated his words to the leader, likely in

the Crow language. The two men exchanged more words with one very recognizable phrase before the Crow leader grunted in seeming approval and spoke again. Beah Nooki translated. "He asked if you are able to do such a thing. I told him you are Niineeni' howouuyooniit. He offers a guide to help you."

Paynter's brow creased. "A guide?"

"Yes. The trail leads to a big lake. We must journey around it to go west. The outlaws chose a foolish path, but there is an easier way. The Crow will show us."

"How much time will that save us?"

Beah Nooki asked the Crow leader, who waved an arm along an arc in the sky. Beah Nooki grinned. "A half day."

Gus and Paynter caught the old man's smile, but Lucien remained grim-faced. "Do you trust these people? I thought they were your enemy."

Beah Nooki shook his head. "They raise an open hand to me instead of a war lance. These men are not my enemies. And the Mountain Crow never speak lies. They would rather die."

Lucien grunted and nodded. "Right, then. Tell him we accept the guide."

"With our thanks," added Paynter.

As the posse moved ahead again, Gus marveled at the idea of a people who never told lies. He was glad he had lived long enough to witness such a wonder.

CHAPTER FORTY-FIVE

THEIR GUIDE WAS CALLED PRETTY FACE, AND FOR GOOD reason. A jawline and cheekbones seemingly chiseled from granite gave way to deep dimples when he smiled, which seemed a frequent occurrence. The young man maintained an unending stream of chatter with Beah Nooki, who answered with short, punchy sentences—patient and amused but not fully engaged. This proved enough for Pretty Face. For a while, he even directed the conversation at Jake as if he understood a word of the Crow language. Jake just nodded and grinned from time to time until the young man refocused his attention on the Shoshone elder.

Here and there, Jake's Arapaho-given name appeared—Niineeni' howouuyooniit. *He Is Merciful.* No matter how often Jake heard the name, it surprised him anew, a disturbance in his gut that stirred a deep well of longing, pride, and shame—longing to live up to the name, pride that some perceived him that way, shame for the times he hadn't deserved such an honor.

Under Pretty Face's guidance, the posse followed a series of connected ridges of rock that funneled them efficiently toward the huge lake shining in the distance, its waters sparkling from the bright sun even though still at least two hours away. Around midafternoon, they met a solitary Crow hunter returning along the trail toward the summer village. As the man spoke to Pretty Face, Beah Nooki translated.

"He saw twenty white people on horses passing through rough country. Toward the lake."

"How long ago?"

Beah Nooki interrupted to ask the question. The man motioned to the sky, marking the sun's location when he saw them. The hair stood on the back of Jake's neck. *An hour ago.* Van Zandt and his captives were only one hour ahead. A ripple of enthusiasm passed through the collective group as they realized the implications of the hand motion.

"Give him our thanks. We need to move if we're to catch van Zandt tomorrow."

The posse moved onward with yet more urgency in its pace, descending toward flatter ground but still caught up in the thrall of mountainous country. They found the outlaw trail an hour later and tracked it until darkness swallowed the world, forcing them to stop for the night. Pretty Face shared their fire, seemingly content to study his hosts and smile—particularly at Stacy. Gus seemed to notice and pushed up next to her. She appeared to enjoy the attention—and Gus's jealousy. Jake shook his head. He'd never seen his old friend so undone, and he couldn't help but find it amusing. A conversation between Emshoff and Lucien drew his attention back to grimmer matters.

"Surely, they would not do such a thing," said Emshoff.

Lucien shook his head flatly. "They would. Those who kidnap children have no qualms about using them as shields."

"But if the children are harmed, van Zandt will lose all

leverage." Emshoff rubbed his chin. "I believe he will do as before. He will ride the children ahead of his men."

Lucien bobbed his head back and forth. "For their sake, and for Rosalyn's, I hope you are right. But I fear what they might do in the belly of a fight. I also fear our shots might find unintended targets."

Uncharacteristically buoyed by rising hope from recovering the outlaw track, Jake decided to wade in. "That's why we mustn't just rush in on 'em. We need to find them, then attack van Zandt's men when and where it suits us. We must set the terms of the battle." He motioned toward Beah Nooki. "You heard his story. Of how he waited for nightfall, killed his enemies, and saved Touches the Fire. We'll do as he did. We will save them all."

The fire on Jake's face faded to ash as he met Beah Nooki's leaden stare. After a stretching silence, the elder squinted toward the fire. "You do not understand."

"Don't understand what?"

The old man heaved a sigh. "It is true I entered my enemies' camp and killed them. But Touches the Fire was already dead by their hands. Perhaps she tried to run." He paused, breathing deeply with eyes a thousand miles distant. "I carried Touches the Fire home to her father, but her spirit had gone to the other side."

Jake's heart seized as if a claw had reached inside his chest to grind it slowly to dust. "I didn't know. I'm sorry."

Beah Nooki lifted his eyes to Jake. "You cannot save everyone, Paynter. You can only try. You bring home those you save and bury the rest. Then you live again, different from before."

The thought of living after losing Rosalyn or Lisbet seemed suddenly like scaling the sky to touch the moon—impossible. A hollow opening in Jake's gut drew him to his feet. "I'm calling it a night."

He left the subdued gathering, found his blanket, and rolled up in it. He stared at the stars for a long time, regretting never having told Rosalyn anything of importance, before sleep took him.

CHAPTER FORTY-SIX

THE NIGHT COULDN'T LAST LONG ENOUGH FOR STACY, knowing what the morrow would bring. And knowing what the morrow would bring, morning couldn't arrive soon enough. Indifferent to her anguished conflict, the sun began rising anyway to stir the posse into motion. They rode an hour before the golden orb cleared the peak behind them. When they passed the remains of the outlaw camp, embers still glowed red in the abandoned campfire. Van Zandt and his men were so close, she could almost smell them on the breeze—although it was probably just her imagination or the still-steaming droppings from the outlaw horses. Paynter pressed the pace harder, and nobody tried to disagree.

As the well-trodden Crow trail opened into a long, straight shot along the hip of a tree-shrouded ridge, she finally saw them. The line of outlaw horses moved along the trail ahead at a similar pace, maybe three hundred yards distant. The fact that she saw no children meant they were either dead or rode at the front of the column. While she was trying to determine which, Paynter pulled his mare to a halt.

"We'll give them some rope," he said to those behind him, "and then attack their camp after dark."

Lucien glared at Paynter for several seconds, gritting his jaw. "To hell with that."

He kicked his horse into a gallop toward the receding outlaws. Blackburn, Sweeney, Svoboda, and McPhail raced after him.

Paynter spat a curse. "He's gonna get the children killed."

He dug his heels into the mare's side and sped after Lucien's crew. A groan escaped Stacy as she realized the truth of what Paynter had said. There would be no element of surprise. No chance to free Rosalyn and the children without bullets flying. Lucien meant to finish the chase in short order, and Paynter seemed determined to make sure the ad hoc plan didn't end the way Beah Nooki's retrieval of Touches the Fire had. Gus burst past Stacy, followed by Jim and Emshoff. She drove her calico into the line behind Beah Nooki as Maddie pulled up the rear.

Only seconds passed before the outlaws noticed the pursuit and began banging shots over their shoulders. Lucien's men pressed ahead, firing wildly across the distance. One of van Zandt's men went limp in the saddle and slipped from his horse to tumble down the slope, a flesh-and-blood construct turned rag doll by a well-placed slug. A second man suffered the same fate, but not before killing McPhail with a parting shot. The body of Lucien's ranch hand cracked as it struck a pair of boulders beside the trail and became wedged in the crevice between them. Stacy leaned low and ducked her head as her horse flew past the broken corpse, trying not to think of how quickly he'd died. She hadn't even pulled her shotgun yet, knowing its lack of value until the fighting grew intimate. Suddenly, Beah Nooki's horse crowded against hers, and his hand gripped her shoulder. She sprang up in the saddle to find him slowing his mount.

"Take my horse!" He thrust the reins into her right hand and slid from the still-moving animal, hitting the ground at a dead run.

"Why?" she called while leaving him behind.

"I remember this place." He threw the shout over a shoulder as he attacked the mountain itself, climbing straight upward perpendicular to the trail. She craned her neck to watch with confusion until he disappeared into the trees.

———

Beah Nooki knew he was far too old for the maneuver he had undertaken. Nevertheless, he chewed up the steep hillside in staccato, knee-lifting strides, running harder than he had in years. Already, his wind was growing short and fire invaded his limbs. However, his heart remembered what it meant to fight, knowing that failure meant death. Sparkling recollections of Touches the Fire dogged him up the slope, reminding him of what could have been. What should have been. His tired old body screamed for him to stop, to fall to his knees in defeat, to let the young men carry the fight. But his heart willed him upward, whispering the vow he'd made sixty winters earlier after failing to save his love—that given another chance, he would retrieve the taken ones even if it killed him.

Just when his legs had become water, Beah Nooki broke across the top of the ridge and lurched down the far slope in bounding strides that brought jolting pain to every bone of his body. While navigating the trees, he caught a glimpse of the trail below as it wrapped the ridge like a snake coiled on itself. Then he spied a horse carrying two small figures. And one with a woman. He pulled his knife from its sheath, a blade taken from a slain enemy twenty years earlier, and leaped from the earth toward the passing outlaw. A war cry ripped from his throat as he descended like a swooping eagle.

The momentum of his jump blindsided the man and propelled him from his saddle. They fell together through space for a time until striking downslope, the outlaw's body breaking the fall. As one, they rolled downward in a clench while Beah Nooki tried to negotiate his knife into flesh but failed. When the tumble stopped, the outlaw threw him aside and reached for his sidearm. However, the man's holster had spun in the fall, forcing him to fumble behind his back. Beah Nooki launched himself through the narrow window of opportunity and plunged his knife into the outlaw's throat even as he swung the revolver around. A shot ran wild, harmless. Beah Nooki rode the dying man to the earth, twisting the knife as they collapsed. The outlaw tried to speak and, finding himself unable to do so, died.

Beah Nooki pushed himself to his feet, wobbling and inhaling deeply before exhaling with ragged heaves of his lungs. He studied the dead outlaw, who seemed surprised by his abrupt and brutal death. Beah Nooki raised his arms, emitted a sharp cry, and swept a hand toward the corpse.

"Your shame is greater than the mountains," he shouted in his native tongue. "For an old man has killed you today!"

He bit off the taunt as pain stabbed his gut in the form of battered ribs. He pressed against the tender spot and winced. No doubt broken. But he wasn't coughing blood, so it could have been worse. Clutching his side, he began climbing toward the trail. The thump of hooves above drove him behind a tree to watch what was coming.

The eruption of distant gunshots had alarmed Rosalyn initially. When shouts and returning gunfire arose among the ranks of van Zandt's men, she had quickly realized the truth. From her position with the children at the front of the line, she couldn't lay eyes on the shooters, but she knew it was him. Paynter had come. He hadn't given up on her.

"Treacle!" Van Zandt shouted to the man riding herd on Rosalyn. "Get the captives clear! We will catch up!"

Treacle slapped the flank of Rosalyn's horse. "You heard the boss! Git!"

Her horse bolted forward, nearly colliding with the pair carrying the children. Driven by panic, the startled horses raced ahead, threatening to dislodge their tiny riders in the dash. Only van Zandt's agreement to stop tying their hands allowed them to remain in the saddle. Rosalyn raced to keep pace, to offer a steadying hand if necessary. However, the trail proved too narrow. Instead, she prayed for a miracle. Her answer arrived in the form of a cry and a crash of underbrush at her back. She reined her mount to a stop and turned to find an empty horse behind her and a pair of bodies tumbling down the slope. The children's horses had drifted to a halt in the confusion. Rosalyn leaped from the saddle and yanked the children from their mounts two by two. She grabbed Lisbet by the shoulders.

"Take the others! Run up the hill into the trees and hide!"

"What about you?"

"Go! I will slow them down."

She propelled Lisbet up the slope and shooed the others after her. When she was certain they would follow her instructions, Rosalyn jumped astride her horse and rode toward the oncoming outlaws. Because the men were so intent on the devil at their back, they didn't see Rosalyn blocking the trail until nearly too late. The lead rider jerked his horse aside and spun from the saddle to land in a heap. In an instant, he was up and with a revolver aimed at Rosalyn's chest.

"Damn you, woman! I'll kill you for that."

A boot to the side of his head from another rider ended his threat. Rosalyn yanked her eyes from the place the gun had occupied to find a red-faced van Zandt. He flared his nostrils when spotting the empty saddles down the trail.

"Where are the children?"

"Gone where you will never find them. And if you stop to search, Paynter will finish all of you."

Van Zandt's eyes went cold. He twisted his upper lip and growled, never more reminiscent of a beast than in that moment. He grabbed her horse's bridle and spun the animal to face down the trail again.

"Ride," he said. "If I see your eyes, I will put a bullet between them."

She believed his threat but had accomplished her mission. She kicked her horse into motion and flew, studiously ignoring the trees above the trail where the children hid.

———————

Beah Nooki watched from cover as Rosalyn flew past, pursued closely by the outlaw boss and what remained of his men. When the last of the riders passed by, he hauled his broken body up the slope with grunts of pain and iron determination. Upon reaching the trail, he peered uphill into the trees to find four partially obscured faces regarding him with wide eyes. He motioned, palm up and toward himself in the white man's gesture.

"Come down."

The tallest child, a white-haired girl with a fierce countenance, emerged from hiding to peer at him. "Are you Paynter's friend?"

"Yes. And your father's friend. They are coming, just now."

She cut her eyes up the trail to find approaching horses. A smile split her face and she bounded down the hill to grab Beah Nooki's hand. "Are you a war chief?"

"Not anymore."

"Did you kill that horrible man, Treacle?"

"I did."

"Then you are still a war chief."

Beah Nooki chuckled until his fractured ribs made him stop. "Perhaps I am."

CHAPTER FORTY-SEVEN

JAKE RACED ALONG THE TRAIL IN THE CLUTCHES OF DARK visions. Burning cabins. Dying children. Sightless eyes. When the battle against van Zandt had been joined without his consent, he had thrown himself into the fray with the understanding that the rash action would probably hasten the death of the captives. He had passed Lucien's men one by one to lead the way, firing carefully at identifiable targets, hoping that a stray bullet wouldn't find a small body but fearing the worst. What met him on the trail, then, nearly threw him from the mare in surprise. Four children huddled together beside Beah Nooki while a pair of horses grazed the slope beside them, a pastoral scene if he'd ever seen one. Jake yanked the mare to a halt and kicked out of the saddle with a bushel of astonishment and a handful of pressing questions. He stared at Beah Nooki in disbelief.

"How'd you get here?"

For a moment, Jake expected talk of spirits, wind walkers, and good medicine. The old man simply pointed up the slope. "I crossed over on foot."

Lisbet released her hold on Beah Nooki's hand and ran toward Jake. In the past, he might've held out an arm to maintain the protective distance between him and anyone offering any form of affection. This time, he swept the little girl into his arms and drew her to his shoulder.

"You came!" she said into his ear. "I knew you would."

"I did come. And look." He turned to find Emshoff sliding from this horse and limping toward his daughter at a hobbled lope. She pushed out of Jake's arms and ran for her father.

"Papa! Papa! You came for me!"

He fell awkwardly to one knee and buried her in an unbreakable embrace. Tears wet his eyes. "Of course, *meine Liebe*. Always."

She pushed him away after a moment to study his leg. "You're hurt."

"I've been shot."

"Will you live?" Her voice trembled with anxiety.

"I will."

A broad smile lit her face. "You got shot! For me!" She embraced him again, fierce as any wild creature.

Jake felt a tug on his shirt and turned to find the boy, Herbie, staring up at him with shining eyes. He pointed to Beah Nooki. "He killed Treacle. Miss Ashley told us to hide. The bad men took her away."

The plainly stated information stirred a flood of emotion within Jake. Pride for the old man. Relief for the children. Fear for Rosalyn. And determination to chase van Zandt to the ends of the earth to bring her home. Alive. But what to do with the children? The remainder of the riders had dismounted and crowded around him, their eyes wide with the terror of the hunt, begging instruction. Indecision had never been a problem for Jake. Right or wrong, he would set his mind to a task and dog its heels until the deed was done. However, he stood frozen to the edge of a sharp knife—torn between ferreting the many to safety or plunging ahead after the one at the risk of all. It was Beah Nooki who noticed his plight, gray-hair that he was. He stepped to Jake and planted a hand on his shoulder.

"My ribs are broken. I am no use in the next fight. I will take the children to the Crow village. They will be safer there. Emshoff will ride with me." He dipped his chin at the German, who still held his daughter in a tight clench. Emshoff returned the nod.

"Thank you," said Jake. "My debt to you grows too large to repay."

The elder chuckled softly. "Not to worry. I will soon join my ancestors on the other side and see again Touches the Fire. Go get your woman. We will await your return at the village."

Jake briefly gripped Beah Nooki's wrist before facing the others. "I'm going after Miss Ashley. Any who wish to return with Beah Nooki and Emshoff are free to go, no hard feelings."

Nobody moved for the space of three heartbeats. Then Stacy punched his shoulder, probably leaving a bruise. "Gosh all Friday, Paynter! We're goin' with you."

"Damn right," said Gus.

"What are we waiting for?" said Lucien impatiently. "They grow farther away with every passing minute."

Jake nodded. "Right. Let's go."

As he climbed aboard the winded mare, Beah Nooki came alongside. "The outlaw runs toward a place of burning waters and steam. As white men call it, Colter's Hell."

"Are you sure?"

"That is the shortest path to the far country beyond these mountains. A half-day's ride from here."

"How do I get there?"

"Follow the outlaw, but beware the burning pools. I will sit with you again beside the fire, Niineeni' howouuyooniit."

Jake tried to smile but failed. "In this life or the next."

He kicked the mare into motion, determined to close the gap before van Zandt reached Beah Nooki's hellscape. Regret nagged him as he rode. He'd miss the old man in the battle to come, and he wondered how quickly the alliance would disintegrate without his adhering presence.

CHAPTER FORTY-EIGHT

DUTCH DROVE HIS MEN ALL AFTERNOON AND DEEP INTO dusk, riding them like he might a prized racehorse. He didn't stop until they lost the second horse where an overpowering scent of sulfur drifted on the breeze. The smell brought to Rosalyn's mind one of her few pleasant childhood memories—a family visit to Loutre Springs two days' travel from St. Louis. The odor of sulfur had permeated the air very near the springs, reminiscent of rotting food but not offsetting the joy of bathing in exquisitely hot water. The fact that no such springs were visible to the eye spoke to the extensive nature of thermal waters in the area.

"Shoot her," said van Zandt. Rosalyn jumped with a start and began to cover her face. However, van Zandt was motioning toward the downed horse. The fallen rider released his injured elbow, withdrew a sidearm, and freed the animal from the agony of a shattered foreleg. The outlaw boss paced for a moment before hurling a colorful curse into the night. He rounded on his men. "We camp here. Two rotations of sentries splitting the night. We ride at the first hint of dawn. If I catch a sentry sleeping, I will kill him."

Despite the threatening nature of van Zandt's orders, Rosalyn breathed a sigh of relief. The stop meant an end to risking their lives while plunging through rugged territory in near darkness. It also meant one less mile separating her from Paynter. However, without the children to shepherd, her mind had run wild throughout the course of the afternoon. Was she now more valuable to van Zandt or less? In helping her fellow captives escape, had she made herself more expendable? Regardless, the absence of children opened avenues of risk she had not considered before. Could she steal a horse and ride it into the perilous night? Or perhaps flee on foot? And if she did, could she find those who followed without getting lost, shot, or killed by the wilds? With these questions plaguing her, Rosalyn led the horse away from the mass of men and began unbuckling the saddle's girth. When she slipped beneath the horse's neck, she collided with a looming figure and jumped back with a swallowed shriek.

"Didn't mean to frighten you, ma'am." The voice was Greely's. "I thought to pull down the saddle for you."

Rosalyn wondered briefly if Greely possessed a darker motive for making the offer, but she dismissed it. He seemed the most fundamentally decent of van Zandt's lot, a bruised apple in a rotting barrel. "Thank you. I'd like that."

Greely lifted the saddle and blanket from the horse's withers and set them aside but lingered, fidgeting with a sleeve of his coat. He worked his jaw back and forth in silence.

"Do you have a question?" she asked finally.

Greely scratched his jaw and frowned. "Yep. About the marshal."

"Mr. Paynter?"

"Him. Yes."

"What's your question?"

Greely dropped his hand and leaned closer. "Now that he's got the young'uns, will he still follow us?"

Rosalyn considered her answer carefully. Did she want Greely at ease? Or instead on edge, intimidated, afraid? She gambled on which would have the greater effect on the man and chose the latter. "Yes, he will. Even if he must do so alone."

Her response produced the desired effect. Greely expelled a breath as the square of his shoulders eroded into the slump of impending defeat. "Is he always this dogged in his pursuit?"

"Always." Rosalyn decided to press her advantage. "I have witnessed him do so on more than one occasion. He never appears to consider the odds against him, only the object of his pursuit. Which now includes you."

"Then just who is this man, anyway, to do what he's done?" said van Zandt as he emerged from darkness behind Rosalyn. She spun to face him, her heart hammering. The outlaw boss grew a thin-lipped smile. "Is he, perhaps, a Greek hero fallen from Olympus and hell-bent on the completion of an impossible quest?"

"No." She stammered the word, betraying her dismay at what van Zandt had overheard. He was beyond intimidation, immune to fear. She tried to render the bold narrative benign. "He's just an ordinary man."

"Just an ordinary man, you say?" Van Zandt cocked his head to one side, regarding Rosalyn. "Ordinary men turn back from the gates of hell, unlike Paynter. What's drives him, do you suppose?"

Rosalyn should say no more, but she knew that silence might also betray the truth. She flipped a hand, feigning indifference. "I don't know. It seems in his nature to repair what others can't fix and to rescue those others can't save. Who can say?"

The hard lines of van Zandt's smile softened, widening the expression as his eyes bored through Rosalyn. "Oh my. I see so clearly now. Why he pursues with such vigor." Rosalyn shrank against the horse, clinging to its neck as van Zandt stepped closer. "It is not for the sake of the children. It is for you. Am I right?"

"I–I don't know what you mean…"

"Of course that's the reason. *You* are his impossible quest. *You* are his Helen of Troy, and he comes in fury like a thousand ships to save you. And you return his affection. You love that irredeemable killer, God knows why."

Rosalyn cursed herself for unwittingly contributing to van Zandt's insight. However, she hadn't even admitted to herself that what the outlaw claimed might be true. The startling thought of her affection for Paynter lent her strength. Resolve welled from the recesses of her flagging spirit to lift her from dismay. She stepped away from the horse, abandoning her cower to stand tall with folded arms.

"Is that so? Then you should let me go. If what you claim is true, Mr. Paynter will turn back when he retrieves me. Afterward, you may travel onward in peace without a hellhound snapping at your heels. Such an outcome would work to everyone's advantage."

Van Zandt hummed quietly and massaged his chin, apparently deep in thought. After a moment, he dropped his hand. "No."

"No?"

"As I said."

"Why? What if Paynter and his people catch up to you?"

He laughed. "We still outgun them, Miss Ashley. And I will still possess you as leverage in the fight. Surely, between your brother and Mr. Paynter, one of them would like to see you survive. And when they lower their hands, I will square the ledger."

"Square the ledger? What do you mean?"

He stepped nearer still until they nearly touched. She craned her neck upward, afraid that he might decide to end immediately any pretense of civility. His hot breath bathed her face with malice. "Your despicable brother betrayed me. Your marshal killed half my men and took from me a fortune. The damage to my reputation is irreparable—unless I am the last man standing. I intend to bury both of them before this journey ends."

She leaned away from van Zandt. "I see. And then you will turn me out, my value undone, to wallow in misery?"

He shook his head. "Oh no, my dear. That is not how this story ends. Your brother betrayed me, and you are the price he will pay. Before I kill Lucien, I want him to know you died for *his* misdeeds. His death will taste all the sweeter for the expression of anguished regret on his face."

Van Zandt spun and walked away to berate his men, leaving Rosalyn trembling—as much with anger as with fear. Her eyes drifted to Greely, who'd remained through the entire conversation. She strode over to him, pressing close, and stabbed a finger into his chest.

"You can't allow this to happen, sir." She kept her voice

to a harsh whisper. "To let him kill me for little more than entertainment. You seem a decent man, despite everything."

Greely stared with eyes wide in his angular face. "I–I don't agree with the boss on this. But…" He paused to expel a pent breath. "It's just that I ain't got no choice. I'm just one man. I'm not even a good man."

She frowned and held his averting eyes. "That is what Mr. Paynter claims about himself. That he is not a good man. But everything he does says otherwise. Men can change, Mr. Greely. It only requires making nobler decisions one opportunity at a time."

Greely stood in silence for a few seconds, his tall frame swaying. Then he abruptly touched the brim of his hat. "I can't. I'm sorry. Good evening, miss."

Greely's departure left Rosalyn bereft of potential allies and with fading hopes. If van Zandt made good on his threat, he'd never allow Paynter near enough to affect a rescue. He'd make certain she died while the marshal was helpless to change the outcome, if for nothing else than to hand the mythic Paynter a historic defeat. Her eyes began to well with tears, but she angrily swiped them away.

No.

She would not go quietly. If Paynter couldn't save her and if Lucien couldn't bargain for her, then she would by the Lord God rescue herself. After securing her horse and rolling out a pallet, Rosalyn retrieved the spur from its hiding place and began grinding the narrowing end to an even finer point.

CHAPTER FORTY-NINE

JAKE ONLY RECENTLY HAD BEGUN TO DISCERN THE unseen but powerful thread that binds human to human, woven over the course of shared experience and meetings of the minds. The connection to Gus had formed long before he'd become aware of it and, more recently, to Stacy, the Emshoffs, and Beah Nooki. However, no thread seemed more substantial yet more tenuous than the link to Rosalyn Ashley. Unlike the others, it pulled him relentlessly, like a persistent knot in his gut, liable to snap at any moment. As predawn propelled his dwindling posse into motion without visible evidence of a trail, the thread showed him the way. He could almost feel her presence, hear her laugh, smell her perfume—just an arm's reach away.

"You smell that?"

Stacy's question caught Jake blinking before he realized she was talking about the odor hanging in the light breeze. Sulfur, like a million spent matches. "I smell it."

"Colter's Hell?"

"No doubt."

"What is it exactly?"

"I don't know."

The posse, winnowed down to Jake, Gus, Stacy, Jim,

Lucien, Sweeney, Svoboda, and Blackburn, pressed through ever-thinning trees as darkness melted into twilight before giving birth to proper dawn. The growing ethereal light illuminated no evidence of the outlaw trail or of the source of the odor—at first. However, they soon found both in the last gasp of trees before what seemed to be a creek bordering an open space.

"They passed through here," said Jim as he slipped from his horse to touch hoofprints. "Several shod horses. Gotta be van Zandt."

"Headed which way?"

"Toward that big meadow."

When Jake lifted his eyes to view the hint of open space beyond the trees, he froze. Something about the sight struck him as odd. He nudged the mare forward, his eyes pinned on what lay beyond the woods. As he emerged into the open space, his jaw fell open. What greeted his eyes was not a meadow but a landscape sculpted from pure fantasy. The ground ran wildly in a chaotic blend of white and yellow earth. An azure pool of impossible blue exhaled steam like a pot of boiling coffee. Across the expanse, odd formations rose like the forgotten ruins of a fallen empire, terraced and steaming. Other pools bubbled in the distance, each of a different fantastical hue stolen from the leftovers of every rainbow in creation. Vapors danced on the creek at his feet, carried away from steaming pools to fade into obscurity. The forest clustered around the entire perimeter of an area at least a mile long and nearly as wide but dared not march into the fairyland expanse. However, an invasion of grass cutting

through the middle of the arid landscape gave host to a clus-
tering herd of buffalo—a hundred or more. As he stared
in fascination, the others rode up beside him with similar
stunned wonder.

"Holy Bejeezus!" whispered Jim at his side. At the sound
of the young man's exclamation, Jake yanked his eyes from
the otherworldly view toward the creek.

"They followed the bank, heading west," he said. "So we
follow too, single file."

Jake led as they hugged the creek for a short distance with
the fantasyland crouching off their collective left shoulders,
a kingdom of the unreal. The creek cut deep banks, every
bit of ten feet, that chewed along the edges of the hellscape.
It meandered west a short distance before whispering an
intention of curving to the right. *Sharply to the right.* As Jim
drifted up beside him, Jake's instincts began shouting for his
attention, but too late. A series of shots rang out from behind
the turn of the creek. Jim rocked back in his saddle and
slumped to the earth with a hole in his cheek. Jake rolled off
the mare and slapped her back into the woods before finding
cover behind a too-narrow pine.

"I told you to stay behind me," he whispered to Jim's
body. Another burden on his tally.

The others had dived into the trees, similarly bereft of
horses. Puffs of smoke flared from the embankment ahead
with each of the outlaw shots, while the acrid smell of smoke
from the posse's returning fire blended with the sulfuric air,
like sugar and spice gone to seed. The sound of a cry drew
Jake's attention to find Svoboda crumpling to the earth

behind a tree. The man thrashed for a few seconds before growing still.

"Fall back!" Jake called. He backed away, firing the Henry as fast as he could yank the lever, until stumbling over a body. He glanced beneath his legs to find Gus sprawled on the ground. Without thinking, he scrambled up to drag his old friend into deeper cover, his thoughts numb.

"Easy, easy, easy."

Gus's pained instruction wrenched Jake from his enveloping fog. "Gus. Where are you hit?"

"Just here." He pressed a hand against his chest just above his heart, and bright blood slipped between his fingers.

"Gus! Gus!" Stacy was at his side, grasping for him. The anguished twist of her face threatened to bring back the fog.

"I ain't dead yet, Anastasia Blue."

Lucien appeared beside them with Sweeney and Blackburn hanging over his shoulders. When Gus looked up at Jake, he still retained the spark. "What happened, Paynter?"

"Van Zandt's crew hid their horses and hit us from behind the creek bank. Jim's dead. Svoboda too."

Gus grimaced. "That's a shame."

"We need to retreat and reconsider," said Lucien. "Before we *all* get killed."

Stacy cut a curse in half before apparently reconsidering her disagreement. "He's right. We gotta help Gus."

The moment threatened to tear Jake down the middle. His oldest friend lay bleeding on the forest floor while van Zandt's men maintained a clear advantage. Meanwhile, his allies were fading from the fight. When Jake froze with inde-cision, Maddie shoved him aside.

"Pardon me, Marshal. I need to look."

With machine-like efficiency, she tore open Gus's shirt and began applying pressure to the wound. "Stacy. Fetch me the bullet forceps and gauze from my bag. I'll need a towel and my canteen as well. And a needle and sutures."

Maddie's certainty drew Jake again into the fight. He peered at Gus in wordless question. Gus narrowed his eyes and flared his nostrils.

"Go get Rosalyn. Kill all them sons a' bitches."

The words of war from his old brother-at-arms roused the darkness, which fed him detailed and oddly specific visions of the violence he would commit. Jake fished in his pockets for cartridges and began loading the Henry by feel while swiveling his gaze over the remaining members of his ill-fated expedition. "I'm going after them, and right now."

"You'll kill us all."

"You misunderstand," he growled. "I'm going alone. Stay put and stay alive until I need you."

As he began slipping away into the trees, Stacy called out, "How will we know when?"

"You'll know."

Jake loped away from the ambush, following the perime-ter of trees as it circled the island of lifeless, steaming earth. After minutes of running, he rounded the far side of the expanse. From his new vantage, he spied van Zandt's men perhaps four hundred yards distant, still pushed up against the bank of the creek with barrels raised to finish off their pursuers should they decide to attack. He paused to slow his breath while studying the enemy position. Rosalyn was not among them, nor was van Zandt. And horses were nowhere to be seen.

As Jake surveyed the battlefield, the earth began spewing a hissing column of water to his right, lifting a gushing spray a hundred feet into the brightening sky. Van Zandt's men craned their necks to watch the awesome display, pointing. Jake's mouth crawled into a tight line across his face and a primal growl escaped his throat. It was time to move. He checked his Kerr, chambered a cartridge in the Henry, and burst from the trees. The outlaws didn't notice him until he'd covered half the distance and come up behind the buffalo herd to launch a blast of his Henry. An old bull regarded him with alarm before turning away toward the creek. Jake cut loose two more shots before the balance of the herd veered away across the narrow swath of grass that pointed like an arrow toward the creek and the outlaws' entrenched position.

Jake became vaguely aware of bullets whistling past as his enemies tried to cut him down, but those stopped when the buffalo barreled through the creek to run over the top of rapidly scattering men. Jake sprinted in behind the massive creatures, death on two legs, and began to empty his rifle against those who hadn't been trampled, stomped, or gored. Men fell before him like summer wheat before the scythe, collapsing into unmoving heaps as he opened their skulls and chests with a steady barrage of .44-caliber slugs. When the Henry came up clicking, Jake flung it aside, pulled out his Kerr, and shot two more outlaws as they fled. His momentum carried him into the waist-deep creek to the figure of a floundering man. He gripped the outlaw's collar and yanked him from the water.

"Where?" His voice felt like gravel in his throat. "Where is van Zandt?"

The man's eyes were wide with fear as blood poured from his neck, measuring his life in minutes. "West. By the hot pools with the horses."

Jake dropped him back into the water to expire just as Lucien scrambled down the creek bank. Without so much as a blink, Lucien shot the outlaw in the head, hastening his inevitable demise.

"That's for Rosalyn, you miserable bastard."

Sweeney and Blackburn dodged stray buffalo and joined them at the edge of the creek. Blackburn whistled softly. "Sons a' Moses, Paynter. You killed 'em all. You're a right proper monster, just like I taught ya."

Jake's finger twitched on the Kerr as he considered adding Blackburn to the list of dead. He exhaled and pulled the finger away. "How's Gus?" It wasn't so much a question as a dare for anyone with enough courage to bring him bad tidings.

Lucien removed his hat to run a hand through his hair. "The woman is still working on him. It didn't look good."

Jake clenched his left fist until he was certain his fingers might break. "Van Zandt's up over this creek bank and to the west. He's got Rosalyn and maybe some help."

Lucien peered at Jake through eyes of primal desolation. "Are you going now?"

"I am."

"Let's do this, then."

As Lucien, Sweeney, and Blackburn scrambled up the bank with him to head west, it occurred to Jake that he had run clean out of allies. Every step forward would suck him deeper into a darkening realm of adversaries—those before him and those at his back. He only hoped to save Rosalyn before dying at the hands of his many enemies.

CHAPTER FIFTY

AFTER SPRINTING ACROSS THE SPUR OF GRASS RECENTLY vacated by the stampeding buffalo, Jake slowed to a loping trot and followed the creek again as it cut back on a westerly course. The ribbon of water bisected another wash of white landscape that scalloped away from the creek on both sides like a vast field of crushed and splintered bone, the horrific remains of an ancient Armageddon. Vapor rose from steaming pools of all hues—cherry red, amber yellow, burnt orange—and water spat from spigots of mineral and mud with stuttering sneezes that echoed on the breeze. Coppery red mineral flows spread toward the creek, bleeding dry the pale corpse of land with dramatic runs of brilliant color. His boots slid with every step as he crossed patches of algae clinging to the ethereal hellscape.

"Watch your step there," he called back.

His temporary allies didn't answer, which was just as well. Distraction could land them in a boiling pool. After a few hundred strides, Jake spied a gathering of horses at the far end of the wash where white faded to brown behind a hardy stand of trees. Halfway between him and the horses, four figures stood beside what appeared to be the largest pool he'd seen so far—maybe fifty feet across. One of the figures wore a dress and was held tightly by a man wearing a three-piece suit and holding a revolver at the ready. The two men flanking him carried rifles but only half aimed. Jake comprehended their stance and slowed to a walk.

"They ain't running," he told Lucien. "Van Zandt wants to negotiate."

Lucien grunted. "Seems so. Let's hear him out."

"But keep your hammers pulled back." Blackburn laughed. The man's high spirits reminded Jake how much his former mentor delighted in the prospect of a bloodletting. Of the wicked mark Blackburn had left on Jake's soul, soiling him for all time, shaping him into a relentless killer. He shook away the recall. Blackburn murdered for sport. In the years since leaving the corrupting man behind, Jake had turned his skills *against* Blackburn's ilk, mowing down those who would trample the helpless for gain, game, or glory. In his impossible grasp for redemption, it was the least he could do.

The gap closed until Rosalyn's expression became clear. Anguished relief. Fearful expectation. Jake and Lucien stopped side by side perhaps fifty feet from the outlaws. He recognized van Zandt's bodyguards—Boggins and Greely. The tall man who'd briefly been Jake's prisoner glared with hooded eyes, his rifle a half second from firing. They stood like four statues before the huge ocher-rimmed pool. Van Zandt smiled broadly, looking every bit the stage actor, and lifted his revolver barrel toward Rosalyn's head.

"Good of you to join us," he said. "But did you have to kill *all* my people?"

"They started it," said Jake.

"I was speaking to Mr. Ashley." He lifted his chin to Lucien. "You may approach. Any other course of action will end your sister's life."

"Don't do it!" shouted Rosalyn. "He won't…"

Van Zandt casually clipped her temple with his revolver. When her knees buckled, Jake lurched forward three steps but halted at the sight of Boggins's and Greely's rifles holding him in their aim. Lucien strode ahead. Van Zandt lifted Rosalyn back to her feet and shoved her toward Boggins.

"Mind her," he said, never allowing his eyes to drift from Lucien. "That's close enough, Ashley."

Lucien stopped. "Let's hear it."

"Hear what?"

"Your proposal."

"Indeed." Van Zandt winked at Boggins, who grinned in return. Van Zandt lifted his revolver to his shoulder, pointing it lazily toward the heavens as if an afterthought. "See here, Ashley. I would remind you of our initial agreement last year when we struck hands. Our pact required mutual aid and mutual trust. However, you saw fit to withdraw both—a most unwelcome unilateral decision."

"We never signed a contract, van Zandt. As a New York City attorney, you should have known better."

The twinkle vacated the outlaw's eyes and his smile flattened. "Funny you should mention New York City. A handshake is as good as a contract on the meaner streets of the five boroughs. Breaking such contracts is nothing short of pure betrayal. There are consequences for betrayal."

Jake began leaning forward, sensing what was coming.

Unlike Lucien. Rosalyn's brother laughed derisively. "Consequences? Like what?"

In a fluid motion, van Zandt brought his revolver forward and put a bullet into Lucien. "Like that."

Rosalyn cried out while Jake dashed forward to catch the staggering Lucien as he fell. Jake crumpled to his knees, and Lucien's head fell into his lap. Blood welled through Lucien's fingers as he clenched the middle of his abdomen.

"Oh God," whispered Lucien. Sweeney and Blackburn stepped up beside them, rifles pointed at the outlaws.

Van Zandt laughed casually. "Tell them to put aside their rifles or Miss Ashley gets a bullet from Mr. Boggins."

Lucien inhaled painfully. "Do as he says."

"But, sir..."

"Do it! Now!" He coughed blood down his chin.

A pair of rifles appeared on the whitewashed ground on either side of Jake, accompanied by muffled curses.

"Gentlemen. Step back if you will," said van Zandt. Sweeney and Blackburn complied, which Jake knew was a mistake. The outlaw shook his head at Lucien. "Now, for the balance of the consequences."

Lucien heaved in Jake's grip. "Don't you dare!"

"You know what's coming, then." Van Zandt grinned. "You will watch your sister die before you pass from this world. On with it, Mr. Boggins."

Boggins pressed the barrel of his rifle beneath Rosalyn's chin. Jake shifted his knees, knowing any action would come too late. As he reached for the Kerr at his hip, though, a sliver of metal appeared in Rosalyn's hand, and she ripped it upward across Boggins's neck. His rifle fell as he gripped his throat, spraying bright blood onto the starchy ground. Jake put a bullet between his eyes and charged van Zandt. When his Kerr clicked empty, Jake figured Greely would end him before he reached the outlaw boss. However, the angular man remained unmoving, his jaw set like stone, and let Jake come.

Van Zandt managed a wild shot before Jake hit him. The force of his momentum drove them headlong toward the boiling pool. The spent Kerr vaulted from his hand to disappear beneath steaming waters, the final baptism for the last residue of Jake's service to Blackburn's heinous mission. Van Zandt went for Jake's eyes, forcing him to roll away. A flying fist struck his jaw, spinning him further, followed by a pair of kicks to the ribs. Jake scrambled to his feet to wrench the revolver from van Zandt's hand even as the outlaw hammered the bridge of his nose and planted a knee in Jake's gut to stagger him backward again.

The demons howled inside, having found a worthy opponent.

As van Zandt descended on him, six and a half feet of villainous fury, Jake launched a fist into the man's neck with such force that the windpipe gave way. The outlaw stumbled to a halt and crossed his hands over a now dysfunctional throat. Jake grabbed him by the well-tailored lapels and rode him toward the ocher pool. Van Zandt only seemed to realize that he was destined for a stew pot before it was too late. Jake flung the man into the boiling muck, catching himself just short of a similar fate on the slick algae. He spun away to his feet to find Blackburn in possession of Rosalyn and Greely bleeding on the ground beneath a madly grinning Sweeney. The Philadelphia masher jerked his head up at Jake and approached with his rifle at the hip.

"I promised you'd pay for killing my boys last year. Now comes the reckoning."

Jake didn't flinch. There was no point. Sweeney would kill him, but Rosalyn was safe. However, Sweeney never pulled the trigger. Instead, a hole opened up in his gut, and he lurched face-first into the slime to slide to a stop against Jake's feet. Jake's eyes flicked upward to find Stacy running to his side, smoking shotgun in hand. She paused to spit on the back of Sweeney's head.

"Bastard."

Jake climbed to his feet, his head ringing hollowly in the aftermath of the fight. "How...how's Gus?"

She peered at him through the tops of her eyes. "Maddie's still workin' on him. She didn't need my help, so I came to do what I could."

He wrapped an arm around her head and pulled it to his chest. "And I'm glad you did, little sister."

She lent him support as they approached Lucien. Rosalyn struggled to join her dying brother, but Blackburn held her at bay with an amused smirk. "Hold still, honey," Blackburn said in her ear. "I got ya now."

Lucien lay flat on his back with blood shimmering down his chin to soak his shirt, a man in the throes of a too-slow death. Jake froze, however, when Lucien lifted his revolver to point it between his eyes. The man coughed a spatter of blood.

"I told you my sister is too good for you, Paynter."

Jake stood unmoving and gently pushed Stacy away from him. "I know she is."

The barrel of the revolver trembled as Lucien pulled back the hammer.

"I'm not even your sister!" Rosalyn's shouted claim drew Lucien's eyes. Then quieter, she said, "Father took me from my real parents. He never told you. You don't have to do this."

Lucien's eyes softened. "I knew about that since the day they brought you home." He coughed again, expelling a darker shade of blood mixed with bile.

Rosalyn pulled away from Blackburn until he held her casually by one arm. "But…but why did you never…"

"I vowed then to take care of you, Rosalyn. To protect you from terrible men. And that's what I intend to do now. One last time."

Jake exhaled, preparing himself to receive a bullet, almost relieved. He flinched, though, when Lucien swung the revolver toward Rosalyn. His entire existence collapsed into a pinpoint of powerless distress. Lucien pulled the trigger and Rosalyn jumped—but didn't fall. Blackburn blinked twice before teetering onto his back, the fresh hole in his forehead condemning him to lie dead on the stark white ground. Rosalyn didn't even look back at the expired body as she rushed to her brother's side. Jake knelt on the other side of Lucien, still stunned. He shook his head in disbelief.

"Lucien. Why'd you do that?"

Lucien's blood-soaked hand rose up to claw the front of Jake's shirt. "Because, despite my disdain for you, I know you will care for Rosalyn as no one else could." He pulled Jake near until their noses nearly touched. "Promise me, Jake Paynter. Promise me you'll do that."

"You have my word."

Rosalyn laid her tearstained cheek against her brother's, sobbing. "I'm sorry, Lucien."

He smiled softly at her. "For what?"

"For always disappointing you."

Lucien closed his eyes. "Sister. I've never been prouder."

The last of his breath leaked away with those final words, but the smile remained for a few seconds like a wisp of dandelion before scattering on the breeze. As Rosalyn wept over her fallen brother, Jake laid a hand gently on her back and sat with her in the ashes of her grief. He didn't know what else to do.

CHAPTER FIFTY-ONE

JAKE HAD NEVER BEEN PARTICULARLY PROFICIENT AT meeting new acquaintances. Farewells, on the other hand, had become second nature for him, like breathing. As he walked up on Gus lying prone on the forest floor, though, Jake's breath caught in his chest. Gus had been his only friend for most of eight years, even when Jake had been the most unlikable and unapproachable. Especially then, in fact. Gus had been the rock he'd clung to repeatedly when darkness had threatened to sweep him into oblivion. He removed his hat and covered the final steps to where Maddie leaned over Gus. His old friend's eyes were closed, his pose almost peaceful.

"Is he…"

"I ain't dead, if that's what you're gonna ask."

At the sound of Gus's mocking tone, Jake exhaled and dropped to a knee. Stacy knelt before Gus and seized one of his hands. Her face grew flush as she fought back tears.

Gus opened his eyes and chuckled before wheezing. "Don't do that," he said. "It might kill me."

"What's his prognosis?" asked Rosalyn. She had remained standing across from Jake.

Maddie lifted a palm. "The bullet lodged high in his chest but missed his heart. I retrieved it and sutured the wound."

"So will he…" She left the question hanging.

"Live? Probably, as long as he doesn't catch a bad fever. He'll need to stay out of trouble for a while, regardless."

Stacy laid her head against Gus's chest as if listening for a heartbeat. "I won't let him die. We got too much unfinished business between us."

Gus coughed again with a grimace. It gave way to a smirk. "Sounds interestin'. Think I'll stick around for that."

Jake impulsively placed a hand against the side of his friend's head. "You good?"

"Not really. I got a hole in my chest. But I've been shot a few times before, so it ain't nothin' new."

"You gotta stop getting shot, Gus."

"Then I gotta stop chasing after you."

Jake cut short a laugh, almost euphoric in his relief. Gus wasn't out of the woods, but he'd made clear his intention to fight. Nobody Jake had ever met fought harder than Gus Rivers. He cut his eyes to Rosalyn to find her watching him, her gaze inscrutable, a mystery. Puffy eyes spoke of her spent grief. She opened her mouth, hesitated, and then asked the question she seemingly didn't want answered.

"What next, Mr. Paynter?"

What next indeed? For his entire adult life, "next" had been a vague notion as day carried him into day and year swept into year. "Next" was nothing but a faint hope for a good tomorrow while expecting worse. The defeat of van Zandt and the demise of his closely held enemies left him nearly adrift. Nearly, but not quite.

"Gus. If we give you a few days to rest here, do you think you can ride?"

"Can a catfish drink water? 'Course I'll be able to ride, but real slow-like."

"All right. I'll bury the dead here first. Then we'll wait three or four days and ride for the Crow village to collect the others and bury anyone we find along the way."

"That's a lot a' diggin'," said Gus. "And I won't be of help."

"Leave it to me, friend. Leave it to me." Jake settled his hat back on his head. "We'll rest a while longer with the Crow if they are so inclined, and then cut over Togwotee Pass to the Wind River country. That's what we'll do."

He became acutely aware that Rosalyn was still watching him, grim-faced. His plan probably didn't sufficiently answer her question. He closed the distance between them, just short of reaching for her. His hands didn't seem to know what to do, so they just clenched and unclenched of their own accord.

"After that..." He paused to consider the blank sky beyond the trees. "Well. It's like this. Not long after I joined the Tenth, some years ago now, I received a letter from an attorney down in Austin. It outlined provisions my grandmother had made for me."

"The grandmother who raised you as a boy?" she whispered.

"The same. Anyway, it turns out her family was something important in Britain. Gentry, I think he called them. People of money. When she married my grandfather and came to America, she brought a dowry with her. Before she died, she arranged for the money to be left to me when I turned eighteen. It's stashed in a bank account in Chicago. With the war on, the news didn't catch up to me for a few years."

"Chicago," said Gus. "That's where you were headed when I tracked you down in Missouri two years ago."

"Yep."

"You were goin' after the money."

"I was."

"I'm doubly sorry I stopped you, then."

Jake smiled at Gus and then Stacy before locking eyes with Rosalyn. "I'm not."

Rosalyn flushed and looked away. "What will you do with the money, then?"

It was a fine question, one that brought a low chuckle from his throat. "First, I'll give away this damnable badge to Gus and Stacy."

"I don't want to be marshal," said Gus.

Stacy nudged him and grinned sharply. "Who said he wanted you to be marshal? I figured he meant me, with you as my deputy."

"Tell you what." Gus coughed a laugh. "We'll flip for it. Loser gets to be marshal. Winner gets the deputy's badge."

"I don't want the marshal's badge either."

"But you said…"

"A joke, Gus. You still gotta sense of humor, right? We'll let Francisco Aguilar keep it and find somethin' better to do."

Gus grinned broadly. "Deal."

Jake shook his head and turned his attention to Rosalyn. She was watching him, her face a mask of uncertainty. Her lips parted in silence briefly before she could muster words. "If you are no longer a marshal, what will you do?"

Jake knew what she was really asking. Would he stay?

Maybe put down roots? Or would he bolt? Would he cross over the next horizon as he'd done for a decade, never looking back? He knew the answer, though. He'd known for a while.

"Think I'll start a ranch," he said. "I hear the Wyoming Territory is prime for horse and cattle."

She held his gaze and bit her lip. "Alone?"

It was the question Jake had been dreading. He knew the right answer but struggled to find the words. "There were times, when we talked, you know, that I thought maybe…" Eloquence failed him, and he averted his eyes. "Look, Miss Ashley. I ain't no good. Your brother was right about that."

Rosalyn rocked forward and grabbed both his hands, startling him. He willed himself to remain in place.

"Look at me, Jacob Paynter."

He found her face and held it in his gaze. Her expression was earnest, as if she guarded all the secrets of the universe in her head. She dipped her chin.

"We may have come from a far distance, you and I, but always toward each other to meet in the vast middle. Me running from my gentle roots to discover what I really am. You running from the monster you see in the mirror but haven't been for a very long time. We both left all that behind when we came west. Out here, all is forgotten. The world is new. We are new. Re-created in better images than we were given, free to discover what wondrous creatures we can yet become."

Jake stared at her for a few seconds before realizing that he believed her. Every word of it. The revelation must have bled through his expression, his very mannerism, because Rosalyn cocked her head wistfully. A smile crept slowly across Jake's face. "You ever been to Chicago?"

Rosalyn's wistfulness faded into wide-eyed wonder. "No. Why?"

"Would you like to see it?"

Her smile grew to match his. "I believe I would."

"All right." He released her hands reluctantly. "Then I need to dig some holes."

He turned away to search for the scattered horses. One of them carried a spade, and he had more than a dozen dead men to bury before moving on to what came next. If he was lucky, he'd bury a bit of the old Paynter while he was at it. After a lifetime of soul-sapping guilt, he'd finally managed to learn one solid truth. A man mired in the past was destined to drown in it eventually. For the first time in his life, then, Jake Paynter found himself no longer running away but running toward.

Do you love historical westerns? Discover more action and adventure in *USA Today* bestselling author Nik James's Caleb Marlowe series

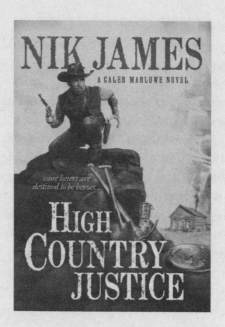

Available now from Sourcebooks Casablanca

CHAPTER ONE

Elkhorn, Colorado, May 1878

CALEB MARLOWE WATCHED THE EMBERS OF THE FIRE throw flickering shadows on his new cabin walls. Outside, a muffled sound drew his attention, and Caleb focused on the door at the same time Bear lifted his great head. The thick, golden fur on the neck of the dog rose, and the low growl told Caleb that his own instincts were not wrong.

In an instant, both man and dog were on their feet.

Caleb signaled for the big, yellow animal to stay and reached for his Winchester '73. The .44-caliber rifle was leaning, dark and deadly, against the new pine boards he'd nailed up not two hours before. If he'd had time to hang the door, whoever was out there might have gotten the drop on him.

Moving with the stealth of a cougar, Caleb crossed quickly to one side of the door and looked out, holding his gun. The broad fields gleamed like undulating waves of silver under the May moon between the wooded ridges that formed the east and west boundaries of his property. Down the slope from the cabin, by a bend in the shallow river, he could see the newly purchased cattle settled for the night. From this distance, the herd looked black as a pool of dried blood in the wide meadow.

He could see nothing amiss there. Nice and quiet. No wolves or mountain lions harrying the herd and stirring them up. The only sound was a pair of hunting owls hooting at each other in the distant pines. Still, something was wrong. His instincts were rarely off, and he had a prickling feeling on the back of his neck. He levered a cartridge into the chamber.

Caleb slipped outside into the cool, mountain air and moved silently along the wall of the nearly finished cabin. Bear moved ahead of him and disappeared into the shadow cast by the building blocking moonlight. The crisp breeze was light and coming out of the north, from the direction of Elkhorn, three miles away as the crow flies.

When Caleb peered around the corner, he was aware of the large, yellow smudge of dog standing alert at his feet. Bear was focused on the dark edge of the woods a couple hundred yards beyond Caleb's wagon and the staked areas where the barn, corral, and Henry's house would eventually set. Bear growled low again.

Caleb smelled them before he saw them. Six riders came out of the tall pines, moving slowly along the eastern edge of the meadow, and he felt six pairs of eyes fixed on the cabin.

He had no doubt as to their intentions. They were rustlers, and they were after his cattle. But this was his property—his and Henry's—and that included those steers.

If they'd been smart enough to come down from Elkhorn on the southwestern road, these dolts could have forded the river far below here and had a damn good chance of making off with the herd. It must have surprised the shit out of them, seeing the cabin.

"Bad luck, fellas," Caleb murmured, assessing the situation.

He needed to get a little closer to these snakes. Standing a couple of inches over six feet, with broad shoulders and solid muscles, he was hardly an insignificant target, even at night. His wagon was fifty yards nearer to them, but with this moon, they'd spot him and come at him before he got half-way there. It'd take a damn good shot on horseback from a hundred and fifty yards, but they could close that distance in a hurry. And Caleb would have no cover at all. Beyond the wagon, there were half a dozen stone outcroppings, but nothing else to stop a bullet.

Just then, the cattle must have smelled them too, because they started grunting and moving restlessly. That was all the distraction he needed.

Staying low, Caleb ran hard, angling his path to get the wagon between him and the rustlers as quickly as he could.

He nearly made it.

The flash from the lead rider's rifle was accompanied by the crack of wood and an explosion of splinters above the sideboard of the wagon. A second shot thudded dead into the ground a few yards to Caleb's right. Immediately, with shouts and guns blazing, they were all coming hard.

If Caleb had entertained even a fleeting thought that this might have been a neighborly visit—which he hadn't—the idea was shot to hell now.

He raised his Winchester and fired, quickly levering and firing again. The second shot caught the leader. He jerked back off his saddle and dropped to the ground like a stone.

Caleb wasn't watching. As he turned his sights on the next rider, a bullet ripped a hot line across Caleb's gut just a few inches above his belt, spinning him back a step. Big mistake. Now he was really angry.

They were not a hundred yards away, close enough that he could see the moon lighting their features.

And close enough that he wouldn't miss.

Setting his feet, he put a bullet square in the face of the nearest man, taking off the rider's hat and half his head.

That was enough to give the other four second thoughts. Reining in sharp, two swung out of their saddles and dove for cover behind a pair of boulders. The other two turned tail, digging in their spurs and riding hard for the pines.

Shots rang out from the stone outcroppings, and the sound of bullets whizzing through the air and thudding into the ground around him sent Caleb scurrying toward the wagon.

Both of the rustlers stopped firing almost simultaneously, and Caleb knew they were loading fifteen more into their rifles. The man on the right seemed to be the better marksman. His bullets had been doing serious damage to the wagon.

Going down on one knee between the front and back axles, Caleb slid the barrel of his rifle across the wagon's reach. Aiming for the spot on the edge of the boulder where he'd last seen the better shooter positioned, he waited.

He didn't have long to wait. The gleaming barrel of the rustler's rifle appeared, immediately followed by a hatless head. Caleb squeezed the trigger of the weapon Buffalo Bill himself called the *Boss*. The shooter's head disappeared, and the rifle dropped into the grass beside the boulder.

Before Caleb could swing his gun around, the other fellow gave up the cover of his boulder and started running for the pines, stopping only once to turn and fire a round. That was his final mistake. A flash of golden fur streaked across the field, and Bear's teeth were in his shoulder even as he bowled the desperado to the ground. Managing to throw the dog off him as he staggered to his feet, the rustler was drawing his revolver from its holster when Caleb's bullet ripped into him, folding him like an old Barlow knife before he fell.

Caleb called off Bear and strode quickly across the field toward the pines, loading cartridges into his Winchester as he moved. He knew the place where the other two entered the forest had put a deep gulch between them and Elkhorn. So, unless they planned to ride their horses straight up the side of the ridge to the east, they'd boxed themselves in.

Caleb entered the pines, listening for any sound of horse or rider. It was dark as a church here, with only a few openings where the moonlight broke through the boughs. The cool smell of pine filled his senses, and he saw Bear disappear off to the right.

Since the dog was following them, he decided to track to the left.

A few minutes later, his foot caught air, and he nearly went over the edge of the gulch. Caleb caught himself and peered into the blackness of the ravine. The spring melt was long over, and there was no sound of running water. And no sound of any riders that might have gone over the ledge either.

No such luck, he thought.

Working his way along the edge, Caleb soon heard the sound of low voices.

"…got to go back down there. Ain't no other way."

"I ain't heard no shots for a while."

Caleb moved closer until he saw them standing with their horses in a small clearing illuminated by the blue light of the moon.

"Maybe they killed the sumbitch."

"Maybe they did, and maybe they didn't."

They froze when their horses both raised their heads in alarm.

"What's that?"

On the far side of the clearing, Bear crept into view, head lowered and teeth bared.

Before either one could draw, Caleb stepped in behind them. "Throw 'em down."

Unfortunately, some fellows never know when to fold a losing hand.

One of them drew his revolver as he whirled toward the voice. Caleb's Winchester barked, dropping the man where he stood.

The other swung his rifle but never got the shot off. Bear leaped, biting down on the hand holding the gunstock. Locking his viselike jaws, the dog shook his head fiercely, eliciting a scream.

Trying to yank his hand and the weapon free, the rustler stumbled and fell backward into the shadow of the tall pines, pulling the yellow dog with him. As Caleb ran toward them, he fired his rifle. The intruder twitched once and lay still.

Even in the dim light, he could see the life go out of the man's eyes. The bullet had caught him under the chin and gone straight up.

"Leave him, Bear," he ordered.

The black-faced dog backed away, shook his golden fur, and stood looking expectantly at his master.

"Done good, boy."

Caleb straightened up and, for the first time, felt the stinging burn from the bullet that had grazed his stomach. Pulling open the rent in his shirt, he examined the wound as well as he could. Some bleeding had occurred, but it had mostly stopped.

Could have been a lot worse, he thought.

A few minutes later, with the two dead men tethered across their saddles, Caleb led the horses single file back down through the pine forest. As they drew near the open meadow, Bear stopped short and raised his nose before focusing on something ahead.

Caleb looped the reins of the lead horse over a low branch and moved stealthily forward.

In the darkness at the edge of the forest, another rider— wearing a bowler and a canvas duster—was peering out at the unfinished cabin and the four saddled horses grazing in the silvery field. Caleb raised his rifle and took dead aim.

"All right. Raise your hands where I can see them."

Slowly, the hands lifted into the air as Bear trotted over and sniffed at the intruder's boot.

"Start talking," Caleb demanded.

As the rider turned in the saddle, a spear of moonlight illuminated her face. A woman's face, and a damn pretty one, at that.

Caleb nearly fell over in surprise.

"I was coming after you, Mr. Marlowe. But the fellows who were riding those horses beat me to it."

CHAPTER TWO

CALEB APPROACHED THE WOMAN CAUTIOUSLY. RIGHT now, he was trying to ignore the empty feeling that always came after killing. And even though his instincts told him this rider had no intention of doing him any harm, he had no assurance she wasn't packing a firearm beneath that duster.

"You are Mr. Marlowe, aren't you?"

"I am. What's your connection with those fellas, ma'am?"

The rider tilted her head slightly as she considered the question. "Oh! I have no connection with them whatsoever. I was coming to find you when I saw them leaving Elkhorn ahead of me."

"And you followed?" His tone was sharp. Following six unfamiliar men in the middle of the night. She was evidently not too smart.

"I heard one of them mention your name." She matched his tone. "I figured following them would be the easiest way to get here. They did look like a rough bunch, however, so I was careful and stayed well behind them."

He wasn't feeling any better about what she'd done but decided to let her talk. The woman wasn't really his concern, but the sooner she had her say, the sooner he could go about his own business. He had more bodies to collect while the moon was still high.

"I must admit, when they turned off the road into the pine forest some ways after leaving town, I got a bit lost. But I heard gunshots and followed the sound. I hope there was no trouble."

Depends on who you ask, he thought. Caleb eyed her horse. "Ain't that Doc Burnett's gelding?"

"Yes, it is."

"Who are you, ma'am, and what are you doing with his horse?"

She took off the bowler, and a thick braid fell down her back. "I'm Sheila Burnett. My father is Dr. Burnett. I know from his letters that he's a friend of yours."

Caleb was taken aback by her words. Doc was indeed a friend of his, about the only one he'd claim as such in Elkhorn. But he'd had the impression that Doc's daughter was a young girl living with his in-laws back East somewhere. This was a grown and confident woman.

Maybe a bit overconfident.

"Why the devil is your father sending you out here in the dark of night, Miss Burnett?" Perhaps his tone was too sharp still, because Bear gave him a look and then trotted off into the pines.

"That's the problem, Mr. Marlowe. He didn't send me. I arrived on the coach from Denver yesterday to find he's gone missing. I need your help finding him."

Caleb had seen Doc only two days ago, and he was just fine. This daughter of his couldn't know it, of course, but the doctor often traveled away from town to look after miners and other folks who needed him. He might be on the road. Curious that the man had said nothing about the imminent arrival of his daughter, though.

Caleb cradled his rifle in the crook of his arm. "Your father can take care of himself, Miss Burnett. But tell me, are you armed?"

"Of course not."

She had the false confidence of a greenhorn.

"Was Doc expecting you?"

"In our recent correspondence, I mentioned my interest in paying him a visit."

"Was your father expecting you?" he repeated.

"Not exactly. Once I decided to come, a letter would have been too slow in arriving. And as you know, the telegraph lines haven't reached Elkhorn as yet."

Caleb shook his head slightly. An overly confident greenhorn with an impetuous disposition. A dangerous combination in these wild Rockies. Someone needed to explain a few things to this young woman about the dangers she'd exposed herself to, but he had six dead blackguards who'd be attracting wolves and coyotes and all kinds of undesirables before sunup.

"If you wouldn't mind moving out into the field there a ways, I'll follow you directly. After I finish up a chore or two, I'll take you back to Elkhorn and—"

"But what about finding my father?"

"We'll talk about that after I deliver you back to town." This woman was trouble he didn't need.

As Caleb turned to retrieve the horses and the dead men lashed to their saddles, he saw his dog trot out ahead of Doc's daughter.

"And what's your name, fellow?"

"That good boy is Bear," Caleb called after her. "But usually he ain't one to offer up his name to folks he don't know."

A few minutes later, he led the two mounts out into the field to find Miss Burnett standing by her horse with Bear sitting and leaning against her leg. Not his dog's customary response to strangers, though maybe it was because she was wearing Doc's bowler and duster, Caleb decided.

She stopped petting the dog's head, and he heard her sharp intake of breath the moment she saw what the horses were carrying.

"These men are dead?" she asked, her voice wavering.

"Yes, Miss Burnett. They are." Not an uncommon outcome for fellows like these.

"You killed them?"

"I did, ma'am," Caleb replied, stopping as he reached her. "Though it could have turned out different. And that would not have been good for either you or me."

"You took their lives."

That was the same as killing, but he didn't feel it was worth dwelling on. "They came to take mine."

"Are you sure that was what they intended? Did you speak to them before…before…?" She waved a hand toward the dead bodies.

"There's no *before* in that situation," he said.

Acknowledgments

I must thank again—at the risk of redundancy—my editor and champion, Christa Désir. She helped shape a decent idea into a compelling story and guided its formation—my personal Beah Nooki. I must also acknowledge again my wife, Karen Nix, whose belief in the story made her the first and most important fan—my Rosalyn.

I would also like to acknowledge those whose love of the historical West leads them to document it thoroughly, creating the rich research base necessary for a man of my era to write a historically accurate tale. Among the many are Candy Moulton (*The Writer's Guide to Everyday Life in the Wild West*); Bill Sniffen (*Wyoming at 125*); H. W. Brands (*Dreams of El Dorado*); John P. Langellier (*Fighting for Uncle Sam: Buffalo Soldiers in the Frontier Army*); Randolph B. Marcy (*Prairie Traveler*); Carol Thiesse, Traci Foutz, and Joe Spriggs (*Images of America: Lander*), and the various YouTubers who demonstrate the loading, firing, and cleaning of vintage firearms.

About the Author

When I was eight, my adventurous parents hauled our young family from the West Coast to a Wyoming mountain town perched on the border of the Wind River reservation. That magical landscape infused my formative years with a wonder of local lore that was both historical and present, and revealed to me that often the greatest stories have been all but forgotten or were never told. After publishing science fiction and historical romance for ten years, it seemed a matter of destiny that I'd eventually return to the tales of my youth. The Jake Paynter series brings together fact and fiction to explore places, people, and themes precious to me.

I've called Austin home since 1998 with my wife and three children. The kids are grown now but remain in and around the heart of Texas and consider themselves honorary Wyomingites. I've been away from that mountain town for a long time now but never really left the place.